RECKLESS
in TEXAS

KARI LYNN DELL

sourcebooks
casablanca

Copyright © 2016 by Kari Lynn Dell
Cover and internal design © 2016 by Sourcebooks, Inc.
Cover art by Craig White

Sourcebooks and the colophon are registered trademarks of Sourcebooks, Inc.

All rights reserved. No part of this book may be reproduced in any form or by any electronic or mechanical means including information storage and retrieval systems—except in the case of brief quotations embodied in critical articles or reviews—without permission in writing from its publisher, Sourcebooks, Inc.

The characters and events portrayed in this book are fictitious or are used fictitiously. Any similarity to real persons, living or dead, is purely coincidental and not intended by the author.

Published by Sourcebooks Casablanca, an imprint of Sourcebooks, Inc.
P.O. Box 4410, Naperville, Illinois 60567-4410
(630) 961-3900
Fax: (630) 961-2168
www.sourcebooks.com

Printed and bound in Canada.
MBP 10 9 8 7 6 5 4 3 2 1

This book is for the stock contractors, committees, sponsors, and contract personnel who make rodeos happen. Without you, we would have nowhere to compete. It is no accident that the hero of this story shares a name with Joe Baumgartner, who changed rodeo bullfighting forever, and provided inspiration for this book in so many ways.

Chapter 1

IT WAS LABOR DAY WEEKEND AND THE NIGHT WAS tailor-made for rodeo. Overhead the sky had darkened to blue velvet, and underfoot the West Texas dirt was groomed to perfection. Music pounded and the wooden bleachers were jammed with every live body within fifty miles, plus a decent number of tourists who'd been lured off the bleak stretch of Highway 20 between Odessa and El Paso by the promise of cold beer, hot barbecue, and a chance to get western.

Violet Jacobs maneuvered her horse, Cadillac, into position, mirroring her cousin on the opposite end of the bucking chutes. She and Cole both wore the Jacobs Livestock pickup rider uniform—a royal blue shirt to match stiff, padded royal-blue-and-white chaps to protect against the banging around and occasional kick that came with the job. Tension prickled through Violet's muscles as they waited for the next cowboy to nod his head.

She and Cole were supposed to be emergency backup during the bull riding, charging in only if the bullfighters—the so-called cowboy lifesavers—failed to get the rider and themselves out of danger. Trouble was, the odds of failure got higher every day. For a bullfighter, speed was key, and if Red got any slower they'd have to set out stakes to tell if he was moving. He'd worn out his last legs two weeks back. What he had left was held together with athletic tape, titanium braces, and sheer stubbornness. At some point, it wasn't going to be enough.

Violet's gaze swung to the younger of the pair of bullfighters. Hank vibrated like a bowstring as the bull rider took his wrap and used his free hand to pound his fist shut around the flat-braided rope. The kid was quicksilver to Red's molasses, as green as Red was wily. If he would just listen, work with Red instead of trying to do it all…

The gate swung wide and the bull blasted out with long, lunging jumps. Red lumbered after him like the Tin Man with rusty hinges. The bull dropped its head and swapped ends, blowing the rider's feet back, flipping the cowboy straight off over his horns. He landed in a pile right under the bull's nose. Hank jumped in from the right, Red from the left, and the two of them got tangled up. When Red stumbled, the Brahma caught his shoulder with one blunt horn and tossed him in the air like he weighed nothing.

Cole already had his rope up and swinging. Violet was three strides behind. The instant Red hit the ground, the bull was on top of him, grinding him into the dirt. When Hank scrambled to his partner's rescue, the bull slung its head and caught the kid under the chin with his other horn, laying him out straight as a poker.

Cole's loop sailed through the air, whipped around the bull's horns, and came tight. He took two quick wraps around the saddle horn with the tail of the rope and spurred his horse, Dozer, into a bounding lope. The big sorrel jerked the bull around and away before it could inflict any more damage. Violet rode in behind shouting, "Hyah! Hyah!" and slapping the bull's hip with her rope. He caught sight of the catch pen gate and stopped fighting to trot out of the arena toward feed and water. Violet wheeled Cadillac around, heart in her throat as she counted bodies. The breath rushed out of her lungs when she saw everyone was mostly upright.

The bull rider leaned over Hank, a hand on his shoulder as a medic knelt in the dirt next to him, attempting to stanch the blood dripping from his chin. A second medic supervised while two cowboys hoisted Red to his feet. He tried a ginger, limping step. Then another. By the third, Violet knew it would take a lot more than a can of oil and a roll of duct tape to fix the Tin Man this time.

—◆—

The Jacobs family gathered in the rodeo office after the show for an emergency staff meeting. The five of them filled the room—her father, Steve, was six-and-a-half feet of stereotypical Texas cowboy in a silver belly hat that matched his hair, and Cole, a younger, darker model cast from the same mold. Even Violet stood five ten in her socks, and none of them were what you'd call a beanpole. It was just as well she'd never set her heart on being the delicate, willowy type. She wasn't bred for it. Her five-year-old son, Beni, had tucked himself into the corner with his video game. Her mother, Iris, was a Shetland pony in a herd of Clydesdales, but could bring them all to heel with a few well-chosen words in that certain tone of voice.

Now she shook her head, *tsking* sadly. "Did y'all see that knee? Looks like five pounds of walnuts stuffed into a two-pound bag."

"He won't be back this year," Violet said.

Her dad *hmphffed*, but no one argued. Even if Red wanted to try, they couldn't put him back out there for the three weeks that were left of the season. It wasn't safe for Red or for the cowboys he was supposed to protect. It was sad to lose one of the old campaigners, but he'd had a good, long run—clear back to the days when the guys who fought bulls were called rodeo clowns, wore face paint and baggy Wranglers, and were expected to tell jokes and put on comedy acts. Nowadays, bullfighters were all about the serious business of saving cowboys' necks. Leave the costumes and the standup comedy to the modern day clowns, pure entertainers who steered well clear of the bulls.

"Saves us havin' to tell Red it's time to hang up the cleats," Cole said, blunt as always. "Who we gonna get to replace him?"

Steve sighed, pulling off his hat to run a hand through his flattened hair. "Violet can make some calls. Maybe Donny can finish out the year."

Oh, come *on*. Donny was even older than Red, if slightly better preserved. Violet opened her mouth to argue, but her mother cut her off.

"It'll have to wait until morning." Iris began stacking paperwork and filing it in plastic boxes. "Y'all go get your stock put up. We've got a date for drinks with the committee president."

And Violet had a date with her smartphone. Fate and Red's bad knees had handed her an opportunity to breathe fresh life into Jacobs Livestock. She just had to persuade the rest of the family to go along.

———

Once the stock was settled for the night, Violet herded Beni to their trailer and got them both showered and into pajamas. She tucked him into his bunk with a stuffed penguin under one arm—a souvenir from a trip to the Calgary Zoo with his dad earlier in the summer.

"Can I call Daddy?" he asked.

She kissed his downy-soft forehead. Lord, he was a beautiful child—not that she could take any credit. The jet-black hair and tawny skin, eyes as dark as bittersweet chocolate…that was all his daddy. "Not tonight, bub. The time is two hours different in Washington, so he's not done riding yet."

"Oh. Yeah." Beni heaved a sigh that was equal parts yawn. "He's still coming home next week, right?"

"He'll meet us at the rodeo on Sunday."

He'd promised, and while Violet wouldn't recommend getting knocked up on a one-night stand, at least she'd had the sense to get drunk and stupid with a really good man. He would not let his son down, especially after he'd been on the road for almost a month in the Pacific Northwest at a run of rich fall rodeos. The rodeos that mattered.

She heaved a sigh of her own. Of course her rodeos mattered—to the small towns, the local folks, they were a chance to hoot and holler and shake off their troubles for a night. The contestants might be mostly weekend cowboys with jobs that kept them close to home, but they left just as big a piece of their heart in the arena as any of the top-level pros. Still, the yearning spiraled through Violet like barbed wire, coiling around her heart and digging in. It cut deep, that yearning. Nights like this were worst of all, in the quiet after the rodeo, when there was nothing left to do but think. Imagine.

At legendary rodeos like Ellensburg, Puyallup, and Lewiston, the best cowboys in North America were going head to head, world championships on the line. Meanwhile, Violet had successfully wrapped up the forty-third annual Puckett County Homesteader Days. Jacobs Livestock had been part of twenty-nine of them. If her dad had his way, they'd continue until the rodeo arena crumbled into the powder-dry West Texas dirt, her mother and Cole trailing contentedly along behind.

How could Violet be the only one who wanted more?

"Night, Mommy." Beni rolled over, tucked the penguin under his chin, and was instantly asleep.

Violet tugged the blanket up to his shoulders, then pulled shut the curtain that separated his bunk from the rest of the trailer. Finally time for dinner. She slicked her dark hair behind her ears, the damp ends brushing her shoulders as she built a sandwich of sliced ham on one of her mother's fat homemade rolls, a dollop of coleslaw on the plate alongside it. Before settling in at the table, she turned the radio on low. The singer's throaty twang vibrated clear down to her heartstrings, reminding her that the only man in her life had yet to hit kindergarten, but it muted the *tick-tick-tick* of another rodeo season winding down with Violet in the exact same place.

She prodded her coleslaw with a fork, brooding. Red had been operating on pure guts for weeks, so she'd made a point of researching every card-carrying professional bullfighter in their price range. Was her prime candidate still available? She opened the Internet browser on her phone and clicked a link to a Facebook page. *Shorty Edwards. Gunnison, Colorado.* His status hadn't changed since the last time she checked. *Good news! Doc says I can get back to work. Any of you out there needing a bullfighter for fall rodeos, give me a call.*

Shorty was exactly what they needed. Young enough to be the bullfighter of their future, but experienced enough to knock Hank into line. Good luck persuading her dad to bring in a complete stranger, though—and not even a Texan, Lord save her. She might as well suggest they hire the devil himself. Violet drummed agitated fingers on the table, staring at Shorty's action photo. Jacobs Livestock needed new blood, an infusion of energy. Fans and committees loved a good bullfighter.

Her dad *had* said she should make some calls. As business manager for Jacobs Livestock, she would write up the contract and sign the paycheck, so why not get a jump on the process? She could discuss it with her parents before making a commitment.

Her heart commenced a low bass beat that echoed in her ears as she dialed his number. He answered. Her voice squeaked when she introduced herself, and she had to clear her throat before explaining their situation.

"Three rodeos?" he asked. "Guaranteed?"

"Uh…yeah."

"And you can give me a firm commitment right now?"

"I…uh…"

"I've got an offer in Nevada for one rodeo. If you can give me three, I'll come to Texas, but I promised them an answer by morning."

Violet's mouth was so dry her lips stuck to her teeth.

She'd never hired anyone without her dad's approval. But it wasn't permanent. Just three rodeos. Sort of like a test-drive. If Shorty turned out to be a lemon, they could just send him back.

"Well?"

"Three rodeos, guaranteed," she blurted.

"Great. Sign me up."

She ironed out the details then hung up the phone, folded her arms on the table, and buried her face in them. When the first wave of panic subsided, she sat up, pressing her palms on the table when her head spun. *Chill, Violet.* She was twenty-eight years old and her dad was always saying the best way to get more responsibility was to show she could handle it. They had a problem. She'd solved it. Once the rest of them saw Shorty in action, they'd have to admit she'd made the right choice.

Because you have such an excellent track record when it comes to picking men...

Violet slapped that demon back into its hidey-hole. This was different. This was business. She was good at business. As long as Shorty Edwards was exactly as advertised, she was golden.

Chapter 2

THE LAST BRAHMA TO BUCK AT THE PUYALLUP, Washington, rodeo was a huge red brindle named Cyberbully. Three jumps out of the chute he launched his rider into the clear blue sky. The cowboy thumped into the dirt like a hundred-and-forty-pound sack of mud and stayed there, motionless, while the bull whipped around, looking to add injury to insult.

Joe Cassidy stepped between them and tapped Cyberbully's fat nose. "Hey, Cy. This way."

The bull took the bait. Joe hauled ass, circling away from the fallen cowboy with the Brahma a scant inch behind. The big son of a bitch was fast. Caught out in the middle of the arena, Joe couldn't outrun him, so he opted to let Cy give him a boost. With a slight hesitation and a perfectly timed hop, he momentarily took a seat between the bull's stubby horns. Startled, Cy threw up his head and Joe pushed off. As he was thrown free, he saw a flash of neon yellow—his partner sprinting in from the opposite direction. "C'mere, Cy, you ugly bastard!"

The bull hesitated, then went after Wyatt. Joe landed on his feet and spun around to see Wyatt vault up and onto the fence next to the exit gate with a stride to spare. The bull feinted at him, then trotted out.

"Ladies and gentlemen, give a hand to our bullfighters, Joe Cassidy and Wyatt Darrington!" the rodeo announcer shouted. "That's why these two are the best team in professional rodeo."

The air vibrated, fans whistling and stomping their appreciation as Joe jogged over to check on the cowboy, who had rolled into a seated position.

"You okay, Rowdy?" Joe asked, extending a hand to help him up.

"Yep. Thanks, guys." Rowdy swiped at the dirt on his chaps and strolled to the chutes, unscathed and unfazed.

Wyatt folded his arms, glaring. "We should let the bulls have the ones that are too dumb to get up and run."

Joe snorted. That'd be the day. Wyatt was hardwired to save the world—even the parts that didn't want saving.

"That wraps up our rodeo for this year, folks!" the announcer declared. "If you have a hankering for more top-of-the-line professional rodeo action, come on out to Pendleton, Oregon, next week for the world-famous Roundup…"

One more rodeo, then six weeks off. Seven days from now, after Pendleton, he was headed home. Fall was Joe's favorite time of year in the high desert of eastern Oregon, weaning this year's crop of colts and calves under the clear, crisp sky.

He twisted around, checking the spot where the bull had tagged his ribs. Not even a flesh wound thanks to his Kevlar vest, but the big bastard had ripped a hole in his long-sleeved jersey. "Damn. That's the third one this month."

Wyatt took off his cowboy hat and wiped sweat from his forehead with a shirtsleeve. "You're gettin' old and slow, pardner."

"Five years less old and slow than you."

"Yeah, but I take better care of myself."

"Says the guy with five shiny new screws in his ankle." Joe nodded toward Wyatt's right leg, supported by a rigid plastic Aircast. "How's it feel?"

"Like they drove the bottom two screws in with a hammer." Wyatt rotated the ankle, wincing. "Still works, though, so they must've got 'em in good and tight."

Joe rubbed the sting from the elbow Cyberbully had smacked with the top of his rock-hard skull. He ached from head to toe with the cumulative fatigue of six straight days of rodeo piled on top of all the other weeks and months of bruises and bodily insults. "What the hell is wrong with us?" he asked.

Wyatt started for the gate. "I'm in it for the women and free booze. Let's go make that stupid shit Rowdy buy us a beer."

"Just remember, you're driving," Joe said, yawning.

Wyatt sent him a sympathetic glance. "Long night, huh?"

"Yeah." Tension crawled up his back at the memory. Goddamn Lyle Browning. Someone should've castrated the bastard by now. His wife had plenty of reasons to cry, but why did she insist on using Joe's shoulder?

Wyatt shook his head. "I shouldn't have left you alone at the bar. You were already upset before the weepy woman."

"I wasn't upset." The tension slithered higher, toward the base of Joe's skull.

"Bullshit. Your old man lives fifteen miles from here and couldn't show up to watch you in action. That sucks."

"I'm thirty years old, not ten. It's not like he skipped

a little league game." But he'd missed plenty. Most of Joe's high school sports career, in fact.

But that was ancient history. Joe tipped off his cowboy hat, peeled the ruined jersey over his head, then balled it up and gave it a mighty heave. It landed three rows up, in the outstretched arms of a little girl in a pink cowboy hat, who squealed her excitement. Joe smiled and waved and kept moving. He wanted to be gone. Far, far away from Puyallup and any expectations he hadn't been able to stomp to death.

"I haven't seen Lyle's wife around today," Wyatt said.

"Probably still hugging the toilet."

Or maybe she'd finally smartened up and left. 'Bout time. Lyle Browning was a sniveling dog, dragging along on the coattails of his dad's successful rodeo company. They'd grown up in the same small town and Joe had started working summers on the Browning Ranch when he was fifteen, but he and Lyle had never been friends. Early on, Joe had had some sympathy. Had to suck for Lyle, his mom dying when he was so young, and his dad not exactly the nurturing type. At some point, though, a guy had to take responsibility for his own life.

As they stepped into the narrow alley behind the bucking chutes, a hand clamped on Joe's shoulder. "Hey, asshole. I need to talk to you."

The words were slurred, the voice a permanent whine. Joe turned and found himself face-to-face with the last person he wanted to see. He brushed off the hand. "Whaddaya want, Lyle?"

Lyle Browning tried to get in Joe's face, but came up short by a good six inches. Even at that distance, his breath was toxic. "You fucking prick. How long you been sneaking around, fucking my wife?"

"Don't be stupid."

Lyle rolled onto his toes, swaying. He smelled like he'd passed out in the bottom of a beer garden dumpster. Looked like it, too. "Everybody saw you leave the bar together, you son of a bitch, and she told me what happened when you got back to her room."

The *fuck* she did. But Joe could think of a dozen reasons Lyle's wife would want her husband to think she'd gone out and gotten a piece. At the very least, it'd sure teach him to screw around every chance he got. Lyle had mastered the art of trading on his daddy's name with the sleaziest of the buckle bunnies who hung around looking for a cowboy-shaped notch for their bedpost. Too bad for them, they got Lyle instead.

"See?" Lyle crowed. "You can't deny it."

Joe ground his teeth. Hell. He couldn't. Not without humiliating her all over again in front of the gathering crowd. "You're drunk. Crawl back into your hole and sleep it off. We'll talk later."

"We'll talk now!"

Joe put a hand on Lyle's chest, making enough space to take a breath without gagging. "Back off, Lyle."

"Don't push me, asshole!" Lyle reared back and took a wild swing.

His right fist plowed into Joe's stomach. Even if Lyle wasn't a weenie-armed drunk, it would've bounced off Joe's Kevlar vest. His left fist grazed Joe's chin, though, and that was too damn much. Joe popped him square in the mouth. Lyle squealed, arms flailing, then toppled straight over backward, his skull smacking the hard-packed dirt. He jerked a couple of times before his eyes rolled back and the lights went out.

Joe barely had time to think *oh shit* before Dick Browning's voice sliced through the crowd. "What the hell is going on here?"

A whole section of the onlookers peeled away to clear a path. Dick crouched over his son and gave him a not-very-gentle tap on the cheek. "Lyle! You okay?"

Lyle moaned, his head lolling off to one side. Dick jumped up and spun around to face Joe. Where Lyle was scrawny, Dick was wiry, tough as a rawhide whip. He was only a hairbreadth taller than his son, but somehow, when Dick decided to get in your face, he made it work.

Joe took a step back and put up his hands. "He took a swing at me."

"What did you expect? You mess with a man's wife—"

Like Lyle was any kind of man, but Joe didn't dare say so. Sweat beaded on his forehead, part heat, part panic, as his gaze bounced off Dick's and around the curious crowd. This was not the time or place to set Dick straight. "Can we talk about this later, in private?"

"You disrespect my family, assault my son—there is no later," Dick snapped. "Consider yourself unemployed. And don't bother showing up at Pendleton, either."

Joe flinched, the words a verbal slap. "That's crazy. You know I wouldn't—"

"Then why would she say so?"

Joe opened his mouth, then clamped it shut. God*damn*it.

Wyatt yanked him backward and slid into the space between Joe and Dick, smooth as butter. "If that piece of shit you call a son could keep his dick in his pants, his wife wouldn't be out at the bar drinking herself into a coma."

"This is none of your business."

"If it's Joe's business, it's mine. We call that friendship—not that you'd know." Wyatt leaned in, got his eyes down on Dick's level. "Don't give me an excuse, Herod, or I'll lay you out in the dirt with your spawn."

Joe grabbed him, afraid Wyatt might actually punch the old man. "You can't—"

Wyatt yanked his arm out of Joe's grasp. "It'd be worth the bail money."

For a long, tense moment they remained locked eye to eye. Then Lyle groaned, rolled over, and puked. Dick jerked around, cursing. "Somebody give me a hand getting him over to my trailer."

Out of reflex, Joe took a step. Wyatt jabbed an elbow into his sternum. "Don't even *think* about it."

He hauled Joe away, around the back of the grandstand, over to the sports medicine trailer that also served as their locker room.

"Who is Herod?" Joe asked, unable to process the rest of the scene.

"The most evil fucking tyrant in the Bible, but only because Matthew never met Dick Browning." Wyatt yanked open the door to the trailer and dragged Joe up the steps.

Matthew. Herod. Christ. "Who says that shit?"

"I'm a preacher's kid," Wyatt said. "I get my gospel up when I'm pissed."

Preacher. Hah. Try *Lord High Bishop of Something or Other.* Wyatt's family learned their gospel at Yale Divinity. He read big fat history books for the fun of it. For two guys who had nothing in common, Joe and Wyatt had been a dream team from the first time they worked in the same arena, and hell on wheels outside those arenas. The mileage added up, though, and a thirty-year-old body didn't bounce back from hangovers the same way it used to. Joe sure didn't miss them, or waking up next to woman whose name was lost in his alcohol-numbed brain.

As they stepped into the trailer, one of the athletic trainers grabbed a gauze pad and slapped it on a split in Joe's knuckle. "You're dripping. Wipe it off, then I'll see if you need stitches."

Wyatt leaned against the counter and folded his arms. "What he needs is a rabies vaccination."

The trainer's head whipped around in alarm. "It's a dog bite?"

"No," Joe said.

"Close enough," Wyatt said. "He cut it on Lyle Browning's face."

The trainer smirked. "So, more like a rat. Better dissect Lyle's brain to see if he's rabid."

"Good luck finding one," Wyatt said. "But I volunteer to knock him over the head. And his little daddy, too."

"Not very Christian for a choir boy," Joe muttered.

Wyatt's grin was all teeth. "One of a long list of reasons the Big Guy and I are no longer on speaking terms."

Fifteen minutes later, the last of the cowboys had cleared out of the trailer and the trainers had gone to have a beer, leaving Joe and Wyatt stretched out on the padded treatment tables. Stripped down to a pair of black soccer shorts with his blond hair slicked back and a bottle of water dangling from long, manicured fingers,

Wyatt looked exactly like what he was—the product of generations-deep East Coast money. When asked how he'd ended up fighting bulls, he liked to say it was the best legal way to be sure his family never spoke to him again. The reporters thought he was joking.

Joe's knuckle was bandaged, but his whole hand throbbed in time with the pounding in his head. His initial shock had morphed into fury, churning like hot, black tar in his gut. He punched the pillow with his uninjured fist. "I *should* skip Pendleton. It'd serve Dick right."

"Don't be an idiot," Wyatt said. "Just because you're his chore boy on the ranch between rodeos doesn't mean Dick has shit to say about when and where you fight bulls."

Joe scowled, but couldn't argue. The mega-rodeos they worked were too much for any one stock contractor to handle. Cheyenne lasted two weeks. Denver had sixteen performances. Rodeos that big hired a main contractor to gather up at least a dozen others, each bringing only their best bulls and horses. The rodeo committee also hired the bullfighters. Down in the bush leagues, you worked for the contractor. At the elite level, they were freelancers. Joe and Wyatt were the most sought-after bullfighters in the country, stars in their own right, which meant they could pick and choose from the most prestigious rodeos.

It irritated Wyatt to no end that Joe chose to stick mostly to the rodeos where Dick Browning had been hired to provide bucking stock, and continued to work on Dick's ranch for what was chump change compared to his bullfighter pay. Wyatt blamed misplaced loyalty.

And yeah, Dick had given him his start, but Joe had paid that debt a long time ago. The ties that bound him were buried deep in the hills and valleys of the High Lonesome Ranch. He loved that land like nothing else except the stock that ran on it.

How could Wyatt understand? He wasn't a cowboy.

He cocked his head, his gaze sharpening. "You're really pissed."

"Wouldn't you be?" Joe shot back.

"Hell yeah, but I would've throat-punched both of them ten years ago. This isn't the first time Dick has blown up in your face. It isn't even the first time he fired you."

"I deserved it most of those other times." When Joe was a showboating twenty-year-old with more guts than common sense. The anger boiled up again. "I'm not a brain-dead kid anymore."

"So tell him to go fuck himself."

Joe shook his head and Wyatt hissed in frustration. "Geezus, Joe. What's it going to take?"

Joe couldn't imagine. The High Lonesome had been the center of his world for too long. Solid ground when his home life was anything but. Dick's great-grandfather had veered south off the Oregon Trail to homestead there. He had given the ranch its name because the rugged miles of sagebrush desert were high in altitude, lonesome in the extreme, and spectacular in a wild, almost savage way that possessed a man's soul. Joe could cut off a limb easier than he could walk away.

"You were right before." Wyatt adjusted the ice pack on his ankle, then reached for his phone. "If Dick wants to shoot off his mouth, slander you in front of half of pro rodeo, you should call his bluff. Let him explain to the committee in Pendleton why you're not there."

Joe bolted upright. "I can't leave the Roundup short a bullfighter."

"You won't." Wyatt's fingers danced over his touch screen before he lifted it to his ear, holding up a palm for silence when Joe tried to speak. "Hey, Shorty! This is Wyatt. I heard you're looking to pick up a rodeo or two before the season ends. How does Pendleton sound?"

Joe opened his mouth, but Wyatt shushed him again.

"Yes, really. Would I joke about something that big?" A pause, then Wyatt grinned. "Oh yeah. I forgot. That was a good one. But I paid you back for the airfare, and I'm serious this time. Joe wants out. You want in?" Another pause, and a frown. "Where, and how much?" Wyatt listened, then grimaced. He covered the phone with his hand and said to Joe, "Shorty Edwards can come to Pendleton in your place, on one condition."

"What condition?" By which Joe meant to say, *Are you fucking crazy?*

"How do you feel about Texas?" Wyatt asked. When Joe only gaped at him, he shrugged and said into the phone. "Guess that means yes. See you in Pendleton, Shorty."

He hung up and tossed the phone aside.

Joe stared at him, horrified. "You did not just do that."

"Bet your ass I did." Suddenly every line of Wyatt's body was as sharply etched as the ice in his blue eyes. "I will do whatever it takes to pry you away from that son of a bitch."

"Dick's not that bad." But there was no conviction in Joe's voice. He was tired and hurting and every time he replayed Dick's words, heard the contempt in his voice, his chest burned with humiliation and fury. How could he stroll into Pendleton and pretend it was all good?

"If you stay, you'll end up just like him—a shriveled up, rancid piece of coyote bait."

Joe stared at the ceiling, sick of arguing. Sick of it all. Silence reigned for a few moments. Then Wyatt sighed, and the pity in his voice cut deeper than Dick's lashing tongue.

"Have some pride, Joe. Go to Texas. Get a little perspective." Wyatt flashed a knife-edged smile. "At least give humanity a chance before you sign over your soul to the devil."

Chapter 3

A HARD BUMP AND THE SCREECH OF RUBBER ON tarmac nudged Joe out of the closest thing to sleep he'd had in the past thirty-six hours. He rubbed the blur from his vision as the plane taxied to the terminal. *"Welcome to Dallas-Fort Worth, where the local time is 1:33 p.m. and the temperature is ninety-seven degrees. Please remain in your seats…"*

Make me. Joe was on his feet before the plane came to a complete stop, shaking the kinks out of legs that had been crammed into coach way too long. Every decent flight out of Sea-Tac had been overbooked, forcing him to hop a commuter flight to Spokane, suffer through a five-hour layover, a four-and-a-half hour flight, then spend what was left of the night and most of the morning in the Minneapolis airport. But by damn, he was on the ground in Dallas on schedule. Jacobs Livestock was expecting a bullfighter to show up by five o'clock this afternoon and they'd get one. They just weren't expecting Joe.

"Easier to ask forgiveness than beg for permission," Wyatt had insisted. "Besides, what are they gonna do, complain you're too good for them?"

Joe wasn't inclined to care if feathers got ruffled. Jacobs was getting double their money's worth, and with every mile, every hour that took him farther from where he was supposed to be, at Pendleton, the needle on his give-a-shit meter dropped another notch. If the point was to punish Dick, why did Joe feel like he'd been sent down to the minor leagues for bad behavior?

He grabbed his battered gear bag from the overhead bin—the luggage handlers could misroute his clothes to China, but they weren't touching his bread and butter—and vibrated in place while he waited for the aisle to clear. An eternity later, he broke free of the shuffling herd. His twitching muscles whimpered with relief when he was able to lengthen his stride, weaving past roller bags and shuffling Bluetooth zombies, down the terminal to the nearest restroom. He took a leak, then sighed wearily at his reflection as he washed his hands and splashed water on his face. Shaving and laundry had fallen by the wayside while he'd scrambled to make last-minute travel arrangements, by turns too pissed off at Dick and assaulted by second thoughts to care how he looked. Besides, the three-day stubble was a nice match for the dark circles under his bloodshot eyes.

Violet Jacobs would just have to take him as he was, scruff and all. In thirty years, only three women had earned the right to tell Joe to clean up his act. Roxy had been his partner in crime, his staunchest supporter and a near-constant exasperation since the day she gave birth to him. Helen, the cook at the High Lonesome, had been trying to put some meat on his bones since he first showed up there as a gangly teenager, and LouEllen at The Mane had been cutting his hair just as long. She had a knack for trimming it so no one but Wyatt noticed. Joe just looked less like he should have an electric guitar slung over his shoulder than a bagful of knee braces and body armor. Unfortunately, she'd been out of town last month when he'd passed through between rodeo runs. No one else touched Joe's hair, regardless of how much Dick bitched.

He ran damp fingers through the straggly mess and called it good. Then he tapped a text into his phone. Arrived gate E-16. Have to grab my bag.

The reply bounced right back. Come straight out the door nearest baggage claim. I've got the yellow car.

Wyatt had arranged this ride from the airport to the first rodeo—four hours west of Dallas—and Joe had been forbidden to offer to pay for gas. Whether Wyatt had called in a personal or professional favor Lord only knew, and Joe hadn't bothered to ask. He snagged his duffel off the carousel, walked out the door, and stopped dead at the sight of the car parked directly across the street, its owner contributing to the traffic congestion in the loading zone as she lounged against the hood, her long, bare legs crossed at the ankles. Oh yeah. Wyatt definitely had personal business with this one. Joe blew out a breath that was half laugh and headed for the car.

He might not make a great first impression, but he was damn sure going to make an entrance.

———∼∼∼———

Violet swiped away a trickle of sweat that oozed down her temple and glared at the last stinking water tank left to be cleaned. Emphasis on the *stink*. Whoever used these stock pens last had left water in the tanks to ferment into foul green soup. Violet's father and Cole drained and upended all of them, propping them on their sides against the fences for Violet and Beni to attack with a hose and a scrub brush while her mother brought up the rear with a bucket of bleach water.

Violet smelled like the Swamp Thing after a hard day, probably looked worse, and their new bullfighter was due to pull in any time now. Not that she had to impress him, but she was nervous enough about bringing a stranger on board that she'd feel better if she at least combed her hair and put on a clean, dry shirt. She scowled at the green-black slime coating the bottom of the tank, steeling herself to move in, when a flash of canary yellow caught her eye. A Corvette turned into the rodeo grounds and crept along the dusty gravel driveway, its engine grumbling in disdain. Violet's heartbeat kicked up. Could this be Shorty? She wouldn't put it past a bullfighter to go for the flash, even if it would be hell to keep the dirt off all that gleaming paint and chrome.

The car stopped and idled for a moment as if the occupants were inspecting their surroundings—a bare dirt parking lot, the old wooden grandstand, a ramshackle hut that functioned as a rodeo office…and Violet. She was tempted to dive for cover behind the tank until the car passed, but the doors opened instead. The driver emerged first and Violet's jaw dropped. *Wow.* Give this woman pom-poms and a pair of miniscule white shorts and she could stroll right onto the sidelines of the next Dallas Cowboys game. Her cloud of brilliant red curls seemed impervious to the humidity, and her elegant nose wrinkled as she surveyed the stock pens. She made a face and what sounded like a joke as a man climbed out of the passenger seat. He responded with a tight smile.

Definitely not their bullfighter. Shorty was, well,

shorter, compact, and dark. Violet judged this guy to be close to six feet, long, lean, and as potentially hazardous as the car he stood beside. His shrewd gaze cataloged every rusty nail and weathered board of the aging rodeo grounds, snagging for a moment on Violet, and then moving on as if she were just part of the scenery. The intensity of that gaze contrasted oddly with his shaggy brown hair, bleached to gold at the tips, and the wrinkled T-shirt that hung loose on broad shoulders. When he turned to reach into the backseat of the car, she wouldn't have been surprised to see him pull out a skateboard instead of a pair of road-weary duffel bags. Who—

"Hey, Mommy!"

A blast of water hit the stock tank and ricocheted, drenching her in slime. She shrieked, whipped around, and a second blast caught her square in the face. Beni cackled in delight as Violet choked and sputtered. She made a lunge for the hose, skidded, slipped, and landed flat on her butt in the middle of a rapidly growing puddle. Beni giggled louder and doused her again as she wallowed around, trying to get her feet under her.

"Beni!" she heard her mother say. "Give Grandma that—"

Then a shriek as Beni hit the trigger on the hose nozzle.

"*Benjamin. Steven. Sanchez.* You stop that right now!" Violet made another grab for him.

Beni ducked and dodged, howling like a hyena with the nozzle gripped in both hands, using the powerful spray to fend her off. Suddenly, the water stopped. Beni shook the nozzle and squeezed the trigger. Nothing happened. His eyes went wide and his mouth made an *uh-oh* shape. He dropped the hose and ran, diving under the fence and tearing past the skater dude, who stood with one hand on the lever of the water hydrant. Violet glanced over at the car then back at the hydrant, at least thirty yards away. He'd covered the distance in the space of a few heartbeats.

So he didn't just *look* fast.

She started to wipe the water from her face before she realized her hands were coated in rancid mud, which she had now smeared across both cheeks. Awesome. She brushed the drips from her eyebrows with one forearm then squelched across the pen to where the stranger stood outside the fence.

"Can I help you?" she asked.

His eyebrows rose. "Looks like it's the other way around to me."

He wasn't from around here. No sign of a Texas drawl in those lazily amused words. His gaze took a stroll from her bedraggled hair, down the front of her sopping-wet denim shirt, and over her mucked-up jeans and boots before returning to her grubby face. Her cheeks heated under the scrutiny.

"Thanks for that." She spared a dark glance for where Beni had disappeared around the end of the bucking chutes, seeking temporary asylum with Cole or his grandpa. "My son and I will be having a chat later. Are you looking for someone?"

"You, I assume."

Violet blinked. "Me?"

"You hired a bullfighter." He spread his hands, inviting inspection. What she saw didn't inspire confidence. His T-shirt was worn through at the collar and the Mint Bar logo was so faded and cracked she could barely read the *Hangovers Installed and Serviced* tag-line. His jeans were, if possible, even more decrepit, and his face was rough with at least a few days' worth of stubble.

"You aren't Shorty," Violet said, confused.

"No kidding. I was…" He stopped, a muscle in his jaw working as if chewing off the end of an unappetizing explanation. "Shorty got an opportunity to work Pendleton. I'm taking his place."

Her gut went alternately cold then hot as she absorbed the implications. No way. This could *not* be happening. The one time she stuck her neck out, acted unilaterally to hire an unknown, and he had left them flat. Her father was going to be furious. Come to think of it, so was she.

"He doesn't bother to call, give us a heads-up, nothing? Just sends"—her voice climbed an octave and she chopped a hand toward him, flicking mud onto the *B* of Mint Bar—"whoever? And I'm supposed to just accept it, assume you're good enough to turn loose in our arena?"

His chin snapped up and his deep-set eyes narrowed. "I'm better than anything that's ever set foot in one of your arenas, sweetheart. But if you want me to leave—"

Violet drew a breath to tell him yes, and provide detailed directions to exactly where he could go, when a small, damp hand closed around her arm, the grip like iron.

"Violet." Her mother's voice was soft, the tone unmistakable. *Mind your manners, young lady.* She extended her other hand to the imposter. "I don't believe I've had the pleasure. I'm Iris Jacobs."

As he accepted the handshake, he angled a smile

at Violet that glinted with a grim sort of triumph. "Joe Cassidy."

Oh. Oh dear God, *no*. She hadn't just… She couldn't have failed to recognize… But of course it was him. So obviously him that she wanted to head-slap herself. Beni had an autographed poster of Joe Cassidy and Wyatt Darrington *on his bedroom wall*, for pity's sake. Violet swore silently, closed her eyes, and prayed the puddle she was standing in would swallow her whole.

Chapter 4

JOE CASSIDY WAS GOING TO BE TROUBLE. VIOLET JUST hadn't figured out what kind yet. Fifteen minutes on Facebook and she'd learned why he was in Texas. Rumors were flying fast and hard about the blowup between Joe and Dick Browning, starting with Joe leaving the bar with Dick's daughter-in-law, and ending with Joe punching Dick's son.

Drinking, fighting, and adultery. Yep, her dad was real impressed with her decision-making skills. And now, to top it all off, their starstruck rodeo announcer had given Joe a wireless microphone, so instead of lounging around behind the chutes until the bull riding—the final event on the program—he was in the arena, schmoozing the fans. Violet tried not to glance over to where he leaned against the fence chatting with a trio of autograph seekers. Female, of course. They flashed a lot of tanned skin, white teeth, and big hair as they shoved their rodeo programs through the fence. He said something that made them giggle.

Violet felt her lip curl. Lord, the man put her teeth on edge, and not just because she'd made a complete fool of herself. He strutted around like he was God's gift to rodeo, radiating energy like those big static electricity balls at the science museum. When one of the buckle bunnies put a hand on his arm, Violet was surprised the girl's bleached hair didn't stand on end. Violet was not surprised to see the blonde scribble on the corner of her rodeo program, tear it off, and tuck it into Joe's hand.

"You're in for a real treat today, folks. Our next bareback rider is a fan favorite…especially with the single ladies," the rodeo announcer declared in a voice that was the equivalent of an exaggerated wink. "Delon Sanchez is a seven-time National Finals Rodeo qualifier, currently number one in the world standings!"

The crowd clapped enthusiastically, enjoying the exceptionally nice view as Delon leaned over the horse. His sleeve was rolled up to the elbow, exposing the muscle that bulged in his forearm. Little wonder his grip on the stiff leather handhold was nearly impossible to break. Riata Rose wasn't nearly as awestruck. The mare slumped against the side of chute, sulking, as he worked his hand into the rigging, the squeak of rosin and leather audible. The chute crew massaged her mane and shoved on her hip as Delon lowered himself onto the horse's back, but Rose wouldn't budge.

Into the lull, the announcer's voice boomed. "Hey, Joe, did you know Violet here is the only female pickup man in Texas?"

Oh hell. Not that again.

"Shouldn't it be pickup *girl*?" Joe made it sound indecent, like she plied her trade on street corners.

The announcer grinned down at her from the crow's nest, oblivious. "Well, now, I'm not sure. Do you prefer pickup girl, Violet?"

She gave an exaggerated shrug, but couldn't stop the sidelong scowl she fired at Joe. He answered with a mocking smile. She snapped her focus back to the chute, but Riata Rose was in a mood and had no intention of cooperating until she felt damn good and ready. The mare sank onto her haunches. Delon shook his head and climbed off. In that position, the mare could flip onto her back in an instant and crush him.

While the crew tried to persuade Riata to play nice, Joe moved down the fence to an older couple, their knobby knees sunburned pink below baggy walking shorts. He held out the clip-on microphone so the woman's strong German accent could be heard over the loudspeakers.

"What do you do? You don't look like a cowboy."

A valid question. If it weren't for his white straw cowboy hat, he could have been mistaken for a soccer player, lean and edgy as a feral cat, in silky black shorts and a long-sleeved red jersey plastered with sponsor logos. His shaggy hair might be a fashion statement or just neglect, but either way it added to his general air of *too cool for you*.

"I'm a bullfighter," he said.

"You fight the bulls? With the sword?" The woman made a stabbing motion, enthusiastic enough to make Joe step back.

"No, ma'am. I just jump in after the ride ends and distract the bull long enough for the cowboy to get away."

"Oh." The woman looked disappointed. "Why don't you ride?"

"Have you seen the horns on those things?" Joe gave an exaggerated shudder. "You couldn't pay me to get on one."

Laughter rippled through the audience, for which Violet was reluctantly grateful. Joe was doing a good job of filling dead air, the same way he chatted with

the cluster of fans that waylaid him every day after the
bull riding. He'd also gone along with the impromptu
autograph session the committee had included in their
pancake breakfast. Three days in, even her dad couldn't
complain about Joe's behavior.

Joe caught Violet's glance—okay, maybe it was
more like a frown—and his eyes narrowed. He held
her gaze as he leaned closer to the German woman, his
voice dropping to a purr. "I might consider climbing on
a bucking horse if it meant Violet would pick me up."

The crowd laughed and cheered in approval. Violet
glared at Joe, kicking Cadillac up a few steps and
angling the horse to turn her back on Joe. Big mistake.

"Hey, Vi?" he called out. "In case you're wonder-
ing…those chaps make your butt look just fine."

Her face went hot as a pancake griddle as every eye
in place tracked straight to the back of her saddle. She
slapped her hand against her thigh as if to encourage
Riata Rose, hoping no one but Joe noticed her middle
finger was extended. Three more horses to buck, then
she could ride out of the arena, march up to the announcer's stand and crank the dials on the sound system until
the feedback fried Joe's ears. And honest to God, if he
made a crack about her not being any shrinking violet,
she and Cadillac would run him down on the way.

One of the crew rattled the sliding gate at the front
of the chute as if to open it and let Riata move forward.
She fell for the fake, straightening. Delon slid into position and nodded his head. The chute gate swung wide
and the mare blew straight in the air, all four hooves off
the ground. The instant she touched down, she launched
again, even higher.

Delon matched her, lick for lick, the loose rowels of his spurs singing as his knees jerked up and back, every stroke precise. Shoulders square, no wild flopping or bouncing, rock solid in the midst of a storm, while the silvery fringe on his chaps whipped around him. Violet kicked her horse into a lope to circle around in front of Riata Rose. The mare followed her lead, bucking in a tight loop in front of the chutes, clear to the eight-second buzzer.

On cue, Rose flattened out into a bounding lope. Cole closed in one side, Violet on the other. As she thundered up alongside, Delon yanked his hand from the rigging and grabbed Violet around the waist. The mare's shoulder slammed into Violet's leg, but the contact was routine, absorbed by her shin guard. She clamped her knees hard against the saddle as she veered left to pull Delon clear, then reined her horse to a stop. He dropped on his feet only a few yards from the bucking chute where he'd started.

"Ladies and gentlemen, let's hear it for Delon Sanchez!" the announcer hollered. "If he keeps riding like that, this will be the year he brings a gold buckle home to Texas!"

Delon tipped his hat to acknowledge the cheers, then held up a fist. Violet bumped hers against it. He smiled up at her, out of breath and breathtaking with those sparkling brown eyes and chiseled cheekbones. His smile made her heart sigh a little, because it was the same one she saw on her son's face every single day.

"And the judges say…eighty-two points!" the announcer boomed. "There's your new leader, folks!"

Riata Rose flung her head up, prancing around the

arena like a total prima donna, then ducked out the catch
pen gate. Delon saluted the crowd then reached back and
down to unbuckle the leg straps on his chaps as he stood
beside Violet's horse.

"Soon as I get my gear packed up, I'm gonna grab
Beni from your mom and hit the road."

"His backpack and suitcase are by the door in my
camper."

"Thanks. Don't worry about picking up milk or
anything—we'll grab some groceries on the way."

Thank the Lord above. They were all going home
for the first time in three weeks. Tonight she'd dither
as long as she wanted in a shower big enough that she
didn't bang her elbows when she shampooed her hair.
"I can't wait to sleep in a bed without wheels under it."

"I hear ya." Delon rolled his shoulders, then angled
a look toward where Joe stood chatting with another
fan, the microphone turned off. "Is he giving you a
hard time?"

"Nothing I haven't heard before." Usually she
could ignore it. Cowboys had been making her the butt
of asinine jokes since she started picking up broncs as
a teenager.

"Joe's not like most of the guys you know."

Yeah. She'd noticed. "We can handle him."

Delon aimed another narrow-eyed look at Joe. Then
he slapped Violet's leather-clad knee. "We're outta here.
I'll see y'all at the ranch."

Chapter 5

JOE LEANED AGAINST THE FENCE, INTRIGUED BY THE cozy chat Delon had with Violet after his ride. What was their deal, anyway? Other than the kid. That part was obvious, but the rest of it was hard to figure. The whole Jacobs family had fallen all over Delon when he'd showed up the night before, like he was one of their own. Even Cole had paused in the middle of his chores long enough to chat, and Cole took strong and silent to a whole new level. Or should that be height? The guy was a beast, just like his uncle. Joe had noticed, though, that Delon had bedded down in Cole's trailer, not Violet's.

It was hard to picture them as a couple, but Joe could definitely see the attraction. Violet wasn't hard to look at when she hadn't been mud wrestling. Joe allowed himself a grin at that memory. Wet or dry, she had that all-American thing going on—tall, strong, the one you'd pick first for your beach volleyball team—but the men's jeans she favored didn't do much for her, and she never slowed down long enough to fuss much with her hair or makeup. Violet was in constant motion, organizing this and fixing that when she wasn't working in the arena… or chasing after Beni. Violet, her parents, Cole, Hank, and the truck drivers all pitched in, tag-team style, to chase Beni. The grown-ups weren't winning. At best, it was a draw.

A hand tapped his arm and he nodded and smiled at

whatever a chubby brunette said as he took the rodeo program she held out. At least the fans in Texas were happy to see him. Violet was still giving him the stink eye, acting like he was putting her out—an NFR bullfighter showing up to work for peanuts at her little Podunk rodeos. Yeah. He could see why that would be annoying.

No one should be more pissed than Joe. Damn his stupid hide for letting Wyatt twist his head around and convince him to give Dick a taste of his own medicine. Right. Like that would work. Nobody forced Dick Browning to do anything. Back him into a corner, and he'd just bellow and sling snot like a belligerent old bull, hooking the shit outta anybody who got too close. Joe had lasted fourteen and a half years longer than anyone else who'd worked at the High Lonesome because he understood Dick. Keep your mouth shut, let all the bluster blow right over your head, and a week from now he wouldn't remember why he was chewing your ass to begin with. Every day that Joe bit his tongue and stuck it out, Dick relied on him more. Put enough of those days together…

But he'd blown it all in Puyallup. Fate had handed Joe a golden opportunity to prove he could and should be the one who picked up the reins when Dick was ready to set them down, and he'd turned it to dust. Why couldn't he just stand there and let Lyle make an ass of himself? But no, Joe had to knock the little bastard on his butt, and compound the problem by running off. Now he had to stand his ground because he'd called Dick out. And because Wyatt's voice kept echoing in his head: *Have some pride, Joe.* Then he remembered all those people in Puyallup watching, listening…

Joe signed his name in savage, illegible slashes, passed the program back to the girl, then stepped down the fence into the shade of the bucking chutes to watch the last couple of bareback riders. A skinny guy from Waxahachie settled onto the back of a buckskin they'd named Thumper, for good reason. The stocky gelding pounded the ground like it had insulted his mama. That kid better be stronger than he looked, or this wasn't going to end well.

The cowboy cocked his arm back and nodded. He spurred the hell out of Thumper clear to the end of the chute gate, then the horse jammed his front feet in the dirt and jacked the kid up onto the rigging. The next lunge whipped his shoulders back and his head slammed off Thumper's butt. He went limp, knocked out cold. Joe sprang away from the chute, racing toward the middle of the arena as Violet and Cole spurred into action.

The cowboy's body flopped off the side of the horse, his weight pinning his gloved hand in the rigging. Thumper dragged him by one arm, boneless, defenseless, the horse's rear hooves crashing down around his legs. Violet rode hard to the horse's left side while Cole came up on the right to flip the catch on the flank strap so the buckskin would stop kicking. They thundered around the end of the arena, three abreast. Violet made a lunging grab and got hold of the back strap of the cowboy's chaps, hauling up hard to lift his body out of harm's way. *Thank God he was a scrawny little shit*, Joe thought as he sprinted to meet them.

Cole bailed onto Thumper's neck the way a steer wrestler would jump a steer. He buried his feet in the dirt, his arm locked around the buckskin's nose, his mass and strength too much for even the stout gelding. As they slid to a stop, Joe leapt to the horse's side, yanking at the latigo of the rigging.

"Got it," Joe said, pulling the strap free.

Cole let go of Thumper, stepping in front of him so the horse stumbled backward, then wheeled and trotted away. The cowboy sagged, his full weight hitting the end of Violet's arm. Joe caught the kid around the chest, Cole grabbed him by the thighs, and Violet let go as the two of them lowered his body gently to the ground, hand still stuck in the rigging. From beginning to end, the whole thing had lasted half a minute—an eternity if you were in the middle of it.

The cowboy opened his eyes, blinking groggily as the EMTs rushed up to hunch over him. Violet circled around and rode up close, her knee nudging Joe's back as she leaned out in her stirrup to watch the medics perform a brisk examination of head, neck, and limbs. Finally, they let the kid sit up. A wave of relieved applause rolled around the bleachers as they helped him to his feet.

Joe turned, and his shoulder bumped up under the edge of Violet's chaps, against a muscled thigh. His body did an instinctive *hmmm*. Instead of moving away, he held up a hand. "Nice catch."

"Thanks." She actually smiled at him as she held out a palm.

Instead of a slap, Joe clasped his hand around hers and gave a congratulatory squeeze just to be contrary. His thumb skimmed her wrist and he felt her hammering pulse, the thrill of the save pounding through her system. He knew the feeling. Hell, he lived and breathed the feeling. Their eyes met, and an electric jolt of shared adrenaline and the flash of awareness in her eyes set his blood humming in a whole different way. His mind jumped straight from the arena to her trailer—or the nearest sturdy, vertical surface. The sex would be incredible when two people were revving that hot.

Violet jerked her hand away like she'd read his mind.

Joe held her gaze as he clicked on the wireless microphone so his voice echoed over the loudspeakers. "Give our pickup girl a hand, folks. She's even better than she looks."

Her eyes narrowed and she yanked the reins, spinning her horse around so its ass slammed into Joe, nearly planting him face-first in the dirt. He laughed for the first time since his fist collided with Lyle's jaw. How 'bout that? Sweet Violet could say *fuck you* plain as day, without even moving her lips.

Chapter 6

HE MIGHT BE AN ARROGANT JERK, BUT VIOLET HAD to admit watching Joe Cassidy fight bulls was worth the price of admission. Knees bent, hands on thighs as he waited for the next bull rider to nod, he was a coiled spring. Violet rubbed her palm down the front of her chaps, trying to massage away the memory of his touch. The sizzle of connection. The way his fingers had tightened when he felt it too.

Violet jerked her hand as if it were still in his grasp. Dammit. Why couldn't she lust after a man's brains for a change? But no, it was always the physical. And not just looks, but how a man moved, the wonder of bone and muscle honed to perfection. Joe Cassidy was all that and more—the indefinable something that elevated a star from merely athletic to exceptional.

Better than anything that's set foot in one of your arenas, sweetheart.

"Take him left," Steve Jacobs called out to Joe. "Right around the end of the chute gate."

A good-natured Brangus they called Carrot Top—named for his orangey color and the tuft of curly hair on his hornless head—peered out between the slats of the chute gate. Joe flashed a thumbs-up and adjusted with a few springy steps, shooting a quick glance over to check Hank's position. Violet released a pent-up sigh. So much for a positive role model. She'd wanted someone who'd teach Hank a little humility. Instead, she got Joe.

As the cowboy took the last wrap of the bull rope around his gloved hand, Joe rocked onto the toes of his cleated shoes, as if the adrenaline was blasting out through the balls of his feet. He'd dumped the wireless mic, added knee and ankle braces and a Kevlar vest under his jersey. Not a whole lot of protection considering the average bull weighed as much as an entire NFL defensive line.

The cowboy nodded, and the gate swung wide. In a flash, Joe was there, tapping Carrot Top on his curly head, drawing him around and into a bounding spin. The rider hung tight for two, three, four jumps, the crowd noise swelling. As the eight-second whistle sounded, the bull threw in a belly roll, whipping the cowboy off the side. Hank stepped in, flicking the bull's ear. Carrot Top swung around to follow him. Hank danced backward, his hand on the bull's head. He did a full pirouette, tapped the bull again, and danced away. Carrot Top did the equivalent of an eye roll and a shrug and lumbered toward the exit gate as Hank tipped his hat to the whistles and cheers of the crowd.

Violet ground her teeth. Carrot Top might not hurt a flea—intentionally—but if Hank kept showboating, one of these days he'd push his luck too far. She could only hope he got hurt just bad enough to teach him a lesson, and not enough to cripple him for life.

Joe watched, arms folded and face expressionless. While the announcer started his spiel about the last cowboy set to ride, Joe strolled over to Hank. He raised his hand, but instead of a high five, he flicked the brim of Hank's cowboy hat, tipping it down over his face. When Hank grabbed for the hat, Joe cuffed the back of his head hard enough to make him stagger.

"Hey!" Hank spun around, hat clutched to his chest. "What was that for?"

"Quit fucking around," Joe said.

"I was just having a little fun!"

"You want to do tricks and take bows, join the circus. You want to be a bullfighter, get your ass over there and pay attention. Use your brain instead of just your feet."

Hank tossed Joe a sulky look, but put his hat on and did as ordered. *Well. That was unexpected.* Violet sat back in her saddle, giving Joe a second look. Then the soundman shifted into a familiar thrumming guitar lick that swelled into a thundering crescendo.

"If you're not already on the edge of your seats, folks, you need to get there." The announcer's voice rose in volume and intensity with every word, until he was shouting. "Right now, in this arena, you're about to see the biggest, the baddest, the number-one bull in all of Texas. In chute number three, it's a legend in the making, the pride and joy of Jacobs Livestock...say hello to Dirt Eater!"

The chute gate swung open and for an instant the bull stood framed, silver-gray hide shading to black on his hump and head, thick horns curved like swords. Then he exploded into a right-hand spin, flinging his massive body through space at an impossible rate of speed. The cowboy hung tough, chest forward, free arm back, in perfect position. Dirt Eater made his signature move, driving his forelegs straight up into the sky, kicking with his hinds, his entire body suspended in midair for an instant. Then his head dropped, his nose swooping so low it brushed the ground and came up crusted with sand. The sheer force snapped the cowboy's chin up, yanked his arm straight, then pile-drove him into the ground.

Before Dirt Eater could take another step, Joe hurdled the fallen rider, shouting, "Hey! Hey! Hey!"

The bull took a swipe and caught his leg with a horn, sending him cartwheeling into the air. He did a full twisting backflip and landed on hands and knees as Hank lured the bull clear. The crowd roared. Dirt Eater stopped, snorted, then threw up his head and sauntered away. Kicking up her horse, Violet tracked the bull out of the arena with one eye on Joe where he crouched, head bowed, hands clenched. Hank jogged over, clapping a concerned hand on his shoulder. After a beat, Joe popped up, shook his leg, then jogged in place. Violet heaved a sigh of relief.

"Ladies and gentlemen, let's hear it for one hell of a bull, and one hell of a bullfighter. Welcome to Texas, Joe Cassidy!"

The crowd roared again, stomping and whistling as Joe tipped his hat.

Cole coiled his rope and dropped it over his saddle horn. "That's all she wrote."

And not a minute too soon. Violet stepped off, loosened the cinches, and patted her horse's chocolate-brown neck. "Good work, Cadillac."

He rubbed his head on her shoulder, leaving a streak of dust-infused sweat on her shirt. She shoved him away, then scratched the spot below his ear. Out back, hooves clattered on steel, the crew already loading bucking

horses onto a truck. A second truck idled nearby, waiting to load the bulls and start the two-hour drive home,
the end of their last long road trip of the year. The
Jacobs Ranch was in the wide-open space north of the
Canadian River, eight miles out of a speck on the map
called Earnest, Texas. The closest town of decent size
was Dumas, ten miles south of Earnest, then Amarillo
another forty-five miles down the road. Lord, it would
be good to set her feet on the red dirt of home.

Violet unbuckled her chaps, peeled them off, and
hung them on her saddle horn before leading Cadillac
out of the gate. She would've preferred to make a
beeline for the trailer, but she schmoozed through the
milling crowd, pausing to shake committee members'
hands, congratulate them on a successful weekend, and
mention how much Jacobs Livestock looked forward
to seeing them again next year. Finally, she escaped to
the trailer that hauled the four pickup horses. She slid
Cadillac's bridle off, pulled on his halter, then gave a
startled squeak as something moved practically under
her feet, in the dense shade beneath the gooseneck of
the trailer.

"Sorry. Didn't mean to scare you," Joe said from his
seat on the ground. He was massaging the thigh he'd
been stretching, and he was…

Violet sucked in a breath, then let it out on what came
perilously close to a giggle. Okay, not quite naked, but
he'd stripped off everything but his soccer shorts and
shoes, baring acres of sweat-slick skin.

Violet swallowed hard. "What are you doing under
there?"

"Hiding from my adoring fans."

Damn good thing or we'd have a riot. "Are you hurt?"

"Just a Charlie horse. Dirt Eater tagged me pretty hard." He touched a reddening welt high on the inside of his thigh.

Too high. Violet dragged her eyes back down, waiting. This was where he'd say something like, *That's some bull.* Everyone did.

Everyone except Joe, who spread his legs wide and bent at the waist, his chest nearly touching the ground, giving Violet ample opportunity to admire the long, sleek muscles of his back.

"You should get some ice on that leg," she said.

He angled a sardonic smile over his shoulder that said, *I see what you're lookin' at.* "Believe me, darlin', I know how to take care of a bruise."

"I am not your darlin'." Violet yanked open the door to the tack compartment, blocking him from view, and jammed the bridle onto the nearest hook. "Or your *girl.*"

For crying out loud. Why was she letting him get to her? Cowboys had been flinging bullshit her direction since she was two weeks old—which was about the time she'd developed a weakness for a man with a wild streak. She turned, then squeaked again when she came face-to-face with Joe. Damn, he was quick. She hadn't even seen him move and now he was right *there*—one hand braced on the open door, the other holding a half-drained bottle of water, and all that bare flesh right under her nose.

Dear sweet heaven, that was one beautiful body. Like the yellow Corvette, designed specifically for impressing the girls and taking curves way too fast. This close, she could smell the clean sweat from the clumps of damp hair around his face. His eyes were green. The color of luck, and money, and the other side of the fence. They gleamed with the same arrogant light as his smile.

"Are you always this cranky? Or are you actually still pissed about the pickup girl thing?"

She stiffened and stuck out her chin. "I'm supposed to enjoy being the butt of your jokes?"

"I was just kidding around."

"Yeah. That's what all the sexist assholes say."

He went still, all hint of sarcasm dropping away as he studied her for a few intense moments. "I'm sorry," he said quietly. "You're right. You were working and I was out of line."

His sincerity flustered her in a way his arrogance couldn't. "Uh…thanks for your help. With that bareback rider, I mean. 'Preciate you being on your toes."

"I'm always on my toes." He waggled the water bottle at her, then himself. "That's why they hire us."

Us. As in *You and I.* Two of a kind. In five simple words, he'd paid her the biggest compliment of her career. He hadn't even tagged on the usual *pretty good… for a girl.*

Surprise and an unmitigated burst of pride turned her brain to mush. She heard herself babbling, "Well, um, thanks. And never mind about the other. No big deal. I'm sure you didn't mean it."

The water bottle paused halfway to his mouth. He lowered it slowly, the gleam in his eyes turning dangerous. "Didn't mean what?"

"Uh, you know. What you said about, um, me. You were just kidding."

"About which part?" His voice lowered to a rough

purr that sent a shiver over her skin despite the heat. And just like that, the energy between them changed again. "Why wouldn't I want you to pick me up?"

Because…because…oh Lord. There went her last functional brain cell. He leaned closer, fully into her space, and she had to fight the instinct to retreat. The even stronger urge to press her palms to his chest and get another hit of energy off his radioactive core. She opened her mouth, but the words jammed in her throat.

He brushed her jaw with his thumb, condensation from the water bottle leaving a damp trail on her skin. "Be careful what you assume, Violet. I might have to prove you wrong."

Then he stepped back, toasting her with the water and a smirk as Cole rode up. It was all Violet could do not to rub off the wet spot on her skin before it was vaporized by the static electricity crackling between them. His eyes laughed at her, even as they glowed with answering heat. Now she knew exactly what kind of trouble Joe Cassidy was—the kind she'd never been able to resist getting into.

Chapter 7

THE LONE STEER SALOON WAS A NEON OASIS halfway between Dumas and Earnest. The Jacobs convoy took up a quarter of the gravel parking lot: two semis loaded with stock, Cole's pickup and horse trailer, and two pickups pulling the camper trailers that housed the rest of the Jacobs family on the road.

Cole, Hank, and Joe were the last to arrive because Cole had to double-check every inch of the arena, chutes, and stock pens for forgotten equipment, even though he'd counted each halter and flank strap as it was hung on its designated hook. Cole had a mental checklist and it was like he had to follow it to the letter or his head would explode. Compulsive—one of Wyatt's pet words. Pain in the ass would have been Joe's choice.

He climbed out of the pickup, wincing. His thigh had tightened up, but it was nothing an ice pack and few days of jogging and stretching wouldn't fix. He kept his limp to a minimum as they crossed the parking lot. Couldn't let Hank think he was a wimp. Or worse…old. Beyond the parking lot, the plains stretched off in every direction, barren and featureless in the moonlight. No comfort for the lonely out there. Joe shivered, goose-flesh rising on his back as if the ghost of a lost soul had trailed its finger down his spine.

Inside, the Lone Steer was classic honky-tonk: rustic wood, a bar that stretched the length of the back wall, and a big dance floor off to one side with a stage crammed into the corner. On a Sunday evening the barstools stood mostly empty, but over half of the tables were full. The prime rib must be as good as it smelled. Cole skirted the edge of the dance floor, nodding a greeting at every table as he crossed the room, but not pausing to chat—big surprise. Through the door to a small banquet room, Joe saw a single long table that held the rest of the Jacobs crew. Steve held court at one end, wife and daughter on his right, a pair of empty seats on his left.

Joe stalled, suddenly claustrophobic. That wasn't his place. These weren't his people. He was sore and bone tired and beyond capable of playing nice with strangers who couldn't figure out what the hell he was doing there. Cole started for the empty seats, glancing over his shoulder when Joe didn't follow.

"I'm gonna grab a beer," Joe said.

Cole absorbed that for a beat, then shrugged and went to sit down.

Joe escaped to a stool at the far end of the bar. When he tried to pay for his beer, the bartender shook him off. "Steve'll take care of it. How do you want your prime rib?"

"Medium rare." Joe tapped his beer glass. "And bring me a refill when this one's gone."

Considering what they were paying him, Jacobs Livestock could afford to kick in a couple of beers. When the bartender handed him the frosty glass, Joe sucked down a third of the ice-cold brew in the first few gulps. Not the best way to rehydrate, but screw it. He had four days to recover what he'd sweated out, and not a damn thing to fill them.

He'd been on the road almost continuously since the Fourth of July. When he did have a break, he made a beeline for the High Lonesome, if only to ride the pastures, check the stock, and let the vast emptiness suck the clutter out of his brain. Even if Steve Jacobs would turn him loose on their ranch, he doubted strange country could work the same magic. And if he'd ever needed to clear his head…

His phone buzzed. He checked the number, contemplated letting it go to voice mail, but answered on the last possible ring. "What?"

"I see Texas is doing wonders for your disposition," Wyatt said.

"Maybe I'm sick of some nosy bastard calling to check on me."

Wyatt clucked his tongue. "It's the first time we've sent you off without even Dickhead for company. We worry."

"What *we*?"

"I lent you my favorite redhead, so I'm having dinner at Hamley's with yours."

"I thought Roxy was going home this morning." Joe frowned, suspicion flaring from long experience. "Are she and Frank having trouble?"

"They're solid. Frank's trip to Japan was extended. The usual."

Meaning someone was gonna lose a billion dollars if Joe's stepfather didn't stay to take care of it personally. One thing Joe had to say for his mother—every time she got married, she did better for herself.

"Why is she still in Pendleton?" Joe asked.

"She wanted to spend some quality time with her other son."

"She's not old enough to be your mother." She was barely old enough to be Joe's mother.

"Unfortunately she *is* your mother, so I have to keep my thoughts in the maternal realm."

Joe groaned. "Just once could you talk like a normal person?"

"No. You really are in a crappy mood. What's up?"

"Besides the mess with Dick?"

Wyatt made a dismissive noise. "After the flogging he got from the Roundup directors, he's ready to kiss your ass."

Or kick it clear to Hell.

"What else?" Wyatt asked.

Joe kept him waiting while he swirled his beer, took a swig, and set the glass down. "Obviously it was a mistake to assume these people would be thrilled to see me."

"Short of going myself, I sent them the best bull-fighter in the country. How is that a problem?"

"Hell if I know."

There was a rattle and Wyatt's voice went muffled, calming. Great. Now Roxy was wound up. Just what Joe needed, his mother on a tear.

Wyatt came back on the line. "From what I hear, Steve Jacobs is a decent guy, but extremely old school. Probably takes a while to warm up to new people."

"I'm not new," Joe snapped. "I'm a pro, and he looks at me like I'm gonna whip out a crack pipe behind the chutes. And his daughter…"

Now *she* had a perfectly good reason to be mad. He'd let his temper get the best of him again, and this time he'd shot off his mouth. Sexually harassed her in the middle of a rodeo performance. His mother would not be impressed. He couldn't erase the damage, but he had apologized, hadn't he?

Right before he did it again.

"I did tell you to get a haircut," Wyatt said. "And Shorty said the daughter seemed high-strung."

"Violet?" Joe snorted. "Hardly."

"So what is she?"

"A pickup man."

"Really?" Wyatt pulled the word out into two syllables, a rare lapse into his New England drawl. "Is she any good?"

"She and her cousin are as solid as any pair I've seen."

"What's she like outside the arena?" Wyatt asked.

Bossy. Busy. All business, with one exception—him. "Pissed off."

What he'd said in the arena was nothing compared to that stunt he'd pulled out back, mocking her, crowding her. Close enough to know that under the dust and horse sweat, she smelled like a fresh-peeled orange, which was a lot sexier than he would have guessed. He guzzled another third of his beer.

Wyatt was talking to Roxy again and hadn't bothered to cover the phone. "I know. They usually aren't like that until after he sleeps with them. Did you sleep with her?" he asked Joe.

"I've only been here three days!"

"He says no. Maybe that's why she's annoyed."

"Thanks for discussing my sex life with my mother," Joe said, then winced when the bartender shot him a startled look. "Tell her I'm fine. I'll call her tomorrow so she can hear just how fine I am."

"He misses you," Wyatt said to Roxy. "And he's homesick."

"I am *not* homesick."

But the ache caught him up under the ribs, sharp as one of Dirt Eater's horns. He could picture them sitting at their usual table at Hamley's, the historic steak house in the heart of downtown Pendleton. East balcony, second floor, right below the red stamped-tin ceiling so Wyatt could observe and critique the sea of humanity in the bar below. Joe dragged in a long breath, then froze. Shit. Oranges. He glanced over his shoulder. Yep. There was Violet, and if she was close enough to smell, she was damn sure close enough to hear.

"I have to go."

He hung up and swiveled around on his stool, prepared to be as much of an asshole as necessary to chase her away. Then he got a good look at her and the words dissolved on his tongue.

She'd tossed the men's Wranglers in favor of dark jeans that rode low on her hips, doing a stellar job of showing off her curves. Holy hopping hell, she had curves. Firm and proud under a snug-fitting, vivid pink shirt. She'd done something with her hair, made it fall around her face in a smooth, shimmery curve, the lights over the bar picking out glints of red in the dark brown. And how had he missed that mouth? Full and soft and shiny with gloss that had just enough color to make him want to take a bite, to see if she tasted as sweet as she looked.

"Joe?"

He dragged his eyes up to meet hers. She'd done some work there, too. Put on more makeup so they looked bigger, darker. Concerned.

"What do you want?" he asked, snapping out the words.

She folded her arms, which only served to lift and frame a particularly stellar set of…curves. "I hope you're not sitting out here alone because of me."

"You? Why?" Although with as much trouble as he was having keeping his eyes from straying, it was probably best he wasn't sitting at that table across from her dad. Steve already acted like he was a convicted goat rapist.

"I called you a sexist asshole," Violet said.

"Oh. That. Nope. Didn't bother me." Much. He spun around and hunched over his beer. "I wanted some space."

He waited for her to go. She hesitated another beat, then settled onto the stool beside him, pointing at Joe's beer to indicate to the bartender that she wanted the same.

He threw her a scowl. "What part of that sounded like *Sit down and stay awhile?*"

"I don't need your permission."

Joe blew out a sigh that rippled the foam on what was left of his beer. "What? You're bored, so you come out here to irritate me?"

"Nope. I came to use the bathroom. Irritating you was a bonus."

He glanced in the direction she waved. Yep, he was sitting by the hallway to the restrooms. "Mission accomplished. You can go back to the party now."

"I'd rather not." She shrugged off his glare. "You're not the only one who could use some space. We've been on the road for a month, practically on top of each other."

Oh geezus. He did not need the rush of heat, imagining what it would be like to be on top of Violet, buried in those killer curves.

The bartender set a beer in front of her. "You want the tab or should I give it to your dad?"

"Me. He'll lose the receipt before he gets out the door."

Joe took a long, slow swallow of his beer. What did she want? Not that it would be hard to figure out. Up close, Violet had the opposite of a poker face. Every thought and emotion played out in those big brown eyes, across that mouth. He'd seen her trying not to look at his bare chest earlier. She was attracted and not the least bit pleased about it. Joe smiled to himself. So that was it. She wanted to prove she could handle him. Fine. Let her try.

He angled her an insolent smile. "If you're gonna sit there, you have to tell me something about yourself."

"I can't imagine there's anything you haven't heard."

"Everybody's got secrets."

"In a town this size? Not hardly." She took a sip of her beer and licked the foam from her top lip, sending another pulse of heat through Joe's system.

"Tell me about your kid."

Her eyes went cool. Protective. "His name is Beni. He's five."

"And you and Delon are…"

"Friends."

"With benefits?"

"Only once," she said, as matter-of-fact as if they were discussing the weather.

Joe felt his jaw drop. Had she just admitted her kid was the result of a one-night stand?

"Like I said, no secrets here." Her mouth curled into a sneer as she glanced past Joe to the tables beyond. "There are a dozen people in this bar who'd be thrilled to tell you the whole story."

Joe glanced around. Sure enough, most of the other patrons were looking back and didn't bother to pretend otherwise. "Why did you hook up that one time?"

Violet gave a slight shrug. "Delon and I were both nursing a case of the blues. Relationships gone wrong, blah, blah, blah. One shot of tequila led to another and… well, you can imagine."

Oh yeah. Joe could imagine. Way too clearly. He gulped down the last of his beer and shoved the glass toward the bartender, who replaced it with a full one.

Violet fixed Joe with a steady gaze. "Anything else you're dying to know?"

Hell yes. "Why don't you want me here?"

She barely blinked. "You're not the person I hired."

"I know. I'm better."

She flashed him a disgusted look. "And I'm sure we should feel blessed, but I was in the market for someone who might come back next year."

"And you figured Shorty was that guy?"

"Sure. Why not?"

Joe lifted his eyebrows. "If he's good enough to replace me at Pendleton, he's out of your league."

This time, she took a beat to recover. "Well. I guess that puts me in my place."

Her voice was husky, with a slight tremble that made Joe feel like a complete prick when he was only telling the truth. "For the record, I'm no happier about it than you are."

"Then why are you here?"

"Same reason you're sitting on that barstool." At her blank look, he added, "Tryin' to prove a point, darlin'."

The reminder sliced at his gut, severing the frayed tether on his always limited supply of discretion. He cocked his head toward her, breathed deep. Her scent was magnified by the warmth of the bar. Along with the beer he'd guzzled on an empty stomach, it made his head do a giddy spin. "Why do you smell like a bowl of oranges?"

She rubbed a hand over her bare arm with a self-conscious smile. "Mandarin cream lotion. Beni gave it to me for Mother's Day. He likes stuff that smells like fruit."

"Me too." Joe let his arm brush hers and got a nice *zing!* at the contact.

She edged away, sliding a quick glance toward the banquet room. "I, um, should…"

"Running off so soon? We were just getting to know each other." He swiveled his stool so his thigh pressed against the warm, firm length of hers and heard the quick catch of her breath. "Besides, I have one more question."

Her eyes were wide, cautious, that soft mouth so close he could practically taste it. "What?"

He leaned in until her hair brushed his cheek as he whispered in her ear. "Can I buy you a shot of tequila?"

Chapter 8

VIOLET WOKE UP MONDAY MORNING EXHAUSTED from beating the crap out of her pillow. Imagining it was Joe. That arrogant *bastard*. She should have punched him in the mouth and told him what he could do with his shot of tequila. But no. She'd stuttered a lame ass *No, thank you* and scurried back to her parents like he was the Big Bad Wolf and she was packin' a basket of her mama's cookies.

Even if he did look as tired and homesick as he swore he wasn't to whoever was on the phone, she shouldn't have parked next to him at the bar. Nothing good could come of it when he appealed so strongly to her worst instincts. He'd been a complete jerk and her stupid skin still hummed where he'd brushed up against her.

What the hell, Violet?

She jammed her toothbrush into the holder and followed the sound of her son's excited chatter to the kitchen. Her single-wide mobile home had a bedroom and a bathroom on each end with the kitchen and living room in the middle. A perfect setup for her not-so-usual living arrangements, especially on the nights when it was more convenient for Delon to crash in the extra bed in Beni's room.

Father and son sat at the table scooping cereal out of matching Sponge Bob bowls. Delon looked disgustingly good in the morning. He looked disgustingly good most of the time. What the man did for a plain white cotton T-shirt should be illegal. So how come she never got hot flashes when *he* brushed up against her?

Again, *What the hell, Violet?*

Delon lifted one dark brow. "Feeling a little rough?"

She curled her lip at him. "Feeling suicidal?"

He jumped up, poured a cup of coffee, and shoved it into her hands.

She inhaled, then drank, then sighed. "Okay. You can live."

"Whew!"

She smiled, relaxing for the first time in days. They'd agreed from the beginning that sex was off the table. Well, not the very beginning. First Delon had insisted they get married. And Violet had asked if he'd lost his ever-loving mind, and he'd sulked for a while. *Then* they'd agreed. There was too much at stake—a lifetime of friendship, the infinite connections between their two families, Beni's happiness—to muddle it up with sex.

Not that they'd never been tempted. What woman wouldn't be tempted by Delon, especially when the rest of the male species seemed hell-bent on proving that she was an idiot to even glance elsewhere? More than once, when one or both of them had been worn to the bone by life and the rodeo road, they'd nearly given in. Offered and accepted the comfort right at their fingertips—but somehow they'd always stopped before crossing the line. Was it crazy to think a relationship should be based on more than mutual respect and love for their child?

Delon pulled a bowl out of the cupboard, filled it with raisin bran, and set it in front of her on the table.

"Hey, Beni, why don't you run over and say good-bye to Grandpa and Grandma?"

"And Katie, too?" Beni asked.

"Sure."

Beni was off like a shot to inflict a hug on Cole's red heeler dog and bum snacks from his grandmother, warding off any chance of starvation on the ten-mile drive into town.

Delon sipped his coffee, letting Violet suck down half of her first cup before he spoke. "So how's it going with Joe?"

Heat climbed into Violet's face. Stupid. She hadn't done anything. And she didn't intend to, dammit. "He's a hell of a bullfighter."

"That's a given." Muscles bunched in Delon's arms as he cradled his mug, suddenly fascinated by his coffee. "How's he fitting in, um…personally?"

Violet paused in the act of pouring milk on her cereal. "How do you mean?"

Delon flicked a glance at her as he rotated the mug between his hands. "I heard you were together at the Lone Steer last night."

"Who told you?" Violet plunked the jug down hard enough to make milk splash out the top.

He hunched a shoulder. "Oh, you know. People."

Yeah. And she could guess which people. Violet jumped up and grabbed a washcloth to swipe at the spilled milk. "I wasn't *with* Joe. I sat by him at the bar while I took care of the tab."

"They said it looked like he was hitting on you."

They should eat shit and die. And since when did Delon give her the third degree? They'd always had an unspoken don't-ask-don't-tell policy when it came to dating. "He was just trying to mess with me."

Delon looked up, frowning. "Why?"

"I'm not sufficiently grateful for his presence. His ego is dented." She stomped to the sink, rinsed the cloth, and wrung it to within an inch of its life. "Don't worry. After that disaster in Hickory Springs, I'm giving up men until my next reincarnation."

"I can see how that would put you off." Delon's lips twitched, just barely, but he flattened out the grin before she could snarl.

Violet wandered over to the table to plop down opposite him. "Sorry. I'm a little out of sorts this morning."

"Anything I can do?"

Tell her Joe was wrong, and Jacobs Livestock wasn't a two-bit rodeo company, living off scraps that were too small for the big shots like Dick Browning? With every sneer, Joe reminded her that next year she'd be producing the same rodeos, in the same dusty, one-horse towns, while he strutted around on a stage bigger than she'd ever experience at this rate.

"Just my usual case of end-of-summer blues." She forced a smile. "Give me a few days to knock some road dust off, get out in the open space, and I'll be good."

Delon knew her too well to fall for her flippant tone, but he only hesitated a beat. "If you say so."

Violet polished off her cereal and left Delon gathering up the belongings Beni had scattered in the few short hours since he'd been home. Outside the air still held a hint of morning freshness, but it would be weeks before the leaves turned from green to gold. Dust puffed around her feet as she crossed the driveway to her mother's blocky frame house, shaded by oak and pecan trees. Past Violet's house stood a bunkhouse that had been refurbished to serve as guest quarters, then Cole's two-room cabin. When Violet had hired Shorty Edwards, it'd made perfect sense to put their temporary bullfighter up in the bunkhouse. Save a few bucks on a motel, win him over with her mother's cooking. Now she had Joe Cassidy camped on her doorstep. This was *so* not going the way she'd planned.

The ranch stretched south, over a series of low bluffs and plateaus, the draws choked with scrubby mesquite and tough native grass. The only real patch of color was Iris Jacobs's yard: lush green set off by splotches of pink, blue, orange, red, and more. Otherwise, the landscape was painted in muted shades: mostly brown, plus the chalky pinks, reds, and whites of the bluff behind the ranch buildings. Not exactly paradise, but Violet wouldn't trade the Panhandle for all the trees in the Piney Woods.

She found her mother in the kitchen, leaning on the sink, head cocked toward the open window. Violet favored her in coloring and features, if not size. Iris's brown hair was short and curly, her body strong through the shoulders but soft in the middle, just like her disposition. She made a shushing motion and gestured toward the window. Violet eased over to peek out.

Beni sat on the picnic table on the covered rear deck, cereal box on his lap. Joe was perched on one side of him and Cole on the other. Cole was in his usual uniform of denim button-down shirt, jeans, and battered straw cowboy hat. Joe wore a Pendleton Whisky T-shirt and a Coors cap. With that lanky body and hair straggling past his collar, he reminded Violet of a major league pitcher—deliberate scruff, lethal speed, a deadly combination.

Beni reached into his box, fished out a few chocolate puffs, and handed one to each of his companions. "Ready?"

They nodded gravely.

"Okay, go."

All three popped the cereal into their mouths and chewed. Beni scrunched his eyes shut as if waiting for a firecracker to explode. After a few seconds, he opened one eye to peek at Cole, who shook his head. Beni opened the other eye to check with Joe, who did the same.

Beni heaved a mournful sigh. "It's not *working.*"

Violet looked at her mother, who shrugged.

Pushing open the screen door, Violet went out onto the deck. "Why the sad face, little man?"

"There's something wrong with this cereal." Beni scowled at the box. "On TV, they said amazing things will happen if you eat it."

Violet had to work to keep an appropriately solemn expression. "What kind of amazing things?"

"I don't know, but we've been eating and eating it—"

"And not one single monkey has flown out of my ass," Joe drawled.

Cole made a noise that sounded like a chocolate puff going down the wrong pipe.

Beni giggled. "You said a bad word."

"Oh sh—I mean, shoot. I didn't mean—"

Violet strangled another laugh and gave Beni a stern look. "Sometimes big people say those words. Doesn't mean you can."

"But, Mommy—"

"No." She turned to Cole before Beni could drag her into a debate about exactly which words were off-limits, requiring him to say all of them. "You still want to gather those two-year-old bulls?"

"Not this morning." Her father strolled out to join them on the deck. "Delon said he'll take a look at that Jake brake on the Peterbilt if I can drop it by their shop by ten. Someone'll have to follow along and give me a ride home."

Cole pushed to his feet. "I'll come. We can swing by the feed store and pick up more mineral for the cows."

Violet mentally revised her schedule, bumping laundry and bookkeeping to the top of the list. "We can gather after lunch."

"Or I can help you now," Joe offered.

Four heads swiveled toward him. Joe met Violet's glare with a bland smile and a gleam in his eye.

"You have to be a cowboy to chase bulls," Beni declared. "You're just a bullfighter."

Violet choked down a snort of laughter at Joe's thunderstruck expression. *Just* a bullfighter. God bless her son.

"I know how to handle stock," Joe said.

"As good as Uncle Cole?" Beni asked.

"Uh—"

Beni patted Joe's arm. "Don't worry. Nobody's as good as Uncle Cole, but you can borrow his horse. Mom says Dozer's been working this ranch so long he can make any idiot look useful."

Cole laughed, a single, loud *hah!* Violet nearly had an aneurysm trying to gag herself. There was a strangled snort from her dad's direction, but when she glanced at him, his face was impassive. Joe did not look amused.

"That's real nice of you, Beni," Violet said. "But we'll wait—"

"If you think you're up to it," her dad said, his words edged with challenge.

Joe didn't blink. "No problem."

"But—" Violet began.

"Okay then." Her father glanced at his watch. "We'd better get a move on, Cole."

As the back door slapped shut behind them, Violet fired a glare at Joe. He smiled, mocking as always, but before either of them could speak, Delon stuck his head out the door. His gaze landed on Joe and cooled. "Joe."

"Delon," Joe answered, in an equally flat voice.

Violet looked from one to the other, catching a whiff of testosterone in the air. What the hell?

"Ready to go, Beni?" Delon asked.

"Yes!" Beni jumped up and ran to his father.

Delon turned him around and gave him a nudge. "Hug your mom good-bye."

Violet leaned down and he threw his arms around her, pressing his silky cheek against hers. "I'll miss you," she said, squeezing hard.

"Miss you, too," he said, and planted a smacking kiss on her face. Then he squirmed free and scampered through the door, dragging his dad by the hand.

"See you Thursday," Delon called over his shoulder.

Then they were gone, and Violet was alone on the deck with Joe.

He flashed a toothy smile. "Looks like it's just you and me, darlin'."

Violet growled under her breath. Hell. Just...*hell*.

Chapter 9

Joe strolled down to the barn, grinning as Violet stomped ahead of him. Aggravating her was turning out to be a decent distraction. Nice of Delon to get the kid out of the way for a few days, so Joe didn't have to watch his step. Or his mouth.

Joe's good mood deflated slightly at the reminder of Beni. Were all kids that wise at his age? Other than scribbling autographs and patting heads, Joe didn't come into contact with many humans under the age of fourteen. He paused in the barn door. "Sorry about the swearing. I'm not used to being around kids."

Violet snagged a pair of halters from a hook. "When Beni isn't behind the bucking chutes, he's hanging around the shop at Sanchez Trucking. He can probably cuss circles around you."

"In English and Spanish?"

"Delon isn't Hispanic." She snatched up a pair of leather gloves and fired them at Joe.

He caught them in self-defense. "But…Sanchez?"

"Their grandfather took his stepdad's name. They're dark because Delon's mother is Navajo."

"So that makes Beni—"

"An American." She slapped a halter into Joe's hand and pointed at a stout sorrel gelding. "That's Dozer. Use the saddle on the first rack. It's the only one that fits him."

The horse was built like his namesake and moved with about as much finesse. Straddling him was not going to feel good on Joe's sore thigh. "I can handle something less idiotproof."

Violet tossed a smirk over her shoulder as she haltered Cadillac. "Better safe than sorry."

"Expecting trouble?"

"With bulls? Always. Too much testosterone… makes them stupid." The bite in her voice made it clear her opinion applied to males in general.

Joe grinned. Say what she wanted, he'd felt the answering flash of heat every time he touched her. His blood still hummed when she got close.

"I'd like to get this done sometime today," she said.

"Yes, ma'am." He gave her a lazy salute before letting himself into Dozer's stall.

When both horses were saddled, Violet handed him a rope and slung one over her own saddle horn. At her whistle, Cole's red heeler, Katie, popped up out of the patch of shade where she'd been keeping a close eye on the proceedings. Joe followed Violet out the back of the barn, through a corral, and down a long, wide lane flanked with square pens, built of heavy oilfield pipe that could take anything a one-ton bull—much less a horse— dished out. The pens were empty now while the rodeo stock enjoyed a few days of well-earned pasture time.

"You said you graduated from college," Joe said as he mounted up. "Where?"

"West Texas A&M, in Canyon."

"They teach Pickup Man 101 there?"

One corner of her mouth twitched. "I have a business degree. You?"

"I worked my first pro rodeo before I graduated from high school. Couldn't see how sleeping through another four years of classes was gonna improve my career prospects."

She snorted, almost a laugh. "You and Cole."

At the end of the lane, Violet pushed the heavy steel gate wide before swinging aboard her horse. Beyond the corrals, barbed wire angled out to either side, forming a funnel that would guide the bulls into the lane. Dust billowed around them as she led the way up through a gap in the rocky bluff and onto the flat above. From there, the land stretched to the horizon on all sides, the neighboring homesteads distant glints of glass and metal in the sunlight.

"I suppose this is pretty barren compared to where you're from."

Joe shook his head. "The high desert is basically like northern Nevada. Not much different from here except the hills are bigger."

She looked at him with a smidgen of curiosity. "Did you move there to work for Browning?"

"Nope. Born and raised."

"You have family there?"

He shook his head again. "Both of my parents moved away."

"Separately?"

"Yeah."

For a few minutes there was nothing but the dull clop of hooves on baked earth and the crunch of dry grass. The sun beat down on Joe's shoulders, hot but not unbearable. The aroma of the mesquite was sharp like sagebrush. The hawk circling overhead was probably a different species, but its cry pierced the air in the same way as those back home. If it weren't for the slightly higher humidity and flatness of the landscape, he could almost imagine he was on the High Lonesome. Close enough to stir up the longing so it swelled inside him until it felt as if his rib cage would explode from the pressure.

Today should've been the first day of his treasured fall break between Pendleton and the circuit finals in Redmond. Weaning day, one of Joe's favorites of the entire year, seeing the future wrapped in coats that were still downy, shining from eyes that held that certain gleam—a spark of wildness bred into their bones. Joe could trace it back through their mothers, fathers, even grandparents. He knew every colt's breeding by the shape of its head, the slope of its shoulder. This was his family tree—planted in borrowed ground.

"I appreciate you setting Hank straight yesterday," Violet said abruptly. "He won't listen to any of us."

"He'll grow out of it eventually. I did."

She raised her eyebrows, a silent *really?*

"Hah. Funny."

"I didn't say a word." But she smirked and Joe smirked back at her. She broke off the eye contact, twisting in her saddle to search for any sign of the bulls.

She'd opted for the man pants and a baggy T-shirt. Whatever she wore underneath had some serious squashing power to hide those mouthwatering curves. She must do it on purpose. What she'd worn at the bar would be a major distraction on the ranch or in the arena. Hell, twelve hours later, Joe was still seeing pink.

"Why isn't it Violet Sanchez?" he asked.

Her gaze jerked back to him. "Excuse me?"

"You and Delon act more married than half of the married people I know. Why not make it official?"

"We don't feel that way about each other."

"He stays in your house."

She fired an irritated look at him. "Why do you care?"

"Before I buy you that shot of tequila, I want to be sure I'm not trespassing."

Her chin came up, her cheeks flushing. "I'm not a piece of property."

"Looks like Delon's staked a claim."

"We share a kid and a friendship. Nothing more."

Right. That explained the *Step the fuck away from my woman* look Delon had given him. Delon had a pretty sweet deal as far as Joe could see. He got to do whatever he wanted on the road, no questions asked, and still come home to his cozy little family. "Not even an occasional booty call?"

She made a sound of disbelief wrapped up in anger. "Are you always this…"

"Curious?"

"Not quite the word I was looking for."

He grinned. She huffed out a breath.

"Not that it's any of your business, but no, no booty calls. It's not worth the risk. There would be feelings, and someone would get hurt, and Beni would be the one who suffered most."

Yeah. Joe knew all about that. His parents had splattered feelings all over the place before, during, and after the divorce. Proof positive that getting married because you were knocked up wasn't such a great plan, either.

"How's your future husband gonna feel about Delon camping in the spare room?"

"That's not an issue." She shot him an assessing glance. "What about the woman in the Corvette?"

"She's Wyatt's problem. I've already hit my quota of incredibly high-maintenance redheads." When Violet raised her eyebrows, he added, "My mother."

"Oh." She jerked her gaze away, holding a hand over the bill of her cap to shade her eyes as she scanned the horizon in search of their prey. "There isn't exactly a stampede of eligible bachelors looking to relocate to Earnest, Texas. And besides, Beni's at a tough age."

"It won't be any easier when he's ten or eleven."

Her gaze shifted to him, sharpening. "Is that how old you were?"

Hell. He hadn't meant to let that slip. He nodded tersely. "Ten the first time they split. Eleven when they got back together. Twelve when they did everybody a favor and made it permanent."

"Why?"

"Personality conflict." As in his mother claimed his father had none, but Joe didn't intend to share that charming detail.

"It was better after they split?" Violet asked.

Joe shifted in the saddle to take pressure off his sore thigh, stretched to the limit by Dozer's broad back and jarring walk. He preferred not to think about those days. Roxy, with her stereotypical redheaded temper tantrums. His dad, the king of the silent treatment. And Joe, left hanging between them like a human piñata, taking all the emotional whacks even though he wasn't their target.

"It wasn't worse," he said.

Violet's eyes darkened with sympathy. Joe braced himself for more questions, but she tilted her head toward the next draw. "Come on. As slow as Dozer walks, we'll be out here until dark if we don't kick up into a lope."

—m—

It figured Joe would sit a horse like he was born to it. He was bound and determined to be everything Violet ever wanted in a man—except available for anything beyond the next two and half weeks. Not that she was looking for permanent. Between Beni, Delon, Cole, and her dad, her life was so full of men she wasn't sure where she'd cram another one in.

The bulls were in the first draw, lounging in the shade of the trees above the water hole, thankfully. The next likely spot was another half mile across the flat, and she'd had enough quality time with Joe. Bad enough she couldn't talk her body out of responding to his physical presence—then he had to go and act semi-human. Imagining him young, confused, and caught in the crossfire between his parents was a whole lot more dangerous than any hot and tinglies, damn her sympathetic heart.

As they started down the side of the draw, Cadillac pushed at the bridle, nudging her back to the job at hand. The bulls' heads came up and they clambered to their feet, a dozen in all, from silver gray to dark red to coal black, all lean, athletic Brahma crossbreds.

"What's the plan?" Joe asked, pulling the rope off his saddle horn and building a loop.

"You know how to use that thing?" Violet asked.

"Well enough."

"Watch that brindle," Violet said, pointing to a black bull with orangey tiger stripes. "He's one of Dirt Eater's calves and he inherited his daddy's jumping ability. Last time we brought them in, he cleared the barbed wire fence and got off down the highway."

Yet another reason she'd wanted Cole along on this mission. Like her, he'd done this so many times he could anticipate almost every move a bull could make. As they started toward the bunch, two of the bulls waded into the water at the edge of the stock pond, belly deep. Violet gestured to the dog. "Come by, Katie."

The dog blasted off like a rocket and bailed into the murky water, swimming out and around the two bulls. When one lowered its head, snorting, she nipped its nose. It bellowed, jumped back, and splashed out of the water. The second followed. Katie chugged after them, picking up speed when she hit shallow water and found the bottom. She paused on the bank long enough to shake off the water and throw Violet a triumphant look.

"Good dog."

Violet kicked Cadillac up to circle the right side of the herd. She raised a hand to direct Joe to the left but he was already there, bringing up the flank and leaving the middle to the dog. Katie zipped forward to nip the heels of a bull that wheeled around to butt heads with one of his buddies.

Violet slapped her hand against her thigh, shouting, "Hyah, hyah!" until they moved out at a brisk trot. Like a bunch of teenage boys, bulls this age would conjure up all kinds of trouble if you gave them time to think. They crossed the flat without problem. Then the bulls hit the trail down off the bluff and broke into a lope, the brindle bull in the lead. Violet urged Cadillac to keep pace as they skidded down the loose dirt path.

As soon as she hit the bottom, she tapped Cadillac with the tail of her rope, pushing him into a gallop. She blew past the lead bull and swung Cadillac around hard on his hocks. The brindle hesitated. Violet swung her loop and shouted as the bull ducked left, then right, then sprinted straight for the fence behind her. She flung a Hail Mary shot as he passed. Miracle of miracles, it dropped over his horns in mid-leap. One hind leg failed to clear the top wire. Wire screeched, stretched, but held. Violet had just enough time to get the tail of her rope wrapped around the saddle horn before the bull kicked loose of the fence.

Cadillac staggered, jerked almost off his feet by the force of a thousand pounds of bovine brought to a halt. The big brown horse dropped his butt and dug in as the bull swung around, and the rope snapped taut, horse on one end, bull on the other…and four strands of barbed wire in between.

"You got him?" Joe yelled, pushing the rest of the herd through the gate.

"For now," Violet yelled back. "Hold 'em, Katie."

The dog plopped on her belly in the middle of the pipe-fenced lane, daring any of the bulls to try to get past her. Joe bailed off his horse and yanked open the wire gate leading out to where the brindle was slinging his head, fighting the rope. Vaulting back onto Dozer, Joe shook out his loop and eased close.

His first attempt snagged only the right horn. He cursed, coiled his rope, and rebuilt the loop. On the second attempt, it fit. He dallied the tail of the rope around his saddle horn and backed Dozer up until it was tight.

"I'll come around to your side and help push him," Violet said, and let go of her rope.

She loped Cadillac to the gate, out, and around. The bull squatted on its haunches, pulling hard against the rope, but he couldn't budge Dozer.

Joe grinned like this was the most fun he'd had in a coon's age. "You should call this one Flight Risk."

Violet couldn't help grinning back. "I'll keep that in mind. Ready?"

"Ready."

Joe reined Dozer around and kicked. The big sorrel lowered his head and grunted, metal-shod hooves carving divots as he plowed ahead, skidding the bull across the hard red clay. Violet rammed Cadillac's chest into the bull's butt. The bull popped to his feet, took three steps, then locked up again. Dozer kept going. After another bump from Violet, the bull weakened, still dragging, but walking now. Joe pulled him through the gate. When the bull spotted his companions clustered at the far end of the lane, he launched for the herd, blowing past Joe and Dozer. The rope burned through Joe's gloved hand, the free end whistling as it spun loose of the saddle horn. Violet heard a pop.

Joe doubled over the front of the saddle. *"Fuck!"*

"What's wrong?" Alarm shot a cold spear into Violet's gut. "Did it catch your hand?"

Joe was too busy cussing to answer. Violet jumped off her horse, swung the big metal gate shut, and slammed the latch into place. Joe slid off his horse, face contorted with pain. He pressed his back against the nearest post and eased down, knees bent, hands clasped tight between his thighs, grinding out curses between clenched teeth. Violet dropped to a crouch between his feet, stomach churning at what she might find. Just a month earlier, she'd seen a team roper lose a thumb by catching it in his rope, and last year one of the tie-down ropers had crushed his wrist in a stray coil.

"Let me see." She took hold of his forearms, trying to pull his hand out to where she could examine it.

"No."

"Yes." She slid her hands down to his wrists, not feeling any gross deformities or blood, but he still had his gloves on. "Is it your thumb?"

"Go. Away."

"Stop being a baby."

His right hand snapped up, whip-quick, and clamped on the back of her head, bringing them nose to nose, eye to eye. "It's not my hand, Violet. It's what's underneath."

"What's—oh!"

Joe's hand was cradling his crotch. That pop she'd heard? It was the knotted end of the rope whacking him where it counted. And her hand was right on top of his.

He bared his teeth. "Still wanna kiss it better?"

Mortification rolled over her, hot as molten lava. She tried to jerk away, but the force of Joe's grip on her nape tipped her off balance. She grabbed his shoulders and her not-inconsiderable weight knocked him sideways. They tumbled to the ground in a tangle of limbs. She scrambled to get her knees under her. One of them made contact with something solid. Joe yelped, twisting hard and fast, flipping Violet onto her back. She arched, bracing to fight him off.

"Stop!"

Violet froze. Joe was sprawled on top of her, his body rigid. Air hissed in and out between his teeth and sweat beaded on his forehead.

"Just…don't…move," he panted. "Honest to God, you knee me in the thigh again, I'm gonna puke right down the front of your shirt."

Violet held her breath. If possible, she would've willed her heart to stop beating, in case the *thud, thud, thud* disturbed his stomach. Motherhood had done nothing to disable her very active gag reflex. As her head cleared, she sorted out what was where. Joe was draped over her, chest to chest, her kneecap flush against the inside of the thigh Dirt Eater had nailed. She carefully rotated her leg, removing the pressure.

"Thank you," Joe breathed. "Just give me a minute to catch my air and I'll get off of you."

Her hands were still clamped on his shoulders, but she couldn't find anyplace else to put them. The longer she stayed put, the more aware she became of all the hard, lovely muscle under his T-shirt. If it were Beni, she would rub his back to make him feel better. She imagined sliding her palm down the sleek curve of Joe's spine. Imagined his reaction. Yeah. He would definitely misinterpret the gesture. Much like her body was beginning to misinterpret their current position, the lean length of him hot against her, his cheek pressed to her collarbone, his face buried in the curve of her neck. Each short puff of air was a hot stroke on her skin.

"You sound like you're in labor," she said.

He huffed a laugh that tickled her ear. "If having a

kid hurts as bad as gettin' whacked on the pecker with a nylon rope, I need to buy my mother flowers."

"More like a new car," Violet said drily. "And I thought it was your thigh."

"It's both now, thanks to you."

"I was *trying* to help."

"Uh-huh. I'm guessing this is why you're a pickup man and not a paramedic."

Degree by degree, the tension eased from his body, even as Violet wound up like a spring. Need coiled hot and low, and the urge to wiggle against him was almost intolerable.

"Up until then you were doing pretty good," she said, by way of casual conversation. "I'll have to tell Beni you can handle stock okay."

"Gee, thanks." She could hear the eye roll in his voice. He blew out a long, slow breath—then nuzzled his face into her hair and inhaled deeply. "You even smell good when you've been rolling in the dirt."

She jerked her head away. "Do you always go around sniffing women like a damn stud horse?"

"Nah. If I were a stud horse, I'd do this." He gave her a quick, light nip at the curve of her neck that electrified every nerve ending and shot a blue-white current straight to where his thigh was pressed between her legs.

She shoved at his shoulder. "Stop that!"

"Just wanted to see if you tasted good, too." He pushed up onto his elbows, groaned, and eased sideways, an excruciating slide of body against body before he rolled clear and flopped onto his back, legs splayed. He lifted one hand in warning. "Stay back. I'll be fine as long as you don't help me anymore."

No problem. Violet couldn't move, paralyzed for a few breaths by the sudden, aching absence of his weight. Then she scrambled to her feet, slapping the dust from her butt and legs. "Take all the time you want, tough guy."

His head snapped up. "You tackled me when I was already down."

"I thought you were actually hurt." She flipped a casual hand at him. "No, don't get up. Katie and I can handle it."

He made a noise like a pissed-off rattlesnake. She shook the dirt out of her hair, tugged her cap down low, and went to deal with the bulls before she lost her head and tackled him again.

Chapter 10

VIOLET SLATHERED MAYONNAISE ONTO TWO PIECES OF squishy white bread, slapped a slice of American cheese between them, and took a huge bite, chewing furiously. She usually ate lunch at her mother's house when Beni was gone, but facing Joe across the table would ruin her appetite. For food, anyway.

She choked down the mouthful, then took another huge bite. Maybe all the triglycerides would gum up her arteries so she couldn't feel that low simmer in her blood. As if. She scowled at her pathetic excuse for lunch. Nothing short of a massive stroke could wipe the imprint of his body off hers. The man was a walking, breathing collection of all her biggest weaknesses, but didn't they say abstinence was good for the soul? If she managed to keep her hands off Joe for two more weeks, she'd qualify for sainthood.

She crammed the rest of the sandwich in her mouth, washed it down with sweet tea, then picked up her phone and tapped out a text message to her best friend. Home sweet home. Got time for lunch tomorrow? Melanie would slap some sense into her. No one knew Violet's baser tendencies better. She'd barely hit Send when the phone rang in her hand.

Violet checked the number and grinned as she answered. "Nothing better to do than hang around waitin' on my call?"

"I wish." Melanie blew out a gusty sigh. "My schedule this week is proof I sinned in a former life. One meeting after another all damn day. But I've got ten minutes before the next hour of hell, so dish."

"About what?"

"Don't play coy. Joe Cassidy. You've had him in your clutches for five days and I haven't heard a peep. Please tell me he's as hot as he looks on TV."

Violet's fingers curled around the phone as a full-body tingle swept over her. "He's okay, I guess, but he's not in my clutches."

"Why the hell not? When fate drops a big ol' hunk of man candy in her lap, a girl's gotta have a taste. And I hear this one isn't afraid to hand out free samples."

"Stop!" Violet scrubbed at the spot on her neck where she could still feel the scrape of Joe's teeth. "Dammit, Mel. You're not supposed to encourage my bad habits."

Melanie gave a little squeal. "I knew it! Has anything good happened yet? He is exactly your type."

"Which is *exactly* why I'm trying to keep my distance." Violet gave a growl of annoyance, more with herself than Melanie. "Everybody's got their eye on Joe, and after that mess in Hickory Springs, the last thing I need is to draw more attention to my love life."

Melanie snorted. "Honey, you don't have a love life. You have a series of unfortunate events."

Violet scowled, dumping her plate and silverware into the sink with a clatter. "I had a perfectly normal relationship."

"Once. In college. Six years ago."

"Well, I've been *busy*. I have this child, in case you hadn't noticed."

"Hard not to, when Xena, Warrior Cowgirl is hiding behind a five-year-old boy to avoid meeting a real man."

Violet cranked the faucet, propping the phone on her shoulder while she scoured the plate like it had been infected with ptomaine. "I have so many real men in my life, I can't take a step without tripping over one of them. Lord save me from testosterone and all of its carriers."

"Uh-huh. Which is why you developed a sudden hankering for Cajun food last spring?"

Violet jammed the plate into the drying rack. "That was a serious error in judgment. When I do decide to date again, it will be someone sensible with zero potential for psycho ex-girlfriends."

"You mean someone like…oh, I don't know…maybe Delon?" Melanie allowed for a thoughtful pause. Violet didn't bother to fill it with an argument they both knew by heart. Melanie blew out a gusty sigh. "The trouble with you, Violet, is you've got a head for business and a heart for thrills, and as far as I can tell, the two of them aren't on speaking terms."

Violet stared glumly at the water circling the drain. "Stupid heart won't listen."

"Maybe it's not your heart that's got it wrong."

Violet scowled. "Gee, Mel, thanks for calling. You've been ever so helpful."

Melanie was laughing as she hung up. Violet tossed the phone aside and stalked into the laundry room, brooding as she stuffed dirty socks into the washing machine. Silly to expect Melanie to be the voice of reason. After all, she was Hank's sister, and blood will tell. Violet and Mel wouldn't have spent half of junior high in detention if either of them knew when to say *Whoa*.

Violet left the socks sloshing in the washer and walked into the living room in time to see Joe stroll across the driveway, apparently none the worse for wear. She waited until he disappeared inside the bunkhouse, then hotfooted it over to her mother's, intending to grab a snack on her way to the office. The lingering scent of pot roast taunted her as she walked into the kitchen. Her stomach gurgled its disappointment. Her parents and Cole were sitting around the table. At the sight of their grim faces, Violet stopped dead, fear skittering cold fingers across her nape. Not again…

"What's wrong?" *Who died?*

"Buck McCloud called," her dad said stiffly. "His heart's getting worse. The doctor says he's gonna have to have an artificial pump implanted to keep it running."

Relief whooshed through her. Bad news, but not the worst. She wasn't sure they could survive the worst again. Violet plunked down in the chair Joe had vacated, vaguely aware that it was still warm. "That sounds scary."

Her mother smoothed a hand over a lace-edged floral place mat. "Any time they go crackin' your chest open, it's a big risk."

Violet's heart clutched in sympathy. Buck was a crusty old bastard, but she'd always liked him. He and her dad were two peas from the same old-school pod. They were close geographically, too, but didn't step on each other's toes business wise. McCloud Rodeo stayed mostly north—Oklahoma and Kansas, with a few shows up in Nebraska. Jacobs Livestock didn't venture outside

Texas, no matter how hard Violet tried to convince her dad to do otherwise.

"Who's gonna take care of his stock until he's back on his feet?"

Buck didn't have any family involved in the business. Like Violet's older sister, Lily, both of his daughters had married town boys.

"He won't be back," her dad said, emotion graveling his voice. "Doc says he has to pack it in."

"Pack it in?" Violet echoed. Buck? And do what? The man lived for his work. "You mean sell out?"

"Yes."

Violet shook her head. Rodeo contractors didn't retire. Look at the legendary Harry Vold, ninety years old and still an active part of the business. And her dad—they'd have to back the hearse up to the arena to haul him away.

"He offered us first shot at the whole string," Iris said.

The quiet declaration was like a bolt of lightning, electrifying Violet. For an instant, she couldn't even form words. Finally she managed to choke out, "That's great."

Her dad glared at her. "A man losing his health and his business?"

"I didn't mean—" Violet stuttered, then pinched off the rest before she stuck her foot in any deeper. Her head spun with the unexpected possibilities. On average, Buck's stock was a little stronger than theirs, though he didn't have anything in Dirt Eater's class. If you put the two strings together…

"How much does he want?" she asked, numbers already dancing in her head.

Her dad shrugged. "I didn't ask. We can't use that

much stock and we're in no position to lay out that much cash."

"But if we picked up his rodeos, too—"

"Who's gonna move up to Kansas for the whole season?" he demanded. "Not you, with Beni starting kindergarten next fall."

But—

Violet looked to Cole for support. He stared back, face implacable. She tried to imagine Cole on his own in Kansas, dealing with the public, and nearly burst out in a fit of giggles. But still…

"We should at least consider it," she insisted.

"Waste of time." Her dad thumped down his coffee cup and stood. "Let's go have a look at those bulls, Cole. Decide what we're gonna buck at the practice session on Wednesday."

Violet grabbed a cookie, crumbling the edge with angry fingers as the men lumbered out. She counted to five after the slap of the screen door before saying, "He won't even think about it."

"Of course not." Her mother pushed back from the table and stood to gather cups and glasses. "He's so set in his ways, the day of the Apocalypse he'll tell the Four Horsemen they can just turn around and ride on back where they came from—he has work to do."

Violet gave a reluctant laugh, then groaned, near bursting with frustration. Finally—*finally*—they had a chance to take a huge step up, out of their niche at the trailing fringe of pro rodeo.

"He isn't completely beyond reasoning," her mother added. "And it would mean a lot to Buck to turn his operation over to a friend."

Violet blinked in surprise. "You think Dad would consider it?"

"If you can figure out a way to make it all work. And if it doesn't put us in too much of a pinch."

Violet leaned back in her chair, forehead puckering in frantic thought. She could call Buck and get a purchase price, hear what kind of terms he'd consider, then check out financing options and rates, run profit and loss projections. The number-cruncher half of her soul danced with delight at the prospect. Then reality kicked it in the shin.

"My proposal will have to be damn near bulletproof to persuade him."

"That it will."

And the whole thing was nothing but pie in the sky until Violet had the figures in front of her. If nothing else, gathering all of their financials would give her a leg up come tax time. The fact that it would give her an excuse to avoid a certain bullfighter for the rest of the day was a bonus.

She leapt to her feet, filched a couple more cookies and a can of Coke. "I'll be in the office."

Ideas zinged around inside her head like bats in a cave as she strode across the lawn to the wood-shingled office out back. The places they could go. The rodeos they could produce. One step up the ladder, then another, until someday…

Fort Worth. Houston. San Antonio. Her heart did a double backflip just thinking about it. She burst into the musty, airless office, threw open a couple of windows, then fired up her old PC, her fingers jittering impatiently on the keys while the computer clicked and hummed and did whatever computers do instead of just starting. She flattened her palms on the desk and took a deep breath, willing herself to calm down.

Don't get ahead of yourself, Violet. She'd already pinned her hopes on one long shot in the past week, and ended up with Joe as the grand prize. And that was a bad thing. Really.

Chapter 11

MONDAY EVENING, LONG AFTER DINNER, JOE SAT ON THE wicker love seat on Violet's tiny front deck, glad for the dense shadows. A porch light would invite the damn moths to fling themselves at his head, along with the occasional mutant beetle the size of his thumb. Cole called them June bugs. Apparently they couldn't read a calendar for shit.

Joe also preferred the lights out so his presence went undetected, especially by Violet's parents, but he hadn't figured on waiting this long. He checked the time on his phone. Almost nine. What was she up to in the office? Not that he had anything better to do. It was only Monday and already he was stir-crazy. He wasn't used to killing time. His rodeo days were usually a whirl of activity: looking after Dick's livestock, autograph sessions, a performance, and more chores, even on the days between rodeos.

Here, there were more days off than on, and fewer bull riders in each performance—eight or ten instead of twelve or fifteen. He felt like he barely got warmed up before it was over. The bulls were easier, too. Less athletic. Like dropping down from the majors to double A in baseball, everything moved slower...except Dirt Eater. That bastard was a hundred-mile-an-hour flame slinger in a bullpen where nobody else's fastball topped eighty-five.

Joe rubbed at the bruise on his leg that had come within a few inches of making him celibate. He'd figured Hank was exaggerating when he bragged that the bull was good enough to buck at the National Finals, but the kid was right on the money. Which begged the question—did anyone on this ranch understand what they were wasting?

Joe shifted and stretched, his muscles twitchy despite a four-mile jog just before dusk. Too much sitting around. Too much thinking. Too much he didn't want to think about. He tilted his head back and stared up at the half-moon that rode too high over the trees, muting the stars so he couldn't even get his bearings by way of the constellations. They'd probably be out of whack down here anyway. Everything else was.

Back home, he wouldn't have wasted a balmy evening sitting around his dinky apartment. He would've saddled a horse out at the High Lonesome and headed for the scrub-filled canyon that curved up the side of Cayuse Butte, where he'd flush a few mule deer, maybe even an elk. When the trail topped out on the plateau, you could see clear to the Nevada border. If a man had to think, that was the place to do it. The mere suggestion of giving it up curled his hands into fists. He *had* to work things out with Dick. The alternative—being barred from the ranch—was unbearable.

Joe forced his rigid muscles to relax, dragging his gaze and his attention to the square of light in the office window. He supposed he could go knock on the door, but talking to her across a desk wasn't anything like what he had in mind. Better to wait. He pulled out his phone and redialed the last number called.

Wyatt answered on the second ring. "Two phone calls in the one day? You are homesick. You got my email with the names you asked for?"

"Yeah. Thanks."

"You're welcome." A spoon clinked on glass, Wyatt stirring whatever he was drinking. Probably one of those god-awful smoothies he made in his thousand-dollar blender. "Who are you buttering up, the old man or the daughter?"

"Just being helpful."

"The daughter, I'm betting." Wyatt's voice sharpened with curiosity. "You haven't chased after a girl since I've known you. Are you smitten, or is this a classic case of avoidance?"

The latter, Joe suspected. Playing tag with Violet was a whole lot better than being pecked to death by what-ifs and worst case scenarios. "I'm bored. I hate twiddling my thumbs between rodeos. That's why I have a job."

"Had a job," Wyatt corrected. "Or did you already call Dickhead and beg to be forgiven?"

"No!" The denial was sharp, its edge honed by every time in the past five days Joe had held his phone in his hand, on the verge of dialing.

"If you're going to cave, do it before Wednesday. After that, I'm out of the betting pool."

A barb aimed for Joe's pride, so blatant he was disgusted that it hit its mark. Better, though, than admitting the truth. He wasn't paralyzed by pride, but fear. What if Dick really meant what he said in Puyallup? What if— panic skittered around inside Joe's rib cage—he could never go back?

He grasped at something to fill the void that

threatened to swallow him from the inside out. "How well do you know Delon Sanchez?"

"Safety Man?"

"What?"

"You've seen him ride. You know what I mean."

"He's strong." Should be—he had a chest and arms like Popeye on a spinach bender. Joe stretched out his legs, slouching into the cushions of the wicker love seat. "Hardly ever see a horse get him out of shape."

"Because he'd rather stay tight and win third than open up and risk getting bucked off."

"He's number one in the world."

Wyatt slurped, and it even sounded disgustingly healthy. "He's been lucky. Drawn the right horses at the right places. His lead won't hold up at the Finals."

"Consistency is good when you're going ten rounds," Joe argued, purely for the sake of winding Wyatt up.

"Head to head against Kaycee Field, Bobby Mote, Steven Peebles? Only if you're consistently awesome. You want to beat those boys, you've got to expose yourself."

"Delon must have exposed himself at least once. He's got a kid."

Wyatt laughed. "Beni. I met him at Houston last year. He's a piece of work."

"No kidding." *Just a bullfighter, my ass.*

"Wait a second." Wyatt snapped his fingers. "Violet Jacobs. I met her, too. You're hitting on Beni's mother? She's…completely unlike you."

"Bullshit," Joe snapped, irritated for no reason he could define. "She's a pickup man. A stock contractor. A damn good hand out in the pasture. She's exactly like me."

Only a whole lot softer. Joe's brain might've been too distracted by the pain to take much notice at the time, but his body had an excellent memory of what it felt like to have Violet stretched out underneath him. His body was very much in favor of trying it again.

There was a long, weighted pause. Joe could practically feel the draft as Wyatt flipped open his skull and tried to poke around inside his head. But when Wyatt spoke, his voice was suspiciously neutral. "I meant she's not like your usual women. Which you just illustrated perfectly."

"Whatever that means," Joe muttered. "From what I saw, Delon has dibs."

Wyatt snorted. "That's gonna come as a shock to Stacy Lyn Reed. She's been knocking a chunk off of him every chance she gets."

"Really?" Joe screwed up his face in disgust.

"She isn't hard to look at."

"She's scary. That woman could have Delon for lunch and toss you and me both down for dessert." Probably simultaneously.

"She makes it hard to refuse."

"I wouldn't know. I make damn sure she never gets close enough to ask the question."

But if Delon was getting his cork popped by the reigning queen of the barrel racers, there was definitely nothing romantic between him and Violet. Mr. Nice Guy would never cheat—and that left the field clear for Joe.

"So…Violet," Wyatt said. "Interesting choice for a guy who prefers his women uncomplicated. She couldn't pack more baggage if you gave her a freight train. The kid, her family, the business, Delon…"

"Violet can handle it." Just like she handled herself in the arena, picking up broncs. And roping that bull today. Capable. Strong. And very, *very* soft in all the right places.

"Joe." Wyatt made it both a question and a warning.

Joe ignored both because just then the light went out in the office and the door opened. He straightened, his pulse kicking up a beat in anticipation. "Gotta go."

"We need to talk about next year," Wyatt said. "At least consider your options—"

"Not now."

"When?" Wyatt demanded.

"Tomorrow. Or maybe the next day. I'll be in touch."

"Dammit, Joe—"

"Later."

Joe hung up, then turned the phone off so Wyatt couldn't call back. He needed to get the drop on her and he had to focus. Violet would not make this easy. Joe had never bothered to practice much finesse outside the arena, but he could fake it. He'd always been quick on his feet.

Violet emerged from the shadows of her parents' backyard and crossed the road with her usual long, no-nonsense strides. She was nearly to the foot of her steps when she faltered, then stopped, spotting Joe on her deck.

Her eyes narrowed from startled to suspicious. "If you came to tell me you're filing a workers' comp claim, save your breath. Roping bulls is not in your contract."

"Nope. That was purely voluntary."

Alarm filtered into her expression. "Are you hurt too bad to work this weekend?"

"Nah. You'll be glad to know my parts are in perfect working order." He picked up his leg, kicked a couple of times to prove it, then gave her a deliberately lewd smile. "All of them."

He watched, entertained by the emotions that trailed across her face as she tried to figure out what to do with that statement. She settled on annoyance, her frown sharpening into a glare. "Well then, what do you want?"

He would've thought that was obvious, but if she preferred to pretend she didn't understand, he was willing to play along. He held up a slip of paper between two fingers. "I brought you a present."

She took a step closer, squinting into the gloom. "A check?"

"Better." He waved the note like a tiny white flag. "Information."

Violet's toes bumped the bottom step. "What kind?"

"Come up here and I'll tell you." Joe patted the seat next to him.

Violet hesitated, her eyes tracking from him to the seat and back again.

"Or you could stand in the middle of your lawn until your dad comes out to see what's going on."

She glanced over her shoulder, then at the security light that cast an orange glow over most of the yard, then back to the seat. Her mouth went flat, but she climbed the steps and plopped down, leaving a deliberate space between them. "Fine. I'm here. What is that?"

Joe held out the paper. She plucked it from his grasp with the tips of her fingers so their hands didn't touch. She peered at it for a few moments. "It's too dark to read. Are these names and phone numbers?"

"Yep. Bullfighters." Joe pointed at the top of the paper. "The first guy is from Missouri, but he wants to relocate. Go figure. He's looking to get on with a contractor so he'll have steady work. Solid, smart, and he'd be a good influence on Hank, according to Wyatt."

Her eyes widened. "Wyatt Darrington?"

The reverence in her voice made Joe twitch. "Yeah. So?"

"He gave you this list?" She looked down at it in amazement. "He lives in Oregon. How does he know this guy?"

"Wyatt knows everyone. And everything. It's annoying."

Violet's mouth curled, amused at his disgust. "But useful."

Especially since it had lured Violet within reach. And scent. He took a deep breath. Oranges again, and a hint of fabric softener from the clean clothes she'd put on. Another baggy T-shirt, but her curves were more pronounced, as if she'd also changed into something less constrictive underneath. Something lacy, maybe. Joe sprawled so his thigh touched hers. She shifted in response, pressing closer to her end of the seat. Joe stretched his arm along the backrest behind her shoulders. Violet slouched away from the contact.

"So now you owe me," he said, letting his voice drop to a significant chord.

She huffed. "I don't need a bullfighter that bad."

"But you want one." *This one.*

Joe lifted a finger to brush back a strand of her hair, savoring the cool slide of it over his skin. She frowned, but didn't slap at his hand, didn't shrink away when he leaned in. Would she let him kiss her? Maybe, but he was enjoying the slow rev of his engine, the lazy swell of heat, all from just sitting next to her, barely touching. He wanted to coax her along, rather than pushing. He traced a line down the side of her neck, watching the skin pebble in response. "Go out with me, Violet."

"Out?" she repeated, blinking. "Like…a date? Dinner and a movie?"

"Sure." Whatever, if it got him close to her.

Her forehead puckered. "But…I don't even like you."

"Yes, you do."

She sucked in an outraged breath, but Joe only smiled wider. He could see the pulse jumping at the base of her throat. And once the pain had eased, he'd felt her reaction out there at the corral, while they were all tangled up.

"You're not scared, are you Violet?" he taunted softly.

"Of you? Hardly." Her chin jerked up, her voice snooty. "I don't date the help."

"That's good, since your truck drivers are married and Hank's a tad young." Joe brushed back her hair again, his fingertip skimming under her ear, smiling when her breath caught.

She squared her jaw. "My dad would not approve."

Joe trailed his thumb along the top of her shoulder, wishing he could reach bare skin. "You still ask Daddy's permission to play with the boys?"

"Yeah." She finally swatted his hand away, then folded her arms. "So go ahead. I'll wait here."

Joe's spine snapped straight and he gaped at her. "You expect me to go over there and ask permission to take you out?"

"Only if you want that date."

Joe's mouth opened. Closed. As he glared, she smirked, smug in her victory.

"You don't think I'll do it," he said.

The smirk faded.

"Be right back." He jumped to his feet, wiping that smirk off her face, and bounded down the stairs, his boots crunching out a rapid tattoo on the gravel driveway.

Have. You. Lost. Your. Mind.

Through the open curtains on the tall windows of the living room, he could see Steve tilted back in his recliner, reading a newspaper while his wife worked some kind of puzzle in a paperback book. Geezus. Was he really dumb enough to walk in there and ask permission to take Violet on a date?

Yep. He was. She'd dared him. Thought she could blow him off by tossing her daddy in his face. Hah. *Nice try, darlin'.* He took the steps two at a time and knocked before he could chicken out.

After an endless count of ten, Iris answered the door. "Joe? Is something wrong?"

"No. I, um, wondered if you and your husband have a few minutes."

Her brows rose but she stepped back. "Come on in."

He followed her through the kitchen, into a living room much like the woman who owned it—cozy and attractive in a welcoming way. The pillows tossed haphazardly on the leather couch were meant to be used, and photos were hung and propped on every available surface. Violet and Beni, her older sister getting married, a much younger and skinnier Cole with what must be his parents and a brother, all mixed in with photos of Jacobs bucking stock in action. Family of all kinds.

Steve dipped his head to peer at Joe over his reading glasses. "Trouble?"

"No." Well, not the kind they imagined. "I, um, wanted to talk to you."

Iris settled back into her chair. "Have a seat."

"No. Thanks. I'll just…"

Steve set his newspaper aside. "What can we do for you?"

Joe opened his mouth, realized he should take off his cap, then did and wished he'd gotten around to that haircut. He scraped the shaggy mess off his forehead and clasped his cap in both hands, rolling the brim between sweaty palms like every tongue-tied suitor in every John Wayne movie he'd ever seen.

"I'd like your permission to date your daughter," he blurted.

They both stared at him. Then they looked at each other. Then back at him.

"Violet?" Steve asked.

Well, duh. Did he think Joe wanted to sleep with the one with the husband?

"Yes. Violet." Joe's heart was beating so loud it was like talking with headphones on, his lips moving but no sound getting back to his own ears. He hoped he wasn't yelling over the racket. "I'm on your payroll for the next couple of weeks, so I figured I should ask first."

Steve shifted in his chair. Frowned. "I don't really think—"

"That would be nice," Iris cut in. "It's been too long since Violet took some time for herself."

She fired off a look that silenced Steve. He scowled, settled back into his chair, and snapped the newspaper tight in front of his face.

Iris gave Joe a bright smile. "Anything else?"

"Uh…no. Thanks. 'Preciate it." Joe retreated a couple of steps, scooped his hair back, and tugged his cap on over it. "Have a good evening."

Steve grunted.

"You too," Iris said.

Joe spun around and hightailed it for the door. Outside, Violet was sitting right where he'd left her, looking stunned and more than a little panicked. Well, good. He wasn't the only one with a head full of scrambled eggs.

He stopped at the edge of the deck, planted his hands on his hips, and flashed a smile that was a lot cockier than he felt. "Satisfied?"

Her chin dropped. "He said yes?"

He hadn't said no, so that was the same thing, right? Joe dodged the question with one of his own. "Know a good barbecue place?"

"I…yeah. There's one in Earnest."

"Is there a movie theater?"

She shook her head. "Dumas is the closest."

"That'll work. Tomorrow night okay for you?"

"Um, sure."

"Great. I'll pick you up at six."

He was halfway to the bunkhouse before she called out, "Joe?"

He turned, pacing backward as he asked, "Yeah?"

"You don't have a car."

He stopped dead. Crap. She was right. "Do you?"

"Yes."

He grinned.

"What?" she snapped.

"Looks like I got you to pick me up after all."

He strolled to the bunkhouse, whistling. Behind him he heard a muttered curse, the thump of footsteps, then the sound of her front door slamming. He laughed. Oh yeah. Good times.

Chapter 12

IF VIOLET HADN'T ALREADY BEEN IN A FOUL MOOD ON Tuesday morning, trailing her mother around the Super Saver warehouse grocery in Dumas would've done it. She could've been trailing horses in from the pasture with her dad and Cole, but no. Because she was the girl, she got stuck dragging around a pair of carts stacked to the brim with everything it took to feed the Jacobs crew on the road. She'd tried arguing that it was sexist and Cole should have to take a turn as her mother's flunky, but Iris only rolled her eyes and said, "Lord, please take me before that desperate day."

So Violet was stuck. In this same damn rut forever, or at least the foreseeable future, because they were not going to be buying out Buck McCloud. She'd twiddled and tweaked the numbers every which way to Sunday, but they refused to line up. Forget convincing her dad— Violet couldn't even persuade herself they could swing it.

Then there was Joe. The one time in her entire life she wanted her parents to disapprove and they'd failed her. Violet glowered in the direction of the produce department, where her mother was molesting cantaloupes in search of perfection. Iris hadn't said a thing about Joe. Not one blessed word. Granted, they'd driven separate cars because Iris had some serious catching up to do with her eldest daughter in Earnest this afternoon, but still. Not. A. Word.

Violet wedged two packs of juice boxes into her cart, tossed a pillowcase-sized bag of raisin bran on top, then nearly mowed down a girl who sashayed past in platform sandals and a flippy little sun dress. Her cart held nothing but a few bunches of leafy green things, a bottle of wine, and a tub of exotic-looking olives. A pang that was not quite envy shot through Violet. She'd never wanted to be that girl—primped, prissy, and obviously starving. It was more about the lack of baggage, literal and figurative. How would it feel, for a day, an hour, even a minute, to think only of herself? To say yes to a date without imagining every possible repercussion?

Even before Beni, family had been woven into every aspect of her life. A solid foundation was awesome, but sometimes it felt as if her feet were set into the concrete.

She appreciated the life she'd be born to. Honest she did. There was maybe a stock contractor in ten who would let a woman pick up broncs, or give her a real say in the business, though it was almost as tough for a man to come in from outside. Contractors were mostly bred, not built, because it took a huge stake to get started— animals, land, trucks, crew. And more than all of that, time and knowledge. Sure, you could buy bucking stock, but the savvy, the horse sense—that took year after year of watching, studying, absorbing, until you developed the instinct that let you look at a two-year-old mare, the tilt of her head, a certain spring in her step, and know, *This one.*

She felt the same way when Joe got too close, except it was more like, *Watch out for this one.*

A shiver of premonition tickled down her spine. She stubbed her toe on the front cart and the rear cart

rolled up on the back of her heel. Her curse earned her a
church lady's glare from down the aisle. A cubic yard of
toilet paper and a bucket of laundry detergent later, she
manhandled the carts to the checkout area, where she
found her mother glaring contemptuously at a rack of
packaged cookies. Violet cast a longing eye at the butter
shortbread but grabbed a Baby Ruth rather than incite
her mother's wrath over prepackaged baked goods.
Ahead of them, a man was raising a fuss about whether
the price on his gross weight of breakfast sausage links
was correct.

The cashier rolled her eyes and reached for the microphone. "Manager to check stand eight…"

Violet blew out an exasperated breath, slumping over
to rest her forearms on her cart.

"I assume things didn't work out last night," her
mother said.

Violet shot her a sulky look. "You were supposed to
say no."

Iris paused in the midst of digging through her purse
for her stray reading glasses. "I was talking about Buck
McCloud's stock, which I assume we can't afford since
you look like somebody kicked your best dog. And
honestly, how could we say no to Joe? He was so cute,
asking our leave that way."

Cute? Joe? Only Iris could think so. "I suppose
Daddy is furious."

"I'd say disgruntled is a better word. Or maybe
consternated. Is that a word?" Iris pursed her lips in
thought. "Consternation was five across in last night's
puzzle, but consternated—"

"Mom. Please." Violet jabbed at a bag of jumbo

marshmallows with one finger. "Doesn't it bother you at all? Joe is working for us. And he's…well…Joe."

Iris cocked her head like a little brown hen. "Mmm. There is that. But he's only temporary and I hardly think he's going to confuse you with one of his buckle bunnies."

"Wow. Thanks," Violet said sourly.

"Oh, stop. You know what I meant. And besides…" Iris clucked her tongue. "It's been three months since that fiasco down in Hickory Springs. Past time you got back on the ol' horse and rode. So to speak."

Violet's face flamed. "Mom!"

"What? I am aware that you sometimes have sex, Violet. Not very often, by my measure. How do you stand the dry spells? Your father and I—"

"Mom!" Violet hissed, as a woman in the next line choked, then sputtered with laughter.

Iris heaved a resigned sigh. "Just like your father. Can't talk about sex unless it involves a cow or a horse." Then she brightened. "Oh, look! They've got a special on raspberry smoothies at the lunch stand."

They loaded all of the groceries into Violet's car, then Iris motored off to hunker down with Lily, who wouldn't hesitate to chat about sex in the grocery store checkout line. Violet shuddered to imagine the degree to which her upcoming date was about to be dissected over sweet tea and baked goods. Homemade, of course. Violet would give it an hour, max, before she got either a call or a text from Lily, telling her what to wear. Given that ninety percent of her wardrobe was still in the laundry hamper, Violet figured Joe would just have to take her as she came, in jeans and a T-shirt. But not actually *take* her. Just…

Oh hell. She was in so much trouble.

Back home, the house was deserted, but dust swirled into the cloudless sky above the corrals. Violet lugged groceries in and stowed them away as quickly as possible, then hotfooted it down to join the men. She found them all in row, elbows braced on the fence as they gazed into the pens, her dad and Cole side by side, and Joe a few paces to the left. The separation struck her as both intentional and unconscious, as if Joe had practiced maintaining his distance for so long it was automatic. Then again, he had no problem invading her space, so what did she know?

A piercing squeal heralded another billow of dust, churned up by a herd of young horses that milled around the largest of the corrals, snorty and wide-eyed from the gathering. The three- and four-year-olds were the junior varsity of the Jacobs string. They'd had the summer off to grow and mature, but their training would start up again now that it was fall. That was the purpose of the Wednesday afternoon practice sessions. Young riders and young stock, learning together. A passel of damn good cowboys had eaten their first dirt in the Jacobs Ranch arena, including one world champion. With any luck, Delon would be their next gold buckle alumni.

Violet's gaze wandered to the next pen and she frowned at the sight of a piebald Appaloosa. "Why is Gunslinger locked up by himself?"

"Got a knot on his shin," her dad said. "Must've got kicked. Nothing serious, but we won't be able to buck him this weekend."

"That'll leave us one short in the saddle bronc," Violet said, ever one to state the obvious.

"Yeah. We were debating what to put in his place."

Not a lot of choices. As a sportscaster would say, they weren't real deep on the bench, especially this year. One good young prospect had washed out, and a solid campaigner had suffered an episode of colic that sidelined him for the season. If they had the McCloud stock, they'd have plenty of depth. And—heavy sigh on Violet's part—no operating budget.

Her dad thumbed his hat back and rubbed his forehead. "It'll have to be Juicy Fruit."

Violet shook her head. "Nobody's won a check on her all summer. Whoever draws her will turn out rather than waste the gas to come and get on."

"Got a better idea?" Cole asked.

She pondered a moment, then said, "Move Kicking Woman from the bareback to the saddle bronc and put Oredigger in her place."

"Oredigger?" Her dad gave a derisive snort. "We didn't even take him on the last trip because he was so flat by the end of July."

"Now he's rested," Violet argued. "The temperature is only supposed to be in the eighties this weekend. And he likes that arena."

Cole stared at Gunslinger for several long moments, face blank. Then he nodded once. "Kicking Woman will fire hard in the saddle bronc. And Delon placed on Oredigger at this rodeo last year. But we gotta buck him Saturday—he's always better at night."

Her dad frowned, considered, then straightened and slapped both hands on the fence rail. "That's settled, then."

"I'll let Mom know so she can update the stock draw," Violet said.

Joe moved abruptly, stepping away from the fence as if he'd suddenly remembered someplace he had to be. "If you don't need me anymore…"

"We're good," Steve said. "'Preciate the help. I can see why Dick Browning likes to keep you close."

Something complicated passed behind Joe's eyes before he turned away. He paused to toss a pointed glance at Violet. "I'll see *you* later."

He was barely out of earshot when Cole said, "You have a date with him?"

"Yes." She shot him a defensive glare. "Is that a problem?"

"Depends. Just so you know, I'm short on cash for bail money."

Great. *Now* Cole decided to have a sense of humor. She ignored him. "I'm sorry, Daddy. I know, I promised—"

He fixed her with the kind of glower only a man with very aggressive eyebrows can achieve. "Bad enough a father has to know his daughter has dates. Spare me the details."

She ducked her head. "I didn't mean to. It just happened."

"You accidentally sent Joe over to talk to us?"

"It was a…um, miscalculation." She angled him a hopeful look from under her lashes. "If you want, I'll say I have to cancel."

"And use me for an excuse?" He *hmmphed* loudly. "You don't want to go out with the man, tell him straight up. Otherwise, you hold to your word."

She cast her eyes down, chastened. "Yes, sir."

"And for hell's sake, keep this stuff to yourself from now on." He made a low rumbling noise like a grumpy old bull. "I assume you didn't have any luck figuring out how to buy Buck's stock since you haven't hounded me about it again."

"No."

He sighed. "Woulda been nice to help out an old friend."

"I asked about just buying a few of the horses," Violet said, even more depressed by the confirmation that her dad would at least have considered the deal. "He's dead set on keeping the herd together."

"Be hard to watch what you've built broke into pieces and scattered across the country."

Violet could only nod. They all stood for a moment, putting themselves in Buck's boots and not liking the view.

Cole squinted toward the house. "I was startin' to think you finally picked one with some sense. Guess I was mistaken."

Violet followed his gaze. Sure enough, Joe was in front of the bunkhouse, standing on one foot while he bent the other leg back to stretch his sore thigh. He wore a pair of green shorts that had lost an altercation with a bottle of bleach, a T-shirt with the sleeves whacked off—presumably with a pocket knife—and he'd tied a pink bandana into a headband over his wild mop of hair. The overall effect had Violet hoping the local sheriff didn't happen by and pick him up as a transient.

Then he shook out his leg and broke into long, loping strides, so easy and graceful it seemed like he barely touched the ground. Violet's heart clenched, mostly in envy. Lord, to be able to run like that, instead of thundering along like a plow horse.

Steve slapped the fence rail again. "No sense standin'
around flappin' our jaws. Let's get these colts sorted
and run them through the chutes a few times so they
remember the way."

It was crowding five o'clock when Violet shuffled
into the house, her clothes, skin, and hair layered with
dust and sweat. She grinned at her reflection in the
living room mirror. Unlike her, the colts looked great.
She flipped her baseball cap onto the hat rack near the
door, anticipation bubbling in her veins. Tomorrow's
practice session would be the first chance to see the
four-year-olds with real live cowboys on their backs.
Hot damn, she couldn't wait.

On the end table, her phone chirped. Violet heaved
a resigned sigh and checked the text message from her
sister. Wear the red shirt I gave you for your birthday.

Violet shook her head as she tapped keys. It's not
really my style.

The response came back before she could set the
phone down. I know. It makes you look like a girl.

Violet stuck her tongue out at the phone, glad Beni
wasn't around to see. It's very…red.

It looks great with your dark hair and it doesn't even
show any cleavage. WEAR THE DAMN SHIRT.

Violet ground her teeth. Whatever, bossy.

Bet your ass. Don't try to blow me off, Violet Jacobs. I
have spies everywhere.

Violet would have laughed, but Lily wasn't kidding.
If Violet didn't follow orders, she would hear from her
sister as soon as she stepped out in public. Funny how
the short people in the Jacobs family packed the biggest
attitudes. She'd let Lily win this one, though. It was just

a stupid shirt and she knew it was clean, seein's how the tags were still on it.

Tossing the phone on the table, Violet headed into her bedroom to strip off her grubby clothes and dive into the shower. When she was scrubbed and dried, slightly more than her bare minimum of makeup slapped on, she dug up a decent set of underwear, pulled the shirt over her head, and studied herself in the mirror. Other than the color, it wasn't so bad. The cap sleeves covered her shoulders and the vee of the wrap front didn't dip very low, but it was really, *really* red. Plus the fabric was stretchy, silky stuff that clung to every curve, and the wrap was held in place by a couple of ties that came loose with a tug. Way more convenient than Violet would've liked, in the interests of her willpower. She turned sideways and winced. The fit didn't exactly downsize her bust.

"For when you want to get someone's attention," Lily had said with a wink, when Violet opened the box.

She wasn't sure she wanted that much of Joe's attention, but it would have to do. She turned her back on the mirror, grabbed her purse and strode out to the kitchen—then froze when she saw Joe walking across her lawn. Her pulse did a mad little jig. Compared to his usual sloppy T-shirts, he looked almost formal, a black polo tucked into his jeans and topped with a belt and buckle. He bounded onto the deck with those springy steps that made it seem like gravity didn't affect him.

Violet took a deep breath, reminded herself that she had, in fact, been on a date before and did know how to act, then went to the front door to answer his knock. "Hi."

"Uh…"

He seemed to get stuck after that, so Violet tried again. "Ready to go?"

He nodded, still mute, his eyes fixed on a spot somewhere below her chin. He smelled heavenly, clean and spicy. Probably cologne some sponsor or other had given him. Joe didn't seem to wear anything but freebies. Even tonight his shirt had a Dodge Trucks logo embroidered above his heart. The trophy buckle, on the other hand, was not something they handed out to just anyone. Montana Silversmiths, personalized in gold letters. *Joe Cassidy, National Finals Rodeo Bullfighter*. He was the best of the best and had the hardware to prove it.

He still hadn't moved.

"Joe?"

He drew in a breath big enough to push his shoulders up a couple of inches, then let it out in a whistle. His green eyes gleamed when they met hers. "I thought pink was my favorite color. I'm going to have to reconsider."

Chapter 13

JOE REELED IN HIS TONGUE AND TOOK THE CAR KEYS Violet held out to him. Considering the way she'd avoided him all day, he'd half expected her to answer the door in the dusty jeans and Texas Rangers cap she'd worn down at the corral. Or to pawn him off with some feeble excuse why she had to cancel. He'd expected damn near anything but that red shirt.

She strode around the far side of the car and climbed into the passenger's seat while he was still trying to adjust his expectations, among other things. He managed to get in the car without slamming anything in the door—barely—but as he put the key in the ignition, Violet reached back for her shoulder belt. Everything lifted and shifted under the red silk and he lost motor function when the scent of warm strawberries washed over him. Screw oranges. He had a new favorite fruit too.

"You dropped the keys," she said.

He nodded, but didn't move to pick them up.

Violet fanned a hand in front of her face, wafting more strawberries his direction. "Kinda hot in here."

He nodded. Then he realized she meant the actual temperature, which was about three hundred degrees inside the sun-baked car. He scrabbled around on the floor, found the keys, and got the car started. Violet reached over to crank up the air conditioner and Joe lost another thousand brain cells when the seat belt pulled tight across her chest.

Cross my heart, darlin'.

Violet frowned at him. "You didn't get too much sun out there jogging, did you? You look a little…glazed."

He blinked, forcing his eyes up and forward. "I'm fine."

Providing he didn't get distracted and run off the road. That would be bad, especially when the prospects for the evening were suddenly looking very, very good. He'd made his intentions perfectly clear and that shirt was Violet's answer. Unless she'd worn it just to torture him. That brought his blood pressure down a notch.

She tapped the gear shift knob between them. "D is for 'Drive'."

Right. He put it in gear. "I was letting the car warm up."

Because that was important when the outside temperature was pushing ninety-five. Geezus. *Get a grip, Joe.* It wasn't like he'd never seen boobs before. Violet's just had a habit of showing up when he least expected them. Catching him off guard. He frowned as he looped the car into a U-turn in the driveway. If he was going to stay one step ahead, he needed to focus on something besides that shirt.

He patted the steering wheel. "Nice car."

"Thanks. I just bought it in June. I've barely been home enough to drive it."

"Got a thing for Cadillacs?" he asked, thinking of her horse.

She smiled slightly. "They both have excellent safety ratings. Plus it's easier to wipe apple juice off leather seats."

He glanced in the rearview mirror. A booster chair

stared at him from the middle of the backseat, radiating waves of disapproval. Joe tilted the mirror up so all he could see was the dust rolling off the road behind them. At the end of the driveway he stopped underneath the black iron gate with a big J set in the middle, then turned toward town. Half a mile down the highway, an identical entrance led to a house and barn nestled against the foot of the bluff, except this gate was shut tight and padlocked. He'd checked it out when he jogged past.

"What's that place? It looks like part of your ranch."

"It belongs to Cole."

"He doesn't live there?"

"Not since his family died."

The declaration was like a bucket of ice water in Joe's face. His foot came off the accelerator and the car slowed abruptly.

"His family?" he repeated. "As in…"

"His parents and his older brother."

"How?"

"Car wreck." Violet delivered the information in a monotone, as if she'd said it so many times the emotion was worn flat. "They were driving home from a Cowboys game in Dallas. A woman dodged an armadillo, lost control, and hit them head on."

"That's…" What? There wasn't a word to describe it, so Joe didn't try. He let the car roll to a stop on the shoulder of the highway as he studied the ranch buildings. Weeds had grown up around the barn and corrals, but the house looked like the owners had only gone away for the weekend. "How long has it been?"

"Fifteen years in November." Violet's eyes were as

dark and flat as her voice. "I was thirteen. Cole was a sophomore in high school."

Which made Cole around thirty years old, same as Joe. Younger than he looked. Or acted. "No wonder he's so, uh…"

"It didn't help."

Joe cocked his head, curious. "He's never been the sociable type?"

"Not really, but it got worse after the accident because, well, you know."

Honestly? No. Joe couldn't possibly know. He'd never had that much to lose. There was really only his mother, and she drove him insane sometimes, but he couldn't imagine…

"We're still recovering. Financially, I mean. The other, well…" The hitch of her shoulders held a pain too deep to express. "They were partners, our dads. Mine was the horse guy, the practical one. Cole's dad was all about the bulls. The big dreamer. Always swore someday one of his bulls would buck in the eliminator pen at the National Finals." She blew out a breath that was half laugh, half sigh. "Dirt Eater is the last of the calves out of his cow herd."

"He gets my vote."

She blinked, clearing the shadows from her eyes. "Really?"

"Sure." Joe gave a shrug of his own, searching for a way to lighten the mood. "But what do I know—I'm just a bullfighter."

She laughed, the sound a little forlorn. "Feel free to pass that vote along to the powers that be, would you? Then maybe I'll get to stand on the back of the chutes in Las Vegas at least once before I'm too old to climb the steps."

He should've taken the bitter edge in her voice as a warning and steered clear of the subject, but once again his curiosity won out. "Your parents were talking about the McCloud stock this morning at breakfast. Sounds like the deal fell through."

"It never got off the ground. We can't come up with enough capital to buy him out."

"Sure you can," Joe said. "You can sell Dirt Eater."

Her jaw dropped, her expression as horrified as if he'd reached out and slapped her. "I...we...*no!* That's insane. When you get a bull like him, you build on those genetics, you don't sell it."

"You do if you've got the opportunity to double up the quality of the rest of your herd." Joe pivoted in his seat, bracing an elbow on the steering wheel as she continued to stare at him as if he'd suggested she put Beni up for auction. "Think like a cowboy, Violet. If you want to put on the best rodeos, you have to attract the best contestants, and they have a lot of options. Why would you choose one rodeo over another?"

"Prize money."

Joe shook his head. "Too simple. You want the best chance at winning the money, which means the best odds of drawing a horse or bull that will take you to the pay window."

"Same thing."

"Not even close. As of now, you've got six solid pay-window bulls." He listed them off, beginning with Carrot Top. "If you average thirty bull riders per rodeo, buck each bull twice, that's less than a fifty-fifty shot at drawing a winner."

Violet's stare morphed into astonishment. "You've worked one rodeo and you've got our whole lineup memorized?"

"It's my job."

She gave her head a shake. "You forgot Dirt Eater."

"When's the last time someone won a check on him?"

Her chin came up, pride sparking in her eyes. "No one has made the whistle on him in two years."

"So he's not exactly a money bull, is he? Not at rodeos like yours. You ride that bastard, you should get paid thousands of dollars, not hundreds."

Violet's chin wobbled a touch. "Are you saying he's too good for us?"

"He's too good for anything but the top twenty rodeos in the country."

She ducked her head. Joe breathed a silent curse. He wasn't trying to be mean. Just practical. And this was a lousy way to start a date.

He made a deliberate effort to sound sympathetic. "I know it's hard to part with a bull like him, but with the money you'd get for that one animal, you could step up the level of your entire herd. I've watched Dick Browning do this three different times over the past fifteen years and look where he's at now."

Exactly where Violet wanted to be. At the top. Or close. Dick hadn't quite made that last leap, but with Joe's help…

"He sold something as good as Dirt Eater?" Violet demanded.

"Ever heard of Lightning Jack?"

"Of course. He's the leading bucking horse sire in the business."

"Well, Dick Browning raised him—and sold him right after his first trip to the National Finals, for major cash. Enough to buy a brand-new semi."

"Seriously?" Violet's nose wrinkled in disgust. "He sold a potential Hall of Fame horse to buy a truck?"

Okay, maybe that wasn't the best example. It still rankled that Dick had ignored every argument Joe mounted against the sale. He sure wouldn't admit that he'd shed a few private tears when Lightning Jack climbed into someone else's trailer.

"This is a business, not a petting zoo." He thumped a finger on the console between them. "Dick needed capital and he didn't let feelings get in the way. That's how you grow."

"You don't sell your legacy."

The set of Violet's mouth was stubborn as she turned her head to gaze at the abandoned ranch, but he'd seen the flicker of speculation in her eyes. She was thinking about it. Imagining the possibilities. Now was the time to back off, let her come around on her own—not that he had any stake in her decisions. But he could feel the frustration, the *wanting*, rolling off her in waves. The least he could do was attempt to point her in the right direction.

He straightened in his seat and pulled the car back onto the highway. "Just an idea."

Violet didn't say anything. Joe counted off her silence in mileposts. *One, two, three…*

"Cole would never agree."

Joe almost smiled, but she'd brought up an angle he hadn't considered. "Does he own Dirt Eater?"

"No more than the rest of us." Violet shifted, adjusting her seat belt, and Joe's vision went red again. So much for distracting himself. "We had a mess on our hands after the accident. No wills, no life insurance, nothing. Once we were back on our feet, I persuaded Daddy to sit down with a financial planning firm. They set us up as a corporation, with the five of us as equal partners."

"Five?"

"Dad, Cole, Mom, Lily, and me." Violet ticked them off on her fingers.

"You all have equal say?"

"In theory."

But in practice, Steve had the final say. He was willing to listen, though, which was a novel experience for Joe. Versions of this afternoon's discussion at the corral had played out a hundred times on the Browning Ranch, but Dick didn't take suggestions or tolerate disagreement. He might eventually come around to Joe's way of thinking. But by then it was always Dick's idea.

He did come around, though. That's what mattered, not who got credit. Not pats on the back and *Atta boys,* no matter how warm and fuzzy Steve's approval made Joe feel. Dick Browning didn't dish out praise. Joe had never needed it. But the stark contrast had stung enough to send him running, pounding out mile after scorching mile. His brain felt blistered by the constant friction of his thoughts grinding around and around and around inside his skull. If he didn't find a way to stop them, he was going to bust an artery.

He took a deep breath full of warm, sweet female. *Here. Now.* For the moment, everything else was out of his control, and he couldn't think of a better way to focus on the present than concentrating on how to get Violet out of that shirt.

———∿∿∿———

Earnest, Texas, was a cluster of buildings ten blocks square, indistinguishable from any other wide spot on the plains. Violet pointed to a street ahead. "Turn left up there. The barbecue place is two blocks down."

Joe followed her directions and parked outside the tiny, shingled building with a plywood sign that read The Smoke Shack. The place was even smaller than it looked from the outside, and the owners seemed to think the heavenly aroma of smoked meat was all the decor it needed. Two lopsided tables the size of checkerboards were shoved against cheap wood paneling. A window was cut into the wall opposite the door, with a counter below and a hand-printed menu above: brisket, ribs, and sausage, pinto beans and potato salad on the side.

The lanky, shaggy-haired teenager behind the counter tore his attention away from a television mounted in the corner of the kitchen. His eyes went wide beneath the brim of his cap and his mouth pursed into an appreciative whistle. "Whoa, Violet. Nice…shirt."

"Shut up, Korby." Her disgusted glare failed to register because his eyes were locked on her chest. "Any chance you could quit staring at my boobs long enough to get us some food?"

He blinked and dragged his gaze up to her face, then over to Joe's. His jaw dropped another notch. "Hey, you're Joe Cassidy. I thought Hank was filling me full of shit when he told me you were coming down here."

"Are you a bullfighter too?"

"Oh, hell no," the kid said.

"Korby thinks he can ride 'em," Violet said.

"Hey, I qualified for the state high school rodeo the last two years!" Korby boasted. "Practice session tomorrow afternoon, right?"

"Every Wednesday till the weather turns."

Korby puffed out his chest. "Then Joe can see for himself."

Violet gave the menu a pointed glance. "Assuming he doesn't starve to death first."

"Oh. Right." Korby grabbed an order pad. "What can I get you?"

Violet ordered brisket with the works and sweet tea. Assuming she knew best, Joe had the same. Korby poured the tea and set it on the counter, allowing himself another leisurely survey of Violet's curves. "What are you all spiffed up for?"

"Dinner," she said, a hint of pink sneaking into her cheeks. "And a movie."

Korby glanced at Joe, then at Violet, then at Joe. His eyes widened again. "*O-oh.*"

Violet's face went a deeper shade of pink. She grabbed her tea and stomped over to plunk down at a table. Korby gave Joe a thumbs up behind her back. Joe responded in kind.

"I saw that," Violet said.

Joe slouched into the chair opposite her and grinned shamelessly. "What, you've got eyes in the back of your head?"

"Yep. They sprouted while I was in labor."

Joe snorted. "Like I tell Roxy, childbirth makes you a mother, not Wonder Woman."

"There's a difference?"

Joe pictured Violet in that metal bra thing and felt a few more brain cells sizzle. "Now that you mention it…"

And she laughed. *Whoa.* That was some laugh. Low and husky, drawing his attention to her throat, and the way that soft, strawberry-scented skin would vibrate under his mouth if he made her laugh again. Or moan. He definitely had to find out where she was ticklish.

The door slammed open and a black-haired missile launched at Violet. "Moommmiieeee!"

Joe grabbed their drinks in the nick of time. As Beni landed in his mother's lap, the rickety table landed in Joe's. Beni gave her a huge, smacking kiss. "I missed you!"

She righted the table with one hand and clutched the neckline of her shirt with the other as Beni's weight tugged it downward. "Missed you too, bub. What are you doing?"

"Me and Daddy been in Amarillo checking out a new Freightliner for Grandpa. It's black and has a computer and the sleeper is totally *awesome.*"

Delon paused just inside the door, his gaze bouncing from Violet to Joe and back again. He got hung up for long beat in the front of Violet's shirt, same as Korby, but the way Delon's eyes narrowed, Joe didn't expect another thumbs up.

"We saw your car outside," Delon said to Violet, patently ignoring Joe. "I assumed you'd run in to pick up dinner."

Combined with the tight set of his jaw, it verged on an accusation.

Violet's face went from pink to red. "We're going to a movie. Anything good showing in Dumas?"

"Dinosaurs!" Beni declared.

Delon put a hand on the back of Violet's chair, staring down at Joe, protective as hell. Of his woman, or his kid's mother? Maybe Delon figured they were the same thing. If so, he'd done a piss-poor job of letting Violet in on the secret. Plus there was that barrel racer.

Beni bounced on his mother's knees, tipping the wobbly table almost into Joe's lap again. "Can I come to the movie with you? The dinosaur one? It is *so* cool!"

"And you know this how?" Violet asked.

"We went yesterday." Delon scooped Beni up and gave him a gentle swat as he deposited him on the floor. "You don't need to go again."

"But I want to see that part where they poop out the eggs—"

"Hush." Delon put a firm hand on each of Beni's shoulders to hold him in place.

"Dinner for two!" Korby plopped a tray onto the counter, then got all bug-eyed when he saw Delon and Beni. "Oh. Hey. Delon. You're um, here."

They all tried not to look at each other for a couple of beats, except for Korby who appeared to be memorizing the moment for retelling. Finally, he said, "You want food or, um, something?"

"No thanks," Delon said. "We ate already."

"Oh. Okay." Korby's eyes darted to Violet, then Joe, then back to Delon. He stayed at the counter, watching them all like he expected the fireworks to start any second.

Joe got up, pried their dinner out of Korby's grasp and set it on the table. "I'm starving. How about you, Violet?"

She gave a stiff little nod. Delon didn't budge. Son of a bitch didn't take a hint for shit. Joe settled into his chair and took a bite of his brisket. The smoked meat melted in his mouth. He didn't have to fake a groan of approval, but he gave it some extra *oomph*.

"Good stuff." He smiled at Violet. "Better eat up if we want to make it to the early show and get you home in plenty of time to tuck you in."

Delon's jaw clenched and his eyes went slitty, but before he could say anything, Beni piped up. "How come you can tuck Mommy in but Daddy can't?"

Crap. Joe had forgotten the kid. "Uh—"

Beni folded his arms and glared, suspicious. For the first time, Joe saw a distinct resemblance to Steve Jacobs. "Grandma Iris says only married people tuck each other in. Like her and Grandpa."

Joe opened his mouth, then glanced at Violet, who gave him a look that shut it again.

"Joe was kidding," she said. "We're just going to a movie. Then home. Alone. I mean, we're driving home together, but then I'll go in my house and he'll go in the bunkhouse…" She trailed off, her face red and her eyes desperate.

"Why do you want to go to the movie with him?" Beni's face squinched up and his voice pitched higher. "Why can't you go with Daddy so I could come, too?"

"You haven't seen Daddy for almost a month. You're having man time, remember?" Panic leaked into her voice, and into the pleading look she gave Delon.

Delon gave them a look that suggested Violet might

be the one who wanted man time, but he backed toward the door, tugging Beni with him, the potential for embarrassment outweighing the need to stick around and thump his chest.

Beni nailed Violet with a pathetic look. "Can I call you at bedtime and say good night?"

A muscle popped in Delon's cheek, like he was grinding his teeth at the thought of what that call might interrupt. "Uh, Beni, it might be late—"

"Sure," Violet said.

Delon shot Joe a glance. *So there, asshole.* Joe gave it right back to him with a cocky *We'll see about that* smile.

"Okay. We can go," Beni said, with tortured sigh.

Violet kissed her fingertips and reached over to tap his cheek. "Talk to you later."

The door slapped shut behind them and the room went silent except for the tinny echo of the baseball commentators from Korby's television.

"Well, that was fun," Joe said brightly.

If looks could kill, there would've been nothing but a pile of smoking ashes on his chair. Yep, now he remembered why he didn't do this dating thing.

Chapter 14

VIOLET HADN'T GONE TO A MOVIE IN A THEATER WITH a man since college. Delon didn't count because Beni was always planted between them. She'd forgotten the hum of anticipation, the intimacy of sitting shoulder to shoulder as the lights went down and the darkness folded in.

Joe was close enough for her to breathe in his spicy aftershave and feel the heat radiating off his body. Prickles of awareness raced across her skin, cranking her nerve endings to maximum sensitivity. Every neuron in her brain tuned into Joe's wavelength like a million tiny antennae, amplifying every breath, the slightest shift of his weight. She braced for the move he was sure to make, anticipation winding tighter and tighter until she thought she'd suffocate from the tension.

And Joe did…*nothing*. No hand on her knee or arm across the back of her chair. Not even an accidental brush of hands over the shared armrest. He just sat there popping Junior Mints into his mouth one at a time and staring at the screen like the stupid movie had a plot. Her emotions spun, whirling from arousal to confusion to irritation and back again. He'd stopped sneaking peeks at the front of her shirt once the silicone princess starting flashing her rack on screen. Not that Violet wanted him to look down her shirt. She just wanted him to want to.

Suspicion hit her like an overripe tomato, splattering

slimy seeds of doubt in every crevice of her brain as she pictured the redhead in the Corvette again. She might be with Wyatt, but Joe could have a woman like that, and he'd chosen Violet instead? Maybe he'd never been all that interested. Just bored. Or on an ego trip. She'd challenged him. He'd won. Damn this shirt. She might as well have answered the door naked. Same message.

And then she had to go parading around town. Forty minutes farther down the road and they could've been in Amarillo, where there wasn't a chance in a million of Delon waltzing in. But hey, at least now Violet didn't have to figure out how to tell him about her date.

She jumped when Joe stuck a hand in front of her face, Junior Mint resting on his palm. "Want the last one?"

"No!" she snapped. The couple two rows ahead glanced over their shoulders. Violet winced and lowered her voice. "I mean, no thank you."

"Okay."

Joe popped it in his mouth, folded the box into thirds and stuffed it into the cup holder. Then he lifted his arm and looped it over her shoulders as casual as if he had a right. Violet's heart revved, stuttered, then took off, pinging around her rib cage like a pinball. The banging inside her chest was so loud it nearly drowned out the explosions on screen as robot aliens laid waste to New York City, which was pretty much a waste to begin with in Violet's opinion, but she'd heard a rumor people there felt the same way about Texas.

Okay, she might be getting a little delirious. Probably because she'd forgotten to breathe. Which she did now, but it made a weird gulping sound that had Joe shooting her a concerned look.

"Are you okay?"

She nodded, but that made her hair slide from under Joe's arm, which left his bare skin pressed against hers and that was *not helping*. "Hiccup."

"Want me to get you a drink?"

Only if it was ice water in a cup big enough to shove her face into. She shook her head, and that caused more rubbing of skin against skin. She was surprised the ends of her hair didn't start smoking, the heat was so…*wow*. Then his fingers stroked her arm, and she thought the top of her head might actually be sizzling. *Breathe, Violet. In. Out. In…oh hell, brain, do* not *go there—*

Crap. Too late.

Joe's fingertip traced a circle over her biceps while his thumb brushed the supersensitive flesh on the inside of her upper arm, and honest to God, her toes actually curled. If he extended that thumb one measly little inch, he'd be touching her breast. Or she could just take a deep breath…

Right. Like her lungs would expand that far, considering they'd gone on strike the second Joe touched her. The least this shitty movie could do was provide a smidgen of distraction, but no, they just ran around swearing and shooting and creating excuses for the leading lady to bend over and give the camera a clear shot down the front of her strategically torn uniform.

Violet tilted the cell phone clipped to her belt, intending to sneak a peek at the time, but it lit up like a strobe light when she touched the button. A man five seats to their left gave her a death glare. And these morons had at least another forty-five minutes of chasing their asses in circles and blowing stuff up before they got around to saving the world. She slapped her hand over the phone, then lifted her head and gave a little squeak of surprise when she found Joe's face only inches from hers.

"Another hour?" he asked.

Violet nodded, rendered mute by his proximity, the way his eyes locked on hers. *Hoo boy. So much for not interested.* His gaze wandered down to her mouth, the arm around her shoulders drawing her in. Slowly. Inevitably. Oh God. He was going to kiss her. And she was going let him, even though the oldest Shackleford girl was sitting right across the aisle, so Lily would get a text message complete with photos before Violet got her tongue untangled from Joe's.

She jerked back and blurted, "Let's get out of here."

All three of their nearest neighbors cranked their heads around to glare. A dozen others stared in avid curiosity.

Joe lowered his voice and leaned in, so close her eyes crossed. "If we do that, we won't get to see how it ends."

"*Boom! Crash!* More boob shots. Defeat is certain until the hero pulls off the impossible save at the last possible second and the robots explode and everyone lives happily ever after."

"You forgot my favorite part." He met her eyes again, his smile a lazy challenge. "Where the guy and the girl sneak off and get naked."

Her pulse thudded hard and her mouth went dry. There were so many ways this could go horribly wrong, and then they'd either be minus a bullfighter again or Joe would be underfoot for another two and a half weeks. If things went sideways, it would be beyond awkward. But if it went well…

When the last rodeo ended, Joe would be on the first

plane back to Oregon and Violet would slide back into her rut with a smile on her face. A big, *big* smile, if the energy crackling between them was any indication.

Joe raised his eyebrows, questioning. "Where are we going, Violet?"

Straight to Hell, probably, but if she was this turned on just sitting next to the man, it might be worth it. She made up her mind. Perhaps she'd made it up days ago. "I know a place…"

Joe's answering smile was hot as Tabasco sauce, burning *all* the way down. He popped to his feet, dragging her with him. "Lead the way, darlin'."

Violet drove, mostly as an excuse to not have to look at him until the car bumped to a stop a few miles out of town, on a patch of beaten dirt at the edge of a bluff. Joe climbed out and stretched, arching that long, lean body. Just watching the man move was more excitement than she'd had in months. Until tonight, she'd seen him in either baggy soccer shorts or loose-fitting grubby jeans with an untucked T-shirt over top. These jeans were not grubby or loose. His belt fit snug around narrow hips, framing what was possibly the nicest butt she'd ever laid eyes on. And would soon be laying hands on.

The thought sent a jolt of lust through her so powerful she checked for scorch marks on the steering wheel before she got out of the car, trailing behind as he strolled to the edge of the bluff, then stopped abruptly. "Whoa. That's quite a drop."

Three feet from the toes of his boots, the flat plain dropped two stories, down to a wide green valley scattered with clumps of trees. The Canadian River meandered through them, more like a sluggish creek this late in the year. Beyond the river, the lowering sun lit up the striated colors of the breaks, row upon row of convoluted ridges and canyons, carved into the earth by centuries of wind and water.

"Hank's family owns all of this?" Joe asked.

"Only down to that curve of the river," Violet said, pointing. "The rest of their property stretches north. The ranch house is a couple miles over that way."

Joe glanced over his shoulder at the rutted dirt road that skirted the top of the bluff. "Their driveway could use some improvement."

"The main road comes in from the west. This is a shortcut."

Joe went back to studying the landscape, shadows skimming across his eyes. "Reminds me of the Painted Hills in Oregon."

He really was homesick. And why wouldn't he be? This land, Violet's home ground, tugged at her soul with an ache that was never quite satisfied, even when it rippled all around her in a sea of earth and sky. Homesick didn't begin to describe how it would feel to be evicted, even temporarily.

She glanced down and vertigo pulled at her, spinning her head and making her feel as if she would tilt into the void. She backed off a couple of steps.

"Don't like heights?" Joe asked.

"Sure. Looks great from here." She allowed herself another long, appreciative look at his body, framed against the glow of the setting sun. "I suppose you're into bungee jumping off bridges and kayaking waterfalls."

"Hell no. Never been a fan of unnecessary pain."

Violet raised her eyebrows. "Interesting choice of careers."

"Totally accidental." He tucked his hands into the pockets of his jeans, gaze fixed on the shadows that crept across the valley floor. "I started working for Dick when I was in high school, stacking hay bales, pitching manure, all the grunt work. One day at practice they needed a bullfighter, so I gave it a shot. Turned out I had a knack for it."

An understatement, if she'd ever heard one. "Are your parents rodeo people?"

Joe laughed. "My dad's an electrician, born and raised in Tacoma. He moved back right after the divorce. And Roxy—my mom—she comes to the rodeos, then hides her face 'cuz she can't stand to watch."

"Did you try competing?"

"Not once I started fighting bulls." He gave a dismissive flick of his fingers. "Riding is a crap shoot—gotta draw good, ride good, hope the judges like you—but the bullfighter always gets paid. A lot better money than what most eighteen-year-olds can make."

"Were you supporting yourself?"

"By choice. Roxy—my mom—was engaged to a financial planner from Portland, and no damn way was I moving to Yuppieville."

"What about your dad?"

His expression didn't change, but somehow all of his edges became harder. "Like I said, I was eighteen. I could take care of myself."

And would rather be on his own, straight out of high school, than ask for help from either of his parents? Just Joe. No family to give him a leg up. Everything he'd done, the career he'd made, he'd built for himself. He'd earned the right to some arrogance. Possibly, he'd needed it to survive.

Possibly, she'd misjudged Joe in a dozen other ways, and suddenly getting to know him felt a whole lot more dangerous than jumping his bones.

She led him to a trail that angled down the side of a narrow, brushy draw, a path worn by ancient feet. This area had been home to the earliest human settlements recorded in the southwest. A side path curved below the rim of the bluff, ending in a room-sized niche scooped out of the crumbling dirt and soft rock. Easy to imagine the natives resting here, high above the river bed in this tiny fortress. The charred remnants of a campfire were fresh, though.

Joe looked around, then gave her a slow, heated smile that said he knew exactly what this place was. "Come here often?"

"Not lately. It's called The Notch." A place for the younger crowd to sneak beer and kisses. Chances of anyone coming along on a weekday were slim, but she assumed the privacy code still applied; see a car, stay clear, in case there was more going down than a few drinks.

Speaking of alcohol…she could use a shot. How was she supposed to do this? Did they chat first, or get right down to business? And crud…condoms. Should she have brought her own instead of assuming a guy like Joe would be prepared? Then she pictured stopping at a store in Dumas and bumping into one of the ladies from her mother's garden club while holding a pack of Trojans in her hand. Oh, *hell* no.

She occupied her jittery hands by spreading the blanket from the trunk of her car at the base of a rock outcropping, the warm, smooth surface providing a decent back rest when she sat down. Her pulse skipped when Joe lowered himself beside her and draped his arm over her shoulders, sending a shimmer of heat across her skin.

He bent one knee and rested his arm on it. "Ah, yeah. Much better than that stupid movie."

She willed herself to relax, tip her head back against his arm and savor the feel of warm, hard muscle against her neck. The sun was a blazing semicircle sliding below the horizon, setting fire to the wispy layers of clouds and reflecting off the ragged edges of the breaks, turning them into a glowing maze of pinks and reds and golds. Violet inhaled. Joe's cologne tickled her nose and made her want to bury her face in the crook of his neck.

"You should see the Palo Duro Canyon," she said, her nerves bubbling over into words. "It's lot more impressive than this. And not very far. Just south of Amarillo."

"Maybe you can show it to me while I'm here." His fingers skimmed over her arm, his voice sliding into a scale that raised goose bumps even though the words were harmless.

The trailing edge of the sun flared, then shrank to a brilliant pinpoint before flickering out. Dusk settled in around them, softening the edges, blurring the lines. Darkness. Yes. That would be good. Much less…revealing. The smell of damp earth and cured grass rose off the riverbed; and birds chittered in the trees, settling in for the night. Joe's arm was a pleasant weight on her shoulders, his hands still for the moment.

"Is your mom still in Portland?" she asked, not ready to move past conversation just yet.

"Boise. Portland was Number Two."

"What number is Boise?"

Joe made a show of counting on the fingers of his free hand. "Five. Well, three and five, if you count marrying the same one twice."

"I take it she doesn't have great taste in men."

"The best. They keep getting richer and smarter, and they're all decent guys who spoil her rotten." Joe's eyebrows lowered in disapproval. "Except Four. He was her one bad call. I think she was so irritated at herself, when Frank came back around she gave him a second shot."

"What went wrong the first time?"

"She has a short attention span." His voice went bone dry. "It's genetic."

The implication was about as subtle as a two-handed shove. Violet echoed his tone. "Guess you're not lookin' to settle down with a little woman and a passel of kids."

"Nope. Roxy has dibs on all the 'I do's' for our family."

Okay, then. They were clear. Crystal. Whatever this turned out to be with Joe, she knew the expiration date. She'd written it on his contract.

"Do you live at Browning's ranch?" she asked.

"Geezus, no." His smile was a razor-edged glint in the half light. "I rent a place in town. Working with Dick and Lyle is enough. I don't need to look at them across the breakfast table every morning."

"If you don't like them, why do you stay?"

The hand that had been dangling on his knee clenched

into a fist, then slowly loosened as if Joe had forced it to relax. "There's no place like the High Lonesome. Ten thousand acres of desert that's never seen a plow. It's... well, you know how it is."

His words were infused with a yearning so fierce, it stabbed at her heart. Her roots were buried deep in this red dirt. She might shrivel right up and die if she was transplanted, but she owned her piece of ground. Joe was at the mercy of a man who, by all accounts, wasn't the merciful kind. It seemed to her that investing his heart and soul in the High Lonesome was asking to be ruined.

"Why do you fight bulls? And don't tell me it's for the money. There's a lot easier ways to make a buck."

"Be the hero. Get the girls. You know..." Then he trailed off, and an odd expression flickered on his face, as if he'd had a sudden realization. His gaze focused on her. "You do the same thing. Make a difference, save the day. Sounds corny as hell, but it's a rush, knowing you're the reason somebody walked out of the arena under their own power."

Yeah. She knew. Felt it even now, quivering in her muscles, though she wasn't sure if she was feeling her own reaction, or his, or both—their bodies vibrating like twin tuning forks striking the same note. Heat zinged from her scalp to her toes, then settled halfway in between. He shifted, rocked onto his hip so his body tilted toward hers.

He rested his hand on her shoulder, his thumb skimming the nape of her neck as his voice dropped to the purr that made her mouth go dry. "I saw you after that save on Sunday. You were fired up."

"It gets your blood pumping," she admitted.

"Darlin', you have no idea." Joe leaned closer, his warm breath fanning across her cheek. Her body tightened. Anticipating. Aching. "Watching you in action… I never knew how hot that could make me. Especially now—" His finger trailed lower, over her collarbone and down to the bottom of the vee of her shirt, and everything adjacent throbbed in response. "That I can see all this."

His fingertip circled, drifting over the inner curves of her breasts as Joe's mouth hovered over hers. "Makes me want to drag you off that horse and shove you up against the nearest fence, see just how hot we could get."

The air shuddered out of Violet's lungs. She barely had a chance to gulp in more before Joe took her mouth in a kiss that felt like it could melt the rock she leaned on. For a beat, all she could do was accept. Adjust. Then she opened up and gave herself to the heat and the sensation. His fingers splayed to cup the back of her head as his tongue toyed with hers. He kissed like he fought bulls. Bold. Aggressive. Advancing, retreating, forcing her to chase him. She curled her hand around the back of his neck, fingers tangled in the ragged ends of his hair, dragging him closer.

He hooked his hand around her bent knee, rolling her into him, taking the kiss deeper as she slid her hand down, palm flat, along the long sleek line of his back. Her body screamed for contact, the hunger immediate, relentless, no time for slow and gentle. He scooped an arm around her shoulders, lifted, turned, and lowered her in one smooth motion, following her down without his mouth missing a beat.

Damn, the man was *good*.

Then she lost the ability to think at all when his thigh slid between hers. His fingers skimmed along the waistband of her jeans, found bare skin beneath her shirt. She arched into his touch, wanting more. *More.* Skin to skin, flesh to flesh. She tugged at his polo shirt, but it was tucked securely into his jeans. Her greedy hands went lower, fingers curling, digging into the hard curve of his butt through taut denim, feeling it flex as he responded to the pressure by rocking his hips into her. The only thing firmer was pressed hard against the front of her jeans. He rocked again and she made a sound that would have been embarrassing if she hadn't been pretty much out of her mind with need.

His nimble fingers found the place where her shirt was tied and, oh thank the Lord, those laces weren't just for decoration. He tugged and they came loose, the shirt falling away at the push of his hands, leaving nothing but a lacy bra in the same shade of red.

He pulled back, looked down at her and sucked in a shaky breath of his own. "Halle-fucking-lujah."

His mouth came down again, planting another hard, hot kiss on her mouth before heading south, sending shockwaves of sensation over her skin as he went. Violet slid her hands around to his hips and at the command of her last functioning brain cell ran her thumbs over the front pockets of his jeans, feeling the gratifying crinkle of plastic.

Joe pulled back, looked down at her.

"Just checking," she said.

"Got it handled."

Hot damn, did he ever. That mouth of his deserved a championship buckle all its own. She tugged at his shirt, hissing her annoyance when it didn't budge. His mouth kept moving, tasting, teasing as he lifted his hips and reached between them to pop first his buckle free, then the button on his jeans before settling over her again. The zipper gave as she shoved her hands down to pull the shirt free and, finally, *finally,* found hot silky skin. Joe stopped just short of the promised land, her breasts aching in protest as he sat up to yank the shirt over his head and toss it aside. His torso gleamed in the near darkness, lean, taut, with smooth flat muscles, like a swimmer's. Violet almost wished he'd stop and let her admire the view. Then he lowered his body onto hers, pressed all that lovely muscle against her and her eyes crossed.

Hallelujah indeed.

She arched and moaned as Joe's mouth and then teeth found her nipple through the lace. Light exploded, glowing red through her eyelids, as if the two of them had generated their own bonfire—

"Violet?"

She froze. Oh dear God, *no.* Her eyes popped open and for a second she couldn't see anything but a bright glare. Then the light bobbed and she heard, "Give me the damn flashlight, Hank!" and it veered skyward and blinked off, leaving pinpricks of brilliant color dancing in front of Violet's eyes. She shoved so hard against Joe's chest she heard the air go out of his lungs in a small *Oof!* He rolled away, blinking like he'd been yanked out of the movie theater into broad daylight.

"What the fuck—"

He followed Violet's stricken gaze up to the two people silhouetted against the darkening sky. She couldn't see their faces, but she knew those voices like her own. Violet fumbled to cover herself as she watched realization dawn on Joe's face.

"Fuck," he said again, with feeling.

Her sentiments exactly.

Chapter 15

AS JOE'S EYES ONCE AGAIN ADJUSTED TO THE twilight, the girl on top of the bluff rammed Hank with her elbow. He just snickered.

"Sorry, Violet," she called down. "I didn't recognize your new car. The sheriff's been getting on us about the underage kids coming out here, so Hank figured we should scare the crap out of a couple of them. I never dreamed…" She trailed off. Cursed. "I'll shut up now. C'mon, Hank, let's go."

"Hope you brought your handcuffs, Joe," he yelled as she grabbed him by the collar and dragged him away.

"Shut *up*, Hank."

Hank laughed. Joe heard a thump and a grunt, as if the girl had gut-punched him. Doors slammed. An engine hummed, something smooth and quiet like Violet's car, the whisper of its tires barely audible on the packed dirt. Joe flopped back on the blanket while Violet fumbled with the laces on her shirt. Wow. Beni wasn't the only one who could swear like a truck driver. She scrambled to her feet, grabbed the edge of the blanket, and cursed again when she realized it was pinned under Joe's weight.

"Bring that with you when you come," she ordered, then strode off into the gloom.

When you come. Yeah, right. That wasn't happening tonight. He propped his hands behind his head, watching the stars brighten, waiting for the hard ache to ease so he could zip his jeans. Above him on the bluff, the car door slammed. He waited, but the engine didn't start so at least Violet must not be planning to drive off and leave him. Not that she had any reason to be mad. Coming out here was her idea. If she'd asked his opinion, they'd be bouncing around on a king-size bed in a motel and Hank wouldn't be fixing to blab to everyone in Texas.

A story that would inevitably reach Violet's parents. Joe pictured Steve's reaction and cringed. What did you say to a man who demanded to know what the hell you were doing with his daughter? *Anything she'd let me* might be the truth, but Joe didn't have much desire to test-drive a body cast.

Son of a bitch. He could get fired for real this time. Now there was a thought to deflate a man. Joe zipped, buttoned, and buckled up, then rolled onto his hands and knees to search for his shirt. A flashlight would've been handy. He should've asked Violet if she had one in the trunk of her car when he saw she intended to lead him off a cliff. Scratch that. He should've gone with his first impulse when he got a load of that red shirt and hauled her into her bedroom, forget the damn date. Let her parents think what they wanted. Along with all those people at the Lone Steer Saloon. The barbecue shack. Every damn place they'd showed their faces.

And if he stuck his hand in a rattlesnake nest fumbling around for his shirt, he was gonna be seriously pissed. He sat back on his haunches, orienting himself. He'd been about here, and Violet had been there. *All* there. That bra had damn near stopped his heart. The image of her in it was permanently etched in his brain.

The feel of her under his hands, that mind-bending combination of softness and strength…

That did it. He was gonna kill Hank just on principle. He located his shirt slung over a rock, yanked it over his head, grabbed the blanket, then eased up the trail, acutely aware of the black void to his left. Violet was slumped on the hood of the car, heels on the front bumper, head between her fisted hands. She wasn't *crying?* No. Mumbling.

Her voice rose and he made out a few words. "…be so stupid, Violet? You *never* learn…"

He cleared his throat and she jerked upright. Her cheeks were dry, thank God, her eyes glittering with anger and a heavy dose of embarrassment. She'd pulled on a jacket—a big, shapeless windbreaker that might as well have had *Don't even think about it* plastered in glow-in-the-dark letters across the front.

Joe shook the dirt off the blanket. "I'll put this in the trunk."

She gave a jerky nod. The keys were in the car so he leaned in, hit the trunk button on the key fob, and went around the back of the car to stow the blanket. Then he opened the passenger door and held it for her. "I'll drive."

She climbed in, her face set in the dim glow of the dome light. Neither of them spoke until he'd turned the car back onto the highway.

"Who was the girl?" he asked.

"Hank's sister." Violet tipped her head back against the seat and closed her eyes, the words hissing out like overheated steam. "Melanie is my best friend. Just my luck, Hank had to be with her."

Violet's phone beeped. She read the text, huffed

once, then tapped out a reply. The response came within seconds. She tapped some more, hit Send, then sighed and dropped the phone in her coat pocket.

"Melanie feels terrible. She swiped Hank's cell phone so he couldn't send out a mass text to all his buddies." Violet turned her face, staring out into the night so Joe could only see her profile. "It'll just delay the inevitable."

Joe opened his mouth, then clamped it shut. He'd almost said he was sorry. For what? Violet was a single adult woman, and he was a single adult man. There was no reason they shouldn't take advantage of each other. Shouldn't have kept taking advantage of each other once Melanie dragged Hank away. So why was there a knot in his gut that felt suspiciously like guilt?

"Take a left up there," she said, pointing to a gravel road. "This road cuts across to our highway."

He did as instructed, then forgot about talking while he navigated the washboards and potholes so big the low Cadillac nearly bottomed out.

"Take a left at the stop sign."

He did. The gate to the abandoned half of the Jacobs Ranch was only fifty yards down the highway, the dirt road the same route he'd jogged that afternoon. He parked the car in front of Violet's house. As she reached for the door, he put a hand on her arm. She froze. The look in her eyes made him pull back while he still had fingers instead of bloody stumps.

"Violet…listen. I'll take care of Hank."

"Really? How?"

"Strangulation preferably, but I don't know my way around here well enough to hide the body."

"Great. Another comedian." She kicked her door open.

Joe did the same, jumping out to look at her over the top of the car. "Look, I know this was embarrassing, but don't you think you're overreacting a little?"

"No." She spun on her heel and stomped toward her house, but her stride hitched when her phone rang. Pausing on the steps, she pulled it from her pocket and checked the screen. Joe saw her take a deep breath and blow it out, making a visible effort to calm down. As she opened the door, she lifted the phone to her ear, her voice soft. "Hey, little man. How's it going?"

For a count of ten Joe stood, staring at the closed door. He'd alienated a lot of women in a lot of ways, but this was new. The women he usually dated didn't give a damn who knew they were having sex…which was why he should've stuck to that kind of women. Then his head filled with visions of soft, round curves and red lace.

Hell.

He dropped into the rusty metal patio chair in front of the bunkhouse, the screech of the springs a nail through his eardrum. He rocked back and made them screech again, the sound a perfect match to the bitter taste of not-quite-guilt at the back of his throat. Down at the corral a bull bellowed, trailing off into a series of low grunts, but there was no answering challenge.

Joe pulled out his phone, frowning when he pushed a key and nothing happened. Oh. Right. He'd turned it off the night before and forgotten to turn it on again. He hit the power button. The second it was functional, it started beeping frantically. One, two, three incoming texts, two voice messages, all from Wyatt except one. Crap. Joe had forgotten to call his mother. He ignored all the messages and dialed Wyatt's number.

"Nice time to turn your phone off, jackass," Wyatt snapped. "I've been trying to reach you all day."

"I saw. What's got your titties twisted?"

"Violet. I kept thinking there was something I'd heard about her."

Joe stopped rocking. "What?"

"Remember a couple years back, when that bronc rider from Louisiana talked the Roundup queen into sneaking up and having sex on the roof of the south grandstand?"

"Sure. It was the worst kept secret in Pendleton." He also remembered that she'd shimmied out of her fringed buckskin skirt long before the last day of her reign, but that was between her and Joe.

"Yeah, well, Violet hooked up with that goofy bastard at a rodeo in Hickory Springs last spring, and his other not-quite-ex-girlfriend showed up at his motel a night earlier than he expected."

Uh-oh. "How bad was it?"

"Shrieking, scratching, catfight ugly, but you know who won."

Violet. Hands down. Then Joe remembered Hank's crack about the handcuffs. "Somebody called the cops?"

"Yep. Violet ended up cuffed and stuffed, and rather than just coughing up the bail, that dumbshit rookie you're working with called her dad."

Joe ground his teeth. Hank definitely had to die. First chance, Joe was feeding him to Dirt Eater, one piece at a time.

"Then the next day, one of the committeemen made a nasty comment and Cole Jacobs offered to plow the arena with the guy's face. Needless to say, they won't be producing that rodeo next year."

Joe slumped deeper, pressing a fist to his forehead. "So I'm probably not the best thing that could've happened to her right now."

A beat of silence, then Wyatt sighed. "What did you do?"

Joe gave him the condensed version, minus the red lace bra. Some things a man wanted to keep all for himself.

Wyatt sighed again. "Well, she picked the spot, so technically it isn't your fault, but her dad could still boot your ass clear back to Oregon. Not the greatest thing for your reputation, given that you just weaseled out of working Pendleton."

"Hey! That was your idea, not mine."

"I know. Just sayin' it would be good to smooth this over if possible."

He felt that jab again—not quite guilt, but a close cousin—and blew out an irritated breath. "This is stupid. We didn't do anything wrong. Just because I told her dad…"

"Told him what?"

"Nothing." Joe swatted at a moth, bouncing it off the side of the bunkhouse. It landed on its back, fluttered around, then righted itself and flew right back at him. Stupid bastard. "I asked if it was okay to go out with her. Period."

Across the yard, a shadow moved behind what he guessed were Violet's bedroom curtains. She would be stripping off that red shirt. Then the bra. He could be there in ten seconds…

He swatted the moth away again, feeling slightly more sympathetic.

"Ah. I see," Wyatt said, in the wise man tone that made Joe want to reach through the airwaves and strangle him. "Basically, you have enough respect for this woman to approach Steve Jacobs, man to man."

"Well, yeah, but I didn't say I wouldn't…"

"The promise was implied. Everyone who's ever seen an old western knows that."

Even Joe. Hadn't he thought almost as much, standing in Steve's living room? And his conscience had been taking potshots at him since the first time he'd touched Violet. She had too many sensitive strings attached— the business, her family, Beni, and yeah, Delon—that could easily be ripped to shreds. Joe had sworn he'd never knowingly inflict that kind of damage. Not after being on the receiving end during the implosion of his parents' marriage, and witnessing the trail of destruction his mother had wrought since.

This wasn't just about some promise he may or may not have made to Violet's parents. Joe had violated his personal code of conduct. This woman was everything he had always avoided, for good reason. Wyatt had tried to tell him—his own gut had tried to tell him—but he'd been too wrapped up in self-pity and anger to listen.

He breathed out a curse. "What the hell do I do now?"

"The honorable thing, of course."

Joe lifted the phone away from his ear to glare at it. "*What?*"

"There's only one way you can put a positive spin on this," Wyatt declared. "You have to be a gentleman and make an honest woman of her."

He laughed outright at Joe's very ungentlemanly response.

Chapter 16

Violet propped her elbows on her sister's granite-topped kitchen island, buried her face in her hands, and groaned. "I can't believe it happened *again*."

"It isn't that bad," Lily said, obnoxiously cheerful over morning coffee. "Y'all didn't even have to get a mug shot."

Violet dropped one hand to give her a baleful glare.

"Oh, come on—if this was someone else, you'd be laughing. You tossed her off the balcony, Violet."

"She was trying to claw my eyes out! And I didn't *toss* her. I just shoved and she fell." And thank God for the ornamental shrubs one floor down.

"Hank said she came out lookin' like she'd been in a cage fight with a porcupine."

"Hank should shut up."

Lily hooted. "Fat chance."

Make that no chance. What Hank knew, everybody in the Panhandle would know within a couple of days. Violet slumped over her coffee cup, groaning again. "How could I be such an idiot?"

"Now there's the million-dollar question."

Violet rolled her eyes up to give Lily a death glare, which her sister ignored in favor of fetching a plate of muffins. Homemade, of course. Fresh blueberries. Real butter. Lily had inherited more than their mother's lack of height and tendency toward plumpness. Lily was the anti-Violet—soft, fluffy, and content. The sisters were closer than they had a right to be, considering. Lily was a cowgirl by default—growing up, everyone had to pitch in—but she'd escaped to the kitchen every chance she got, the same way Violet had dodged housework in favor of trailing after her dad. Lily set the plate between them, mouth pursed thoughtfully as she picked out a muffin and peeled off the wrapper.

Violet hissed out a long breath that did nothing for her frustrated hormones. "I'm cursed when it comes to this stuff."

"No. You're stupid."

Violet jerked her head up. "*Excuse* me?"

Lily gazed back at her, unapologetic. "You should be sittin' there basking in the afterglow. Hank's gonna run his mouth regardless—you might as well've stuck around and got your money's worth."

Violet gaped at her. "Awesome advice from the minister's wife."

"And now you know why I haven't been invited to lead the ladies' prayer group." Lily plunked down her muffin and leveled a gaze that matched her unflinching tone. "How many times have we had this conversation, Violet?"

"I…um…a few."

"Starting with the Earnest Fun Days Rodeo when you were sixteen," Lily reminded her. "You and Clayton James, up in the announcer's stand after the Saturday night rodeo."

Otherwise known as The Night Violet Lost Her Virginity. An urban legend in Earnest. Violet had chosen their hometown rodeo to finally give in to Clayton's persistent efforts to get her out of her jeans, so everyone from three counties was right there handy to witness her downfall. And his.

"You didn't have to dump him," Lily said. "Was it his fault he was so weak in the knees after you got done with him that he fell down the stairs?"

Violet felt her mouth pushing into a pout. "No, but if he hadn't gone to squealing like a stuck pig, everybody might not've figured out what we'd been doing up there."

"His ankle was broken."

"So? He could've sucked it up until we got him back to his camper."

"Harsh, Violet." Lily turned the muffin with her fingers, studying it like a crystal ball. "That's where it started, with poor ol' Clayton. And a month later, the accident happened."

Violet endured the usual wash of grief, muted by the years but never gone. "That's got nothing to do with my dating habits."

"It's got everything to do with all of us." Lily picked a blueberry out of her muffin and smashed it between her fingers. "Cole turned into, well, Cole. I was in such a rush to grow up I got hitched to my junior high boyfriend when I was nineteen, and you were so focused on helping Daddy save the ranch, you never got around to figuring out who *you* are."

Violet's jaw came unhinged. "*What?*"

"You want to think you're so sensible, but let's look at the evidence." Lily cocked her head, doing a great impression of their mother at her most persistent. "After knowing Delon your whole life and having no desire to jump him, why that night?"

"I was on the rebound."

"*Pfft!*" Lily gave a dismissive flick of her fingers. "You knew that would end when the big doofus graduated and went back to Wyoming. What else? Something made you take a second look at Delon."

Violet made herself think back to a night she generally preferred to forget. "He was drinking like he meant it. And he was in a mood. Dark. A little crazy. Like he wanted to inflict some damage."

"In other words, he reminded you of his big brother." Lily laughed at the heat that flared in Violet's cheeks. "Like you were the only one who had a crush on Gil back then."

Sure—back when Gil Sanchez was still fun, still flirted with every female from eight to eighty and wasn't mad at the world and the majority of the people in it.

"I didn't sleep with Delon because I wanted his brother," Violet said, pretty sure it was the honest truth. "I was worried. I thought I'd just sit down and make conversation, but he bought me a shot of tequila, then he asked me to dance…"

"He was lettin' his badass side out," Lily finished. "And you've never been one to say no to anything that looks remotely like trouble."

The snippy remark pushed Violet over the edge from irritation to anger. "Go ahead, Lil. Rub it in. I'm an idiot when it comes to men."

"I didn't say that."

"But you meant it." She pitched her voice into a snotty drawl. "*Why doesn't that Violet Jacobs find some nice, sensible man to be a father to that boy of hers?*"

"That boy already has an amazing daddy, and if you

had any interest in nice and sensible, Delon wouldn't still be sleeping in Beni's room."

Violet bunched her fist and knocked it against the granite. "I *know*. He is such a great guy, it's stupid that I don't feel…"

"No. Stupid would be convincing yourself to settle for playing Mommy and Daddy with a man who's like a brother to us." Lily pushed her mutilated muffin aside and propped her elbows on the bar. "Are you looking for a forever guy?"

"Right now? No." Violet threaded her fingers through her hair, massaging her aching brain. "I'd just like to go out once in a while, have some fun, maybe get lucky. Is that so horrible?"

"Not if it's what you want and nobody's getting hurt…other than the occasional crazy ex-girlfriend."

Violet curled her lip into a snarl.

Lily laughed. Then she got serious. "The problem isn't that you're dating the wrong guys, Violet. It's that you won't accept that you're a sucker for the renegades, and you refuse to meet them on the dark side."

"The…what?"

Lily waved an impatient hand. "You can't date a wild-ass Cajun bronc rider in a sensible manner. It's a violation of the natural order and it raises hell with your karma."

Violet rolled her eyes. "Whatever you say, Great Guru."

"The point is, some people are good at being bad. If you're gonna dance with the devil, you should let him lead." Lily propped her chin on her hand. "That Cajun hottie had been flirting with you for weeks. Whose idea was it to hold off until the Hickory Springs rodeo to do the nasty?"

Violet scowled, but muttered, "I wanted to wait until Beni was with Delon."

"Uh-huh. And if the Cajun had had his way?"

"He tried to talk me into a midnight run to Galveston Island to go skinny dipping."

"And you said no because that sounds risky, but it turns out the most dangerous place you could have sex with this man is in a respectable motel in Hickory Springs. You see?" Lily flashed a self-satisfied grin. "Where would you have gone last night if you'd left it to Joe?"

Heat shuddered through Violet at the memory of the look in his eyes when she met him at her front door. His voice hot in her ear at the Notch. *Makes me want to shove you up against the nearest fence…*

Lily jabbed a finger skyward, triumphant. "See? If you'd let him decide, you'da been golden, no one the wiser."

"Except Mama, Daddy, and Cole."

"Who are gonna know anyway. So…"

Damn. She hated when Lily had a point. Violet slumped over her mug, the coffee turning sour in her stomach. She'd made nothing but wrong moves since the day Joe showed up.

Lily reached over to squeeze her arm, voice softer but no less insistent. "You've gotta own it, Violet. Hold your head up, date whoever you damn well please, and let the world kiss your rear. You're a smart, strong, amazing woman. You shouldn't be asking anybody's permission to live how you want."

"Not even Beni's?"

Lily gave her a crooked smile. "Not until he's old

enough to understand what 'Mama's gettin' lucky tonight' means."

"So next week," Violet said drily.

Lily laughed. "Knowin' Beni, that's about right."

Violet straightened, feeling oddly better. "What about how I'm wasting my best years and someday I'll regret not settling down while I can still snag a decent man?"

"That's church lady talk." Lily's mouth curled into an impish smile. "Besides, one of these times you're gonna slip and get tangled up with a guy who's more than what you thought, and then we'll see."

The words echoed in Violet's head as she drove home, sending a shiver of premonition up her spine. She shook it off. Her heart had proved to be a tough nut. A few scuffs here and there, but no real cracks. Joe Cassidy wasn't gonna change that in two short weeks. But maybe—just maybe—she'd give her sister's advice some thought. Stop fighting the inevitable and enjoy the men who attracted her. Her body heated instantly at the memory of Joe moving against her. Oh yeah. She could really, really enjoy Joe. Too bad he wasn't likely to volunteer to repeat the experience after last night.

Chapter 17

OF ALL THE DAMN TIMES FOR A WOMAN TO DECIDE NOT TO hang around the morning after. Joe had heard Violet's car start, but short of jumping out of bed and running into the yard in his underwear, he couldn't stop her. And since Steve was glowering more than usual over pancakes and bacon, Joe didn't dare ask where she'd gone.

Back in the bunkhouse, the cell phone on the table taunted him. *One quick call. Just to touch base with Dick.* He called his mother instead and listened to a blow-by-blow recitation of Frank's business deal in Japan. That was why these men adored her. She didn't pretend to listen—she paid attention, asked questions. By her next divorce she could probably take over as CEO…assuming it paid better than marrying the guy who already had the job.

"When are you coming home?" she asked when she'd exhausted the topic of international trade barriers.

"A week from Sunday. I'm flying into Pendleton, picking up my car, and heading straight home."

Roxy was silent for a few beats. Then she said, very quietly, "I wish you wouldn't go back, Joe."

To work for Dick, she meant. Roxy hated Dick. Had said it a thousand times, usually at the top of her lungs, and in not very polite terms, but this was different. This felt like a plea, verging on begging. *Please, Joe, don't make me worry about you.* That wasn't like her at all.

Roxy might express her opinions, but she never threw her maternal weight around.

"I'm still considering my options."

"Well. That's good then." She forced a silvery laugh. "If you need more space to think, let me know. I hear Mexico is amazing this time of year."

Joe grimaced, imagining the two of them lounging on a beach while the cabana boys leered at him, assuming he was a rich cougar's catch of the day—a common misconception when you had a very young, very hot mother. But it would be nice to spend some real time with her. And when he put the phone down, the temptation to pick it up and call Dick had passed.

Lunch came and went with no sign or mention of Violet. Joe was so wound up he barely choked down the exceptional meat loaf. It was impossible to save the day if a woman didn't have the basic damn decency to show up for her own rescue. At first, he'd figured Wyatt was off his rocker. Joe's initial, powerful instinct was to stay far, far away from Violet. But the more he thought about it, the more Wyatt's plan grew on him. The damage was already done, so what was the worst that could happen? He'd have to spend a lot of time with her. Not exactly a downside, and it would definitely stave off the boredom. He grinned, thinking of pink shirts, red lace and wrangling bulls. Violet was never, ever boring. To do the job right they'd have to make everyone believe she'd sent him home with a broken heart, but his pride could take the punishment, and when he was gone her life would go back to normal, no harm done.

Assuming he could talk her into playing along at all.

After lunch, Joe ping-ponged around the bunk-house, picking up magazines, tossing them down, turning the television on, then off, then on again. He'd found the number for Hank's parents in the creased bunkhouse phone book, tried it several times and got no answer. He couldn't call Violet because he didn't have her cell number.

He did another lap around the bunkhouse, glaring at the Earnest Feed and Seed wall clock. One thirty. At this rate, he wouldn't get a shot at a private conversation with either Hank or Violet before the afternoon practice session. At two, he decided the hell with both of them, then he bolted to the window at the sound of tires on gravel. The car was a sun-bleached blue Taurus jammed with wanna-be bull riders and their gear, an equally battered pickup close behind. Hell. No chance of waylaying Violet now. Might as well get changed.

Joe went with his usual practice gear: thigh-length black compression shorts, then cotton athletic shorts, faded from years of wash and wear. He pulled on an Extreme Bulls Tour T-shirt with the sleeves whacked off, folded a bandana and tied it on sweatband style. His cleats crunched on the gravel as he strolled to the arena, trying not to give himself whiplash every time a car turned into the driveway.

Cole came out of the barn leading a platter-footed roan named Hammer with a head like his namesake only narrower between the eyes. Bastard could run, though, and would pull down a grandstand if you asked him. Cole stopped dead when he saw Joe. "Where ya goin'?"

"Uh…the arena?"

"Why?"

Joe looked around, confused. Had he misunderstood? "You're bucking bulls today, aren't you?"

"Yeah."

"So…"

Cole frowned. "Red never came to practice."

"Maybe Red had something better to do," Joe snapped, his last nerve frayed to a thread.

Cole pondered that, studying Joe like he was trying to figure out if there was a catch. He stood there long enough for Violet's Cadillac to pull into the drive. She stepped out and froze, staring first at Joe, then the gear bag slung over his shoulder. Damn her chicken-livered hide. She hadn't expected him to be at the arena, either. She'd hung back until the last possible second figuring she could avoid him.

Nice try, darlin'.

"Guess we could use you," Cole said. "Hank's trailing cows today and might be late, and the other kid who helps out has football practice."

"I'll try not to get in the way," Joe said, and stomped on down to the arena.

A dozen cowboys had shown up, mostly high school and college kids, along with a few parents. Joe veered away from the crowd and down the fence a few yards where he dropped his bag on the ground and finished gearing up, then spread his feet, grabbed one ankle and pulled his chest to his knee, holding for a slow count of sixty. Hooves thudded on the packed dirt behind him and he looked upside down through his legs to see Violet aboard a stocky gray gelding. She was looking back, and she was not admiring his face. He held the stretch for another ten seconds, then latched his hands behind his head as he unrolled his spine, one vertebra at a time, then turned his head to look directly at Violet. "Ahh yeah. Hurts so good."

Violet's face went beet red, and she kicked her horse on through the gate.

"Hey, Joe. How's it going?" a voice asked.

He dragged his attention away from Violet, struggling to place the vaguely familiar face. Teenager. Dopey grin. The kid from the barbecue joint. "Korby. Hey. Ready to ride the hair off one?"

Korby grinned ear to ear. "You betcha."

The kid sauntered off to join the crowd behind the chutes, adding to the chorus of hollow clanking as ropes and bells were dragged out of gear bags. Metal gates banged, voices called, and bulls rumbled low challenges as they were sorted and loaded—a rodeo symphony. Violet retreated to the far end of the arena. She could probably look worse, but she'd have to work at it. Her cap was yanked down so far he could barely see her nose, those jeans were god-awful, and whatever she was wearing under her long-sleeved denim shirt was an insult to her curves. And still Joe's head filled up with red lace and the scent of warm strawberries.

Joe was in the arena, warmed up and ready to go, when Hank vaulted the fence and jogged over to the front of the chutes. "How's it hanging, Joe?"

"Fine."

"I bet, after last night." And the little pinhead had the nerve to wink.

"Hey, Hank!" Korby had a foot braced on either side of the nearest chute, straddling a high-horned black bull as he worked a gloved hand up and down his rope to heat the rosin. "I thought you were gonna call me last night."

"I meant to. I got distracted." Hank's grin turned sly as he angled a glance at Joe.

"Yeah? By what?" Korby waggled his eyebrows. "Or should I say who?"

Screw finesse. Joe whipped an arm around Hank's neck and yanked him into a headlock tight enough to make his eyes bug out. He kept his voice low but deadly. "Shut the fuck up or I'll shove your head so far up your ass you'll be able to lick your own tonsils."

Hank clawed at Joe's arm, fighting for oxygen. Joe tightened his grip. "You say one word that embarrasses Violet and you and I are going to have a serious problem. Understand?"

He loosened his hold enough to allow Hank a jerky nod and a gulp of air. Joe slapped him hard on the chest with his free hand and flashed a smile that was closer to a snarl. "I knew you were smarter than everybody says."

Hank gulped again and nodded harder. Joe let him go, stepped back, and looked over to find Violet watching, eyes huge. He lifted a hand and gave her a cocky, two-fingered salute. She looked away. Hah. If that made her nervous, she was gonna hate what came next.

Steve gave a gun-shot clap of his big hands. "All right, boys! Let's ride some bulls."

Joe shoved Hank into position. "Take the lead. And pay attention. We're gonna do some schooling tonight."

Joe rode him hard, pushing, hounding, drilling the kid, bull after bull, so Hank didn't have a chance to think about anything but the job at hand. Korby's black bull made three tentative jumps straight down the arena, each more aggressive. On the fourth jump he launched straight in the air and dove right, whipping the kid off the side, hand still in the rope. The unaccustomed weight tipped the smallish Brahma off balance and jerked him flat on his side. *Whomp!* Right on top of his passenger.

Hank leapt at the bull's head as it wallowed around, trying to get up. Joe yanked the tail of the rope to free Korby's hand. The bull staggered to its feet, leaving the kid curled in the dirt, wheezing.

As Violet and Cole herded the bull clear, Hank dropped to his knees. "Hey, buddy, you all right?"

Korby nodded with a sound like a whoop, only in reverse. "No…air…"

"He okay?" Violet asked, peering from horseback over the huddle of cowboys that had gathered.

"He will be when he gets his wind." Joe stepped back, braced himself, then draped his arm across the cantle of Violet's saddle, around her hips. She sucked in a sharp, outraged breath, her leg flexing as if to kick her horse. He tightened his hold. "Stay, Violet."

"What are you *doing*?" she hissed down at him.

He put his free hand on her thigh and tilted his head toward her like they were whispering sweet nothings. "Try to pretend you like me. Otherwise people are gonna think you're just after my body."

Her mouth dropped open and he could practically see the curses piling up on her tongue. "Are you nuts?"

"Most likely."

Hank and one of the dads hoisted Korby to his feet and helped him out of the arena. He staggered over to the fence, then collapsed into a heap, sweat trickling through the dirt on his face as he drew in slow, careful breaths. The rest of the cowboys scattered to get ready for the next pen of bulls—except Steve Jacobs. He stood on the back of the chutes, glaring at Violet and Joe. Seeing him, Violet let one of those curses slip and lifted her hand, as if to rein her horse away. Joe caught her wrist.

"*Stop it.*"

"No." Joe forced another smile. "We need to talk, Violet."

Her gaze jumped away, skimmed over the increasing number of curious faces aimed their direction, then came back to Joe. "Fine. Meet me at the other place after practice."

Joe let go, his fingers trailing down her thigh as if he had the right. "I'll be there."

After helping Cole gather the flank straps and hang them in a neat row behind the chutes, Joe was the last one to walk out of the arena. Steve Jacobs was waiting outside the gate. The part of Joe that was apparently still ten years old whispered, *Run!* Joe ignored it and kept walking, until he was close enough to maintain his manly dignity, but still out of reach of those big fists.

"You want to date Violet, that's up to her, but you keep that crap outta the arena." Steve jabbed a thick finger toward the gate. "Hard enough for her to get the respect she deserves without you droolin' all over her."

"Yes, sir," Joe said, because disagreeing wasn't an option, and Steve wasn't wrong.

Steve gave a curt nod.

"That's it?" Joe blurted.

Steve Jacobs laughed. A single *hah!* like a sonic boom that rocked Joe in his cleats. "If you make my girl mad, she won't need my help rearranging your body parts." The amusement lurked in his eyes as he thumbed his hat onto the back of his head. "But I should say that I appreciate what you're doin' with Hank. Kid needs his butt busted."

"Yes, sir."

Steve gave another nod and ambled away, leaving Joe to consider how it was the first time in his life he'd voluntarily called a man *sir,* not once, but twice. And meant it both times.

Chapter 18

STRETCHED OUT FLAT ON HER BACK IN THE SOFT grass of Cole's parents' lawn, Violet stared up at the sky and willed the shift of light through the fluttering leaves of the sugar maple to smooth away her rough edges. Geezus, what a day. She'd gone to Lily expecting sympathy, and got a kick in the gut instead. And then Joe. She should've known he'd show up for practice. What else did he have to do? And thanks to Lily, she was now intensely aware of how juvenile her reaction had been. *Hello, Violet, welcome to ninth grade.*

She dragged in another breath and tried to absorb the serenity of her surroundings through her pores. The house was tucked into an indentation of the bluff with a wall of rock curving around the yard, the red and cream of the chalky stone mimicked by the stucco of the house and the brick patio. In the shade under the maple the evening air was cool, laced with the sweetness of roses and the spice of mesquite. A perfect oasis, with only the occasional ghost for company. Violet pushed her focus outward to the lazy buzz of insects and trill of birds. The tickle of grass against her bare arms. The quiet scuff of footsteps on brick.

She rolled her head to find Joe standing on the patio, sweat glistening on arms and shoulders exposed by the whacked off sleeves of his T-shirt. His bandana was printed with *Tough Enough to Wear Pink* breast cancer awareness ribbons, clashing with the flame-breathing red-and-black bull on his T-shirt. The shorts might have been yellow early in their existence, but had faded to something that looked like it came out the wrong end of a sick calf. And he still made her mouth water.

"Do you buy any of your own clothes?" she asked.

He glanced down and fingered the logo on his shirt. "Why would I? People give me stuff."

He ran his gaze around the cozy backyard, taking in the neatly pruned rose bushes, thick clumps of hydrangeas with dusky blue blooms the size of Cole's fist, clusters of red, yellow, and orange flowers in niches along the base of the bluff. Thick trunks of maples and mulberry trees enclosed it all, everything as lush and lovingly tended as if the owners had only been gone a day.

"Nice place," he said.

"My aunt's pride and joy. Mom makes sure it's kept up, even if we're between renters like now. Her version of a memorial."

He grabbed the hem of his shirt, lifting it to mop his face, and Violet's pulse jumped. His shorts hung low on his hips, baring the upper curve of his hipbones, his navel and an expanse of taut skin above and below, dusted with golden hair. One good tug and she could have those shorts down around his ankles.

Violet forced her gaze back to the maple tree, watching a tiny brown bird flit from branch to branch. Joe plopped down beside her and propped his forearms on bent knees. Her head spun at his proximity, her vertigo magnified by a rogue breeze that danced through the leaves above with a dizzying swirl of light and shadow.

"What did you say to Hank?" she asked.

"I suggested he keep his mouth shut."

"Did your suggestion include the threat of physical violence?"

"Yep."

"Good." She wiggled her shoulders to scratch an itch where the grass prickled the middle of her back, concentrating on the leaves, the bird, keeping her cool. "Why the big show back there at the arena?"

"I thought it was better than ignoring each other and acting like we're ashamed. I don't know about you, but I'm damn sure not."

Oh. Well. That was…almost chivalrous. But still unacceptable. "You can't do that stuff when I'm working."

"Yeah. Your dad mentioned that, too."

"Daddy?" Violet's gaze snapped to Joe's face, but he didn't seem upset at being dressed down. "You should know—I tend to be more trouble than I'm worth."

Joe's gaze took the slow route all the way down her body, then back up again. His mouth quirked. "I wouldn't say that."

Her system lit up like he'd detonated a series of fireworks under her skin. She tore her gaze away from him and pinned it to the tree branches until she could take a normal breath. "I acted like a jerk last night."

He flashed a lazy grin that did more odd things to her ability to breathe. "I guess you had your reasons."

Well, crap. The ghost of Hickory Springs rises again. Violet closed her eyes, fighting off a wave of embarrassment. "Heard about that, did you?"

"A thing or two."

More than enough. She heaved a massive sigh. "Go ahead. Make your handcuff joke. Get it out of your system."

"Can't now. You ruined it."

She opened her eyes to squint up at him. He was definitely laughing at her, but different than before. Not softer—he had too many rough edges for that—but not mocking, either. This wasn't the arrogant, sarcastic Joe from the night at the Lone Steer. Which had to make her wonder—

"Why are you pretending to be so nice?" she demanded.

His forehead creased in affront. "What do you mean? I'm a nice guy."

Violet snorted.

"What? I am." He frowned at her, looking truly offended. When Violet only arched her brows, his eyes dropped, his frown turning sulky. "I've been in a bad mood, all right?"

"I guess you've had your reasons," she said.

One corner of his mouth curled at the echo of his own words. "Heard about that, did you?"

"A thing or two."

He huffed out a laugh, then ducked his chin to stare at the grass between his feet. "So if we agree that we've both been jerks, can we start fresh?"

"Uh, sure. I guess." Violet was still for several thuds of her heart. "Start what?"

"You. Me. All of this." He waggled a hand back and forth between them, angling his head to give her a look that, for Joe, verged on bashful. "I am sorry about butting in here without asking, and then…well, everything else. I've been so twisted up in my own problems, I wasn't paying attention, and I caused a lot of headaches for you. So if there's a way I can make it better…"

"Can you fix the trouble back in Oregon?"

"I hope so." His expression went grim. "Things got out of hand in Puyallup. I over-reacted. So did Dick."

Violet hesitated, then decided she might as well just get it out in the open. "Did *he* have good reason?"

Joe's chin jerked up and once again he looked insulted. "Like I said…I don't believe in trespassing. And I hope I'm not dumb enough to piss in my own pot. Lyle's wife was a mess that night. I didn't touch her other than to make sure she got back to her room before she did something she'd regret."

Because he might not be your typical nice guy, but Violet was beginning to suspect he was an honorable one. "Does Dick know that?"

"He should after fifteen years." Anger flared in Joe's eyes, then died back to regret. "Blowing a fuse and running off to Texas wasn't a smart move. It made him look bad, and there's nothing he hates more."

"But he fired you!"

"He would've backed down if I'd just let him cool off and then apologized."

Violet twisted onto her side to gape at him, incredulous. "For *what?* You didn't do anything wrong."

"That's not the point."

"It's totally the point!" She wanted to reach out and shake him. Where was his pride? His self-respect? "How can you let him treat you that way?"

His shrug was tight. Defensive. "That's just Dick. It's not personal."

"And it's worth putting up with his bullshit to be on that ranch?"

"Yes." The reply was immediate, unequivocal, and left no room for argument.

She settled onto her back, scowling up at the tree. *Not your business, Violet.* But it rubbed every inch of her the wrong way.

"So?" Joe asked. "What do you say? Can we try again?"

The shadows flitted across his face and over the exposed skin of his shoulders and arms, lighting here then there like butterflies. She fought the urge to reach out and trap one, to see if she could feel it flutter under her fingertip. A muscle beneath his taut, golden skin twitched as if he read her thoughts.

"I suppose that depends on what you have in mind," she said.

The muscle twitched again, then relaxed, and he gave her a smile that drop-kicked *nice* right out of the stadium. "Wyatt says I need to court you."

"*Court* me?" Violet let out an embarrassingly loud guffaw. "Oh, please. Like you'd even know where to start."

"I'll figure it out." He flashed an impish grin. "I'm pretty quick, you know."

He plucked a blade of grass and trailed the tip of it across the back of her hand. She shivered. He laughed, unholy intent glowing in those green eyes. Violet rolled away, then jack-knifed into a seated position. When Joe made to move closer, she pointed a finger as if commanding a dog.

"You! Down!"

"Why?" He cast a deliberate gaze around the yard. "Nobody here but us and the birds."

"Until you lay a hand on me. Then a troop of girl scouts will march through here on a bird-watching expedition. With cameras. That's just my luck." She scuttled out of reach, shaking her finger when he scooted after her. "Uh-uh-uh. No touching. We're both covered in sweat and arena dirt and I smell like a horse."

He grinned. "My next favorite perfume after oranges and strawberries."

"Lord, you are shameless." Violet sputtered a laugh. "But unless you've got a condom tucked in your shoe, we're out of luck, so don't even start."

"Afraid you can't control yourself?"

"Yep." She scrambled to her feet, her hand extended to ward him off. "You just stand back and keep your hands where I can see them, *hombre*."

He laughed, then sprang to his feet with an ease that made Violet feel like a gravity-challenged hippo. She kept a full arm's length between them as they walked around the side of the house and out front to her car. Owning her womanhood would have to wait until she'd had a shower. And a door with a deadbolt.

When she opened the car door, Joe propped his hands on the frame and looked at her over the top, his expression grave. "What I did today...your dad was right. That stuff doesn't belong in the arena. It won't happen again."

Again his sincerity unbalanced her. "Okay. Thanks."

"And I'll watch myself around Beni. I've had the pleasure of watching my mother date. I won't inflict that on a kid."

"I appreciate it." Her head bobbed as if it was on a string.

"My pleasure." His voice had that deep, suggestive rumble again. The one that made certain parts of her body hum in anticipation.

She climbed into the car, squeezing her thighs tight against the ache. He shut the door behind her.

"So does this mean we're going steady?" she joked.

"I guess it does, for as long as I'm here." He smiled, a warm, wide-open smile that knocked her senseless. He braced both hands on the open driver's window, his gaze taking liberties with her body before returning to her face. "How in the hell does Delon stay at his own end of the house?"

"He, um, isn't attracted to me that way."

Joe leaned in until they were nose to nose, eye to eye. "Delon is an idiot."

He kissed her, his mouth quick and hungry. Before she could react, he danced out of reach like a kid playing tag, both palms in the air.

"No hands," he said, and tossed her one last triumphant grin before bounding off down the driveway.

Violet sat frozen behind the wheel, her system in utter chaos as she watched those effortless, gravity-defying strides carry him away. Hoo-boy. This was gonna get interesting.

Chapter 19

HALFWAY THROUGH BREAKFAST ON THURSDAY morning, Joe got up to help himself to more coffee. "Anybody else?" he asked.

Cole waved his mug. As Joe did the honors, he realized he no longer felt like a guest in their kitchen. In less than a week, they'd converted him. Made him, if not part of the family, at least a temporary part of their whole. He suddenly had a bizarre urge to drop the coffee pot and run, as if an invisible trap was closing around him. But there was only Iris's homey kitchen, with the long wooden trestle table and a flowering plant on every windowsill. Steve, engrossed in the weekly newspaper, and Iris, scribbling out a grocery list. Normal family stuff. Maybe that explained the weird twinge of panic. He was totally out of his element.

He poured the coffee and took what had already become his designated seat at the table. Violet didn't make an appearance, which was also standard procedure. He was beginning to suspect she wasn't a morning person. Joe, on the other hand, had popped out of bed before dawn and considered wandering over to see what she wore for pajamas. He went for a run instead. Steve Jacobs had temporarily stopped looking at him like he had *degenerate* tattooed on his forehead. He should try to keep it that way.

Joe kept his head down, letting Iris's chatter and the

men's grunted replies wash past him while he plowed through four pieces of golden French toast with crisp hash browns and fluffy scrambled eggs on the side. Even the coffee was perfect. At this rate, he'd be packing a spare tire back to the High Lonesome. Helen's food was amazing, but Iris Jacobs gave her a run for her money.

Cole speared another piece of French toast, centered it on his plate, and buttered it precisely, edge to edge. Then he cut it into sixteen equal squares and drizzled it with syrup in four parallel lines, exactly like every previous slice, the steps as precise as if they were programmed into his brain. "I'm gonna check the south fence this morning and find where those cows crawled out."

"Need help?" Joe asked. Even fixing fence was better than another day of twiddling his thumbs. And thinking.

Cole took his time considering the offer, no doubt weighing the benefit of an extra pair of hands against having to tolerate the presence of another human being. "If you want."

Joe didn't particularly. He'd strung miles of barbed wire in his lifetime and always came away looking like he'd wrestled a porcupine. "Might as well make myself useful. Mind if I make a phone call first?"

"It'll take me a few minutes to pack some snacks," Iris said, pulling out a full-sized cooler. "I'll leave cold cuts in the refrigerator for lunch. We'll be gone over to Childress until this evening."

And God forbid anybody went more than an hour without sustenance.

Joe excused himself and pulled out his phone as he made a beeline to the bunkhouse. He was about to make a very Wyatt kind of move. Interfering where he hadn't been invited felt wrong, but also right. He couldn't help Violet reach her goals for Jacobs Livestock if they weren't willing to make the necessary sacrifices, but he could give one small dream a nudge toward reality. Joe understood dreams. He ached with them. The things he could do if Dick would give him a tiny bit of rein...

Besides, he hated to see a truly great bull fail to get his due, and that was something Joe might be able to fix. Dirt Eater deserved to buck at the National Finals. Joe knew the person who selected the bulls that would be invited to perform there. Why not put a bug in Vince Grant's ear? It wouldn't cost more than a few minutes of Joe's time, and if anything, he was doing Vince a favor. After all, he wanted the absolute best.

"Son of a bitch," Vince declared by way of greeting. "Joe Cassidy. Didn't figure on hearing from you in a while."

"Why's that?"

"Rumor is you're not really in Texas. Some folks figure you had to be on something to punch Lyle Browning, and Wyatt packed you off to rehab."

"Rehab?" Joe echoed in disbelief. For Christ's sake, he hadn't even laid on a good drunk in over a year. "What for?"

"Pain meds. Everybody assumes you bullfighters live on 'em."

"Not lately," Joe said, fighting the urge to snarl. "I really am in Texas, and there's a bull down here you need to look at."

"Yeah? Who's got him?"

"Jacobs Livestock. Bull named Dirt Eater."

Vince took a minute to search the database inside

his head. Far as Joe could tell, he recalled every bull he'd ever seen. "I've heard of him, but it's hard to bring a bull to the Finals when none of the top guys have ever been on him. You think he's really as good as they say?"

"Yes."

"The money pen?" Which meant the bunch of bulls that were smooth spinners, the kind cowboys could ride for big points.

"The eliminators." The fifteen baddest asses of all the bulls in the country.

"No kidding? Then I better put him on my short list." Joe missed a step and stumbled over the threshold into the bunkhouse. "You're just gonna take my word for it?"

"Ain't nobody in the country knows bucking bulls better. Lord knows you see 'em all, right up close." Vince paused, and his voice dropped a key. "Listen, Joe, what happened in Puyallup was pure bullshit. I have no idea what's going on in your head, but you should know there are at least half a dozen contractors hoping they've got a shot at stealing you from Dick now."

"I…you mean as a bullfighter?"

"No. As a stock man. You gotta stop underestimating yourself. Dick's up shit creek if you walk. He can wheel and deal, but he has lousy instincts when it comes to bucking stock and he sure as hell can't count on Lyle."

"I can't take credit—"

"And Dick ain't gonna give you any, but he proved he don't have a clue when he sold Lightning Jack. Dumbest move in the history of rodeo." Vince's sneer was audible. "Imagine where Browning Rodeo would be right now if he had all the bucking sons o' bitches that stud has sired."

And Joe had used Lightning Jack as an example of why Violet should consider putting Dirt Eater on the auction block. No wonder she'd blown off his suggestion. Outside, the old chore pickup rumbled to life, the signal that Cole was ready to go.

"Gotta run," Joe said. Literally, or Cole might drive off without him.

"I'll spread the word that you're not locked up in detox," Vince said. "Tell Jacobs to send me video of their bull. You got my email address?"

"Yeah. Thanks, Vince. I appreciate the vote of confidence."

Joe was still pissed about the rehab thing. The other stuff Vince had said—about him, about Dick—that was gonna take some time to digest. Either way, pounding on something with a hammer sounded like just the ticket, so he tossed the phone on the table by the door, grabbed a pair of leather gloves, and hustled out to the pickup.

Katie was planted in the middle of the bench seat of the pickup. The dog and Cole each spared Joe one disinterested glance. They bounced south along a dirt track that topped a rise, giving them an unobstructed view across thousands of acres of mostly nothing. Now, though, Joe knew the fold and crinkle of the landscape to the southeast was the Canadian River breaks, with its red dirt and grassy valleys so reminiscent of central Oregon—a familiarity that dug into his soul with razor-tipped claws.

He propped his arm on the open window frame, drew in a deep lungful of dust-tinged air, and gave himself permission to wallow in the melancholy. Lord knew Cole wouldn't force him to make conversation. But after ten minutes, Joe was sick of listening to nothing but his own muddled thoughts.

"What's the deal with Delon?" he asked.

Cole gave him a blank look.

"Delon and Violet," Joe added. "For a guy who's just Beni's dad, he's got some serious attitude."

"About what?"

"Me."

Cole looked, if possible, even more blank.

"Me and Violet," Joe clarified, on the off chance Cole actually hadn't noticed what was going on.

"Dunno," Cole said. "Ain't like *you're* gonna marry her."

True, so why did the assumption sting? "And Delon is?"

"Wants to."

Joe examined Cole's expression closely, to see if there was any chance he was kidding. "Why?"

Cole gave him a look that did not speak highly of Joe's intelligence.

"Well yeah, Beni," Joe said. "But Violet is sure Delon doesn't have the hots for her, and I sorta think she would've noticed by now. So why get married?"

"'Cuz of Gil."

Joe waited, but Cole didn't elaborate. "Gil?"

"His brother."

Gil Sanchez. The name trickled down into Joe's brain, setting off faint sparks of recognition. He got a vague image, dark like Delon but taller, skinnier. More…whoa.

"Gil Sanchez is Delon's brother? I haven't seen him in, wow, it must be ten years, at least." Joe's fingers drummed the window frame as his mind fired off random images. "Bareback rider. Had feet like lightning, could spur anything with hair. Made the National Finals his rookie year."

"Yep."

The picture came clearer as his memory painted in the details of the last time he'd seen Gil. Joe had been nineteen, working for Dick behind the chutes at the Finals. Gil had ridden the hell out of nine head, and only had to make the whistle on the tenth horse to win the whole shittin' shebang, but he came out spurring like he had to be ninety-five points. The horse had jerked his hand out of the rigging at seven and half seconds.

"I never saw him again. What happened?"

Cole shook his head, then frowned, in what, for him, was an outpouring of emotion. "Wrecked a motorcycle a couple months later, messed up his hip. Typical Gil. Going too damn fast."

For an instant, Cole sounded exactly like his uncle. Same inflection, same tone, the words borrowed from an earlier conversation. Or years of the same conversation. Joe got a blast of déjà vu, as if he'd heard it before. Or something similar. Where though? The memory dodged him, sliding farther away the harder he tried to catch it.

"Gil was a crazy son of a bitch. I remember one night in Red Bluff—" Then Joe stopped, because he also recalled that Gil hadn't been the only one dancing on a pickup tailgate, stripping for dollar bills.

"Always was wilder than an acre of snakes," Cole said, still channeling Steve.

"No kidding. He didn't know the meaning of…"

Safety up. That's what Wyatt had said about Delon. How he put more stock in being safe than being first. And no wonder. He must've had a front row seat, watching his brother crash and burn. Literally.

"What's all that got to do with Violet and Beni?" Joe asked.

"Gil's got a kid." Cole's jaw tightened, his big hands clenching around the steering wheel. "Lives up in Oklahoma with his mother and a stepdad. Gil's lucky to see him a couple times a month."

Lucky? Funny, Joe's dad had never seen it that way. "Who's the mother?"

"Rich girl from Guthrie, figured she'd burn off some crazy with a cowboy. Stopped being fun when she got knocked up. She ran home to Daddy, then married one of her own kind and tried to cut Gil out of the picture. Lawyers bled him dry in the custody fight but he wouldn't weaken."

"So what's he doing now?" Joe asked.

"He's the dispatcher for Sanchez Trucking."

That had to suck, for a guy who'd had gold buckle dreams and the talent to back them up. The pickup lurched into a hole, snapping Joe's teeth together and nearly nose-planting the dog into the dashboard, except for the hand Cole stuck out to catch her. She scrabbled back to her place and stuck her nose in the air, once again the Queen of Cool. "That's why Delon wants to marry Violet?" Joe asked. "So he doesn't risk losing his kid the way his brother did?"

"Can't blame a man for wanting to give his son a stable home."

"Like a wedding's gonna guarantee that," Joe said, with enough of a sneer to draw a considering look from Cole.

"You don't believe in marriage?"

Joe shrugged. "It hasn't worked out for most of the people I know."

Roxy went without saying, but she was only the start. By all reports, Dick's marriage had been a war zone before his wife was diagnosed with breast cancer, and he'd shown no inclination to remarry after she died. Helen worked at the High Lonesome because her husband had run off with her cousin and left two kids to raise. Lyle fucked around, and Wyatt's wife had given him a *Get Out of Jail Free* card for their first anniversary. No, Joe didn't have a lot of experience with wedded bliss.

"Maybe you need to hang around some different people," Cole said.

He wouldn't have a choice if he couldn't go back to the High Lonesome. Joe focused on Cole. "I notice you don't have a wife."

The dog curled her lip, as if the mere suggestion made her want to growl.

"Women don't exactly stand in line to put up with a guy like me," Cole said.

Cole said *a guy like me* with the same mix of resignation and defiance as Joe had heard in the voices of soldiers he and Wyatt had met at the Army rehab unit at Fort Lewis. Somewhere between, *I'm broken and I can't be fixed* and *Fuck the world if it can't take me as I am.*

"There's probably a woman somewhere who doesn't like to talk," Joe said.

Cole gave the dog's head a rub. "Already found her."

He stopped the pickup beside a spot where the fence was down and turned off the motor. They climbed out to inspect the damage. The top strand of wire was busted, the second and third pulled loose from the posts, mashed down and wound together into a prickly double-helix by the cattle that had crawled over, leaving a few telltale tufts of hair behind in the barbs.

"Grab the roll of wire," Cole said. "I'll get the fence stretcher."

Joe set the heavy spool down in the middle of the gap, then reeled in the broken wire on his side. The end snagged on a weed. He yanked. It popped loose and sprang at him like a snake, whipping around his calf and inflicting half a dozen pinpricks through his jeans. Geezus, he hated barbed wire.

"So Delon figures when Violet gets tired of the single life she'll marry him, since he's right there handy?" Joe asked.

"Seems like."

"Think it'll work?"

"Dunno." Cole clamped the fence stretcher onto the wire and gave it a tug to test that it was secure. "Violet doesn't have much luck with men. Seems to like having you snortin' around her flanks, though."

Joe's fingers slipped and a barb raked across the tender skin on the underside of his wrist, right above his glove. He strangled a curse and sucked off the beads of blood that welled along the scratch. "How's your uncle feel about all that?"

"He likes Delon."

Cole gave no indication whether the same could be

said for Joe. Not that it should matter. He might never see Steve Jacobs again when he left Texas. But there was something about the man—a quiet dignity, his reserve less standoffish than selective. He wasn't stingy with his praise, but when you got it, you knew you deserved it, and that made earning his respect feel like a necessity. Especially when Joe was so damn uncertain of everything else. "I could use some help getting on Steve's good side."

Cole drove a staple in with one powerful smack of his hammer then turned to squint at Joe. After a long count of ten, Cole turned back to the post, pinched another staple between his fingers, and centered it over the next wire.

"Haircut wouldn't hurt," he said, and gave the staple a mighty whack.

Chapter 20

VIOLET'S LEFT BOOB VIBRATED, STARTLING HER SO she nearly stabbed herself in the foot with a pitchfork. She propped the fork against the side of the stall she was mucking out and fished the phone out of her breast pocket.

"I have *got* to know what happened at practice last night," Melanie declared. "Whatever y'all did, it's got Hank goggle-eyed and afraid to make a peep, which is damned inconvenient the one time I actually want him to talk."

"Joe tried to pinch his head off," Violet said, pressing a hand into her lower back and arching to stretch out the kinks. "Promised to finish the job if Hank blabbed."

She'd surprised herself by sleeping like a rock once she'd finally gone to bed at just after midnight, having deduced that Joe wasn't going to come knocking on her door. Damn him. Just once could the man do what she expected?

"Anyone who can put the fear of God into my lunkhead brother is a friend of mine. I can't believe I have to leave on this asinine business trip tomorrow morning and won't be back before Joe leaves."

Violet imagined introducing Melanie to Joe, counted at least five ways she could end up humiliated beyond words, and decided she was in favor of the business trip. "He wants to court me."

"To…*what?*"

"That's what I said. And then he got all huffy, like I insulted his manly pride."

"So you're going to let him?"

"Might as well." Violet shivered a little at the prospect of being the target of Joe's formidable concentration. "By the time he leaves, no one will care what Hank has to say. And imagine what it will do for my reputation, being wooed by the great Joe Cassidy who, from all reports, does not chase girls. He just stands back and lets them come to him. If nothing else, it oughta be entertaining. I'd be amazed if he ever courted anything but trouble his whole life."

And it was also amazing how little that bothered Violet today. Once she'd decided to take Lily's advice to heart, she felt like a whole new person. No more fretting and fussing at herself. No pretending Joe wasn't exactly what she wanted, and possibly more. Just the fizz and pop of anticipation, like champagne trickling through her veins. Ten whole days before Joe left. Two weekends. Nine nights. And he'd wasted one of them already.

Melanie huffed out a disgruntled sigh. "I'm gonna miss it all, as usual. Remind me again why I haven't let some sugar daddy sweep me off my feet so I can quit this damn job?"

"Because we are modern, independent women who don't need a man to support us."

"Been there, done that, getting pretty damn sick of it," Melanie said. "I wanna see how the spoiled half lives."

Violet laughed, because everybody knew how much Melanie loved her job. As an events coordinator for the fairgrounds in Amarillo, she helped plan everything from rock concerts to rodeos to monster truck rallies. Violet soothed her by promising to report any and all juicy details at the earliest possible moment. As she hung up, she heard a roar. The chore pickup, unmistakable thanks to a muffler that'd died a painful death when her dad hit a dry wash a few years back.

She set her pitchfork aside, walked to the barn door, and leaned a shoulder against the frame while she waited for the pickup to cough and die in front of the shop. Both men climbed out, Katie right on Cole's heels. Joe caught sight of Violet, raised a hand in greeting, and walked toward her, leaving Cole to unload the tools.

"If I'd known barn cleaning was an option, I wouldn't have offered to go fencing." Joe held up his arm so she could see the angry red scratch on his wrist. "I usually don't need a tetanus shot when I'm done shoveling manure."

Violet winced. "I can run you to the walk-in clinic in Dumas."

"Just kidding. I had one in June. Took a horn in the chops at Prineville." He touched a crescent-shaped scar on his jaw, then glanced over her shoulder at the pile of manure she'd scooped out of the stall. "Need a hand?"

Violet hesitated. She couldn't help feeling like this new, considerate version of Joe was some kind of joke he was playing on her, and any minute he'd nail her with one of those mocking smiles.

"I have to talk to Cole," she said.

Joe blocked her path with an arm across the door. He tilted his face into the crook of her neck and inhaled deeply, stirring the hair on her nape. "Oranges. My second favorite."

The champagne bubbles burst en masse at the play of his breath on her skin, a wave of pure sensation rolling through her body and short-circuiting her brain.

Joe dropped his arm, motioning for her to pass, a knowing glint in his eyes. "Take as long as you want. I'll be down here knee-deep in shit, as usual."

Violet nodded, struck mute. She walked slowly over to the shop, sorting out the neurons he'd scrambled. *Focus, Violet.* She couldn't just blunder into this conversation with Cole. The subject was beyond touchy. His head was buried under the raised hood of the chore pickup. He glanced over at the sound of her footsteps in the gravel and looked down again without a word.

"You found the hole in the fence?" she asked.

He pulled the dipstick free, squinted at it, then wiped it clean with the old sock he used as a rag. "Same place as always. First low spot past the gate."

"Figures." She folded her arms and leaned them on the pickup, watching Cole thread the dipstick back into the skinny metal tube. "I can't stop thinking about the McCloud stock. They've got some real buckers."

"Yep." Cole walked into the shop to fetch oil, leaving Violet hanging. When he returned, he said nothing—just stuck a funnel in the truck's filler tube and started to pour from a silver can.

"Like I was saying," she continued. "McCloud's got some good stuff."

"That we can't afford."

"I've been thinking about that, too." Couldn't stop thinking about it, since Joe had planted the idea in her brain. "We do have some assets we could liquidate. At least one very valuable asset."

Cole made no visible attempt to follow her to the obvious conclusion. He was gonna force her to come right out and say it.

"What I mean is…would you ever consider selling Dirt Eater?"

"No."

Yeah. That's what she figured. She blew out a sigh. "I knew better than to ask. It's just…well, sometimes I feel like we aren't doing him justice. Putting him on the stage he deserves. If he spends most of his life at our rodeos, he'll never get the kind of recognition he could."

"If we sell him, he'll get recognized under some other contractor's name," Cole said flatly.

And that was the deal breaker. If Dirt Eater was going to get famous, it had to be as a Jacobs Livestock bull, or it didn't count. They'd be selling the dream. The only living piece Cole had left of his father.

"I'm sorry. You're right. I shouldn't have said anything. The McCloud thing got me going, and I was already feeling restless. Wishful, you know?"

If he had any inkling, he hid it well. Cole set the oil can aside, pulled out the dipstick again to examine it, then shoved it back into place, satisfied. Violet jerked her arms back just before he slammed the hood.

He finally looked her in the eye, his brow puckered. "Is this one of those change of life things?"

"Excuse me?"

"They say women get kinda crazy when they go through that stuff."

Violet had never realized a person could feel their own eyes bug out. "Change of life is menopause, Cole. That's in your fifties."

"Oh." He tilted his head, thoughtful, as if filing that tidbit away for future reference. "Maybe it's a midlife crisis."

"I am not having a crisis!" But an aneurism was a possibility. The arteries in her brain had to be bulging.

"Well, what would you call it?" Cole asked, so damn obtuse she wanted to smack him.

"Suffocation! There hasn't been a breath of fresh air around this place in years!"

He sucked in a noisy lungful, then let it out in a blast that stirred the dust on the hood of the pickup. "Seems fine to me."

He strolled back into the shop to put the oil can away. Violet started after him, then stopped short. Better stay out of there. It'd be too tempting to grab a wrench and try to pound some sense into that thick skull. She flexed and relaxed her fists, breathing deep, trying to clear the red haze from her eyes. Honest to freaking God. *Men!* And people wondered why she didn't want another one in her life.

A flash of sky blue in the driveway yanked her attention away from Cole. Her fury ebbed, replaced by puzzlement. She squinted, then let out a low whistle, tinged with envy. She'd always wanted a Mustang— back before she worried about things like safety ratings and juice-repellant seats—and this one looked like it had just rolled off the lot. Must be a tourist, lost and looking for quickest route to Amarillo. As she started toward the car, Joe poked his head out of the barn, then set the pitchfork aside and came striding up the driveway.

The driver stepped out as Violet approached. The first thing she noticed was his shoes—canvas loafers that looked like they were made for lounging on the deck of a yacht. Definitely a tourist. She started to smirk, but then she got a load of the rest as he unwound from the low-slung car. Tall. Broad-shouldered. Blond. Wow. His short-sleeved sports shirt was the color of ripe cantaloupe, worn loose over perfectly creased golfer's shorts, the blue stripe in the plaid the exact same shade as his car.

He looked like a guy who'd color coordinate. He also looked familiar. Weird, given that Violet didn't know many male model types and definitely wouldn't have forgotten this one. He posed—one hand propped on the open car door, the other on his hip—surveying the yard and buildings before turning his attention to Violet with an orthodontist-perfect smile. Suddenly, it clicked. "Oh! Hi, you're—"

Joe's voice cut between them. "What the fuck are you doing here, Wyatt?"

———∾∾∾———

Joe should've realized something was up. Wyatt hadn't called since Tuesday night and it wasn't like him to butt out.

Wyatt answered his question with a lazy shrug. "I was in the neighborhood."

"You're supposed to be in Omaha tonight. Since when is Nebraska next door to here?"

"I had that fundraiser in Tucson last night, remember? I practically had to fly right over, so I figured I might as well stop." Wyatt focused on Violet, so charming Joe wanted to knock out a few of his perfect teeth. "Nice to see you again."

"Uh…yeah. I mean, yes. Likewise." She was blushing. And stammering, for Christ's sake. Joe had never made her stammer.

"What do you want?" Joe snapped.

Wyatt lifted the hand draped over the car door, revealing a manila envelope dangling between his fingers. "If you can't make time for me, I'll come to you."

Contracts. Hell. Wyatt was not going to back off until Joe considered every rodeo in the country that wasn't produced by Dick Browning.

Joe ignored the envelope and sneered at the Mustang, instead. "Why can't you rent a normal car?"

"Unlike you, I prefer to enjoy the ride," Wyatt said, wrinkling his nose.

"My Jeep gets me where I need to go." And it had been paid off for years.

"So does this, and it actually has a sound system and functional air conditioning."

Violet tapped a finger against her chin, adding up the evidence. "Tucson to Amarillo to Omaha? You're not flying commercial."

"I have my own plane. Just a little twin engine Cessna." As offhandedly as if owning and piloting a plane were a matter of convenience, like having a smartphone. Wyatt pushed the door shut on the Mustang. "I hope I didn't show up at a bad time?"

"Always," Joe said.

Violet's gaze slid down the driveway to the road, then back again. "Delon's flying to Omaha today, too. He'll be bringing Beni home any time now."

And she would clearly be a whole lot happier if Joe made himself scarce so they could avoid a replay of that cozy scene at the barbecue shack. He'd just drag Wyatt over to the bunkhouse…

Too late.

Delon's car turned in off the highway. Why did Joe have a sinking feeling that this was exactly as Wyatt had planned it? The silver Taurus pulled to a stop behind Wyatt's rental. Nothing flashy for Delon. He drove with the same attitude as he rode—safety first. The wheels had barely stopped rolling when the back door swung open and Beni leapt out.

"Mommy! That car is *so cool!* Who does it—" He skidded to a stop when he saw Wyatt, his eyes going big. "Is that your car?"

"Just for today."

"Can I have a ride?"

"Sure."

"With the top down?"

"Naturally." Wyatt held out a hand. "You probably don't remember me. I'm Wyatt."

Beni accepted the handshake, vibrating with excitement. "You're the best bullfighter in the whole world. My mommy says so."

"That's real nice of her," Wyatt drawled, tossing a triumphant grin toward Joe.

"My mommy is always nice," Beni said, serious now. "Except when I don't listen. Or when she scrubs my ears and makes me dress up for church." He leaned closer to Wyatt and lowered his voice. "Did your mommy make you wear those clothes?"

"Beni!" Violet exclaimed.

Joe busted out laughing.

Delon stepped out of the car, ignoring Joe and

working up a polite smile for Wyatt. "What brings you down here?"

"Joe and I have some business, so I popped in on my way to Omaha," Wyatt said.

"You're working the rodeo up there?"

"Heading north soon as I'm done here. Need a lift?" Wyatt asked.

"No. Thanks. I'm flying out of Amarillo with a couple of other guys." Delon shifted and shot Violet a glance. Pretty obvious he wanted to get her alone. To grill her about Joe? Remind her that she'd have an impressionable child watching her every move? And Joe's. Beni circled the Mustang, running his fingers over the sleek curve of the hood. A pained look flashed over Wyatt's face, but he didn't say a word. If it had been his own car, he would've pitched a fit.

Wyatt focused his *vote for me* smile on Delon. "If you can wait until after the bull riding, I'll buy you a beer tonight. I assume you'll stick around for the barrel racing since Stacie Lyn is up tonight. Unless the two of you have other plans…"

Violet's chin jerked up like a coyote catching a whiff of blood.

"We don't…I mean, we're not…" Delon stammered.

Wyatt faked an embarrassed wince. "Sorry. After I saw you together at Greeley and then again at Casper, I just assumed…"

"Funny, you never mentioned her," Violet drawled, her mouth twitching with the beginnings of a smirk.

Delon's face went a shade darker as he sidled toward his car. "I, ah, should get going. I'll pick Beni up next Wednesday morning, okay? We'll see you at the rodeo Saturday night."

"Fine." Violet gave him a bright, toothy smile. "Have a *great* time."

As the car door slammed behind him, Beni frowned at his mother. "You didn't tell him good luck."

She snorted. "I'm guessing he'll get plenty lucky anyway."

"Whaddaya mean—"

"Hey, Beni," Wyatt said. "Give me five minutes to talk to Joe, then you and I can go for that ride, okay?"

Beni pumped a fist. "Awesome!"

Joe spun around and made a beeline for the bunkhouse. Wyatt sauntered in behind him, looking pleased with himself. The instant the door closed Joe turned on him.

"What the hell was that?" he demanded.

"You were worried Delon would give Violet a hard time about you, so I took care of it. The last subject he wants to bring up now is anybody's sex life." Wyatt paused to study a black-and-white photo that hung by the door, a Jacobs bucking horse in action from back in the seventies.

"Do you get some kind of sick thrill from screwing with people?"

Wyatt moved on the next framed picture, this one in faded color. "Didn't seem to bother Violet."

His nonchalance only stoked Joe's temper. "So, what? You were bored, so you dropped by to see what you could stir up here?"

"No." When he turned, Wyatt's expression was flat and hard. "Lyle is gone."

Joe's whirling thoughts caught like tumbleweeds piling up against a fence. "What do you mean, gone?"

"His wife gave him an ultimatum. Her and rehab, or Browning Rodeo. He chose her."

Joe stepped back, felt for the arm of the couch with one hand, and sank down onto it. "How do you know?"

"Helen called. She was worried." Wyatt folded his arms, all stern and disapproving. "The woman fusses over you like you're one of her own and you can't take five minutes to let her know where you are?"

"I didn't think of it." Guilt clenched a knotty fist in Joe's gut. He usually kept Helen up-to-date on his schedule so she knew when to lay an extra place at the table. "She could've called me."

"She said you don't like her trying to mother you."

"I didn't say that." But he'd thought it. Not that he didn't appreciate Helen's intentions. He sure didn't mind the brown paper bags of cookies he found in his car at the end of particularly long days on the ranch. Between that and a more personal relationship was an invisible but vital space, though, and it made Joe feel twitchy and uncomfortable when she crossed it. He could barter for snickerdoodles by taking out the trash. What would she expect in return for affection? Something he didn't have to give.

But that wasn't the most important thing right now.

"Lyle is really gone for good?"

"As long as he wants a chance at keeping his wife."

Joe scrubbed the back his hand over his forehead. "I can't believe she's still trying to save their marriage."

"She's trying to save his life," Wyatt said. "Another five years with Dick and he'll either be dead in a ditch or pickled beyond repair. The man is toxic."

To Lyle, maybe. There was a whole dynamic between

a father and a son, the grinding need for approval, that didn't apply to Joe. Not where Dick was concerned. Joe didn't need a father figure any more than he needed a second mother. The parents he'd been blessed with were more than plenty, thank you very much. He did need the ranch, and the stock, and the opportunity to be more than a hired hand. And now the heir apparent had stepped aside.

"I don't suppose you'll even bother to look at these now." Wyatt flicked the envelope at him like a Frisbee.

Joe snatched it out of the air. He peeled back the flap and pulled out a half-inch thick stack of contracts, neatly stapled—a who's who of the biggest rodeos in the country. While Joe flipped pages, blinking at the numbers, Wyatt wandered the room studying the collection of photos, some dating clear back to the fifties when Steve's dad started the bucking string. The bunkhouse consisted of a living room, bedroom, and bathroom, all done up in rustic barn wood and western odds and ends. No kitchen. Who needed one with Iris right across the road?

Joe dropped the stack of papers on the coffee table, overwhelmed. "I can't do this."

"Because of Dick." Wyatt's voice was ripe with disgust.

Not entirely. Joe grabbed a fringed leather pillow from the couch and kneaded it between his hands. "I can't bounce all over the country doing nothing but showing up when it's time to fight bulls. I need more than that."

"So go to work for another contractor. Somebody who appreciates you."

"It wouldn't be the same." It wouldn't be the scrub

and sage of the High Lonesome. It wouldn't be the Browning stock he'd helped raise.

"You would trade anything for that ranch." Wyatt's voice was sucked dry of emotion. "Pride, self-respect, basic human decency. I think you prefer it that way. Is being empty easier?"

Joe stiffened. "What is that supposed to mean?"

"You live in a town where you have no family, work for a man you don't like—you don't have to care how anyone feels about you. Caring is scary. Sometimes it hurts. Empty is a lot safer. Maybe you and Delon aren't so different after all."

Joe's hands clenched around the pillow, resisting the urge to fling it at Wyatt's head. He'd always wondered why they were called throw pillows. "At least I'm not locked up in a condo between rodeos. I like my town. I like the ranch. If you would quit fucking with me I'd be at home living happily ever after."

"Happily?" Wyatt snorted. "Real happiness requires having a soul, compassion, actual relationships. Dick will suck all of that out of you eventually. You'll end up a gnarly, cussed old man like all the Brownings, dying alone on the High Lonesome."

"At least they died in a place they loved."

Wyatt stared at him for a long moment. Then he closed his eyes and shook his head. "The trouble with places, Joe? They don't love you back."

Yeah, well, neither did people. Not enough that you could count on them to stick around. Wyatt, of all people, should understand. At least Joe had his mother. Wyatt had an endless list of casual acquaintances and business contacts who admired him but wouldn't be inviting him over for the holidays. Wyatt wasn't easy to be around, though in a totally different way than Dick Browning. People didn't enjoy being dissected. It had never bothered Joe much, but it left him as Wyatt's only true friend.

Joe sighed. "If I promise to look through the contracts, will you get back in your plane and go away?"

"As soon as I take Beni for that ride."

Joe smiled, imagining Beni tossing the *just a bullfighter* line at Wyatt. That'd teach him to butt in.

"You have fun with that," Joe said, and held the door so Wyatt could leave.

Chapter 21

VIOLET SHOVED OFF WITH HER TOE, SETTING HER mother's lawn swing swaying. Wyatt Darrington was at her house. Had her kid off somewhere joyriding in a Mustang GT. He and Joe were obviously good friends, and Joe was just as obviously not happy to see him. Whatever business they'd discussed down there in the bunkhouse, it hadn't ended on a particularly pleasant note. Joe had shoved Wyatt out the door then stomped back to the barn, where she could see the occasional pitchfork full of manure fly past the door. Working off a temper, she'd bet.

And Delon…what was up with his attitude? He'd never acted like that with any guy she'd dated. What was it about Joe that had him bristling up like a cowdog at a rattlesnake? Not that Joe was any better, goading Delon at the barbecue shack. Honest to ever-loving God. Men.

The silky rumble of the Mustang's engine alerted her to its imminent arrival, easily distinguished from the rattles and roars of the usual local traffic. As the car scooted around the corner, down the driveway, and stopped in front of her, she made an effort to look cool and serene.

Beni scrambled out over the unopened door, beaming. "That was awesome, Mommy! Can I have lunch now?"

"I left it on the table for you," she said.

"Is it my favorite?"

"Yep."

"All right!" He punched a fist in the air and sprinted for the house as Wyatt climbed out of the car.

"Must be good stuff."

"Frozen dinner," Violet said. "He only gets them when my mom is gone. Might kill her if she knew her grandson was eating fake mashed potatoes."

Wyatt laughed, but instead of getting in his car and on his way, he strolled over and sat down. She caught a whiff of aftershave: crisp, sporty, and expensive. Hoo boy, he was pretty. In the close confines of the swing, she could count the golden hairs on his tanned thighs and forearms. The man of every cowgirl's fantasies was only inches away, and not one teensy little tingle. Damn Joe Cassidy.

Wyatt angled his body to face her, expression screened by dark glasses. "Joe is afraid I caused trouble between you and Delon."

"I assumed that was your intention."

His mouth quirked, acknowledging a point in her favor. "Stacy Lyn's not a candidate to be Beni's stepmother."

"More like Delon's not a candidate to further her career. Sanchez Trucking is doing okay, but he can't plunk down a hundred grand for a new barrel horse." She flashed him an arch look. "I bet *you* know her pretty well."

Wyatt smiled.

"Joe, too, I suppose," Violet said, and regretted the words when Wyatt's smile widened.

Then he shook his head. "Joe calls her the honey badger. Says he'd feel safer sticking his dick in a wood chipper."

Violet laughed, then settled back, studying him closely. "What?"

"You flew here to check me out. I'm trying to figure out what dog you have in this hunt."

She couldn't see his eyes, but she was pretty sure he blinked. "I've been looking for an excuse since Joe told me about you."

"What did he say?" It felt like a dangerous question.

"I could tell he was impressed, and that doesn't happen often. I wanted to see why. Now I do."

Violet thought about blushing prettily, but the likelihood that he was filling her full of bull was too high.

"I always thought when Joe fell for a girl, it would be someone like his mother," Wyatt said. "I should've known better."

Violet's heart stuttered at *when Joe fell for a girl,* but she wouldn't let herself even consider it. Wyatt was using her, or wanted to. But for what?

"What's his mother like?" she asked.

"A beautiful mess." The words were softened by affection and a smile. "But better than she has a right to be. Roxy's mother was a bar whore, sure the next guy who came along would take her away from all that. She chased them to hell and back and dragged her kids along with her, including six months living in their car in Denver after the latest love of her life left them cold."

"Ouch."

"Yeah. And it's fair to assume a few of these guys had no business anywhere near a kid, especially one who looked like Roxy."

Violet cringed. "I guess that explains all the husbands."

Wyatt's head jerked a tiny fraction. "Joe told you about them?"

"It came up."

"Well, that's new." Wyatt folded his arms and gave the swing a nudge. He might look relaxed, but Violet could practically feel the breeze from how fast his mental wheels were spinning. "Roxy inherited her mother's belief that a man can make all her problems go away. The difference is, it works for her. Right up until she realizes she's falling for them. Then she cuts and runs."

"Is that what she did to Joe's dad?"

Wyatt did another double take. "He told you about his dad?"

"Enough." Even from behind the sunglasses, Wyatt's stare was so intense it made Violet want to squirm like a bug under a magnifying glass. "I take it he usually doesn't talk much about his family."

"Never."

But Wyatt might, so Violet asked the question that had been nagging at her. "What's the problem with his dad?"

"He's a spineless little worm who'd rather blow off his own son than risk the wrath of his second wife, so he lives his happy little life in the suburbs with his shiny new family and lets Joe think he's the problem."

"Wait. Family? He has other kids?"

"Two daughters who barely know Joe. Their mother is so intimidated by Roxy, she refuses to let them have any contact for fear it'll open the door to the she-devil."

Joe had sisters? Violet couldn't begin to imagine a female version of him. She glanced toward the barn and saw another forkful of manure sail past the door. Joe had to see them sitting here talking. Dimes to dollars he was not pleased about it.

"He doesn't have anything to do with his dad?"

Wyatt grimaced. "I wish, but Joe can't seem to walk away, and his dad reciprocates just enough to keep stringing him along. That's part of why Joe was punching things last week. The Worm usually comes to at least one performance at Puyallup—it's only thirty minutes from his house, for Christ's sake—but this year he didn't show up."

Violet ground her teeth. "With all your connections, you can't hire a decent hit man?"

"If only. I'd go for the volume discount and rid the world of the Brownings, too."

Aha. That explained so much. "I bet you jumped on the chance to shoo him off to Texas."

"I was hoping if he got some distance he'd come to his senses and tell them all to fuck off. Permanently." Wyatt leaned closer, his voice and his gaze penetrating, as if he could inject his intensity into her. "Every year Joe spends with that man, he gives up a piece of himself, and he can't even see what's happening."

Okay, wow. She was not prepared for this conversation. Violet angled her head away, letting it all sink in. Wyatt wasn't just gossiping. He obviously had an agenda. She'd bet Wyatt didn't go out for coffee without an agenda. Then she remembered Joe, the passion and conviction in his eyes and his voice when he talked about the High Lonesome Ranch. "He can't just walk away."

"It might not be easy," Wyatt conceded. "But with the right motivation…"

Violet stiffened at his implication. "Do not look at me. I'm not in the market for a man."

"Joe isn't just any man, and the two of you have a lot in common. He could fit in pretty well around here."

He already did, but that didn't change the facts. "Here isn't where he wants to be. That ranch is everything to him, and I'm not dumb enough to think I can come between them."

Wyatt absorbed the flat, uncompromising answer. Then he slapped his hands on his bare knees. "Well, I wasted a trip, then."

"Did you?" She had a feeling he'd accomplished something. She just wasn't sure what.

Wyatt sat very still for a few beats. Then he smiled and pulled off his sunglasses. His blue eyes were as sharp and focused as laser beams. "No. I got to meet you. And it was a pleasure."

"Sure it was."

He laughed. "I can be a manipulative bastard, Violet, but I hardly ever lie, especially to someone I respect."

"You don't even know me."

"Yes, I do." Those blue eyes held hers in a grip impossible to break. "Saving cowboys from their own stupidity is your job description. Ours, too. Bullfighters, pickup men—we're all the same in here." He tapped a finger over his heart. "That's why Joe trusts you. You're one of us."

She opened her mouth, then closed it again because she had no answer. A part of her immediately wondered if he'd only said all that as part of his sales pitch.

Wyatt slid his sunglasses back into place. "No, I'm not buttering you up. It wouldn't work anyway. Which is another reason Joe can't stay away from you."

Dammit. She wished he'd quit saying that stuff. She didn't need any encouragement to be stupid about Joe. She stood, so abruptly the swing lurched sideways, and extended a hand. "Well, thanks for stopping by and all. It's been…interesting."

Wyatt took the hint, springing lightly to his feet to accept her handshake. His grip was strong, smooth, with just the right amount of pressure. And still no tingles. "I apologize if sending Joe down here caused you grief. If there's any way I can make it up to you, let me know."

Violet nodded, smiled, and waved as he drove away, all the while thinking she wasn't sure how much of Wyatt's brand of help she could handle.

Chapter 22

IF THERE WAS ANYTHING BETTER TO DO ON A Saturday morning than prepping for a rodeo, Joe couldn't imagine what it would be. He stood in the alley behind the bucking chutes watching the last three horses clatter down the loading chute from the truck and smiled from pure pleasure. The sound of hooves on metal and wood always got his juices flowing. Following Cole's hand signals, he let the stud horse trot on past, then stepped out and waved his sorting stick to turn the two geldings into an open pen on his left.

Hank swung the gate shut behind them and secured the chain, then strolled over to Joe and did a double take. "Did you get a haircut?"

"Yeah." Joe plucked his hat off and ruffled a hand over his head, feeling naked with parts of his neck exposed that hadn't seen daylight in years. "I told him to just take a little off the ends."

"You musta got it done at the barber shop in Earnest. Ol' Leroy learned to cut hair back when high and tight was in style and he's never bothered to learn anything else. But hey, if you get a sudden urge to enlist in the Army…"

Joe glared, but it didn't take any of the shine off Hank's grin.

"So…did you and Violet go out again last night?" Hank's blatant emphasis on *out* made it clear he wasn't asking if they'd caught another movie.

"Beni was home," Joe said. "And Violet's busy catching up on her book work."

When Beni wasn't two steps behind her, she'd been holed up in the office. Frustrating, but it had given Joe a chance to borrow her car to go get the haircut and few other odds and ends. He was flying blind when it came to courting, but ever since she'd laughed when he declared his intentions, he'd been bound and determined to prove her wrong.

"You going out tonight?" Hank persisted. "Assuming she still wants to be seen with you and that hair."

"She said it looked fine."

And she was a lousy liar, especially when she couldn't stop smirking. Otherwise the day had clicked along right on schedule. No breakdowns or meltdowns in the process of transferring the stock to today's rodeo, only an hour and a half from the ranch. Nice drive, through wide-open country. Violet had barely blinked when Joe climbed in her pickup. With Beni in the backseat, they'd had to watch what they said, but it turned out to be easy. They had plenty to talk about. Bucking stock, rodeos, ranches…a few times during the drive Joe had almost forgotten she was a girl. Almost.

"My sister said to tell you there's a place called the Bootlegger on the south side of town," Hank said. "It's kind of a dump, but the music is good and the beer is cold."

"I think I like your sister."

"She's a pain in the ass, but she'd know if it's the place to party. She and Violet used to hit 'em all."

Really? Now there was a side of Violet that Joe would like to see. He handed his sorting stick to Hank. "Give this to Cole so he doesn't have a conniption because he came up one short. I'm gonna grab some lunch."

Hank took the stick, grinning again. "If I was you, I'd keep my hat on."

Joe snarled, but it was hard to put much behind it when Hank had a point. He swung by one of the semis first to grab a shopping bag he'd left in the sleeper along with his duffel. He'd declined Violet's offer of a motel room, preferring to stay at the rodeo grounds when they'd only be here óne night. Saved running back and forth. Kept him closer to Violet. Not that he craved her company, but he'd staked a claim that day at practice. Now people would expect to see them together.

His next stop was Iris's trailer. She'd left a pair of huge coolers under the awning, one packed with iced-down sodas and jugs of homemade sweet tea, the other with tubs of potato salad and roast beef sandwiches on thick slices of homemade bread. It was worth working for Jacobs Livestock just for Iris's food, as long as you made sure you got to it ahead of Cole. Joe loaded up his bag with lunch for two, tossed in a few oatmeal cookies and headed for Violet's trailer. Either by chance or intent, she'd parked right next door to Joe's Peterbilt bedroom, which might be more temptation than he could handle if Beni weren't camped in her trailer, too.

Even that couldn't dampen Joe's mood. A cool front had eased in, dropping the temperature ten degrees and taking the humidity down with it, making it a damn near perfect day. He had a sackful of good food and a hot chick to share it with—not that he'd ever let Violet hear him call her a chick. She was out in the arena, with Beni and his pony bouncing along behind as she helped pen the timed-event cattle.

Beni had wolfed down his lunch while everyone else was unloading. When the last of the steers were sorted, instead of following his mother, he switched to trotting circles around Cole as he walked the fences, examining every gate, post, and fence rail for potential hazards to his precious stock. Soon as everyone else got some chow, the horses and bulls would have their turn for a lap or two around the arena to get a feel for the ground and where to find the exit gate. Animals handled easier and performed better when they knew where they were going and what to expect. Sort of like people.

Joe set his bag down and went to work, unrolling the awning on Violet's trailer and pulling an outdoor carpet and folding chairs from the storage bin underneath. Behind him, the tractor fired up, rolling into the arena with a plow attached. They'd dig the ground deep first, water it, then work it again with the groomer, packing it for traction and speed. The smell of diesel fumes, damp earth, and manure was like a snort of cocaine, pumping up Joe's system. For a few hours, before the contestants or the fans rolled in, the rodeo grounds belonged solely to the contractor.

Joe loved this part. He loved all the parts. Beginning, middle, and end, there was nothing about any rodeo he wanted to skip. At the big shows, where the committee just expected him and Wyatt to show up for the bull riding, he didn't get to help with any of the good stuff. Yeah, Pendleton and Ellensburg and Red Bluff were great rodeos, but Joe would be perfectly satisfied with what Jacobs Livestock had, at least as a start.

He'd been working toward that start since the first summer on Dick's ranch, soaking up every iota of knowledge that Dick was willing to share or Joe could steal. He scraped and scrimped, living in a dingy one-room apartment above the Mint Bar, driving a fifteen-year-old car, signing autographs at western stores in exchange for free jeans while he stashed every extra dime, all with an eye to the day he could offer Dick Browning the one thing he could never resist—a big chunk of cold hard cash. And now, with Lyle gone, Joe's chances had more than doubled, unless Dick decided to hold a grudge.

But he wasn't going to waste this spectacular day brooding about Dick. He was pushing at the little portable table, trying to find a spot where it didn't rock, when Violet came out of the arena. She stopped short when she saw him. Compared to her ranch attire, she looked dressed up with her sleeveless denim blouse tucked into dark jeans and her hair loose around her face, glistening in the sunlight.

"Is this part of the courting?" she asked, both cautious and amused, as she joined him under the awning.

He jerked his head toward where the others were gathering at Iris's trailer. "I know more about stock than women, so I figured I'd make like a stud horse and cut you out of the herd."

Violet laughed. "Sweet talk like that, hard to believe you've never done this before."

"What can I say? I'm a natural."

He set out sandwiches, salad, and drinks on the table and they settled in, hungry enough to put food ahead of conversation. Joe wolfed down both of his sandwiches, polished off his potato salad, and washed it all down with sweet tea, then leaned back and gave a heartfelt sigh of contentment.

Violet offered Joe a cookie, then broke off a small piece of her own. "So, Wyatt. He's sort of…"

"An ass?"

"I was going to say scary."

Joe paused mid-bite. "Most women think he's cool."

"Only if that's what he wants them to think."

Joe lowered his cookie, surprised. Wyatt's charm was generally foolproof. "You don't like him?"

"Like is too simple. A person who likes Wyatt hasn't bothered to look past what he wants them to see." She shook her head again. "I can't imagine living with someone like that."

"Neither could his wife."

Her eyebrows shot up. "He was married?"

"For eighteen months, to a stripper he met during the Reno rodeo. Picture Wyatt playing house with a woman named Bambi, and you can guess how well that worked out."

"Was he temporarily insane?"

Joe shrugged. "She was okay. Smarter than you'd expect. She just needed a chance."

"And Wyatt rescued her."

"It's the frustrated preacher in him. He's gotta have someone to save." Joe savored the first caramel-crisp bite of his cookie, then asked, ever so casually, "What did the two of you talk about?"

"Nothing important." Violet was suddenly too busy cleaning up the table to meet his eye, but she paused in the midst of stacking their empty plates to give him a grave look. "He's got your back, Joe. Always."

Joe dropped his gaze to his cookie. "I know."

Damn Wyatt. He'd told her things, probably stuff that would make Joe squirm. He could pry it out of her, but then he'd have to talk about whatever it was, so he reached down for the shopping bag instead.

"I bought you something."

Violet froze, then set the plates back on the table. "Like…a present?"

"Yes. I saw it in the window of one of those places in the mall and I thought it was perfect for you."

He reached into the bag, pulled out a box and set it on the table. She stared at it like he'd dished up a live snake. Even without the logo, there wasn't much doubt what store it came from.

Violet's cheeks went as pink as the box. "I, ah, you shouldn't have. Really."

Joe pushed it closer to her. "You don't even know what it is."

But she was making educated guesses that turned her cheeks even pinker. She glanced around quickly to see if anyone was watching, then snatched the box off the table and plunked it on her lap, trying to cover it with her hands.

"Aren't you going to open it?"

"Sure. Later."

Joe folded his arms and gave her his best wounded look. "At least read the card."

Her jaw worked a few times, then clamped hard as she tore open the little white envelope. Joe watched her expression as she deciphered his crappy handwriting. *Rose's are red, Violet's are blue…*

She slapped her hands down on the box again, crushing the card. "That is *not funny*."

Joe grinned. "Actually, it is. See for yourself."

She yanked the ribbon off the box, fumbled the lid open, and ripped out the tissue paper. Her face went blank. Then she burst out laughing. "You bought me Wonder Woman underwear?"

Joe stood and leaned close to her, breathing in the fruit of the day, crisp green apples. Different. Nice. "Like I said, they're perfect for you. And there's something else in there for you. Don't throw away the paper until you find it."

He kissed her cheek and sauntered away, feeling pretty damn proud of himself. He might not be a natural, but he didn't completely suck.

Chapter 23

IT WAS GONNA BE ONE OF THOSE NIGHTS. VIOLET could feel the anticipation simmering in the hum of voices from the bleachers, see it in the quivering muscles of horses and bulls, the glint in the contestants' eyes. From the soft, golden stillness of the evening air to the mouthwatering scent of hamburgers grilling at the concession stand, it was all movie-scene perfect. Magic time.

The cowboys rose to the occasion. Every one of them spurred and roped and wrestled like it was the last round of the National Finals. Every horse bucked like it was determined to kick the highest, score the most points. Even the buck offs were spectacular. The crowd hung on every jump, screamed and groaned and cheered like each contestant was their only child. And then the bulls rumbled into the chutes.

Through it all, Violet was intensely aware of Joe's note in her breast pocket. *Vince Grant wants video of Dirt Eater. Here's his email.* Just like that, Joe had put a lifetime dream within reach. A Jacobs bull bucking at the National Finals. It was like being picked to play on the Olympic basketball team. Joe had warned her it was only a chance, not a foregone conclusion, but Violet refused to be discouraged. Dirt Eater was good enough to be invited to the biggest rodeo of 'em all. Any fool would know the minute they saw him buck. Vince was no fool, and he *would* see Dirt Eater thanks to Joe.

Violet's pulse thumped in time to the heavy rock beat the rodeo announcer's girlfriend cued up to usher in the bull riding. Joe appeared beside her, dancing from foot to foot and shaking his hands at his sides, so charged with energy that tingles swept over Violet's skin from mere proximity.

When the gate in front of them swung open, Joe looked up and gave her a smile that turned the tingles into a heat wave. "Party time."

He bounded in to the announcer's introduction and the roar of the fans. Caught up in the moment, Violet spurred Cadillac and galloped around the arena to slide to a stop in her usual position. She ignored Cole's *What the hell?* look. Once in a while, a girl had to cut loose.

The bulls fed off the electricity arcing around the arena, launching their muscle-bound bodies into space, twisting, rolling, flinging dust and riders and glistening streamers of snot into the night sky. It was a beautiful thing. Joe was a flash of constant motion—darting, dancing, dodging horns and hooves and flying bodies, his eyes gleaming with an exhilaration so potent, Violet got high on the secondhand thrill. Damn, it must be something to be able to move like that.

The fifth rider out was a rookie from San Angelo. Tough kid. The kind that never let go, even when his heels were kissing the clouds and his head skimming the dirt. The bull whipped around hard to the right and jerked him down into the well on the inside of the spin. His hand wedged in the rope, and in a blink the kid was hung up on the side of a ton of stomping, hooking bovine.

Hank slapped the bull on the head as Joe threw

himself onto the bull's shoulders opposite the rider, one hand grabbing the kid's elbow to hold him up, the other hand catching the tail of the rope and yanking. The wrap came free as the bull leapt again. The rock hard mass of its shoulder slammed into Joe and sent him flying as the cowboy tucked and rolled and hit his feet running for the fence. Joe landed on his butt and skidded across the dirt. The bull stopped, tossed his head in a gesture of pure, arrogant *Take that!*, then sauntered out the exit gate.

For an instant, the crowd was silent. Then Joe popped to his feet and pumped an arm over his head and the grandstand exploded, wave after thundering wave of applause washing over the arena. Violet shivered in pure delight. Nights like this should never end.

As the announcer wrapped up the show, wishing the crowd a good night and safe travels, Joe threw his head back and howled like a wolf, thumping a fist on his chest. "Now *that* was a rodeo!"

Violet laughed as she stepped off her horse. Hot damn. What a show. Even Cole was smiling. She peeled off her chaps and hung them on her saddle, but as she stepped toward the gate, Joe snagged her around the waist and spun her into his arms.

"Come dancing with me, Violet."

Temptation tugged at her sleeve, whispered in her ear. How long had it been since she'd danced until closing time? She heard a wolf whistle and a couple of hoots and tried to wriggle free. "I can't. Beni—"

"He can stay the night with us," her mother called down from the announcer's stand above them, where she was packing away stopwatches and clipboards. "You go. Have fun."

Violet's pulse jumped at the prospect, her system already revved from the rodeo. She looked down at her blue shirt and dusty jeans. "I'm not—"

"You can be by the time I get out of the shower," Joe said.

"But I have to help—"

"Cole, take Violet's horse," her mother ordered. "Y'all can manage without her tonight."

"Yes, ma'am." Cole plucked the reins out of Violet's hand as he passed.

Joe planted his index finger under her chin and pushed it up to look her in the eye. "Get your dancin' shoes on, Violet. We're gonna show this town how it's done."

———

Driving one of the Jacobs Livestock pickups, Joe bypassed the bar designated as the site of the official rodeo after-party and headed across town to a low-slung concrete block building that could have doubled as a bomb shelter, which was probably the only reason it had outlasted decades of rowdy cowboys. The infamous Bootlegger.

Violet shot him a baffled look as he pulled into a parking space. "How did you know about this place?"

"Hank told me, on orders from his sister."

Violet laughed. "Of course. This is where Melanie and I used to go when we had serious trouble to get into."

"Then we're in the right place," Joe said, with a smile so full of the devil it was probably illegal in some parts of the Bible Belt.

She stepped out into the silky evening air, almost

cool enough to raise goose bumps on her bare arms. She'd changed into her best jeans and a sleeveless white blouse, and added some turquoise and silver jewelry. Boots would've been smarter, but she'd opted for flat black canvas shoes that made the most of the small difference between her height and Joe's. Once in a while it was nice to feel like the girl, and she'd come prepared this weekend, not knowing what Joe's idea of courting would necessitate.

Joe grabbed her hand and towed her through the front door, pausing just inside. Not much to see—scarred tables, scuffed floor, dingy walls. The Bootlegger never had pretended to be about anything but drinking and dancing, and since it was after eleven, the crowd had a sizable head start on them in the drinking department. Violet scanned the mass of humanity. Plenty of cowboy hats, plenty of familiar faces. Joe plowed through the crowd, dragging her in his wake. At the bar, he waved a hand at the nearest bartender, pointed at a beer and held up two fingers. The bartender nodded and grabbed a pair of glasses. While Joe dug in his pocket for cash, Violet took the opportunity to enjoy the view. He was wearing his cowboy hat, thank God. That haircut was worse than the scalping she'd given Beni with the clippers from the As Seen on TV store. Joe had worn his boots and the same jeans from Tuesday night that made his butt look so spectacular, but he hadn't bothered with a belt and buckle or tucked in his short-sleeved sports shirt.

Wait a minute. Violet inspected him waist to collar, then leaned to the side and craned her neck to examine his chest. Not a logo in sight.

"What?" he asked.

She plucked at the silky sleeve of his shirt. "I thought you didn't buy clothes."

"It looked like something Wyatt would wear on a date." He smoothed his palm over the geometric black and turquoise print. "I figured I should get something nice if I was gonna take you out dancing."

"Oh. Thank you."

As if he'd bought it for her. But, well, he had, and it was the sweetest damn thing any man had done for her in a very long time—except maybe the Wonder Woman underwear, and that was…well, not exactly sweet, but special. Which pretty much described Joe. At least the version of him that had been hanging around the last couple of days.

The band kicked into a better-than-average rendition of Toby Keith's "Shoulda Been a Cowboy," and the thump of the bass sent energy pulsing through her muscles. When the bartender plunked their beers down, Joe paid without letting go of her hand. He passed one beer to her, then took a big gulp of his own. She did the same, the first taste so cold, crisp, and perfect that she took a second, bigger gulp. She started to lick a dab of foam from the corner of her mouth, but Joe beat her to it, his tongue flicking over her upper lip. Then he moved to her ear and nipped at the lobe.

"You smell like apples. Makes me want to nibble."

Before she could catch her breath, he kissed her. She tensed instinctively, thinking of all those watching eyes. Then she remembered she wasn't going to worry about them anymore and kissed him back, savoring the cool-on-warm tanginess of the beer on his tongue. He pulled her closer, hip to hip, and she had to remind herself to watch where her hand wandered because she probably shouldn't grab his butt in public. Especially this public, with all the curious eyes and wagging tongues. She dragged herself out of the kiss, resenting every millimeter of the retreat.

"I think we're warmed up now." Joe took another big gulp of his beer and set the glass on the bar.

Violet followed suit. Then he was off again, dragging her onto the dance floor and into a whirl of perpetual motion. The man just never stopped. At the beginning of the fourth—or maybe fifth—song, Joe twirled her, caught her close, and rocked her into a quick two-step. Violet's head was spinning faster than the music, but she matched his rhythm without missing a beat.

He grinned his approval. "You're good."

"*Pfft!* Down here we learn the two-step in the crib."

"God bless Texas," he said, and twirled her again.

Like in the arena, Joe was a step quicker than anyone on the floor, his hands sure and strong, spinning her, swinging her, those laughing green eyes daring her to strut her stuff. She held back a little at first, self-conscious, but with every twirl her give-a-shit level slipped a tiny bit more until finally she just let go. The hell with it. Let the devil lead her where he would.

And lead he did. It was like jumping feet first into a tornado, bolts of lightning crackling around her, through her, sending her nervous system into overload. She was surprised her skin didn't glow every place he'd touched her. If it did, she would have illuminated the entire bar, because there wasn't a whole lot of her Joe hadn't managed to brush up against. As the band crashed to the end of "Sweet Home Alabama" he spun her out, then back, and caught her tight against him on the final note, a whole lot of her parts pressed up nice and cozy against a whole lot of his. Hers lit up like a neon sign, flashing *Take me now.*

"Time for a break, folks," the lead singer declared. "But we'll be back for one last set."

Joe's hand splayed over her lower back, holding her so close she could see the flecks of gold around the irises of his eyes. He brushed a kiss over her mouth as the other dancers melted away toward the bar or the tables.

"Thirsty?"

"I could use a glass of water." The colder the better. With a bucket of ice on the side to dump down the back of her shirt. She suspected it might evaporate, and only a fraction of her elevated body heat was due to exertion. Joe kissed her again, lingering for a moment, his hand curving her hips into his. Then he stepped back and all those parts of hers whimpered in protest at his absence. He steered her over to a narrow counter along the wall and commandeered the lone empty stool. "I'll be right back."

Then he was off, weaving and dodging through the crowd like it was an obstacle course he had to conquer. Violet grabbed a napkin from a chrome dispenser and dabbed at her forehead. Her feet throbbed like she'd run a half marathon, and the band still had another set to go.

Without Joe to overwhelm her senses, her awareness of the rest of the world seeped back in. Oh Lord. When had those three guys come in? Some of Delon's buddies. At least one of them would be on the phone to him before closing time—assuming he wasn't too busy with Stacy Lyn to answer. She met their gazes head on, chin up, challenging. They looked away first.

She searched Joe out in the mob and watched as cowboys passed by, clapped his shoulder, shook his hand, probably offered to buy him a beer from the way he shook his head and waved them off. There was more of the same as he edged through the crowd. He smiled and spoke to all of them, but kept moving, as if getting back to Violet was his one and only goal. When he handed her the plastic cup of ice water, she guzzled most of it without taking a breath. Lord, did that hit the spot. Joe skimmed his hand up to lift the hair from the back of her neck, his fingertips cold and damp. The brush of them sent goose bumps racing over her skin. She shifted, acutely aware that if he looked down, he might see what else had puckered.

He touched the rim of his glass to her bottom lip, like a toast. "Having fun?"

"Boy howdy."

He laughed. She gulped down the last of her water. Joe did the same, stacked his empty plastic cup with Violet's, and set them on the counter behind her, then nudged a space for his thighs between her knees, bracing his hands on either side of her. "You up for more?"

Oh yeah. An image of what they could do in that position if they were alone sent heat searing through her. Joe smiled as if he read her mind, his eyes glowing like a green light on the highway straight to hell. He had her surrounded, but he wasn't touching her except for those two throbbing spots where the insides of her thighs pressed against his. The rest of her body was one giant nerve, quivering in anticipation.

Joe trailed his fingers down her bare arm and wrapped them around her wrist as the band blasted out the opening of the next song. "Time for round two."

He yanked her off the stool and onto the dance floor and kept her there for every single song. Two-step, swing, the Cotton-Eyed Joe—they did it all. Her feet were screaming for mercy by the time the band polished off a foot-stompin' extended version of a Turnpike Troubadours song.

The lead singer mopped his face with a towel, then said, "Hate to tell ya', folks, but it's time to say good night. Grab your Mr. Right—or Mr. Right Now—and let's slow it on down for the last song."

Not just any song. The most disgustingly romantic love song Kenny Chesney had ever recorded, and that was saying something. Violet didn't resist as Joe molded her against him, hands on her hips, just enough taller that she could rest her cheek on his shoulder. Finally, he slowed down. *Way* down, the shift and sway of their bodies producing a nearly unbearable friction where they rubbed up against each other. He started to hum along, then sing, his voice low and amazingly good, vibrating against her cheek. She tilted her head back in surprise.

"What?" he asked.

Violet stared at him a beat, then said, "Nothing."

He reached up to push a strand of damp hair off her forehead. The scratch on his wrist looked sore, puckered, and red. Without thinking, she brushed her lips across it. Joe stumbled slightly, eyes going dark.

"I was just kissing it better," she said, embarrassed.

His smile came slow, so sweet it made her ache. "Then I expect it'll be healed by morning."

He slid a hand up to the nape of her neck, tilting her cheek back onto his shoulder. She closed her eyes and let herself be swallowed up by the moment—the two of them alone on the crowded floor with Joe's arms strong around her, the lean grace of his body hard against hers, his fingers stroking circles low on her back and his voice singing softly in her ear, a song about how he could never let her go. The hunger hit her low and hard, an ache so powerful her hands clenched in his shirt. *Her* shirt. His arms tightened in response, and he brushed a kiss across her eyebrow, nearly taking out her knees.

Dear sweet Lord, she wanted him, with an intensity unlike anything she'd ever experienced. And with Beni safely stowed in her mother's camper for the night, there was no reason she couldn't have him.

Chapter 24

JOE NOSED THE PICKUP INTO THE GAP BETWEEN VIOLET'S trailer and the semi he was calling home and turned off the engine. Violet hopped out of the pickup and met him at the front, letting him catch her wrist and slide his hand down to lace his fingers through hers. He walked her to her door, then leaned against the side of the camper, pulling her into the circle of his arms. The drive home had left him wishing for the old bench-style pickup seats where there was no console to keep her from snuggling. She nestled her face into the crook of his neck.

"Tired?" he asked.

"Mmm. Been a while since I danced holes in my shoes."

I could rub your feet for you. And work his way up from there. She shifted, her mouth brushing his skin, and the jolt of lust wiped his mind clean. Sweet Jesus. He had to get her naked. But first, he had to get her inside. She nibbled along his jaw and he nearly groaned out loud. Just one kiss…but her mouth was so soft, so willing, he had to go back for more. His palms flattened, molding her against him so he could feel every inch of her warm flesh through his thin shirt.

He wanted to memorize her taste, the shape of her body, that little catch in her breath when he touched her just right. Something pulled deep inside him—a hard, tight ache that was more than physical: a craving to be a part of all that was Violet. Solid, strong, sure of her place in the world. Working beside her, laughing with her, sliding into her bed and all that heat at the end of the day—a man could get used to that life.

The thought had barely formed when something entirely different flared in his gut. A sharp sizzle, like an emergency flare, warning him of danger ahead. Suddenly, he couldn't breathe, as if his heart had jumped up and crammed itself into the space behind his Adam's apple.

Violet eased out of the kiss, glancing over her shoulder. "What's wrong?"

Joe's gaze fell upon her parents' trailer. Was Iris sitting up, waiting to be sure Violet got home safely? Her dad peering out from one of those darkened windows, watching to see if Joe went inside with Violet? Or, God help him, Beni. *How come you were kissing my Mommy? Did you tuck her in?* Joe's stomach twisted up and wrung itself out like a sponge at the thought of *that* conversation. Dammit to hell. He couldn't do it. He could not drag Violet up those steps if there was the slightest chance any of her family would see and think less of him—or worse, of her. He had an amazing woman in his arms, hot and willing and ten steps from a bed, and he could… not…do it. A howl of frustration welled up, scorching his lungs when he refused to let it loose. He'd survived for thirty years without giving a damn what anyone thought. Why now, for Christ's sake? Why these very temporary people? It made absolutely zero sense.

And none of that mattered, because this inconvenient conscience or sense of propriety or whatever he'd suddenly developed wasn't listening. "Joe?"

He leaned in, groaning as he rested his forehead against hers. "I can't."

"Can't what?"

"This." He ran his hands up and down her back, torturing himself with the possibilities. "Your family would know. And everybody else."

Irritation crackled through the heat in her eyes, like lightning in storm clouds. "If it doesn't bother me, what do you care?"

Hell if he knew, but being able to look Steve and Iris square in the eye in the morning mattered a whole lot, and there wasn't a damn thing he could about it. "I'm sorry. I just…there's something about your parents. Knowing they're right over there, maybe even watching us right now? I'm sorry, but I can't come in."

She pulled her head back and stared at him with patent disbelief. "You have *got* to be kidding me."

"I wish I was." He blew out a long, defeated breath. "I'm sorry. This is not like me."

She continued to stare at him for what felt like eternity. Then she closed her eyes, gritted her teeth, and shook her head. "I do *not* believe this. I finally decide to do whatever the hell I want, and what I want won't let me do him. Honest to God. It's like I'm cursed."

"It's not you, Violet, it's—"

"You?" She lifted a hand and curled her fingers into a fist and for a second Joe thought she might clock him. "Believe me, I know."

"I'd better go." Before he ended up with a black eye. Or worse. He gave her a swift kiss, then pushed her to arms' length, even though the separation was like peeling off a layer of his own skin. "I'll see you bright and early, for the timed-event slack. Sleep tight."

"Sure. Great. *Whatever.*" She shook off his hands

and yanked her door open. The trailer rocked as she stomped up the steps and slammed the door behind her. Joe plastered both hands over his face and rubbed hard. Geezus. What was *wrong* with him?

He jammed his hands in his pockets and strode around the stock pens, into the space behind the bucking chutes. Horses stirred, the orange security lights gleaming like reflected fire in their eyes. He hoisted himself onto the platform on the back of the chutes and let his legs dangle. Untethered. Like he felt. He dug his thumb and forefinger into his temples, which throbbed in time with the rest of his seriously annoyed body. A tiny square of light blinked on in Violet's trailer. The water pump kicked on, a low, gravelly hum. She would be washing her face, brushing her teeth, peeling off her shirt and jeans and pulling on…what?

He touched a finger to the scratch on his wrist. *Kiss it better.* His own crude joke turned on its head. He felt the brush of her lips and his heart did that thing again, like out on the dance floor, as if it were gasping for air. Or blood. Joe swore. Dirt Eater turned his head and blinked, annoyed at the disturbance.

"Sorry," Joe muttered.

The bull shook his head, long ears flapping, and slurped his tongue into one nostril, as if expressing his opinion.

The light in Violet's window went dark. *Snap!* The last, tiny link between them was broken, leaving Joe to float away, up and up into a sky that was nothing but a black void beyond the security lights. The sense of weightlessness was so strong he scooted back, away from the edge, until his spine was pressed against the solid steel bars of the bucking chute. He could go back, knock on her door and say he'd changed his mind. Except his damn mind was the whole problem. Since when did it mess with him like this? He dug the phone out of his pocket and checked the time. Ten after two. He punched a button, tipped his head back, and closed his eyes.

"This better be good," Wyatt snarled.

Joe heard a television in the background, the sound of gunfire and squealing tires. "Why are you awake?"

"Just popped a couple pain pills. I was watching Bruce Willis kill everyone while I waited for them to kick in."

Uh-oh. "New pain or old?"

"Both. Rowdy did another dead man's flop. I tripped over him and the bull stepped on my sore ankle."

Joe winced in sympathy. "Bad?"

"Swelled up some. I'll see the doc when I get back to Pendleton if it hasn't settled down."

Standard cowboy medical protocol. If it wasn't dangling or hemorrhaging, it would keep. "Think you'll be ready by the circuit finals?"

"I'd be ready tomorrow if I had to. And speaking of working together…"

"I haven't decided." Joe felt himself coming loose again, all the options in front of him, the conflicting needs warring inside of him. "You know George, the pickup man for Flying 5? What's his kid's name?"

"Peter," Wyatt said, following the change of subject without missing a beat.

Peter. Not Pete or Petey because, as he'd informed them solemnly, that wasn't his name. "You know how before he goes to bed, he makes his dad walk around with him to be sure all the horses are in their pens and the gates are locked? And how when you talk to him, he quotes his dad word for word, even does his voice? Cole Jacobs is just like that."

Wyatt was silent for a few beats. "Do they know?"

"Violet says he's always been different, but worse since the accident." Joe assumed Wyatt knew Cole's history. He knew everything else.

"If he doesn't have post-traumatic stress, I'd be amazed. Have you asked him about it?"

"Yeah, 'cuz I've always wanted to have my face smashed."

Wyatt made one of his thinking noises, taking his time about it. "You could toss some information at Cole on your way out the door—let him do with it what he will."

No heart-to-heart chat, just a magazine article, or some brochures. Joe could manage that much. "I assume you know just the thing. What's it gonna cost me?"

"What's it worth to you?"

More than he would have expected, and the price wouldn't be that hard to bear. Wyatt's contracts added up to more dollars than Joe could stand to leave on the table. "Three rodeos."

"Ten."

"No way. I'd be away from the ranch the whole season."

"Exactly." When Joe remained stubbornly silent, Wyatt let loose an aggravated sigh. "Okay, five, but I get to pick 'em."

A scary proposition, but there were no bad choices in that pile. "Deal."

"Even if I pick five rodeos within a day's drive of Amarillo?"

Joe stared at Violet's dark trailer, enduring the low, hard ache when he imagined being in there with her. Self-deprivation really, *really* was not like him. He might as well admit it—he was a mess, and would be until he settled things with Dick. But once he got his life settled and was steady on his feet, he'd be able to handle it—handle her and her family—without feeling like he was teetering on the edge of some unknown abyss, in danger of losing his balance. And then, if she'd let him, he could come back for a visit. Or two.

"I could live with that."

Wyatt let out an amazed whistle. "If I were still a praying man I'd praise the Lord, but I'm not, so I'll be damned instead. I intend to start making calls at daybreak, so don't bother trying to back out."

"Wouldn't think of it," Joe said, but the panic was already closing his throat as Wyatt hung up.

Five rodeos. Five more degrees of separation from Dick. How many before he couldn't go back? He sat for a good long while, until fatigue dragged his eyelids to half-mast. Once in his bed, though, sleep only taunted him, letting him doze off, then jolt awake as panic slammed into his chest. What had he done, promising those rodeos to Wyatt? Dick would come unglued when Joe gave him a list of dates he'd be unavailable. Dread washed over him, cold and dark as a winter lake.

He kicked at the thin blanket, the weight of it too much against his sweat-sheened skin. Then he thought about Violet and a whole different kind of panic grabbed him by the throat. If he told her he wanted to come back and see her after he left, she might expect…stuff. Things he wasn't capable of delivering.

His reconstructed knee started to ache from all the dancing and thrashing. Finally, as the eastern sky began to lighten, he broke down and popped a pain pill. Mixed with the exhaustion, it knocked him out cold.

Chapter 25

DANCE WITH THE DEVIL AND WHAT DO YOU GET? Shin splints. Violet hobbled of out the arena gate toward the rodeo office muttering silent curses. Every step was like a knife in her arches and shot fire up her legs, despite the fistful of ibuprofen she'd washed down with her half-gallon mug of coffee. And there'd been thousands of steps. Saturday night's performance might've been perfect, but Sunday morning slack was the equivalent of pushing a rope uphill through a patch of prickly pear cactus. No matter how she tried, Violet couldn't get the damn thing moving.

To top it off, her dad was sick. Her mother said it was something he ate and he'd be fine as soon as the medicine took hold. He just didn't dare get too far from the bathroom in the meantime, which left Violet to deal with the stock, the committee, the contestants, the judges, and Cole, and she was not in the mood. Her eyeballs felt like she'd fallen and scraped them on the sidewalk and her head throbbed, each beat of her heart a steel-tipped hammer blow to the inside of her skull.

Imagine how much worse it would've been if Joe had stayed.

Her face burned at the fresh slap of humiliation. The man had kissed her like she was water and he'd been crawling across the desert for a week, and he'd been as turned on as she was. Hard to hide that not-so-small detail when she was plastered up against him. Then *bam!* He pushed her off and walked away. What the *fuck?* Or not, as the case may be.

Violet repeated the curse out loud as she stumbled over a beer bottle tossed in the grass behind the bleachers. *Jerk slob littering assholes.* She'd like to smack them upside the head with their own trash, along with the moron who was supposed to be opening the chute for the timed events. By rule, the job was not supposed to change hands for the entire length of the rodeo, but this gate man had staggered in still drunk from the night before. She'd had a dozen ropers, five committee members, and three judges arguing about who would replace him.

Slack had started eventually—fifteen minutes late— then screeched to halt again when a hinge broke on the chute gate. A local welder was now attempting to repair the damage while agitated ropers paced and bitched about how they had to hurry up and get to the afternoon performance at another rodeo down the road. Well, they'd just have to hold their horses, literally and figuratively. She was doing the best she could, and now that the drunk had staggered away to sleep it off, she was doing it one man short.

And despite what he'd said about seeing her in the morning, Joe had yet to show his face. Figured. Just when she thought she could count on him, he left her wanting in every way possible. She hustled around the back of the stock pens and into the ramshackle rodeo office. Cole was there alone, rooting through a portable file box filled with Iris's paperwork.

"What are you doing?" Violet demanded, jerking the

box away from him. "Mom will have your hide if you mess those up."

Cole swiped a sleeve across his sweaty face. "One of the steers is coughing. Just dusty hay I think, but the judges want him pulled. They need the numbers for the extras to draw a replacement."

Great. Now the ropers would have something else to bitch about.

"Where's Mom?" Violet asked, flipping through the file box to find the folder with the morning's draw sheets.

"She ran over to check on your dad. And Beni's being a pain, too."

Of course. With a kid's perfect sense of timing, Beni had been impossible from the moment he popped out of bed. He wanted pancakes. No, waffles. No, French toast. With juice. Or maybe milk. Then he was full after three whole bites. Then he started whining about being bored. He was tired of this game. He wanted his other game, the one she couldn't find. He wanted to be home. He wanted his daddy. Violet would have gladly handed him over except *whoops!,* Delon was probably still handcuffed to a bed in Omaha if Stacy Lyn had had her way with him. Men. Not one of 'em Violet wouldn't trade for a good horse and a foot massage.

She found the team roping draw sheet and held it out to Cole. He lifted his hands, backing away. "You can take it down there."

"I need to go get Beni." And grab another handful of ibuprofen while she was at it.

Cole's face went stubborn. "I'm almost twenty minutes late graining the horses."

Lord knew she didn't dare suggest the horses could wait another ten minutes. Cole already looked like he might hyperventilate. "Get Hank to do it."

"He took off last night with some girl. Where's Joe?" Cole looked around like maybe Joe was hiding behind one of the dusty cobwebs in the corner of the office.

"Sleeping, I assume." Violet shoved the draw sheet at Cole. "It'll take you two minutes to drop this down at the roping chutes."

Cole shook his head. "They'll all start yakking at me and I hate that."

Violet stomped her foot in sheer frustration, then paid the price as pain shot clear to her hip. "Gawd! You are such a butthead."

But the words only bounced off Cole's retreating back.

Her mother hustled into the space he'd vacated, Beni in tow. "Did they get the roping chute fixed yet?"

"I'm going to check right now." She fluttered the piece of paper in her hand. "And take this draw sheet down there, while I'm at it."

"I want to stay in the trailer and play my big video game," Beni whined. "It's *boring* in here."

Violet scooped Beni up to prop him on her hip like when he was a toddler. Sheesh. He must've gained ten pounds in the last month. "How 'bout you help me take this draw sheet to the roping chutes, then we'll go get a snack. What sounds good?"

"Popcorn!"

At nine-thirty in the morning, when he hadn't finished his breakfast? Oh, what the hell? She'd be Mom of the Year some other day. "Can do."

She gave him a squeeze and a smacking kiss, then continued on her way, albeit more slowly. Packing the extra weight did nothing for the pain in her shins. Praise the Lord, though, the welder was dragging his equipment out of the arena and they were back in business. At this rate, they might get this slack run off before Joe got around to crawling out of bed.

She gave the draw sheet to the judges and watched to be sure the next few tie-down ropers got out of the box without the chute gate falling off. Then she gathered up Beni and swung by her trailer, where she popped a bag of microwave popcorn, grabbed a Coke—if she was gonna be the worst mom ever, might as well do it right—and deposited him back at the office while she went to see what else had gone to hell in her brief absence.

An eternity later, she trudged back to the office to get her kid, her stomach rumbling. Cowboys strolled past with horses trailing along behind, ropes slung over their saddle horns. Engines rumbled as the slack contestants rolled out and those slated for the afternoon performance began to trickle in. Violet had, at most, an hour to grab lunch and put her feet up before it all started over again.

She rounded the last corner to the office and there was Joe, sitting on a bench outside the rodeo office with… Beni? They were bent over Joe's phone and Beni was showing him something—either the latest version of Angry Birds or another of the porn sites he'd stumbled across despite every parental control she'd put in place on her phone. Lord only knew with Beni. Joe took the phone, poked at the screen a few times, typed something in, then handed it back.

Beni's face lit up. "Whoa. That is *awesome*."

Then Joe spotted her and sprang to his feet with a tentative smile. "It's educational, I swear."

He was wearing his cowboy hat, one of those threadbare chopped up T-shirts, wrinkled jeans, and running shoes, and looked as if his night had been even worse than hers. In other words, he was perfect.

Right there, right then, Violet's previously undented heart cracked wide open. She felt it, the same as when she broke her arm. She had that same instant to think, *Oh crap, this is gonna hurt*, and wonder if she could somehow eject from her own body before the pain blinded her. But it was too late. She'd fallen head over heels, and just like when that damn Shetland pony took a hard right and threw her into the fence, this was not going to end well.

Joe wasn't ever going to stay in Texas. Not for her. Not for the world. When his three rodeos were done, he'd hightail it straight back to Oregon and the only true love in his life—that damn High Lonesome Ranch. There was nothing Violet could do or say to stop him. She could only try to limit the damage.

Chapter 26

As soon as the announcer's voice woke Joe, he knew he was screwed. He'd promised to help Violet this morning, and one glance at the clock told him he'd slept through most of the slack. He dragged on the first clothes he found and bailed out of the truck. Violet was nowhere in sight, but Beni was slouched on a bench outside the rodeo office, looking like an abandoned puppy.

Joe hesitated. He was a total novice when it came to kids, and this one struck him as advanced-class material, but he couldn't just walk past without saying anything. "What's the problem, big guy?"

Beni rolled his eyes up to give Joe a sullen look. "Grandma's too busy to get me a snack."

Joe glanced into the office. Iris was tapping at the keys of her laptop, a cell phone stuck to her ear and a frown on her face.

"Where's your mom?" Joe asked, like he was only trying to be helpful and not desperate to see her.

"Sorting steers because the gate man is drunk."

Crap. That didn't sound good. Iris hung up the phone, muttering something under her breath that wasn't appropriate Sunday morning talk. Her eyes lit up when she spotted Joe.

"Could you watch Beni while I find Cole? Steve's got…well, he's not feeling so hot, and now next week's committee wants to add a rookie bareback riding event, and I can't give them an answer."

"Uh—"

"Thank you." She shut and locked the office door, hustling away before he had a chance to utter a complete word.

Joe looked at Beni. Beni looked back, equally skeptical about the arrangement. Then he heaved another sigh. "I'm still hungry."

Oh hell. He could at least buy the kid a snack. Come to think of it, he was starving, too. "We can grab something at the concession stand. What do you want?"

Beni perked up. "A Snickers."

"How 'bout a pancake?" Joe countered.

"I already had one of those." His eyes narrowed, wheels spinning in his head. The word conniving crossed Joe's mind, but geez, the kid was five. "Maybe some popcorn?"

Well, it wasn't candy, and it was made of corn, which made it a vegetable. That was good, right? They went to the nearest concession stand, got a bag of popcorn for Beni and a burger for Joe, and brought it back to the bench in front of the rodeo office. Beni munched happily. Joe swallowed his burger in three bites and fidgeted, impatient. If Iris would come back and cut him loose, he could at least help pen and sort the stock for the performance.

"Grandma said you and my mommy went on a date," Beni said.

Joe snapped to attention. Oh hell. What was he supposed to say? "Uh…yeah."

"And you stayed out real late. That's why Mommy's cranky today."

"I…guess?" Joe winced at the pathetic reply. Geezus. He really sucked at this.

Beni's eyebrows scrunched in accusation. "You better not've tried any funny business."

Joe made a sound halfway between a choke and a laugh. He was tempted to ask what a five-year-old knew about funny business, but he was afraid of the answer. And the follow-up questions. He met Beni's gaze, keeping his own steady and somber. "No funny business."

Beni did a classic Eastwood squint, a half-pint badass. Joe didn't flinch. *This*, he realized suddenly. This was the reason he'd had to walk away from Violet last night. So he could look her son in the eye this morning and not blink. Not lie. It was worth every aching, miserable minute since. For the first time in very long time, Joe felt…clean.

Or at least cleaner.

Beni gave him a half-nod, then slouched against the wall and shoveled in a fistful of popcorn. "Got anything good on your phone?" he mumbled through a full mouth.

"Huh?"

"Games and stuff. I get in trouble when I'm bored."

It sounded like a threat. Having seen Beni in action, Joe was prepared to take it seriously. He pulled out his phone and handed it over. "We can download something from the app store."

"Cool." In less time than it took Joe to pull up a number on speed dial, Beni found what he wanted and handed the phone back to Joe. *Zombies vs. Aliens.* "Your mom lets you play this?"

"She never said I couldn't."

Which was pretty much what Joe had told Violet after

asking her dad if they could date. *Nice try, kid.* Joe tried a different tack, opening a browser and pulling up a site Wyatt had found that showed all of the wind currents rippling and eddying across the United States. The effect was mesmerizing, and would hopefully distract Beni long enough for his grandmother to get back.

"Here. Check this out."

As Beni took the phone, Joe glanced up and saw Violet watching them. Hair straggled out of her ponytail, stuck to the sweat on her neck, and her face was flushed, a streak of dirt across one cheek and a smear of calf shit on one thigh. She stared at him as if he was holding Beni at gunpoint, then her expression went weird, sort of queasy, like she'd been punched in the stomach. Her gaze slid, fixed on Beni, and her eyes narrowed.

"Where did you get that?" She stalked over and snatched the nearly empty bag of popcorn out of Beni's hand.

"He gave it to me," Beni whined, like Joe had forced him to take it.

Joe froze like a jackrabbit caught out in the open desert. If he kept still enough, she might find another target.

Violet crushed the bag into a ball and slam-dunked it with enough force to rock the aluminum trash can. "Did I not say you couldn't have any more today? Are you trying to make yourself sick?"

Beni ducked his head and pushed out his bottom lip. "I was hungry."

"Because you didn't eat your breakfast, which is why I told you no more snacks until lunch."

"I'm sorry," Joe said. "I didn't know—"

Violet nailed him to the bench with a disgusted

glare. "That's why he hit you up. You're the only one
he could con."

Perfect. First he'd been a no-show for the slack, then
he'd been played by a preschooler.

Violet grabbed Beni's hand and hauled him off the
bench. "You're going to the trailer, mister." As she
dragged him away, she looked over her shoulder at Joe.
"And you…stay right there."

Any man who'd ever had a mother knew that tone
of voice. Joe stayed. Iris came back, her gaze falling on
the empty space beside him, then rising with a question.

"Violet took him to the camper," Joe said.

"Then the slack must be over. Thank God." She gave
him a weary smile and went on inside.

Contestants came and went, glancing curiously at
Joe, some lingering to chat with Iris. Hank wandered
back from wherever he'd spent the night and made himself comfortable, flirting with a couple of barrel racers
while they checked the time sheets from the slack. Cole
wandered in with his dog and they kicked back in the
corner to share a sandwich. When Violet reappeared,
Joe got up to meet her out of earshot of the crowd. She
led him around the back side of the building.

"Is Beni okay?" he asked.

"Fine, until all that popcorn starts coming out the
other end."

"Oh." Shit. Literally. Joe took off his hat, scooped his
fingers over his head, then frowned when there was no
hair to push out of his face. "Listen, Violet—"

She gave a quick, hard shake of her head. "Beni's a
pro. Everybody falls for his song and dance somewhere
along the line."

Joe rolled the brim of his hat in his hands, unease skittering up his spine at her stony face. Not just angry. Closed. Distant. "I should have been here to help this morning. I'm sorry. I slept right through my alarm."

"We hired you to fight bulls, not push roping calves."

"Well yeah, but I promised—"

She folded her arms tight across her chest, her gaze glued stubbornly to the ground between them. "We've managed to get by this long without you."

Joe slapped the hat back on his head, stung by the ice in her voice. "I'll just get out of your way, then."

"Wait." She reached out a hand to grab his arm, then snatched it away as if the touch burned her fingers. "We need to…talk." She swallowed. Twice. And still her voice was husky. "I can't do this, Joe."

His heart stuttered. "Do what?"

"This." She circled a hand in the air to indicate the two of them. "There's not enough of me to go around right now. I need to tend to business."

He stared at her, incredulous. "You're dumping me because I slept in?"

"No! I'm not…we weren't…" She bit her lip and averted her face. "You're leaving next week. I'm only cutting things a little short. It's just…it's better this way. Now if you'll excuse me, I need to go take care of my kid."

She turned on her heel and made a beeline for her trailer, those long strides sure and swift. No hesitation. No looking back. Joe could only stare after her, stunned to the verge of paralysis. The quiet clearing of a throat pulled him out of the stupor. Hank stood at the corner of the rodeo office and the look on his face said it all.

Humiliation rained down, deepening the chill settling into Joe's bones. "You heard?"

Hank nodded toward an old swamp cooler set in the wall of the building, right next to where Joe was standing. "Sound comes right through that thing."

Great. Once again, Violet had found a way to go public with her love life, but this time she wouldn't be the butt of the joke.

—◦◦◦—

No one was in any mood to howl and pound their chest that afternoon. Steve prowled the back of the chutes like a mountain lion with a bad tooth, taking swipes at anyone who moved too slow, and Violet was stone-faced and silent behind her sunglasses. Iris's smile was strained around the edges. Even Hank was subdued. All of them kept a safe distance from Joe, as if he'd sprouted a mysterious rash and it might be contagious. The crew was in such a rush to load up and get gone, he barely had time to grab his bag out of the truck before it hit the highway.

When Cole was finally satisfied that he hadn't left so much as a spare kernel of grain behind, Hank reached for the door to the front passenger seat of the pickup. One hard look from Joe had his hand dropping. "I'll, uh, ride in back."

For thirty minutes there was no sound in the cab except the voice of the weekly country music count-down host. Must take some powerful drugs to be that cheerful. Whatever it was, Joe needed some.

"Bull riding sucked today," Hank said, unable to stand the silence any longer.

Cole grunted. Joe nodded. No one had made the eight-second whistle. Even the reigning Texas Circuit champion had round-assed off a belly-kicking hopper. Good thing none of them had needed help, because Joe couldn't seem to focus, a beat late with every move. Worthless as tits on a bull.

"You okay, Joe?" Hank asked.

Except for feeling like he'd thrown himself on the ground and let Dirt Eater stomp on his guts? Yeah, he was fine and dandy. He nodded again.

Another mile passed, the hiss of the air conditioner and the thump-thump of tires over the ridges in the concrete road provided accompaniment to the number twenty-three song in the countdown, while Joe stared out the window at an endless stretch of parched grass and red dirt. He'd always loved big, empty spaces. Today the infinite stretch of prairie made him feel insignificant. Invisible. Like he could walk off into all that nothing and no one would notice until he failed to show up for the next rodeo.

"Violet was having a really bad day," Hank said. "She probably didn't mean it like she sounded. I bet if you bought her flowers or something—"

Joe cut him off with another hard stare.

Hank hunched his shoulders and looked out his own window. "You're still going home next weekend?"

"Yeah."

The last rodeo was only fifty miles northeast of the Dallas-Fort Worth airport. The performances were Friday night and Saturday night. No reason Joe shouldn't be on the first possible flight on Sunday morning. Hell, why wait until Sunday to make himself scarce? Violet had made it clear they didn't want or need his help, so why hang around the ranch all week?

"Too bad you couldn't stay a while," Hank said. "I bet if you did, you and Violet could—"

"Shut up, Hank," Cole said.

Joe smiled grimly. There really was a first time for everything. For once, Cole Jacobs had managed to say exactly the right thing.

Chapter 27

"CAN I GO NOW?" BENI ASKED, FOR THE NINETEENTH time.

Violet gave her son a *don't mess with me* look. "You're not leaving that chair until you eat every bite."

Beni scowled into his Monday morning cereal bowl, shoveled in the last three spoonfuls and mumbled through his full mouth, "*Now* can I go?"

"Is that how you ask?"

"Please?"

Since he'd managed to say it without an eye roll, she said, "Yes."

He launched out of the chair and through the door at his usual breakneck speed, yesterday's popcorn overdose already a distant memory. Must be nice. If Violet's attention span were that short, she might be able to forget that, with her usual, impeccable timing, she'd blown Joe off in front of half of the Jacobs crew and a sizable number of contestants. *Nice work, Violet.* Not that she'd changed her mind about ending their… whatever it was. She'd already let it go way too far. She had to save herself. But that expression on his face…

She'd put a another dent in his ego, that's all. And she shouldn't have implied that they didn't appreciate all the extra work he'd done. She owed him an apology and the sooner the better, so she could get on with patching up the gaping hole in her heart. She set the dishes in the sink, then headed outside. The sound of shrill giggles led her around to the backyard. Cole gave Beni a shove on the swing and sent him flying so high it made Violet's breath catch. They were both grinning like fools.

The empty parking space beside Cole's cabin drew her attention and she frowned. "Where's your pickup?"

"Joe took it for a couple of days."

She very nearly gasped again. "To go where?"

"Dunno. Said he wanted to tour around a little." Cole shrugged. "He said he'd be careful."

And he handed over the keys, just like that. Cole, who wouldn't even let Violet hook the thing up to the horse trailer for fear she'd scratch the bumper. "What… now you're best buddies?"

"He's good with the stock." Cole threw an accusing glance over his shoulder. "But apparently we don't need his help, so he took off."

Violet stared, stunned, as he gave Beni another one-handed shove that nearly launched him into orbit. Cole was *mad* at her. Because of Joe. What the freaking hell? Where was the family loyalty? Cole was supposed to defend her honor, especially against fly-by-night rodeo Romeos like Joe Cassidy.

Suddenly it was all just too damn much. Tears burned at the back of her eyes. She blinked them back and gave Cole a stern look. "I'm going to the office. Try to be a little bit careful. You break that kid, you're taking him to the emergency room. *And* paying the bill."

Joe didn't come back Monday night. Or Tuesday. The hours crept by, worry and uncertainty spiraling tighter and tighter until by Wednesday, Violet was strung so tight if she'd had a bow, she could've played her nerves like a fiddle. Where had he gone? Was he alone? Had he dialed one of those phone numbers women constantly forced on him? She couldn't get the vision of that red-head in the Corvette out of her head. Someone like that would be just his speed...

The whole ranch had gone into a stall, as if Joe had siphoned off all the energy when he left. Her dad was still recovering from the stomach virus that had laid him low over the weekend, Cole patrolled the far reaches of the ranch, checking and repairing fences, and Iris was helping Lily organize the annual fall church bazaar. Violet had gone through all of the good-quality video they had of Dirt Eater, chosen the five best, and sent them off to Vince Grant but got only an automated confirmation in return, with no indication of when he might actually look at it.

Which left Violet...nowhere. With nobody. Usually, when she was sick of her own company, she and Beni would make a date for pizza with Delon, but for the first time ever, she wasn't sure he'd want to see her. Or if she wanted to see him. Another situation she had to resolve, but not when her emotions were raw as fresh road rash. So she went to the office and ran the McCloud figures again. She checked and rechecked all her numbers, but she couldn't conjure up cash out of nowhere.

And despite what Joe thought, she couldn't force Cole to let Dirt Eater go. She doubted she could persuade anyone else in the family to agree, either, even though they wouldn't be losing his genetics. They'd been collecting and selling Dirt Eater's semen for the past two years—making a nice little profit and setting plenty aside for themselves for future use. Plus, they had five damn good bull calves out of him, including the one permanently dubbed Flight Risk thanks to Joe. But Dirt Eater would never buck as anything but a Jacobs Livestock bull.

She smoothed the folder closed, stuffed it in the bottom drawer of her desk, and slammed it shut. She had two hours to kill before the Wednesday afternoon practice session, and a house that had been sadly neglected. As long as she was in the mood to attack something, it might as well be dirt and clutter.

Starting with Beni's room. Earbuds in place and her favorite kick-ass playlist cranked, she pulled the bed away from the wall and grimaced into the void. Good Lord. Was that a hotdog? She shuddered, scooping up the petrified wiener and aiming the vacuum hose at the crumbled remains of the bun. Why the place wasn't crawling with roaches, she'd never know.

Delon's side of the room only needed vacuuming and dusting, as usual. He never left a mess. Only one of a hundred ways he made her life better. Too bad he couldn't make her life complete.

Once their bathroom was sparkling, she stowed her cleaning supplies and traded her T-shirt for a faded plaid button down with long sleeves, yanking her hair into a ponytail as she strode out her front door. But at the bottom of the steps, she slammed on the brakes, her heart smacking into her ribs at the sudden stop.

Joe was back. He sat in the rusty metal chair on the porch of the bunkhouse adjusting the straps on his knee brace, dressed in his usual practice gear. Same T-shirt with the whacked off sleeves. Same ugly yellow gym shorts. Same god-awful haircut that looked even worse with the pink bandana headband. Same beautiful body.

A hysterical giggle welled inside her and threatened to bubble out. Why this guy? Violet Jacobs, with her previously iron-clad heart and shiny new vow to just have some fun, falling for a man determined to haul ass for another state as soon as humanly possible. She was tempted to thrust a middle finger at the sky, voicing her opinion of whatever sadistic whim of fate had dropped Joe Cassidy smack dab in the middle of her life.

He didn't acknowledge her presence, even though she'd slammed her front door and thundered like a buffalo across her deck. Was he going to pretend she didn't exist? He tugged one last strap tight, then finally looked up to meet Violet's gaze, but with the shadow of the porch roof falling across his face, she couldn't read his expression.

"You're back," she blurted.

He stood, hitched his gear bag onto one shoulder and stepped out into the sunlight as he drawled, "Miss me, Violet?"

His smile was sharp as a razor, slicing into her heart. She was paralyzed by the brilliant arc of pain, unable to speak or move as he sauntered off toward the arena. Yeah, he was back all right. The old Joe. Arrogant. Mocking. Armed and willing to inflict damage. Forget silly gifts and that *come play with me* smile. They belonged to the other Joe. Her Joe. The one she'd chased away. Suddenly she understood what Wyatt had been trying to tell her, why he was willing to go to any lengths to pry Joe loose from the High Lonesome.

This Joe—the cold, sarcastic bastard—was exactly the man Dick Browning had made him.

And Violet, with her stupid, hurtful words, had resurrected him.

—⁂—

Two hours later, Violet jerked the saddle off her horse and slammed it onto a rack in the barn, her eyes so hot with unshed tears they felt like they'd been fried in lard. Her Joe. What a complete crock. That man was a figment of her imagination. The original Joe had been in fine form today, though. Laughing, bouncing around the arena, exchanging insults with Hank and tossing Violet the occasional smirk as if to say, *Hah! You think you actually hurt me?*

It was all a game to him. He hadn't even tried to pretend otherwise. Joe had told her flat-out he was just fooling around and she'd been dumb enough to fall for him anyway. *Stupid, stupid Violet.* She clenched her fists, squashing down the tears one more time before striding out of the barn, making for the refuge of her house.

She slammed through the door, both glad and sorry that Beni was with his dad. She could use the company and the distraction, but her boy saw way too much. Forget sobbing into her pillow anyway. Swollen eyes and a miserable, crying-binge headache never made anything better. She shucked her dusty clothes in favor of shorts and a tank top, and donned a pair of rubber gloves instead. Her refrigerator was past due for purging. Nicely symbolic. Wash that man right out of her veggie drawer.

She jolted at the shrill of her landline, banging her

head on the top shelf. Rubbing the knot, she crawled out of the bowels of the fridge to check the number on caller ID. Her mother.

"Could you run over and check the sprinklers at the other house?" Iris asked. "The automatic timer is giving me fits and I just started a batch of cinnamon rolls for breakfast."

"Sure." Anything to put distance between her and Joe and blow some fresh air through her addled brain.

The sun hung a scant few inches above the horizon, stretching the shadows into undulating fingers that caressed the landscape. The earlier breeze had died, the air settling cool as water in the hollows, heavy with the scent of mesquite. It streamed through the car window, playing over Violet's skin, and she pulled it deep into her lungs, letting the feel and the smell of it filter into her system like a narcotic, soothing her pain, leveling her emotions. This—the air, the sky, the land—was real. As long as she respected it, appreciated it, the land would always be here for her.

The quiet hiss of sprinklers greeted her when she stepped out of her car. The timer must have started on schedule. She strolled around the back of the house anyway. No reason to rush home to her empty house to imagine what Joe was doing next door. Except Joe wasn't in the bunkhouse. Joe had gone jogging…and made a pit stop. When she rounded the corner onto the patio his eyes went wary, his body tense, like a stray cat caught on the back step.

Violet forced a breath through the tangle of pain and need that clogged her throat. "I suppose my mother sent you."

His eyebrows furrowed. "How'd you know?"

"The Lord works in mysterious ways. Iris Jacobs does not."

He frowned, confused, as Violet settled into the second Adirondack chair, set at an angle so they weren't forced to look each other square in the eye, thank the Lord for small favors.

"Why would she do that?"

"Because I behaved badly and she's gonna make damn sure I have a chance to apologize." Violet folded her hands over her churning stomach and fixed her gaze on a brilliant cluster of red chrysanthemums. She could do this. She'd practiced all night, every night while Joe was gone. "I'm sorry I was so…abrupt. I'd had the morning from hell, but that's no excuse for making you think we don't appreciate everything you've done. Like Cole said, you're really good with the stock."

"Cole said that?"

Violet flicked the slightest of smiles his direction. "You should be flattered. The last time Cole complimented someone was around the same time he lent out his pickup. Meaning never."

Joe let that lay, either indifferent or struck dumb. They sat in silence, Violet staring so hard at the flowers she'd be seeing red for a week, but it was either that or look at Joe and she wasn't sure her heart could take an undiluted dose of bare, glistening skin and sleek muscle.

When he did speak, his voice was completely tone-less, the lack of any emotion almost worse than his sarcasm. "If I'm ever late again, just pound on my door and yell until I wake up."

"I'll keep that in mind." Not likely to be an issue,

with only one more rodeo before he left. The thought drove another nail in her heart. "Thanks for coming back for the practice session today. The more time you spend with Hank, the better he gets."

Joe let another few beats of silence pass. "I invited him to come up and work out with me and Wyatt while we're getting ready for the winter rodeos."

"Wow. I bet he's thrilled." Her voice was wooden, like the slivers jabbing into her heart. At least Hank got to see Joe again. "Are you going back to work for Dick Browning?"

Joe's mouth flattened into a hard line. "You don't toss fifteen years of hard work into the trash can because someone hurt your feelings."

What about your self-respect? Violet wanted to shout. *Your precious ego that was so quick to jump up and snap my head off?* "Is it really worth it?" she asked, fighting to keep the any hint of judgment out of her voice.

Joe lifted his chin and swept an arm in a wide arc. "What's all of this worth to you, Violet? How much would you tolerate to keep from leaving this ranch?"

Minimum? One badly broken heart. But it wasn't like he'd asked her to follow him anyway. "It's not that simple. Home is more than a piece of ground. This is where my family lives, and Beni's father. It's impossible to separate those things from how I feel about the ranch."

"Yeah, well, not everybody is lucky enough to be born into the place where they belong. Some of us have to make our own."

His eyes were so bleak, his face so grim, her heart ached in a whole different way. The High Lonesome might be Joe's dream, but it could so easily turn into a nightmare. Or worse, turn Joe into a man she couldn't even like, let alone admire, and that was unspeakably sad.

"I am sorry for embarrassing you," she said quietly. "I did warn you that I have a knack."

His chin came up, his jaw tightening. "In other words, you're sorry everybody heard, but not sorry you dumped me."

Was that hurt in his voice? Or just wishful thinking on her part? "You're leaving. And it's not like you were planning to jump my bones, since you've decided to be honorable or whatever."

"And if I won't put out, you're not interested?"

"I didn't say—" Then she caught the glint of humor in his eyes and stopped before she gave him more reason to mock her. "I had a really good time the other night. Thanks for the dancing. It's been a while."

"For me, too."

She believed him, which probably made her several more kinds of a fool. Joe scrubbed his hands over his face, quick and hard. When he raised his head the humor was gone, replaced by resignation and a hint of regret. Or maybe that was her imagination, too.

Violet shoved up and out of her chair, locking knees that wanted to wobble. She hadn't humiliated herself yet. No sense pushing her luck by staying any longer. Joe followed suit, trailing a couple steps behind as she circled the house and went out the front gate to her car. As she reached the door, he cleared his throat. She paused, looking back to find him standing beside the hood of the Cadillac, fingers dancing on the gleaming paint.

His eyes almost met hers, then dodged away. He cleared his throat again. "Wyatt talked me into doing more rodeos with him, so I'll probably be getting down this direction a few times next year. In case you wanted to…you know. Go dancing or something."

A sneaky burst of hope got past her guard, flaring so bright it nearly blinded her to what he was really asking. Not *Can I call you?* Not *I'd like to keep in touch.* Not, God help her wildest dreams, *I have to go home but I'll be back as soon as I can.*

Just *Hey, darlin', if I happen to be in the neighborhood in a few months…*

Her mouth was so dry the words came out as a whisper. "It's hard for me to get away with our rodeos and Beni and…everything."

Which was a really weak excuse, but it was all she had. As much as he could expect. He was the one dead set on going back to Oregon, to a place that didn't belong to him and a boss he couldn't trust, instead of considering that there were plenty of stock contractors bigger and better than Dick Browning who would love to have him, with ranches a whole lot closer to Earnest, Texas.

There was even a contractor *in* Earnest that could make room for him.

Violet ducked her head and squeezed her eyes shut. She couldn't start thinking that way or she would delude herself into saying *Yes, please, do stop by whenever the mood strikes you,* praying he might eventually decide the High Lonesome wasn't the only piece of ground in the world. Talk about emotional suicide. She was still figuring out how to survive watching Joe leave her once. It wouldn't get easier with practice.

"I'm sorry," she said again.

He nodded, head bowed, eyes fixed on his dancing fingers. "Thought it was worth asking."

For a few excruciating moments they were stuck, neither knowing how to leave. Then Joe lifted his head and stepped back from the car. The smile he gave her as he turned away was a twisted shadow of the real thing. She stared numbly as he set off down the driveway, the sense of déjà vu so intense it curled her toes. Every time she turned around, she was watching Joe Cassidy run away from her. But today…

She squinted, frowning. Something was different. Joe's strides were as long and graceful as ever, eating up the distance to the gate. Not a hitch or a glitch that she could tell. Then it hit her: the bounce was gone.

For the first time since she'd known him, Joe moved like he was carrying the full weight of the world.

Chapter 28

IT WAS GONNA GET UGLY BEFORE THE NIGHT WAS over. Forty-five minutes before the scheduled start of the Saturday night performance, Joe sat in the front of the truck he was once again using as a bedroom and watched a line of churning black clouds bear down on the rodeo grounds.

As an Oregon boy, he had no idea what a tornado cloud looked like, but Cole had shrugged off his concern. "The energy patterns in this system are not conducive to the development of severe weather or tornados," he said, a perfect, monotone imitation of the guy on the weather alert radio station. "But I will continue to monitor conditions closely."

There went Joe's last hope for getting plucked off the face of the earth and away from his hammering thoughts. He'd intended to drown them when he left the ranch on Monday, but he didn't even finish the first beer at a bar in Amarillo before the presence of other human beings drove him back out into the sunlight. He'd blown a few bucks on cheap camping gear, spent a whole day hiking the Palo Duro Canyon, and slept in a tent deep in its heart, but he still felt Violet's absence clear down to his bones. No matter how far or how fast he hiked, he couldn't leave the ache behind.

The second day, he drove around until he found the back road to Hank's ranch. He left Cole's pickup in the same spot Violet had parked the night of their date, followed the ancient trail clear down to the river bottom, and wandered for miles through the river breaks. At dusk, he made his way back to pitch his tent in the place she called the Notch. Fuck it. If he insisted on torturing himself with memories of how good she felt and smelled and tasted, he might as well do it right.

He had come away determined to at least salvage some pride. He'd show them all he didn't give a damn. Everyone knew he wasn't built for her kind of life. Home. Kids. Neck deep in family. She'd done them both a favor by saying no when he asked to see her again. At least he'd made sure she knew Wyatt was in charge of his schedule. Couldn't have her thinking she was the reason Joe had suddenly developed a fondness for the Lone Star state.

He stared at the boiling clouds, hands clenched on the truck's steering wheel. Within forty-eight hours, he would be in Oregon. The time for avoidance was long gone. He took a long, steadying breath, then picked up his phone and pushed the Send button. As he waited for it to ring, the breeze freshened, whistling around the truck cab.

On the other end of the line, the receiver was snatched out of the cradle with a clatter. "Browning," the voice growled.

"Dick. It's Joe."

There was a beat of silence, then, "You home?"

"No. Flying back tomorrow." Joe fought the urge to clear his throat. That would be a sign of weakness. "We need to talk about next year's schedule."

Another couple of beats. Then, "Come out for lunch Tuesday."

"Okay. See you then." Joe clicked off, petty enough to be sure he hung up first.

Then he stared out the window, his gut tumbling and churning like the clouds. He'd expected to feel better once he talked to Dick. Now he wondered why. Had he expected an apology? A speech about how much they'd missed him and thank God he was coming back? Not unless the old bastard had had a lobotomy since he left. Or a heart transplant.

Joe tossed his phone into the sleeper and hopped down out of the truck. Tonight there was a rodeo to put on. A few blessed hours when he wouldn't have time to brood. A violent gust scooped up fistfuls of dirt and flung it at him. He ducked his head to avoid a face full of grit and bowled into Violet as she strode out from between two parked pickups.

"Sorry." He tried not to care that she immediately put space between them.

"Gonna be messy," she said as they moved on down the road, parallel but not together. She shot a quick glance at Joe's hooded sweatshirt. "Mom's got extra slickers in the office if you need one."

"I do. Thanks."

And that was it. Nothing more to say. Hadn't been since that excruciating moment when he'd scraped up every ounce of his guts and laid them out there, asked if he could see her again, and she'd turned him down flat. Her quiet rejection had sliced deeper than the public humiliation. She wasn't tired or cranky or frustrated beyond measure and lashing out at the first available target. In the hushed solitude of the empty homestead, there had been only him, and even though he'd seen the regret in her eyes, Violet was smart enough to recognize a bad investment.

They hadn't really spoken again except for a few awkward moments on Thursday morning when Violet brought him a bulky envelope from Wyatt. Joe had started to rip it open, then remembered it wasn't anything he wanted Violet to see. He'd stood there holding it, looking guilty as hell. She probably assumed the DVD was porn instead of a copy of the movie *Temple Grandin*, the goddess of livestock handling—who was also autistic and, in some ways, very much like Cole. Before he left, he'd find time to slip that package into Cole's pickup—where it wouldn't be found until Joe was long gone.

The first fat drops of rain smacked him in the face as they rounded the corner of the office and jogged up the steps. Violet slammed on the brakes and Joe had to grab an arm to keep from knocking her flat. She stumbled, caught her balance, and pulled free. When she stepped aside, Joe saw Delon kicked back in a folding chair, arms crossed, feet propped on the table. Black hat, black shirt with white sponsor logos stitched down the arms and over the breast pocket, sleeves rolled to the elbow, looking like he'd stepped straight out of one of the ads he did for a Western wear company—which, no doubt, ended up taped inside high school girls' lockers.

"When did you take over as the secretary?" Violet asked, easing farther away from Joe.

"The judges are having trouble with the electronic timer for the barrel racing. I'm holding down the fort while your mom helps them set it up."

Despite his posture, Delon didn't look the least bit

relaxed. He didn't look at Joe at all. Another gust of wind shook the building, peppering the windows with gravel.

"Where's Beni?" Violet asked.

"With my dad, over in your mom's trailer."

More drops splatted against the windows like miniature water balloons. Violet grabbed a yellow rain slicker from the pile in the corner and shrugged into the stiff, rubberized canvas. The long tails hung past her knees, split in the back for riding. She scraped up pieces of hair the wind had pried loose and jammed them back in her ponytail, then pulled a beat-up straw hat down tight. Her mud hat. Joe wished he had his along. If the rain kept up through the bull riding, his good one would be ruined, and he refused to wear a plastic rain cover that looked like an old lady's shower cap.

Violet started for the door, the slicker swishing around her legs as the rain thickened to a steady rumble on the tin roof. "I have to go saddle up."

She spoke to the air somewhere between Joe and Delon, not looking at either of them. A week earlier, Joe would have offered to help her. Now he just nodded.

"I drew Pepper Belly," Delon said. "How does she buck in the mud?"

"Not worth a crap."

Violet dove out into the storm, leaving Joe and Delon alone. Great. As if to punctuate his discomfort, the sky opened up, and a solid sheet of water poured down. Joe would be tossing his leather cleats in the trash after this one. He dug a slicker out of the pile and pulled it on, his nostrils twitching at its musty scent. Delon stared down at his hands, thumb tracing the ridge of calluses at the base of the fingers of his riding hand, built up from years of being wedged into a bareback rigging. A muscle worked in his jaw like there were a whole lot of words jammed in his craw that he was trying not to say.

Join the club, buddy.

Best if Joe got the hell out of there before either one of them popped off. He got one foot out the door before his temper got the better of his good sense. He spun around to face Delon. "What exactly is your problem with me?"

Delon's black eyebrows drew into a sharp vee. "Who says I have one?"

"Anyone with a pair of eyeballs." Joe shoved his hands into the pockets of the raincoat and found a couple of stray coins and what felt like a dirt-crusted Lifesaver, gifts from the previous owner. "Whatever. It doesn't matter. I'm out of here tomorrow, so you can move back into the spare room and keep your pieces of ass on the side. Sweet deal all around…except maybe for Violet."

Delon's feet dropped to the floor with a thud, every overdeveloped muscle in his body clenching. Anybody else might have come across the table. Delon only stared Joe down. "You think you're what she needs? What Beni needs?"

Scorn dripped from the words and stung like acid. The truth always did, and everybody in the room knew Joe Cassidy was the last guy any woman needed in her life full time, let alone a mother or her son.

Iris scurried in, shaking off the rain like a chubby cocker spaniel, her gaze flicking from Joe to Delon. "Well, this is going to be fun," she said, her smile a touch too bright.

"Good times," Joe agreed, and splashed down the

steps and into an ankle-deep puddle, the water oozing through the seams in his boots and soaking his jeans nearly to the knees. He cursed, then plowed straight through the next puddle on purpose. One way or the other, he was gonna be soaked before the night was done. A couple of hours and it would be over.

All of it. When the rodeo was over, he'd pack up his gear, hunker down alone in the semi, and first thing tomorrow morning he'd be on his way to DFW Airport with Cole. By afternoon, he'd be setting foot on Oregon soil—the moment he'd been dreaming of since his flight took off from Sea-Tac.

So why did he feel more like punching something than dancing in the rain?

Chapter 29

As Violet hauled Delon off Pepper Belly, she felt Cadillac's hind feet skid. The rain had turned the arena into a mud-pocked lake, but there was plenty of sand mixed with the native clay, leaving only a few treacherous spots along the fences. Instead of dropping to the ground, Delon slung a leg over Cadillac's rump and let Violet carry him back to the bucking chute.

"As you know, folks, half of the cowboy's score is for how well he spurs the horse," the announcer explained. "The other half is how hard the horse bucks, and since Pepper Belly didn't hold up her end of the deal, he'll have the option for a re-ride."

Delon grimaced, knocking water from the brim of his hat, but nodded at the judges. Violet had a limited amount of sympathy. Between the stiff protective vest and his chaps, only the sleeves of his shirt and the butt of his jeans were wet. Unlike Violet. Despite her slicker, her back was soaked from the rain that trickled off the brim of her hat and inside her collar. She could feel specks of it on her cheeks and taste the grit between her teeth. Her boots, chaps, and calves were caked with the stuff, splattered from under Cadillac's hooves as they chased bucking horses that kicked more mud in their faces.

"What's in the re-ride pen?" Delon asked.

"Blue Duck."

Delon eyed the arena, churned into a foot of slop in front of the chutes. "Is he gonna fire in this mess?"

"Why do you think we call him Duck?"

As Delon grabbed the top rail of the chute and hauled himself over without touching the soupy mud, Violet looked west. A streak of light glowed along the horizon, the lowering sun peeking under the back edge of the storm.

"We'll hold you until the bull riding. The rain will be done by then."

As she predicted, the rain stopped midway through the rodeo. The fans who'd stuck it out huddled in clusters under the cover of the grandstand. They cheered mightily when, after being introduced, Joe tiptoed three steps into the arena, then jumped as high as he could and splashed down into a huge puddle.

"Might as well get it over with," he told Hank, who followed suit, grinning like a baboon.

"We're bucking Delon's re-ride first," Violet reminded them.

They both backed off to lean on the fence to the side of the first chute. Violet joined Cole in the middle of the arena. The rain had washed every particle of dust from the air, leaving nothing to dull the edges of the scene playing out under the lights. The hollow clank of bells as the bull riders tied ropes onto their bulls. The steel-gray gleam of Blue Duck's rump, shifting as Delon settled down on his back. The glitter of the horse's eye from beneath a tangle of jet-black mane when he shoved his nose up and over the top rail of the chute. The smell of mud, wet horse, and musty rubber slicker.

The metallic bang of the latch as Delon nodded and

the gate swung wide. Blue Duck didn't tiptoe through the mud—he blasted, grunting as fountains of water sprayed from beneath his hooves. Delon was the eye of the storm, steady and calm, heels snapping into the horse's neck an instant before hooves met mud, chaps flashing under the lights. Just as the eight-second whistle blew, they reached the fence. Blue Duck threw on the brakes, intending to roll back on his hocks, but he hit one of the slick spots. His rear hooves skidded, momentum carrying his butt up under his shoulders until he was vertical.

For an instant he hung there, at the edge of his balance. Violet gasped along with the crowd, sure the horse would fall straight over backward, onto Delon. Blue Duck twisted midair and flopped onto his side. When the horse scrambled to his feet, Delon was still aboard, but cocked off to the left, both hands clamped around the handle of the rigging. Blue Duck bolted, Cole in close pursuit and Violet only a few strides behind. Delon's rigging slipped, dropping him even farther onto the horse's side, his head dangerously exposed to the rapidly approaching posts.

Violet had to keep Blue Duck off the fence. She kicked hard, driving Cadillac into the rapidly closing gap as Cole stood out in his left stirrup, grabbing for Delon's arm but missing. Cadillac plowed through the mud, his nose coming even with the roan's flank. Almost there…

Delon's hand popped out of the rigging and he fell—directly into her path. She had no time to react. Cadillac's forelegs slammed into Delon's body, drove him into the mud, pummeled by steel-shod hooves packing the force of a thousand pounds of horseflesh. Violet heard the shrieks from the fans as Cadillac stumbled, slipped, and fell, vaulting her over the front of the saddle. The side of her head hit first, then her shoulder. She braced for the impact of Cadillac's massive body rolling over her, but it didn't come. She'd been thrown clear.

She lay where she'd fallen, stunned. *Wow. Stars.* She stayed perfectly still, waiting for them to clear, trying to assess how much damage had been done.

Hands cupped her face, urgent but careful. "Violet? Can you hear me?"

She opened her eyes. Joe's face wobbled, wavered, then came into focus, only inches from hers. She pulled in a careful breath. Wiggled her fingers. Then her toes. "I'm okay."

"You're sure? You went down pretty hard."

"Yeah, but the landing strip is really squishy."

Joe laughed, but it was shaky, and either her vision was still wobbly or his fingers were trembling when he scraped mud from her cheek and held it up for her inspection. "And a free facial to boot."

Cole splattered up behind Joe and vaulted off his horse, eyes glittering, jaw clenched. "Anything broken?"

Violet shook her head and her vision blurred, then cleared.

Cole fisted his reins in his hand, glaring at her. "What the hell were you trying to do?"

Joe was on his feet and in Cole's face before Violet could open her mouth. He planted a hand in the middle of Cole's chest and shoved. "Back off, asshole."

Cole lifted a hand to return the shove but they were interrupted by the arrival of the emergency medical technicians, slogging through mud. The tall, lanky one started to peel off and head their direction, but Cole cut him off, grabbing the largest of the bags he was lugging. Violet shoved into a seated position and winced at the twinge in her neck. Delon was on his hands and one knee, a cluster of cowboys hunched around him. His left leg was extended, as if too painful to bend.

Shit. Shit. Shit. Please don't let it be serious. Not now. Not when he was so close to a world title he could see his reflection in the gold buckle. Joe crouched beside Violet again. She let him wipe mud from her neck and shirt as she watched the EMTs quiz Delon, poking and prodding, heads bent low to hear his answers to their questions. Finally they hooked their hands under Delon's armpits and eased him to his feet. He didn't put any weight on the left leg.

They took one tentative step. Then another. On the third, Delon's uninjured knee buckled. He clamped his arm across his ribs, face contorted, the noise he made part groan, part gurgle. Fear shot ice into Violet's veins when he folded, crumpling like a broken puppet. The techs lowered him to the ground and knelt over him, movements urgent, faces grim. As they worked, a single, plaintive voice echoed across the hushed arena.

"Daddeeee!"

Chapter 30

THEY BURST THROUGH THE EMERGENCY ROOM DOORS, Violet carrying a tear-soaked Beni with Delon's dad on her heels. Merle Sanchez erupted, a frantic jumble of words about mud and horses and passing out and where the hell was Delon. The prune-faced nurse at the reception desk grimaced at the mud they tracked in and began rattling off the usual bullshit about patient privacy.

"I want to see my daddy," Beni whined, cutting through the din.

The nurse eyed him with slightly less indifference. "Is he the one who got hurt at the rodeo?"

Beni swiped at his nose with his shirt sleeve as he nodded. "Mommy ran him over with Cadillac."

"I didn't do it on purpose, Beni!" Violet protested. "He fell right in front of me."

The nurse took a step back, one hand reaching for the phone as if she might call for backup. What the hell? Did she think Violet had run him down with her car?

Delon's dad went halfway over the counter and into the woman's face. "I want to know how my son is *right now*."

"I'll check." The nurse gave them all a scathing once-over and escaped into the bowels of the emergency room.

Beni whimpered against Violet's neck. "Is Daddy okay?"

"He will be, sugar," Violet said, her throat closing behind the words. *Please, God, let him be okay.* Terror coiled around her heart and squeezed it dry. She'd seen them through the open ambulance door, yanking Delon's vest and shirt open to expose his chest, shoving a tube down his throat, pumping air into him with a big rubber-ball gizmo. Footsteps squeaked on tile and the EMTs appeared, their uniforms caked with mud.

Merle pounced. "What is wrong with him?"

They exchanged a glance, as if uncertain whether they were allowed to tell.

"I'm his father, dammit. Tell me." The final two words were hissed between bared teeth.

"Traumatic pneumothorax," the shorter one said.

At Merle's impatient curse, the second tech hurried to add, "He broke a couple of ribs and one of them punctured his lung. We intubated him immediately, and he's stable. He never even lost consciousness."

Relief washed through Violet like a riptide, sweeping her almost off her feet. She plunked Beni down and grabbed onto the edge of the desk as the room did a slow spin.

"Hey," the tall, skinny EMT said. "You don't look so good. Did you get hurt out there?"

Violet tried to shake her head, but the movement shot an arrow of pain from her left shoulder blade to the base of her skull. Maybe her landing hadn't been as soft as she thought. The tech took her arm and eased her back a couple of steps, to the nearest chair. Her butt hit the seat with an audible smack.

"Just a little shaky."

Heat and pressure built behind her eyes. Dammit.

She couldn't let Beni see her cry. The radio on the EMTs belt beeped, followed by a stream of dispatcher lingo. The shorter man answered, while the skinny one frowned at Violet.

"We've got another call. Are you sure you're okay?"

"Yes."

He stood, reluctant, but his partner was already moving toward the door. "If you start feeling worse…"

"I'm in the right place."

He gave her one last, worried look, then trotted after his partner as the nurse came bustling back. She avoided Violet's gaze, addressing Merle as she repeated what the EMTs had said and added, "The doctor said you can come back while they're waiting for the radiologist on call to get here and do a CAT scan."

"CAT scan?" Merle echoed, alarmed.

"Just a precaution. So if you'll follow me…"

Merle caught an arm as Beni tried to dash past. "Slow down, pardner."

The nurse finally looked at Violet, eyes narrowed and suspicious, as if convinced she had a severe case of spousal abuse on her hands. "You're his wife?"

"Um, no."

"Significant other?"

"No. I'm his…we're…"

"Violet is Beni's mother," Merle said.

"Beni isn't the one in my ER," the nurse said, her jaw squaring.

"That's ridiculous," Merle protested. "Violet is family."

"Our privacy policy states—"

"It's okay," Violet said. And meant it, because a pair of vise grips had clamped tight on her left trapezius muscle and now that she was down, she wasn't sure she could get up again. "I'll wait here."

Delon's dad started to argue, but Beni tugged on his hand. "Come *on*, Grandpa."

He gave Violet a helpless look. She waved them away and paid the price with another stab of pain. When they were gone she let out a long, shaky sigh, closed her eyes and let the tears brim over, hot and silent, sliding down her cheeks and dripping off her chin. She was too weak with relief and pain to wipe them away. Her baby wasn't going to lose his father. Not tonight. *Thank you, God.*

She couldn't have said how much time passed before she heard the whoosh and slide of the emergency room doors. She'd expected her parents at any minute. Some of Delon's friends, if there were any who hadn't left after the bareback riding ended. She hadn't expected Joe.

"Why are you out here alone?" he demanded.

"I'm not a relative." Another shiver rocked her body and her face screwed up in pain. "Ouch."

Joe started to reach for her, then froze with his hand hovering above her shoulder. "Where?"

"My neck. Muscle spasm. Why are you here? Where is everyone else?"

"Your dad and Cole are putting up the stock and your mother had to finish the payout. She sent me to be sure a doctor took a look at you." He scanned the empty front desk. "Where is the receptionist?"

"Probably calling the cops to come haul me away."

He blinked, opened his mouth, then shut it again. "Wait here."

"Like anything short of a forklift is getting me up," she muttered.

He pounded the buzzer on the desk. The nurse scurried out from a door down the hall, scowl firmly in place. She took one look at Joe's cowboy hat and declared, "Unless you're a family member, I can't tell you anything."

"I don't give a shit about him," Joe said. "You've got a woman sitting in your waiting room with a possible cervical spine injury. Somebody better get their ass out here before I pitch a fit they'll hear clear down in Dallas."

The nurse bolted like he'd hit her with a cattle prod, apologizing all over herself while she dragged a rumpled physician's assistant from somewhere in the back. Violet tried to protest that she was fine, but Joe refused to let anyone listen. He took one arm, the physician's assistant took the other, and they hauled her upright. She hissed in pain and called Joe a very bad name.

He patted her butt. "You've probably got that right, but you're still having X-rays."

While they loaded her on a gurney and carted her off to the radiology department, Joe planted himself on a rolling stool in her assigned cubicle to call Iris with a preliminary report. When the X-rays were done, a younger, friendlier nurse wheeled Violet into the cubicle and helped her perch on the end of the treatment table. She was still wearing her damp jeans but they'd made her swap her shirt for a thin hospital gown.

"Waste of damn money. I'd know if I broke anything." She tucked her arms across her ribs and shivered. "Least they could do is use my hundred bucks to turn on the heat in this place."

"Here." Joe shrugged out of his jacket and held it

while she eased her arms into the sleeves. Then he buttoned it clear to her chin and flicked mud off her ear with one forefinger. "Better?"

"Yeah. Thanks."

He cupped her shoulders and held on for a moment, as if assuring himself she was in one piece. She slid her hands into the pockets of the letterman-style jacket, feeling like a high school girl wearing her boyfriend's coat. Her gaze dropped to the sponsor logo plastered across the chest of the mud-speckled jersey that Joe hadn't bothered to change.

"Did you, um, talk to anyone while I was getting x-rayed?"

"About Delon? Yes. There's no sign of internal injuries other than the punctured lung. They'll have to keep him here for two or three days." Of course the nurses would talk to Joe. So much for their stupid privacy policy. He hesitated, then added, "They also think the ACL is torn in his knee."

Violet squeezed her eyes shut and cursed. A torn anterior cruciate ligament meant surgery and a whole lot longer recuperation than the twelve weeks between now and the National Finals Rodeo.

"He could still ride," Joe said. "Wyatt tore his up at Omaha three years ago and fought bulls at the NFR."

"He only made it through four rounds."

Joe could try to argue that Delon just had to ride one horse a night, not fight fifteen bulls, but they weren't ordinary horses and it wasn't an ordinary rodeo. To win the world, you had to make ten damn good rides on the rankest bucking horses in North America. Even if they started out healthy, by midpoint of the NFR the bareback riders looked like victims of drive-by beatings. Violet pressed her mouth into a tight line, fighting to keep everything bottled up.

Joe gripped her chin, staring intently into her eyes. "This was not your fault."

She tried to avoid his gaze, but he leaned in until their noses were nearly touching. "Listen to me, Violet. *Not. Your. Fault.*"

"I should have—"

"What?" he interrupted. "Sat back and waited to see if Cole got ahold of him before his skull bounced off a fence post? Bullshit. You had to make a move. And this is Delon. No one would expect him to lose his grip. You did what any good pickup man would've done under the circumstances."

Emotions churned in her gut—guilt, uncertainty, and a healthy dose of leftover terror. The whole scene played over and over in her head, a jumble of images and sounds muddled by the throbbing in her neck that radiated through her skull.

Joe skimmed his thumb gently along her jaw. "We can only do our best, Violet. We can't save 'em all."

She examined his face, searching for any sign that he was patronizing her, then let out a weary sigh. "That sucks."

"Believe me, I know."

Behind them, the physician's assistant cleared his throat. Joe gave Violet's shoulder one last careful squeeze, then backed away.

"The X-rays are clear and your reflexes are normal, no sign of nerve damage. Looks like a muscle strain." The PA held up syringe. "I recommend a shot of Toradol for your immediate pain, and a prescription muscle relaxant and a cervical collar for the next couple of days."

Violet set her jaw. "I am not walking around looking like a crash test dummy. Beni's had enough of a fright."

"It's for your own comfort. You can try heat and ice but—"

"We know the routine," Joe said.

The PA shrugged and waved the syringe. "Unbutton your jeans. This goes in your gluteus."

She scowled at Joe. "You can leave now."

"Do I have to?"

She snarled. Joe grinned, but left. As the PA swabbed her butt with alcohol, it occurred to Violet that the good Joe, 'her' Joe, was back in full force.

God, she'd missed him.

—✺—

When Joe stepped into the hall, the curtain to Delon's cubicle twitched open, held by Merle Sanchez. Delon's dad was ginger-haired, wiry, and looked like his last name should be O'Malley. He cut his eyes toward where Violet was telling the PA she wouldn't take the muscle relaxants because they made her dizzy. Obviously she'd never had Toradol or she wouldn't be dropping her drawers.

"Is Violet all right?" Delon's dad asked.

"Yeah. Just a stiff neck and a hard head."

Delon, on the other hand, looked like hell, pasty and gray. A tube snaked from under his hospital gown, attached to a suction pump that hissed and slurped. His leg was propped on a foam wedge with the knee packed in ice. Beni had crawled up onto the bed and was tucked under his daddy's arm, curled against his uninjured side. Joe pitied the nurse that tried to move him.

Delon's gaze met Joe's, the antagonism muted by shock and pain. "What was I?" he whispered hoarsely.

"Eighty-three points. You won it by two."

Delon smiled faintly. "Damn. If I'd only stuck the dismount."

Violet's parents blew around the corner and into her cubicle, dragging Joe with them. Iris plucked the prescription from the doctor's fingers and handed it to Joe.

"Take care of that." Then she threw her arms around Violet and hugged her hard enough to make her whimper. "Scared the hell out of me, girl."

"I'm fine. Honest."

"Yeah, I can see that," her mother said dryly.

The nurse had made an effort to clean her up, but Violet's hair was tangled and streaked with the mud that smudged her cheek and neck and caked her jeans. She held herself stiff, her body language screaming *Ouch*.

"She *will* be fine," Joe corrected.

How, he didn't know. His muscles still felt wobbly as overstretched rubber from the sheer terror of seeing her slam to the ground only inches from the fence, her horse so nearly rolling over her. Behind Iris, Steve hovered like a massive thundercloud, his face mirroring Joe's mixture of relief and horror at what had almost happened.

"I need to get Beni." Violet stood, swaying, either from shock or the drugs.

Joe put out a hand to steady her. "He's asleep."

"He can stay with us tonight," Iris said. "Joe will drive you back."

Steve shot her a look but didn't argue. Joe looked from one to the other, baffled. They were trusting him to look after Violet? So soon after she'd almost…come so close to…

A molecular-level shudder wracked his body.

Violet's forehead creased as if she wanted to protest, but her eyes were coming unfocused. "Dammit. Why didn't they tell me that stuff had a kick like a mule?"

"Because you wouldn't have let them give it to you." Iris prodded Steve toward Delon's cubicle, calling back over her shoulder, "Take care of her, Joe. We'll see you in the morning."

Violet took two quick steps, hissed, and swayed. Joe grabbed her arm. "Easy there, darlin'."

"I just need to see—"

Joe pivoted her toward the waiting room. "Tomorrow. You can come back first thing."

"But I have to—"

"In the morning."

He braced a hand on either side of her hips and pushed her down the hall like a balky wheelbarrow. Halfway to the exit, they met the sour-faced nurse. She gave them a curt nod and the evil eye as she passed. Violet stopped, spun around, and tilted back on her heels so far Joe had to throw both arms around her waist.

"Cadillac is a *horse*!" she yelled over his shoulder at the nurse.

The woman's stride hitched, then she scurried into a door marked *Staff*. Violet teetered again, so Joe forgot about explanations and wrestled her around to face the door.

"We'd better get you out of here."

And into bed. That oughta be fun.

The parking lot outside the emergency room had a wicked tilt to it. Or maybe that was Violet, because when Joe wrapped his arm around her shoulders and tipped her to the left, the ground flattened out.

"You're a mess."

She wanted to smack him for laughing at her, but she needed all her concentration to climb into the pickup without braining herself on the door frame.

Joe buckled her seat belt and shut the door. When he climbed behind the wheel, he asked, "Are you hungry?"

"Nope."

"Do you mind if I swing through a hamburger stand on the way?"

"Nope."

He cranked the engine and she hunkered into her seat, letting her eyelids droop so the lights along the main drag zoomed past in streaks like when a movie spaceship jumps into hyperspeed. She was stoned. More stoned than she'd ever been in her life, including the day she gave birth and the night her son was conceived. And the second one didn't count because she was drunk, not stoned, and they were totally different. Weren't they? Except in that Johnny Cash song about Sunday morning, but she was kinda young and naïve back then, so maybe she just thought he was stoned on beer.

Anyway, this was nothing like being drunk. More like floating. *Really* high. She could still feel the pain in her neck—the real pain, not Joe, who was annoying her with the bossing and pushing and all—but neither pain bothered her if she didn't move too fast. Joe didn't ask if she wanted her prescription filled, just pulled into an all-night pharmacy and left her in the pickup while he jogged inside. Just for that, she ate most of his French fries while she waited.

When he parked at the rodeo grounds, she slid out of the pickup only to discover her leg muscles had gone on strike. Joe caught her, propped her up, and steered her in the direction of her trailer. Violet yelped when something popped out from under the fender and went straight for her knee. Katie jammed her head under Violet's hand, stubby tail doing double time. Joe scratched the dog's ears while Violet turned her head one careful degree at a time. Where Katie went…

Cole unfolded from one of the lawn chairs in the black void under the awning. He looked at Violet, frowned, then looked at Joe. "What's wrong with her?"

"She's got whiplash and she's zonked to the eyeballs on pain meds."

"And they left her with you?"

Joe made a face as if he couldn't believe his bad luck, either.

"How's Delon?" Cole asked.

"Good enough to ask if he won a check," Joe said.

"Guess he'll live then."

The rigid set of Cole's shoulders relaxed a touch, which was the equivalent of a normal person's giddy smile. Violet ground her teeth. Of course he hadn't come to the emergency room. Instead, he'd sat alone in the dark, brooding. The big dumbass. She shrugged free of Joe's arm and stumbled over to plant a hand square in the middle of Cole's chest, both for balance and emphasis.

"You are a jerk," she said, giving each word its own space.

"I know."

She slid her arms around his waist and burrowed her head into his shoulder. "I love you anyway."

He stood, stiff as a statue, as she clung to him. After a few seconds his hand came to rest on her back, patting awkwardly. "You scared the shit outta me."

"Join the club." She gave him another squeeze then let go and turned on her heel, sending her head spinning off into hyperspace again.

Joe grabbed an arm and swung her around to face the steps. "Up you go. Say good night, Violet."

"G'night, Violet," she repeated, then giggled.

"Geezus. She's wrecked." Cole whistled to his dog. "Let's get outta here, Katie."

"Appreciate the help, buddy," Joe called after him, then manhandled Violet up the steps and through the door, propping her against the nearest wall while he found a light switch. "Which bed is yours?"

"I need to clean up first."

Joe made an exasperated noise, but helped her to the bathroom door. He inspected the interior and grunted. "It's so small you probably can't fall over."

But she could faint, and almost did when she got a look at herself in the mirror. She peeled off Joe's coat, hung it on a towel hook and shrugged off the hospital gown. A shower was beyond her. She'd have to settle for combing the mud out of her hair and swabbing her face and neck with a washcloth. First, though, she had to lose the sports bra. The clammy elastic dug into her shoulders and rib cage like steel cable. She hooked her fingers under the bottom band of the bra and tried to peel it up. The bra didn't budge. She pulled harder, gritting her teeth against the arrow of pain that shot down her neck. Her fingers popped loose and her hand flew up to cold-cock her square in the chin. She stumbled and the toilet hit her legs, buckling her knees. Her shoulders slammed into the wall and she slid down like a bird on a windshield.

Joe yanked the door open as her butt hit the toilet lid. "What the hell—"

Violet squinted up at him. Them. Multiple versions of his face wobbled though her field of vision. "I believe I'm gonna need a hand here," she said.

Chapter 31

A HAND. OR TWO. ON VIOLET. WHEN SHE WAS HALF naked and getting more so. Somewhere the devil was laughing his ass off. Joe eased her into the bedroom and braced her against the wall, trying to study the bra while trying not to study what was inside the bra. What in the *hell* were her parents thinking, sending him to tuck her in?

First he had to get her out of that god-awful bra—steel gray and industrial strength. Joe wouldn't have been surprised to see rivets.

Violet squeezed her eyes shut, sliding past the fun part of the Toradol high and into exhaustion. "Just get it off of me."

"With what, a cutting torch?"

"Hah. Jokes. Very helpful."

"Fine. I'll use a pocketknife instead."

Violet's eyes popped open and she clapped her hands over her chest. "No! Do you have any idea how much these things cost?"

"I'll buy you a new one." Hell, he'd buy her two if it meant not having to strip that thing off and force himself not to catch what fell out.

Violet got her mulish look. "You have no idea how hard it is to find good bras."

Thank God. Joe could see why women were tough to figure sometimes. It must be hard to be reasonable when you were being tortured by your own underwear.

Violet slumped a little farther down the wall, a breath away from passing out. "Don't have all night."

"Pajamas?"

"Drawer."

He found a nightshirt—dark blue with a silver Dallas Cowboys star—and laid it on the bed. Then he peeled Violet off the wall. "How do you want to do this?"

She wobbled around until her back was to him and lifted her arms. "Pull on the bottom, out and up."

He reached around but stopped short of grabbing anything. "I'll close my eyes if you want."

"You've seen it all before."

And thanks so much for the reminder. Joe took a deep breath, which wasn't the best move, since his face was buried in the curve of her neck and oh, man…oranges again. He worked his fingertips under the elastic, which was no small feat since it seemed to be the same stuff used to tie down oversized loads. Her flesh was warm and soft against the backs of his fingers, the full weight of her breasts resting on the heels of his hands. He had to remind himself how to breathe.

"Out and up," Violet ordered.

He did, and all that soft, warm flesh spilled out. He scrunched his eyes tight and pushed the bra up to her elbows.

She lowered her arms to cover her chest. "You can go now."

He went, shutting the bedroom door behind him. When she opened it a minute later she was wearing the nightshirt and a pair of sweatpants. "What are you doing?"

"Looking for an ice pack."

And shoving his head in the freezer before his brain boiled over. He pulled out the gel pack, then reconsidered and put it back when he saw Violet was hunched into herself like she was cold. Her eyes drooped but she fought them open again.

A shot of something a whole lot more dangerous than lust hit Joe square in the chest. He took her shoulders, turned her around, and guided her to the bed. "Lay down, Violet."

He flipped back the comforter and she eased down, letting him pull the blanket up to her waist. He perched on the edge of the bed like his mother used to when he was sick, smoothing the hair off her forehead.

"Thank you for all your help, even if you were a pain in the ass." Her smile was a little sloppy. "It's your turn to kiss it better."

Geezus. She was killing him. He leaned down, intending to give her a quick peck on the cheek, but she turned her face and caught his mouth with hers, pulling him into the sweet, soft heat. He had to force his palms to stay flat on the bed when they would much rather have curled around what was running loose under that nightshirt. Hunger churned through him, leaving him spinning in its wake. He ignored the need but let the heat roll where it would, thawing the corners of his soul chilled by how unbearably close she'd come to getting seriously hurt. Or worse. God, what would he have done if it had been the worst?

He buried his face in her neck, trying to smother the unthinkable in her smell, treasuring the steady beat of her pulse against his lips. When he finally dragged himself away, Violet looked pretty toasty, her cheeks glowing. She reached up and brushed her fingers over his hair. "I liked it long."

"I was trying to look respectable."

Her fingers drifted down, traced his eyebrow and skimmed over his cheek, her gaze following their path. "Don't. It doesn't suit you."

He caught her hand and kissed the palm. "Go to sleep, Violet."

He started to stand, but her fingers curled around his. "Stay with me."

His body screamed, *Yes.* His brain said, *She's high as a kite, moron. Don't even think about it.* "I can't. It'd be taking advantage."

"Not the naked kind of stay." Her eyes were huge, dark with the shadows of the same fear that lurked in his gut. "I don't want to be alone. I might not wake up if something happens."

He hadn't thought of that. There could be another storm. And what if she got up during the night and keeled over in the bathroom again? Or worse, wandered outside. He'd heard of people on medication walking in their sleep. She could stumble into one of the stock pens. Fall in the mud and get hypothermia. In fact, now that Joe thought about it, there really was only one way to be sure she was safe.

He toed off his boots and turned out the lights before he climbed over her to settle on the inside half of the bed—on top of the blankets. He wasn't a total glutton for punishment. He slid his arm around her waist and kissed her shoulder because he didn't dare go anywhere near that mouth again.

"Happy now?" he asked.

She sighed, wiggling her butt up snug against him, killing him all over again. "Yes."

"Good. Go to *sleep*, Violet."

She closed her eyes. Joe watched her face sharpen from a pale blur into identifiable features as his eyes adjusted to the orangish glow of the arena security lights filtering through the blinds. Beneath his arm, the rise and fall of her rib cage slowed as she finally surrendered. He relaxed, too, all the odds and ends flying around inside him settling like a pile of dry leaves floating back to earth after a dust devil passed through. He eased his arm up until it pressed against the weight and warmth of the bottom curve of her breasts. A man could only take the gentleman thing so far.

He tucked his body around her, filling his nose with the scent that was so thoroughly Violet. Dirt and horses and fruit. Feelings he couldn't—wouldn't—name swelled inside him. He pressed a kiss to her temple, and then he settled in to savor the only night he'd ever get to spend with Violet in his arms.

Chapter 32

VIOLET SHIFTED, THEN GROANED AT THE DULL clench of pain at the base of her skull. Her muzzy brain dredged up images from the night before. Delon. The ambulance. Those awful, scary minutes when they'd feared the worst. And Joe. He'd been the first to reach her side in the arena. The first to arrive at the hospital. Taking charge, taking care of her, tucking her in and holding her so close, so gently…

And then leaving. She slid a hand across the empty bed beside her. When? Outside, one of the trucks roared to life. Sunlight stabbed through the blinds and voices called. Cole. The truck driver. Hank. Loading up to go home. Violet rolled onto her side, then pushed up slowly until she was sitting, feet on the floor. Her mind felt fuzzy and her tongue was cemented to the roof of her mouth. After a minute, she tried standing. Her whole body ached, but as long as she didn't turn her head there was no serious pain.

She braced one hand on the wall as she shuffled to the bathroom, wincing at her reflection in the mirror. Dear Lord. She looked like death, only grubbier. She sat on the closed toilet seat and eased her nightshirt over her head, suffering only a few sharp twinges in the process. She could shower sitting down in the tiny bathroom, and she sure wasn't letting Joe see her like…

The nightshirt fell from her hand. Oh hell. It was

Sunday. She popped the bathroom door open and squinted at the clock. Her heart dropped to the pit of her empty stomach. Eight forty-seven.

Joe had to leave by eight.

She pulled the door shut and sat, stunned. So that was it. Just...*poof!* Gone. She could still feel his body curled around hers, still smell him on her skin, and he was already halfway to the airport. Hadn't even bothered to kiss her good-bye.

Well. It was probably best. Like ripping off a bandage with one quick yank.

She'd like to call bullshit on that theory. Faster didn't hurt one damn bit less.

She cranked the taps and let the tears flow fast and hot with the water. She'd give herself ten minutes to wallow in self-pity, then she had to suck it up. Fifteen minutes later, she was scrubbed and dressed in a sleeveless blouse and shorts. Her eyes were only a little pink and the hot water had helped loosen her neck muscles, reducing the pain to darts instead of flaming daggers.

She glared at the prescription bottle strategically placed in the middle of her table. There was a note propped against it. *Take me.* What was this, *Alice in Wonderland*? She picked up the note, turned it over to see it had been scribbled on a chunk torn off last night's rodeo program. No signature. No *Nice knowing you.* But hey, it was probably more than most women got from Joe after he'd snuck out of their beds at the crack of dawn. She tucked the paper into her pocket, ignored the medicine bottle to reach for the door handle, then jerked back when a knock sounded under her hand.

"Violet? Are you awake?"

She shoved the door open so fast she would've knocked Joe flat on his back if he weren't quicker than the average cat. "What are you doing here?"

He held up a foam cup and a paper bag. "You didn't eat last night."

"But your flight—"

"I changed it to the same one tomorrow." He started up the stairs, forcing her to step back. "The last thing anyone needed to worry about this morning was getting me to the airport."

She snatched the coffee out of his hand and sucked down the first three swallows, craving the kick. Plus it hid her idiotic smile. *He stayed, he stayed, he stayed!*

Joe fished breakfast burritos out of the bag and dropped them on the table, careful not to look her square in the eye. "Your parents and Beni are up at the hospital. Cole even stopped in long enough to see with his own eyes that Delon was gonna live. He and the trucks are headed home as soon as they're loaded." He shoved a burrito toward her. "Eat your breakfast. Then take your medicine. I'm gonna go help Cole load the trucks."

She didn't want a damn burrito. Or her medicine. She wanted a smile. A touch. A kiss. Something. She folded her arms, feeling her face settle into a sulk worthy of her son. "Who made you the boss of me?"

His smile flashed, quick but real. "Your mother."

The hell she did. Violet glared after Joe until her stomach growled at the scent of sausage and eggs. Okay, fine. Maybe she did want a burrito, but she was not taking the muscle relaxants. She couldn't wander around in a rubber-kneed haze all day. She ate both burritos, polished off the coffee, then shoved her feet into her muddy boots.

Hank cut her off at the gate to the stock pens. "Can't let you in here."

"Says who?"

"Miz Iris. She left strict orders. And Joe said he'd kick my ass if you set foot anywhere near a horse or a bull." He gave an apologetic shrug, but didn't budge. "We're almost done anyway."

Violet glared at Hank, then over his shoulder at Joe, who swung open a gate to let Blue Duck into the alley. Mud caked the roan's side and hip and hung in clumps from his mane, a stark reminder of the previous night's misadventures. Hank followed her line of sight.

"Someone in the crowd recorded the whole thing and posted it online." He fished his phone out of his pocket, poked a few buttons and handed it to Violet. "You should go sit down and watch it."

Violet resisted the temptation to snatch the sorting stick out of his hand and whack him. Little punk, telling her what she couldn't do. Instead, she stomped back to plunk down under her awning and squint at the palm-sized screen. The action played out as Violet remembered it—the ride, then the slip and the rear, Blue Duck falling onto his side. She watched herself spur Cadillac up from behind, into the gap between bucking horse and fence, coming straight at the camera.

Her breath caught as Delon fell, Cadillac's feet and legs pummeling him. The big horse stumbled and fought to recover, scrambling on his knees with his nose plowing into the mud as Violet was launched over his head. The picture wobbled, the person holding it gasping as

Violet's skull missed a post by less than the width of her hand, her body sandwiched into the impossibly narrow gap between the fence and Cadillac's hurtling mass. Holy shit. Violet's vision blurred, then went white. She'd almost…she'd come within inches of…it could have been gone in that instant. Her life. *Everything.* Oh God, Beni would've…

Her chest heaved, but still there wasn't enough air. Never enough air. The phone fell from her hand and she grabbed the arms of the chair as the earth tilted beneath her.

"Violet!" Joe's face loomed out of the haze, his voice echoing from far away. "Slow down, darlin'. You're hyperventilating. Just…slow…down…" His fingers stroked her cheek in time with his words, giving her a point of focus. "Slow. Calm. That's it. Easy now."

Her lungs took up the rhythm of his caress and the words he continued to croon. Her vision gradually cleared, but all she could see was Joe. He was definitely looking at her now. From three inches away.

"What happened?" he asked, green eyes dark with worry as he ran a gentle hand over her hair. "Do you have a headache? Are you gonna puke?"

"No. I just…I saw the video…" She dropped her gaze to where Hank's phone had landed.

Joe hissed out a curse.

"I didn't realize it was…it looked so bad. Did you see…"

"Yeah. Every time I close my eyes."

Violet laughed, a shrill, hysterical sound. "Cadillac… how did he not roll right over me?"

"Pure try," Joe said. "He gets extra grain. Forever."

He crouched in front of her, stroking her arms. When she was steady he scooped up Hank's phone. "I'm supposed to drive you to the hospital, but I have to go kill Hank first."

He jumped up and strode back to the stock pens, where he waved the phone under Hank's nose then tossed it over the fence into the ankle deep muck. While Hank scrambled after it, Joe bundled Violet into the pickup. As he drove across town, she slouched in her seat, staring out the window. The storm had left its mark, scattering leaves and small branches across the pavement. Joe propped his arm on the center console. Violet shifted her gaze to watch him tap a jittery beat on the gearshift knob. If she put her hand on his would he turn it over to lace his fingers through hers? Or stiffen and pull away?

They met her parents in the lobby of the hospital, Beni in tow. He launched into her arms, the jolt nearly making her weep. She hugged him hard anyway, savoring the feel of his dense little body in her arms, his clean-scrubbed scent in her nostrils.

"Well, you're looking better this morning," Iris declared, examining Violet. "You should be okay to drive by tomorrow."

"Tomorrow?"

"Someone's gotta take Joe to the airport."

"I'll just get a rental—" he began.

"Don't be ridiculous," Iris said. "Violet will drive you down in the morning. We're going to find her a motel room. You can stay out at the rodeo grounds in her trailer."

"But—"

"Go on and see Delon," her mother said with a

shooing motion. "Down that hall, third room on the left. Then come on back to the fairgrounds for lunch."

Joe looked like he'd been leveled by a freight train. Violet sighed. No sense trying to fight—her mother would roll right over both of them.

"I'll wait here," he said, and took himself off to a couch in the corner of the lobby.

Violet found Delon's room, took a deep breath, and pushed open the door. He was alone, his eyes closed. She pressed her fingers to her mouth to stifle a gasp at the sight of all the tubes and pumps.

"I'll live," he said, his voice raspy. He opened his eyes to watch her sidle up to the bed, hands clasped so they couldn't flutter around.

"How are you feeling?" she asked.

"Great, as long as I don't breathe."

She cringed. "I guess there's not much they can do for the broken ribs."

"Just this." Delon held up a small remote control with a single button. "Shoots morphine into my IV."

Violet twisted one palm against the other. Studied the pattern of blue flowers on Delon's hospital gown. Shifted her weight to one foot then the other. "I'm so sorry," she blurted.

Delon shook his head. "Not your fault. The arena was a mess. It was stupid to even get on. I should've said no to the re-ride."

"You won first."

"Big damn deal." He squeezed his eyes shut. "You stop breathing for a minute or two, you get a whole new perspective on what's important. There's not a buckle in the world worth more than seeing Beni grow up."

Violet dropped her gaze to her hands, rubbing a bruise on her knuckles she hadn't noticed until then, once again struck mute. The stark, residual fear was too big to reduce to words.

Delon thumbed the calluses on his riding hand the way he always did when he was thinking hard. "So… Joe's still here."

"Only for a day," Violet said, hating how defensive she sounded. "He's flying out tomorrow."

"When's he coming back?"

"He's not."

Delon studied her face, eyes darker than usual. "You sure about that?"

"Yeah."

Lord, her head was starting to pound. She reached out to squeeze Delon's arm, the feel of hard, warm muscle a welcome reminder that he was alive and would eventually be well. "We can talk when you're feeling better. Push that magic morphine button, tough guy, and get some rest."

Pain simmered in her neck, radiating into her shoulder and arm and jacking up the throb in her temples as she walked back to the waiting room. Beni scrambled out of his chair and ran to meet her. Her eyes watered when he tugged on her arm.

"Mommy! Grandma got a motel with a pool!"

Violet's body whimpered at the thought of thrashing around in the water with a rambunctious kid. "That's great."

"I'll take him to the pool," Joe said. "You need a nap."

"You can swim?" Beni asked.

"Yeah," Joe said drily. "Even though I'm just a bullfighter."

If she were a better person, Violet would warn him that swimming with Beni was a contact sport, but a nap sounded heavenly so she smiled instead. "Thanks. You really are a lifesaver."

Chapter 33

Joe sat beside Violet on the bed at the motel and slid the collar of her shirt aside. His fingers trailed over her skin and he felt her quiver in response. God, he wanted to put his mouth right there…

"What's that?" Beni asked, standing on tiptoe to peek over Violet's shoulder while she tried to snap the buckles on his life jacket.

"A muscle stimulator," Violet said. "To make my neck feel better."

She scooped her hair up and out of the way as Joe peeled a gel-backed electrode off a plastic sheet and pressed it onto the nape of her neck. Then he placed the other three electrodes on the surrounding muscles, hooked up the wire leads, and set the dials to low.

"You know how to run this thing?" he asked.

"Yes."

Joe handed her the unit he kept in his gear bag, the size and shape of a pack of cigarettes, then fished a couple of the muscle relaxants from his pocket and held them out.

She pushed his hand away. "No."

"Yes." He slapped them into her palm and grabbed a bottle of water off the nightstand. "Relax. Take a nap. The muscle stim will shut off after twenty minutes. I promise I won't break your kid."

"I wasn't really worried about *you* breaking *him*."

Oh, come on. The kid was five. Joe could handle him. Probably.

"Take your medicine," he told Violet. "We'll be fine."

The instant they cleared the pool gate Beni shot out of Joe's grasp, took a flying leap and splashed down like a miniature hippo. He came up sputtering and coughing, despite the life jacket. Joe bailed in after him and took an elbow in the throat and a knee in the gut as he grabbed the slippery, thrashing body.

Beni gagged, spit, and choked out, "Again!"

Hoo boy. Joe hauled him to the side of the pool by the straps of his life jacket, planted his butt on the concrete deck and said, "Stay."

Beni stuck out his bottom lip, but stayed put.

Joe peeled off his soaked T-shirt and lobbed it toward the nearest lounge chair, then braced a hand on either side of Beni, pinning the squirming kid in place while he leaned in, nose to nose. "So here's the deal, sport. You want to swim, you follow my rules."

Beni's forehead did a mutinous pucker. "My daddy lets me make the rules."

"Bullshit." Even Joe wasn't falling for that line. "We got a deal, or do we go back to the room?"

Beni chewed his bottom lip, considering. Geezus, he was something. Really, it didn't matter that Joe knew nothing about kids. Beni was a fifty-year-old con man stuffed into a four-foot-tall package.

"Oh-kay," Beni said, stretching the word into two pained syllables and tossing in an eye roll for good measure.

"Great. Rule number one. *No running.*"

—᷑᷑᷑—

Violet was still alone in the room when she woke up. She rubbed the sleep from her eyes and checked the clock as her brain slowly came unmuddled. She'd been asleep for two hours? Where was Beni? Even Joe must've run out of energy by now. She went to the bathroom, splashed cold water on her face, then shuffled outside. The air slurped around her like hot molasses when she stepped out the door.

Beni's voice echoed across the parking lot. "You can't beat me this time!"

"Wanna bet?"

They were halfway down the pool when Violet reached the fence, Joe gliding easily while Beni churned water like an egg beater with bad gears. Violet's mother lounged poolside in the shade of a huge red-striped umbrella, head buried in a book.

"Have they been swimming this whole time?" Violet asked, easing into a chair beside her.

"They take a break every half hour to reapply sunscreen. Joe has a timer set on his phone to be sure they don't go over." Iris tilted her head toward where it sat on the table, beside a small cooler. "There's sweet tea in there. And cookies in that plastic tub."

Violet pulled out a jug of tea, guzzled a third, then got herself a peanut butter cookie.

Her mother studied her closely. "Looks like you're moving better."

"Mmm-hmmm," Violet mumbled through the first chewy bite. The pain in her neck had been reduced to a dull ache. "I didn't mean to keep you waiting. Why didn't you wake me?"

"You needed the rest. And it's nice to just sit here and listen to Beni laugh."

Because they were so damn lucky both of his parents were alive to hear him. Violet nodded, the second bite of cookie hanging up on the lump that swelled in her throat.

"I win!" Beni yelled, finally reaching the shallow end of the pool.

Joe stood, water sliding off his body, and Violet got choked up all over again. His soccer shorts were plastered to his body, the weight of the water dragging them down to expose the curve of his hipbones and a stretch of taut skin below his navel, a regular smorgasbord of lean, tanned muscle glistening in the sun. Violet could damn near taste the water on his skin.

Her face went hot. Geezus. Her mother was sitting *right there*. Violet took another bite of cookie before her mouth did or said something completely inappropriate. Beni spotted her and scrambled onto the pool deck. Joe lunged, snatching Beni up by the straps of his life jacket, leaving his feet spinning in midair.

"What's rule number one?"

Beni scowled, but went limp. "No running."

Joe set him on his feet. Beni marched over to Violet and planted his hands on his hips, forty-five pounds of perturbed boy child. "Mommy, Joe is mean."

Violet swiped wet hair off his forehead, trying not to stare as Joe hoisted himself out of the pool and strolled over to join them, dripping and shameless. Damn. He even had nice feet. It would not be good if she gave in to the urge to lick the water out of his navel with her son and her mother watching.

Violet forced her eyes to focus on Beni. "Looks like you were having fun to me."

"He wouldn't let me do any of the good stuff." Beni ticked off the injustices on his fingers. "No flips. Or jumping off the diving board. He wouldn't even throw me like Daddy does. We wasted *hours.*"

"We made up for it." Joe flopped onto the next chaise lounge, scooping a hand over his head as if to push back the hair he didn't have any more. He slid Violet another of those wary looks. "Your mom said it was okay."

"It's great. Thanks." Her voice sounded chirpy. Nervous. She shifted her gaze to the pool, squinting against the glitter of sunlight on the water. "I didn't expect you to spend the whole day out here."

Joe hitched a shoulder. "It's been fun."

Violet raised her eyebrows.

"The water's nice and cool," he amended, his smile as fleeting as the eye contact before his gaze dropped.

"Time to get dried off. Soon as your grandpa gets back, he'll want to leave," Iris told Beni.

He grabbed a cookie, then plunked back down on the foot of his mother's chaise lounge, giving her the sad puppy eyes. "Can't you come with us?"

"I have to stay and give Joe a ride to the airport in the morning." She combed her fingers through his wet hair. "And the next day, Daddy gets to come home."

"Is he gonna be all better by then?"

"He will be before you know it," Iris said, then turned to Violet. "Gil borrowed an RV to take Delon home."

Violet could hardly fathom that Gil hadn't broken every speed limit between here and Earnest when he heard about Delon's injury, but that damn motorcycle had busted more than Gil's body. It had shattered a bond between two brothers that Violet would have said was unbreakable.

Beni wolfed down the last of his cookie, then scrambled to his feet. "Come on, Joe. I wanna swim some more before Grandpa gets here."

Joe stood and scooped Beni up in one swift, seamless motion. At the side of the pool he swung Beni like a sack of feed. "One, two…" He hesitated just long enough to let Beni plug his nose, then, "Three!"

Joe launched Beni out over the water, then jumped in after him, splashing down simultaneously to the tune of Beni's delighted shriek. Joe looped an arm around Beni's waist while he sputtered, "Again!"

Joe gave him another toss, laughing as Beni squealed. She never would've guessed Joe could be so patient. So careful. He looked so…so…

Perfect. Still. Violet's heart spasmed, the pain arcing through her chest. But as her head cleared from the nap and the drugs, something tickled her memory—a glimpse, a fleeting image not quite registered before it was gone. With one eye on Beni and Joe, she swiped and tapped on her phone until she located the video Hank had shown her that morning. She kept her face schooled— *nothing to see here, just checking my email*—while she fast-forwarded past the wreck, to the point where she was sprawled in the mud and Joe came into view.

The hard glare of the arena lights revealed all. As he dropped to his knees and reached for her, he was totally exposed—every thought, every emotion drawn in stark lines on his face. And what she saw made Violet's heart ring as true and sweet as a Sunday church bell.

Joe wasn't pretending. Not in that moment. Maybe not in any of the moments.

She let the phone drop into her lap, blinking hard behind her sunglasses to hold back the tears. Of joy? Hope? Delusion? He was still determined to leave. Did it matter how he felt if he didn't want her more than his precious Oregon desert?

A hand squeezed her arm. Her mother smiled, but it was sad around the edges, a mother feeling her child's potential pain. "It won't be easy, baby girl, but you have to try."

Violet drew in a long, shaky breath, her fingers clenching around the phone as she watched the man she loved laughing with her son. Yes. She had to try. She couldn't let him walk away without a fight. This Joe—yes, dammit, *her* Joe, whether he would admit it or not—was worth saving. She just had to figure out how. And soon. She had to stake her claim before he stepped on that plane tomorrow.

Dragging him away once had taken all of Wyatt's considerable power. If Dick Browning got his hooks back into Joe, Violet feared she might never be able to pry him loose again.

Chapter 34

VIOLET WRESTLED CLOTHES ONTO BENI'S WATER-LOGGED body and walked him out to her parents' rig where Joe was stowing the cooler in the pickup for her mother. He'd pulled on a damp, wrinkled T-shirt over his wet soccer shorts and shoved his feet into unlaced running shoes. Maybe she could just offer to help him get out of those wet clothes.

She nudged Beni. "You should thank Joe."

Beni marched over and stuck out his hand. "Thank you for swimming with me. You're not *so* bad."

"You're welcome." Joe gave the offered hand a brisk shake. "You're not so bad either."

Beni grinned, then scampered off to climb in the pickup. Joe stepped forward and offered his hand to Steve Jacobs. "It's been good working for you. Thanks for having me."

"We appreciate you coming down. You ever need another job, give us a call." Then Steve grinned. "Long as you're willing to work cheap."

Joe laughed and let Iris hug him, which Violet chose to take as a good sign. She'd take anything right now. She and Joe watched the rig disappear around the corner, then shuffled their feet and tried to figure out where to look.

"Guess I'll go shower and get dressed," Joe said.

He didn't ask if she wanted to scrub his back. "I'm gonna grab a Coke. You want one?"

"Sure."

She strolled to the convenience store down the block with one eye on her watch. How long would it take him to shower and dress? Fifteen minutes? Half an hour? She flipped through a couple of magazines and engaged in a lengthy internal debate over what kind of snacks to buy. She had no idea what kind of chips Joe liked. The thought brought her up short. How could she imagine she was in love with a man when she didn't even know if he preferred smoked almonds or cashews? Hell, for all she knew he was allergic to nuts. No, wait, he'd had three peanut butter cookies, so she was safe there.

Okay, deep breath. If she didn't relax she would walk into that motel room and blurt out something that scared him clean out of town. She might not know how Joe felt about banana versus chocolate Moon Pies, but she had no doubt how he'd take a declaration of undying devotion. She could practically smell the burning rubber. She could just say she'd changed her mind and would like to see him next time he was down this way. But what if he said "Great," and that was that? The earliest of the rodeos he might possibly work was in February. Scratch the hell out of that plan.

She grabbed almonds and cashews plus three kinds of chips, then tossed in a pack of mint gum. Forget talking. Guys hated that stuff. She should just show Joe how she felt. He'd understand what it meant if she asked him to get naked.

Naked. With Joe. She breathed through the heart palpitations, ignoring a curious look from the teenager behind the cash register. Okay, she had a plan. Step one—don't hyperventilate and pass out at Joe's feet.

That would be humiliating. Unless he gave her mouth to mouth, and she really was losing it if she thought that might work as an ice breaker. Step two—make her move, whatever that was gonna be. Honestly, once she and Joe and a queen-sized bed were alone in a motel room, how hard could it be?

She filled two large Cokes from the fountain, gathered up her pile of snacks and started for the cashier only to be brought up short by a rack of condoms. Oh Lord. Should she? She couldn't. But what if Joe didn't?

Oh, grow up, Violet, Lily's voice said inside her ear. *Own it.*

She snagged a box off the rack, marched up to the front of the store and dumped the works on the counter, chin up. Let the greasy worm of a cashier think whatever he wanted. He took a step back, eyes going wide. Hmm. Maybe she shouldn't own it quite that hard.

Her heart thumped a little louder with every step she took back to the motel. She stopped outside the door, staring at the gold metal numbers, stymied. She had a key card, but she couldn't go busting in. What if Joe wasn't dressed? That would be…bad? She waited a few more moments, hoping the door might magically open. It didn't. She wandered over and sat down on a bench outside the motel office. She would've figured Joe for a five-minute shower kind of guy, but what did she know?

Within a few minutes her hair was plastered to the back of her neck. How stupid would it be to sit out here basting if Joe was waiting for her to knock? So she did. Softly at first. Then a little louder. No response. She waited a few beats, listening with all her might, then tried again. Still nothing. The pickup was still parked in the lot, but there was a burger joint around the corner. He might have gone for food.

She pulled the key card out of her pocket, slid it into the lock, and eased the door open a crack. "Joe?" she called softly.

No answer. She pushed the door all the way open, then stopped, then let out the breath she'd been holding. So much for worrying how to kill time. Joe was sprawled facedown on the bed, sound asleep.

He couldn't believe he'd slept most of the afternoon. 'Course it might have something to do with spending the previous night curled up with Violet, afraid to doze off for fear of where his hands would wander in his sleep. Now she sat across from him at the motel café, chasing a cherry tomato around her plate with a fork. She'd barely touched her salad and her eyes were shinier than usual. On the verge of glassy, like a rookie bronc rider about to crawl down into the bucking chute for the first round of the National Finals.

"Are you okay?" he asked.

Her fork jerked. Joe caught her wayward tomato as it rolled across the table and set it on his empty plate.

"I'm great. Almost back to normal." She turned her head slowly side to side to prove it. "Why?"

"You didn't eat. And you look hot." When she blinked, he hustled to add, "Uh, feverish I mean."

"I had snacks while you were sleeping." She dropped her chin and went back to molesting her tomatoes. And God, he was in bad shape when even that sounded dirty. "Have you talked to Dick?"

His gut tightened at the reminder. "Yesterday."

"And?"

"He wants to get together and talk about next year's schedule."

She pulverized a crouton with her fork. "Business as usual?"

"Sort of." He'd see when he was face-to-face with the old man.

The red-haired waitress strolled over and propped a hand on an ample hip as she eyed Joe's plate. "Guess I don't have to ask if the chicken fried steak was good— you licked off everything but the shine on the fork." She switched to her attention to Violet. "Somethin' wrong with the salad, honey?"

"No, it's fine. I wasn't hungry."

The waitress cleared away the plates, leaving nothing between them but an empty table and an ocean of unspoken words. All the important stuff had been said. He had to go home. She didn't want him to come back. End of discussion. She put the salt and pepper shakers in their chrome rack and lined it up precisely with the square ceramic trays that held paper packets of sugar and non-dairy creamer. Fidgeting. Violet never fidgeted.

The waitress came back and slapped the check down on the table. When Joe reached for it, Violet grabbed his hand, trapping the check underneath. He could swear he heard a *crack* of live voltage at the contact, the current sizzling up his arm. Her breath caught as if she felt it too. Their eyes met, held, hers swirling with emotions Joe couldn't identify.

She turned his hand over, the slip of paper trapped between their palms. "I'll get that," she said, voice husky.

"No." His fingers curled around the check, stroking the tender skin of her wrist in the process, making her breath catch again. He couldn't resist the temptation to trace the edge of her palm, his voice going low. "And don't try to say I'm still on the payroll."

Her lips parted, but no words came out. God, those lips. He wanted them on his. On him. Everywhere. His fingers tightened. He could pull her out of the booth and drag her across the parking lot to her room. She'd come with him. He knew she would. And he'd make damn sure she came, too…

"Y'all don't need to fight over lil' ol' me," the waitress drawled.

Violet snatched her hand away and tucked it into her lap, face flaming. Joe was so cross-eyed with lust he couldn't even read the total on the bill let alone figure a tip, so he fumbled a pair of twenties out of his pocket and shoved them at the waitress.

"I'll be right back with your change," she said.

"Keep it," Joe said, unable to tear his eyes off the way the creamy skin of Violet's throat moved when she swallowed.

If he put his mouth right there, he'd feel her pulse. Know if it was pounding like his. Violet lifted her hand, fingertips pressed to the exact spot he wanted to taste. No doubt what was in her eyes now. The heat rolled in a wave across the table, washing over him, dragging him under.

"Well, if you're in a hurry," the waitress said with a knowing smirk. "Y'all have a nice night, now."

Joe nodded. Or meant to. All of his parts that weren't throbbing had gone numb from blood loss. He wasn't

exactly sure how he got across the restaurant to the door. As he held it for Violet, he glanced back to see the waitress leaning against the counter, watching them. She grinned and fanned herself with a menu. Outside, the evening air was thick and smooth as silk against his hypersensitive skin. Violet walked silently beside him, close enough that her arm almost brushed his, dialing up his awareness to the point of pain. They paused at her door. She fumbled the key card into the lock and pushed the door open, but didn't go inside. Joe's gaze went straight to the bed.

He cleared his throat. "I should head out to the camper—"

"And what? Play Beni's video games?" She lifted her chin, the challenge clear in her eyes. "You're not scared, are you, Joe?"

His own words thrown back at him, from the night he'd first asked her out. If he had a brain in his head he'd laugh, concede the point, and go on his merry way. "'Course not."

She leaned in, the scent of sun-kissed oranges flooding his senses. "Then stay."

Go! Now! a voice hissed in his head. His body swayed toward hers, tugged by the gravitational force of his need.

Her voice dropped to a near whisper. "The naked kind of stay, Joe."

The wave of lust knocked him back a step.

Violet flinched and dropped her chin. "Forget I asked—"

"No!" Dear sweet Jesus, no. *Don't screw this up, asshole.* He'd walked away from her once. He might burst into flames if he did it again. He waved a jerky hand toward the pickup. "I just…I need my bag and…stuff. If I'm going to, you know…stay."

"Oh." Her smile flashed again, bright with relief. "Well, I brought my own, um, stuff. But I'll wait inside while you get yours."

"Right. Okay." She'd brought her *own?* Joe took another step back, hooked his heel on a crack in the pavement and nearly landed flat on his butt. "Be right back."

He dropped the pickup keys twice attempting to unlock the door. His nerves jumped at the beep of the horn when he pressed the key fob. Dear God. He felt like someone had implanted an entire drum set in his chest. *Crash! Boom! Bang! Rat-a-tat-a-tat-tat-tat.* He locked the pickup, plunked his duffel onto the hood, and yanked the zipper open, digging for the box of condoms just to be sure. Yep, still there. Brand new. He'd bought them for his first date with Violet. Cocky son of a bitch. And now she'd brought her own. His heart did another extended drum solo.

He tucked the box into the pocket of his cargo shorts, slung the bag over his shoulder, turned…and froze. Glued to the ground, panic slithering cold through his gut. If he went back in there…

If? What was he, crazy? Of course he was going in. He was dying, possibly literally, to get his hands on Violet. To have her hands on him. Besides, if he left now, she'd be hurt. Think he didn't want her, as if that was remotely possible. And since when was he scared of a girl? Never. It was just nerves. Or what was that called? Performance anxiety. Yeah. Because this was Violet, not just someone he'd met in a bar. Plus he'd endured all those hours of what amounted to foreplay last night and there was a good chance he might explode the second she touched him.

Well, fine. The humiliation would be worth it, and he had until eight o'clock tomorrow morning to make it up to her.

He eased through the door she'd left open a crack, elbowing it shut with more force than he'd intended. Violet started at the slam, perched on the edge of the bed with her hands folded in her lap. Joe stalled again. Violet raised her eyebrows in question.

"I'm not sure I know how to do this without a few beers first," he blurted, then winced at how bad it sounded. Worse because it was true.

"Make it tequila and I'm right there with you," she said with a shaky laugh.

He laughed, too, even though it was a painful reminder of how crude he'd been that night at the Lone Steer Saloon. What was she doing here with him? She should have punted his sorry ass back to Oregon two days after he showed up.

"I'm guessing it'll work better if we're both on the same side of the room," Violet said.

Joe nodded, but his feet were nailed down, like the first time he tried jumping off the high dive. One more step and he'd be over the edge, except this time he was blindfolded, and he had no clue how far it was to the bottom, or whether there was even water in the pool. Violet took a deep breath, braced her hands on her knees, and pushed to her feet. Air backed up in Joe's lungs, the pressure building with every step she took. She stopped in front of him and reached up to lay her hand on his jaw.

"How 'bout we pick up where we left off?" And then she kissed him.

The ball of pressure ignited, expanded, blue flame licking down every nerve, jolting his body into action. He inhaled her muffled squeak as he hauled her hard against him—chest to thigh—desperate for contact. It wasn't enough. He swung her around, his mouth devouring hers as he mashed her against the wall and cupped his hands around her butt, lifting her to her toes where he could rock his hips into her. Their nearly equal heights made all the right parts line up in all the right places, the friction too much to stand and still not even close to enough. She moaned, her hands flattening on his back and sliding down to his butt, urging him even closer.

Slow down, slow down...

Fuck that. He had to have her *now*. Here. Her hands dove under his T-shirt, pushing it up. He broke the kiss, his breath rasping loud as he raised his arms to let her peel the shirt over his head, cursing when it tangled in the strap of the duffel still slung over his shoulder. He wrestled free and let the whole works thump to the floor.

Violet's smile gleamed with pure female triumph. "I guess you're sure about this."

"Damn sure." He planted a hand on the wall beside her head, a whole new set of flames licking up his spine as she trailed her fingers low across his back, smiling as his hips jerked in response. "Brace yourself, Violet. I've wanted you too hard for too damn long to make this pretty."

"I can handle down and dirty." She ducked under his arm, grabbing his wrist when he reached for her, backing toward the bed and pulling him along. "We'd better take this horizontal—I'm already weak in the knees."

She skimmed her fingers along the top of his shoulder then down, over his chest, his stomach, his muscles twitching at the featherlight touch. Air hissed between his teeth when she trailed a fingertip along the waistband of his cargo shorts to the button and popped it open with one easy twist.

"Slick," he said.

"I get a lot of practice undressing boys." Before he could think too much about that, she sank to the side of the bed and tugged the zipper down. He nearly passed out when she put her mouth on the exposed skin right below his navel and licked. Her hum of approval was hot against his skin. "I've been wanting to do that for *days*."

She slid her hands inside his cargo shorts and peeled them off his hips. He snatched the box of condoms out of the pocket and tossed them on the bed as she pushed the shorts past his knees, where he could kick them loose along with his shoes. Then she looked up…and burst out laughing.

Joe froze, looked down, then grinned when he remembered his underwear. Black boxers with a bronc rider on the front and the Pendleton Roundup slogan in bright red: *Let 'er Buck.*

"Sounds good to me," he said.

"Damn straight."

She popped the first button of her blouse free. Then the next. And the next. The blouse fell open and Joe was looking straight down into heaven, wrapped in peach-colored satin. He gave a long, slow whistle, stunned into reverence. Halle-fucking-lujah all over again. His hands

shook as he fumbled the blouse off her shoulders, as if
he'd never undressed a woman before. She reached up
to flick open the front clasp of her bra, and this time
Joe's hands were right there to play catch. He groaned,
watching her eyelids drift downward as he cupped her
breasts, exploring the weight and the curve of them with
his fingers and palming the nipples.

She scooted back, the gleam in her eyes dangerous
beneath her lashes as she shrugged off the bra, then
stretched out on her back in a slow, sinuous move that
made his heart skid sideways. Her gaze never left his
face as he unbuttoned and unzipped her shorts, then
sucked in a laugh when he saw her underwear. Blue with
silver stars. *Mine.*

He swatted off that wayward thought and grinned,
pausing to drink in the sight of her. "I never thought
you'd wear 'em."

"I needed all the superpower I could get." Something
flickered across her face—uncertain, vulnerable—there
and gone. "You gonna just stand there admirin' the
scenery or what?"

What. Definitely what. He stripped off his boxers and
braced a knee on the bed between her legs to lean down,
palms cradling her hips, thumbs tracing the points of
one star, then another, then another, working toward the
center, her breath coming faster with each touch. She
lifted her hips and he slid the soft cotton down and off.

He planted a hand on either side of her head to lower
himself inch by inch, drawing out the anticipation of
that instant when they would be skin to skin. Head to toe
and every gorgeous, excruciating inch in between. He
stopped just short, eyes locked with hers, and shuddered

when she raked her fingernails lightly down the length of his back. The moment crystallized in his mind like the first time he stepped out into the arena at Pendleton, looked around at the legendary grandstands and every rodeo he'd ever worked before faded into irrelevance. This was *it*. The real thing.

Her hands curved around his butt, squeezed, and he buckled, his full weight pressing into her, the feel of soft skin and firm muscle nearly enough to make him come undone. He pressed his eyes shut and held his breath, fighting the undertow. If he went under, he might never surface again.

"Hey," she said softly. He opened his eyes and gazed into hers only inches away, steady as the arms she wrapped around him. "I'm the pickup girl, remember? I've got you."

He felt himself slipping, the last shred of his control sliding through his fingers. And then he lost it. He took her mouth, deep and hungry, like she was his first meal in a week. She took it all and gave back more, arching and sliding, hips, breasts, thighs, reminding him of all the other hot, sweet places he had to explore. His hands couldn't decide where to go first. How could he touch enough, taste enough, feel enough in only this one night? Then she moved against him again, obliterating his ability to think at all.

She gave him everything, no holds barred, and left him no choice but to do the same. The force of his need stripped him bare, exposed even that piece of himself he always kept apart. Safe. His mind wanted to retreat, but Violet wouldn't let him go. She didn't wait, just took him, dragged him into her warmth then cranked up the

heat and the speed until he imploded, a thousand sizzling points of light bursting behind his eyes, then arcing
away and fading into the darkness.

And then there was nothing but the two of them,
closer than Joe had ever been to a woman, as if their
souls were touching. He kept very still, his afterglow
disturbed by growing ripples of unease. What had just
happened...it was too much. Too far. How did he get
back to solid ground? His mind scrambled, picking
through the lust-clouded details. Did he say anything in
the heat of the moment he couldn't take back?

Nothing he could remember. There were some long,
hazy stretches when he'd been completely out of his
mind, but he was pretty sure he hadn't been capable
of speech.

Now that he'd blown off the steam that'd been building for two weeks, he could be cool. Prove he was
capable of a little finesse. Violet had made it clear she
wanted him here and now, and equally clear she was
done with him when he stepped on that plane. They had
this one night. No promises, no demands. He just had to
keep his head screwed on straight and his mouth shut,
so he didn't break down and beg her to let him come
back for more.

He opened his eyes and found Violet watching him,
her expression guarded. "You okay?"

"I'm awesome." He worked up a cocky grin. "Give
me few minutes and I'll prove it."

Chapter 35

Violet was awake to see the light around the motel curtains soften from phosphorescent blue into golden sunrise, torn between watching Joe sleep and waking him so they could make the most of every precious moment. She'd given it her all and then some. Was this what it would feel like to cast a spell? Toss in your heart, your soul, a huge dollop of pure sexual desire and a pinch of desperation—then wait, barely breathing, to see if it had worked its magic?

She had hoped she would know by now. That he would say something, *anything*, during the long, hot night to let her know what he was thinking. The sex had been everything she'd expected, a mind-blowing whirlwind that had spun her nearly to the edge of endurance, only to bring her back to earth cradled in his arms like a treasure too precious for words.

But she needed those words, and they were the one thing, the only thing, he hadn't given her. There was still time, though, for her to work up the courage to ask for what he hadn't freely given.

She rolled onto her side and flattened her palm between his shoulder blades, savoring the warm gold of his skin, the sleek lines of the muscle beneath, as she slid her hand down his back to the base of his spine.

"Mmmm." He shifted, then gave a low, appreciative

groan when she increased the pressure on the return trip. "I'll give you a day and half to stop doing that."

She kneaded the ridge of muscle along his spine, earning another approving groan. He opened his eyes, gave her a drowsy smile, and Violet's heart jerked.

There he was. Her Joe. His eyes warm, his smile sweet and open. "Mornin', sunshine."

"Mornin'." Not easy to say when you're holding your breath. Afraid to move or speak in case she scared him into hiding again.

He reached up to trace a line along the side of her neck and down her shoulder. His eyes followed his fingers along her collarbone then down, skimming the side of her breast. He paused where the skin was faintly mottled.

"Stretch marks," she said.

His hand hesitated then drifted lower, over her stomach. "But not here?"

"Beni was two months premature. I didn't have time to get that big."

His palm flattened against her skin, the gesture protective, almost fearful. "But you were okay? And him?"

"I was fine. He had to spend some time in neonatal ICU before he could come home, but we were lucky. He's perfectly normal. Health-wise, anyway."

Joe's smile flashed, then faded, pushed aside by a troubled expression. "Could you have another baby?"

"I'd have to be careful, pay close attention to the signs, but…yes."

She watched the light brighten like dawn in his eyes—hope, possibility, a future so full…

Then suddenly it blinked out. Joe's face went blank, his eyes glassy with panic, like a horse cornered by a pack of dogs. When he moved, it was with the same explosive swiftness, jerking away from her and scrambling out of bed with none of his usual grace.

"I need to go."

Violet gaped at him. "Where?"

He snatched his boxers and shorts from the floor and dragged them on with quick, jerky movements. "Out. For a run. Before it's too late."

He grabbed his bag and was gone, the door slamming behind him.

What the *hell*?

Hot tears pooled at the corners of her eyes and she sat, paralyzed by shock, while they trickled down her cheeks. *So close.* She'd been so very close to reaching him, taking hold. And then, like a mustang sniffing the wind, he'd scented danger and bolted.

Eventually, she scrubbed away the tears with a corner of the sheet and went to take a shower, cranking the knobs until the water was just short of scalding. By the time it went cold, she had smoothed down the frayed spots in her nerves. She dried her hair, did a more particular job than usual with her makeup, and ran through all the channels on the television four times before Joe knocked. Her heart thumped, tight and painful, as she opened the door.

Sweat dripped from his face and arms, soaking through his shirt and shorts as if he'd tried to run himself to death. His gaze dodged hers. "I forgot to grab a key."

Violet stood back. He edged past like he expected her to make a grab for him. Their eyes met for an instant and her breath caught at the depth of the panic and guilt she saw in his. She reacted from a horse handler's instinct, not wanting to provoke another stampede. If she was too aggressive, she might chase him right back to Dick Browning, this time to stay. But if she didn't press the issue, if she let him go without declaring herself…

Maybe he'd find his way back to her.

She crossed her fingers and retreated, praying it was the right choice. "We have to leave in fifteen minutes. I'll wait out by the pool."

He blinked. Then nodded and relaxed ever so slightly, as if he'd been braced for an attack. He came out in five minutes, dressed in jeans and a T-shirt, his cowboy hat pulled low over his eyes and his bag slung over his shoulder. Violet met him at the pickup, ignoring the desperation clawing at her throat as the clock ticked down. Pushing might just send him over the edge, if he wasn't already there. The next move had to be Joe's.

She walked straight up to him, cringing at the way he stiffened, and handed him the pickup keys. "You drive. I'm worn plumb out for some reason."

He stared at her, mouth jacked open, while she strolled around and climbed in the passenger's seat. She settled in, tilted the seat back and closed her eyes. After a long moment, Joe started the pickup and pulled out of the lot. As they turned onto the highway, he found a radio station to fill the empty, echoing space in the cab. She felt his occasional glances, as if he were trying to tell if she was really asleep or just faking it to avoid him.

Her head throbbed with the effort of pretending to doze by the time she felt the pickup downshift and slow. Violet sat up, rubbing her eyes as Joe took the exit to the Northwest terminal. He parked in a zone labeled *Loading and Unloading Only* and turned off the engine, then sat with both hands on the wheel, staring out through the windshield. "We're here."

Violet nodded.

Joe climbed out, grabbed his bag from the backseat, and circled around the rear of the pickup. She kicked the door open and jumped down in time to meet him on the curb. *Say something. Anything. Don't let him go.*

She folded her arms tight across her ribs and gave him a tense smile. "Well. Thanks. For, um…everything."

He nodded. Their gazes caught, held, the moment stretching to the point of pain. His eyes were dark. Desperate. For what? She'd give it to him. Anything he wanted, anything he needed, if it would make him stay, or at least leave the door open for him to come back.

"Joe—"

He cut her off with a kiss. Deep, then even deeper, his hunger a wild, frantic thing that threatened to devour her. On and on, until a cluster of teenagers a few yards away began pointing and giggling.

He eased back to cup her face in his hands and kissed her again, gently. Then he closed his eyes and pressed his forehead to hers. "I'm sorry. I can't…I have to…"

She swallowed hard and whispered, "I know."

Joe pushed her chin up with his thumbs, his voice low, strained to the edge of breaking. "Take care of yourself. And Beni."

She nodded. He let his hands drop and stared at her like he was trying to memorize her face. Then he stepped back. "I have to go."

And he did, his strides long and swift, dodging through the crowd as if it were a race to see who could get the most gone. Violet waited, hoping, but he never looked

back. A horn honked, echoing in the concrete bunker of
the terminal. The wheels of a luggage cart clattered on
the pavement. People scurried around her, rushing to and
fro, caught up in their own lives, their own problems,
oblivious to the quiet shattering of Violet's heart as she
watched Joe run away one more time.

Chapter 36

THE SCRAPE OF KNIFE AGAINST PLATE IN DICK Browning's otherwise silent kitchen grated like a serrated blade on Joe's nerves. Which, granted, were so raw he could barely tolerate the sound of his own breathing. He set his fork aside and swabbed up the last of his gravy with one of Helen's home-baked rolls, the likes of which he'd never had until he met Iris Jacobs.

Of course, if good company really made everything taste better, it wasn't a fair comparison. Helen had given up trying to make conversation five minutes into the meal and Dick Browning was stubbornly silent, his mere presence as abrasive as the shaved stubble of gray hair on his head. If he'd ever had any soft edges, they'd been worn away a million miles ago, leaving only gristle and bone.

He pushed his plate aside, stuck a toothpick between his teeth, and tipped his chair back. "I'm finishing up next year's contracts. I assume we can plan on you for all the usual rodeos?"

As if the fight in Puyallup had never happened. Dick intended to just go on, business as usual, and expected everyone else to do the same. No harm. No foul. And why not? It had always worked that way before.

Joe's knuckles went white around his coffee mug. Goddamn Wyatt and his *perspective*. He'd known—or at least hoped—that this would happen. They'd ruined him down there in Texas. Stripped away his layers of protective cynicism with their hospitality and honest regard, and left him wide open. Too sensitive. Too aware. Now, sitting in a kitchen that managed to be cold and dingy despite all of Helen's efforts to the contrary, he could see the future much too clearly.

Yeah, Joe could step right back into his place here at the ranch, and at Dick's rodeos. All it would cost was everything he wanted to be as a man. A human being. Dick wasn't going to bend an inch. Wouldn't, couldn't—it didn't matter which anymore. Joe had run out of excuses, justifications, tolerance. As he'd always said, Dick was Dick, take him or leave him.

So now, Joe had to leave.

He let the thought settle, grim and undeniable, like a frozen rock in the pit of his stomach. Then he peeled his hand off the mug, crossed his arms and leaned back, mimicking Dick's posture. His pulse pounded in his temples and his lungs burned as he held a match to the fuse that would blow this particular bridge out of the water, but he sounded amazingly calm. "I've had a lot of offers. Accepted a few. I'll have to see what else I can squeeze in."

Dick's eyes went squinty, the grooves around his mouth digging so deep they nearly cut through the leathery flesh. The legs of his chair thumped to the floor and he spit his toothpick onto his plate. "Is this your way of tryin' to squeeze more money out of me?"

"No."

Dick's head jerked at the flat tone, as if Joe had thrown a legitimate offer back in his face. Joe shouldn't have been surprised. It always came down to the money with Dick. "Well, I can't twiddle my thumbs while you're dithering around, waiting for the highest bid," Dick snapped.

"Then find someone else." The words felt like jagged pieces of his soul, ripped out one by one.

For a moment, Dick just glared. Then he stood, grabbed his hat from the rack and jammed it onto his head. "I've got work to do."

He didn't ask if Joe planned to help, which pretty much said it all. The door cracked into the frame behind him, followed by the bang of Helen's coffee mug onto the table. "That miserable old bastard. He'd cut his tongue out of his head before he'd admit how much he needs you around here."

She heaved out of her chair, multiple chins quivering in fury. The eyes that usually sparkled with good humor were spitting fire as she snatched up plates and slapped silverware on top. She dumped the pile of dishes in the sink with a clatter loud enough to make Joe flinch.

"A man who can't admit he made a mistake doesn't deserve to call himself one. Best thing for you, getting out of here."

Tell that to his gut when it felt like it was turning inside out, threatening to reject everything he'd just eaten. He shoved his chair back and stood, knowing there were things he should say, but at a loss. The end had come too quickly, and too quietly. After all the years, all the miles, there should be more. Shaking fists, shouting, a decade and a half of suppressed rage and frustration, exploding into words.

He should have known Dick wouldn't even allow him that much satisfaction. That much importance.

A long, weary sigh trickled out of him. He didn't have the energy to fake a smile. "Thanks for lunch. I'm going to miss your pot roast. I probably will waste away to nothing without you to feed me."

Helen studied him for a long moment. Then she dropped her dish towel, walked over and gave him a hug, wrapping her bulk around him like a warm blanket. When she stepped back, tears glistened in her eyes. "You've been the best thing about this place for a long time, Joe Cassidy. I'm not sure if I'll be able to stand it with you gone."

While he tried to muster a response, she grabbed the leftover beef off the table, carried it to the counter and covered it with aluminum foil, her movements swift and efficient.

"I don't know when I'll get your dish back to you," Joe said, as she pressed the plate into his hands.

"Leave it at the bar. I'll pick it up." She squeezed his arm. "Take care, Joe. Better yet, break down and let someone else give it a try."

Yeah. Like people were lining up for that job. He lifted the plate. "Thanks for this. I'll see you…around."

Helen patted his shoulder. "Be sure to say hello. And Joe? If you ever need anything—a meal, an ear to bend—you just let me know."

"I'll keep it in mind."

He walked outside, set the plate on the hood of his Jeep and braced his hands on the car as he drank in the landscape. Clouds hung low, trailing shreds of fog through the draws, the sky a solid sheet of gray that sucked what little color there was out of the parched brown hills. The air was dry and brittle in his lungs, the chilly breeze whistling across the flat and through the yard. Joe hunched his shoulders against its bite, but still he stood, trying to imprint the scene on his mind. Down in the corral, the newly weaned colts wandered around, bickering amongst themselves and nosing at the hay in the feeder, bewildered by their unexpected change in circumstances.

Joe could relate. It didn't hurt as bad as he'd expected, though. It was worse. Like having his guts carved out, leaving nothing inside him but a massive, hemorrhaging wound. A giant vise squeezing his chest until it cracked right down the middle. He dragged in a lungful of the sage-scented air, held it as if he could absorb the molecules into his bones, but it wasn't his to keep any more than the land. It never had been. Judging by the way he felt right now, losing it all might actually kill him.

His gaze was glued to the rearview mirror as he drove slowly away, until he topped the last rise and the High Lonesome disappeared.

Back in town, Main Street was scattered with the usual assortment of battered ranch pickups and dusty SUVs, nobody in a big hurry to get anywhere on a Thursday afternoon. Joe flipped his turn signal on to circle around to his parking space in the alley behind the Mint Bar, then flipped it off again when he caught a flash of gleaming, fire engine red at the curb out front. A '69 Camaro with a broad white racing stripe up the middle and *BLLDNCR* on the vanity plates.

Bull dancer. Hell.

Joe parked behind the Camaro. He felt weird walking in the front door of the Mint instead of the back hallway, adjacent to the stairs down from his apartment. He paused on the threshold to nod hello to the bartender and take note of the crutches leaning beside the only man sitting at the battered wooden bar.

"Nice haircut," Wyatt said. "Planning to buy a suit and go door-to-door selling Bibles?"

Joe pulled off his hat and ran a hand over his head. "It isn't any shorter than yours."

"Yeah, but I've got choir boy in my genes. It suits me."

Joe slid onto the next barstool and nodded at Wyatt's ankle. "Is it broken?"

"Just a chip off the end of my ankle bone. The plate held where it was broken before."

So no surgery. Some good news in an otherwise shitty day.

"Whatcha need, Joe?" the bartender called down, with an eye still on the television.

"Coke." Joe assumed Wyatt's glass held the same. They'd outgrown the days of afternoon drinking that stretched into an all-night binge. "Did you drive all the way down here to insult my hair?"

"Nah, but that was almost worth the trip." Wyatt plugged one end of his straw with a finger, lifted it from his glass, and sucked it dry, his gaze dissecting Joe the whole time. "How'd it go with Dick?"

"I quit." When Wyatt didn't say anything, Joe slanted him a bitter smile. "What? No victory dance?"

"I've got a broken ankle and you look like you just had to shoot your best horse."

Joe jabbed his straw into his glass. Wondered what the bartender would say if he asked for a shot of grenadine, like the Rob Roys his mother used to buy for him here when they had something to celebrate. Yee-haw. He was moving on up whether he wanted to or not.

"Fifteen years," he said, stabbing an ice cube. "Half my life, I've worked on that ranch. I saw most of those horses and bulls born. Watched them grow up. I've hiked or ridden every inch of that ground, strung damn near every strand of barbed wire on the place. How do you expect me to feel?"

Wyatt didn't answer right away. When he did, his voice was quiet. "It's hard for me to relate. I've never felt that way about a chunk of land."

A chunk of land—like it was just dirt and didn't have a soul of its own. Joe almost felt bad for Wyatt. Wouldn't it be worse to have never felt grounded, even if being uprooted ripped you in two? Joe watched bubbles weave between the ice cubes in his glass, wishing it was something stronger than Coke. What did it matter? Wasn't like he had any place to be tomorrow. Or the next day.

They sat in silence, listening to the clink of ice in their glasses, the bartender grumbling under his breath at a defendant on one of those afternoon Judge Somebody shows.

"I'm still not sorry I sent you down there," Wyatt said. "It was good for you."

Yeah, just fucking great. It wasn't enough, losing the High Lonesome. Might as well toss in those cold sweats every time he let himself remember how he'd put his hand on Violet's stomach, imagined a baby there, and thought *Mine*. Icy fingers clamped around his windpipe and it was all he could do not to claw at his throat.

He jammed his hand into his pocket, dragged out a few dollars, and slapped them on the bar. "Hey, Chuck, toss me a bag of cashews, would ya?"

With a side of whiskey. Booze wouldn't fix anything, but if he drank enough of it he might stop smelling and tasting and feeling Violet with every cell in his body.

"There are other ranches," Wyatt said.

"Perfect. I could get my ass kicked down the road again in another five or ten years."

"Not if you're part owner." Wyatt shot an arm out and intercepted the bag of cashews the bartender tossed to Joe, ripped it open and helped himself to a few before passing it on. "There are plenty of contractors out there who'd be willing to take on a partner in exchange for an infusion of cash."

"I don't have that kind of money." Yet.

"Close enough to borrow the difference."

Joe froze, cashews scattering onto the bar from the bag he'd upended onto his palm. "How do you know?"

"You leave your statements sitting around. How can I not look? What do you live on, peanut butter and ramen noodles?" Wyatt made a thoughtful face, ignoring Joe's glare. "Frank's been kicking my broker's ass for the past three years. I don't suppose he'd consider managing my portfolio?"

"Only if he marries your mother."

Wyatt grimaced. "I wouldn't even wish that on Dickhead. But if you need more capital, Frank would finance you in a heartbeat. He probably keeps that much in his checking account."

Joe wouldn't be surprised. He also wouldn't dream of

asking. Too damn awkward to be in business with Frank when Roxy decided to bail again. A smart man didn't get his money tangled up with his personal life.

Wyatt took a slow, casual sip, then said, "I heard there's an outfit in Texas looking to expand."

The icy claws drove straight into Joe's spinal cord. "They don't want my money."

Could he even buy his way back into Violet's good graces after what he'd done, lighting out of her bed like a stray cat with a belly full of gunpowder and a fuse up his ass? Except she hadn't been pissed. Hadn't seemed fazed at all. She'd just shrugged it off, like it didn't matter. Like he didn't matter.

"Why not? Violet is perfect—"

"And I'm not. I've got nothing she needs."

Wyatt popped a cashew in his mouth, chewed, eyeing Joe as he lined up his argument. "A woman doesn't need a man who's honest, reliable, works hard, and is crazy about her?"

"I'm not—"

"Bullshit. On top of all that, you're damn good with bucking stock."

Joe stabbed viciously at an ice cube with his straw. "And I suck at relationships."

"How do you know? You've never had one."

"My point exactly. I don't even have a role model. Every relationship I've been anywhere near has gone to hell." He shot a glare at Wyatt. "Including yours, brain child. And I'm not gonna practice on Violet, even if she was interested in letting me."

Wyatt's mouth twitched. "So…what? You're saving yourself for a girl you don't like?"

Joe shoved him off the barstool. Wyatt landed on his feet, cursing when his injured ankle had to bear weight.

"Hey! No picking on the wounded."

Joe dumped the last of the cashews into his mouth and ground them to a paste between his teeth. "Then get off my ass."

"Fine. I'll shut up…for now." Wyatt eased back onto his stool and sat sipping his Coke and contemplating the dusty jars of pickled eggs and pigs feet behind the bar, quiet for a few blissful moments. Then he dug out his money clip, waved the bartender over and flipped a fifty down in front of him.

"Top us off with a shot of Pendleton. And leave the bottle." When Chuck hesitated, Wyatt reached over and plucked Joe's keys off the bar, dangling them along with his own from one finger. "I'll toss these in, if it makes you feel better. I think we can manage to walk home."

"That's what you said last time," Chuck said, taking the keys. "But I'm off at six so someone else can haul you up those damn stairs."

He doused both glasses with whiskey and thumped the half full bottle between them on the bar. Wyatt swiped a couple of dollar bills from Joe's pile of change and hobbled over to the jukebox. Joe picked up his glass, sniffed, then took a healthy gulp of pure alcohol off the top. As it burned a trail to his stomach, Wyatt punched in a set of numbers. The jukebox twanged to life and George Strait sang, *Amarillo by morning…*

"I hate you," Joe said, and took another long pull off his drink.

Chapter 37

Violet climbed out of her car and trudged up the metal stairs to Delon's apartment over the office of Sanchez Trucking, her body sluggish, as if drained by the bucket loads of tears she'd shed since Joe left. She'd told herself he'd come to his senses once the plane left the ground, call her the instant he landed, but the hours had passed without a peep. Then she'd said okay, maybe when he got home, but the sun set and the phone stayed silent all through the cold, endless night. And the next. And the next.

She'd scoured the social media sites, Googled herself blind in the wee hours when sleep wasn't an option, but hadn't found a single current mention of Joe Cassidy or Dick Browning. She assumed no news was bad news.

She'd put all her cards on the table, gone all in, and it wasn't enough. She'd lost. The High Lonesome had won. And it didn't even help knowing that Joe was hurting, too, probably even more than she was. After all, she'd put him in an impossible situation. Forced him to choose between two futures. Two loves.

And she'd lost. At least she didn't have to try to put on a happy face. Smiles had been thin on the ground at the Jacobs Ranch since the orthopedic surgeon had confirmed their worst fears. Delon's knee was wrecked—medial collateral, anterior cruciate, cartilage. Forget the National Finals and any chance at the world title. He'd be lucky to ride again by the middle of next season. Delon was taking it as well as could be expected. Beni was heartbroken. Violet couldn't do a damn thing to fix them, either.

She paused, made a concerted effort to wipe the doom and gloom off her face, and knocked on the door.

"It's open!" Delon yelled.

She stepped inside and found him trying to maneuver into a seated position on the faded tweed couch. "Don't get up on my account."

He ignored her, gritting his teeth against the pain in his ribs as he swung his injured leg to the floor, strapped up from hip to ankle in a rigid brace. "Beni was bouncing off the walls so I sent him over to play at Gil's with one of the drivers' kids."

Gil had a house out behind the shop, with a swing set and a basketball hoop and an actual white picket fence—a caricature of the perfect family home. No lawyer would ever accuse him of not providing a good environment for his son.

"You look better today," she said.

"Finally got a decent night's sleep."

"That's good." God, could this conversation get any more trivial? All the years they'd been friends and suddenly they had nothing to talk about. "I'll get Beni's stuff gathered up."

Delon reached out and snagged her wrist. "Would you sit for a minute? Please? I…we should talk."

Oh. Hell. The fatal words. She hesitated, then gave in, sinking down beside him.

He scooted around to face her, cradling her hand in his. "I've had a lot of time to think, Violet. Seeing that video, knowing how much worse it could have been for me or for you—well, it makes me realize maybe we don't have all the time in the world."

She nodded, dread gathering like a slow-moving cold front deep in her gut. *Oh no. Not now.*

"You and Beni are the center of my world, Violet. I couldn't tell you how many times I was alone somewhere, too far from home, beat to hell and bone-tired, when being able to pick up the phone and talk to you was the only thing that kept me going." He folded both hands around hers, his grip tight. "I know it's not all sizzle and fireworks, but what we do have is real, and it's good. If we just give it a chance…"

Violet could only stare at him. By Delon's standards, he was a mess. Two days of stubble on his chin, his T-shirt, gym shorts, and hair all rumpled. And still, he was gorgeous. Solid. And here. Always here, whatever she needed. Maybe he couldn't give her fireworks, but Delon would never blow her heart to pieces and disappear into the smoke. She had a sudden, powerful urge to crawl into his arms. It would be so easy to let him soothe away some of the pain…

And so completely unfair to both of them.

"Delon…"

"Just think about it. Please." His voice dropped to a low, pleading note.

"I can't."

His grip loosened, animosity darkening his eyes. "Because of Joe."

It would be easier if she lied, but only in the short term. This was another of those bandages that had to be ripped off, and it *would* have to happen when they were both so wounded. She clamped her teeth over her bottom lip to stop the trembling and said, quiet but final, "No."

"So it's just me." His hands dropped hers and he slumped back against the couch.

"No! Lord, Delon. Look at yourself." She sketched a frame in the air around him. "You're amazing—a helluva bareback rider, a great guy, a wonderful father, and gorgeous on top of it. I've gotta be some kind of fool *not* to be in love with you."

He gave a harsh laugh. "Apparently, there are a lot of foolish women in the world."

Her tattered heart shredded a little bit more because he had given her so much, and she did love him—just not in the way they both deserved. And here she was, kicking him when he was down.

"I'm sorry," she said.

As sorry as she'd ever been in her life, but she couldn't fix this, either, any more than she could conjure up the cash to buy out Buck McCloud, or be woman enough to make Joe turn his back on Dick Browning and the High Lonesome. Everything she touched lately seemed to crumble into dust and trickle through her fingers, leaving her with nothing but the gritty taste of failure on her tongue.

Footsteps hammered on the metal stairs and they both had time to brace themselves before Beni burst in the door. "Mommy! You're finally here! Can we go right now so I can ride my pony and…"

Beni chattered the entire time she gathered his things, so excited to get home to the ranch he never noticed that his parents didn't say a word.

She stopped to fetch the mail out of her box before continuing on down the driveway. The minute she parked, Beni was off and running to beg his grandpa or Cole to saddle up his pony. Violet went inside and slumped on the couch to sort through the mail. Junk mail. Junk mail. Grocery store sale flyer. Credit card bill. Phone bill. Pro Rodeo Sports News. She flipped the magazine over and sucked in a breath, the headline another punch in the gut.

Sanchez finishes strong. The cover photo was classic Delon, from the rodeo in Ellensburg, Washington. The magazine had gone to print before his wreck. Violet blew out a long, defeated breath. Lord, she could use a break. Just a tiny ray of light in this long, cold tunnel. Tears welled, blurring the words as she paged through the magazine half-heartedly, mostly stories about the cowboys on the bubble, just above or below the magical fifteenth slot in the standings that would get them to the National Finals.

And whoo-hoo. Another big-name contractor had hit the jackpot, selling shares in one of his top bulls to some country singer who'd divvied up major cash to be listed as owner, corner bragging rights, while the contractor kept hauling and bucking the bull as usual. Too bad Jacobs Livestock wasn't in a position to tap that market. She could sell a piece of Dirt Eater for enough to finance the McCloud sale and then some. Celebrities and rich dabblers wanted the bright lights, though, not the back roads. It was all about hearing your name announced on television and…

Violet lowered the magazine to her lap. *It was all about hearing your name…*

What if she turned that concept on its head? She mentally poked at the idea, rearranging the pieces, chucking one here and adding another there until she had something worth considering. It could work. It *would* work for sure if Dirt Eater got selected to go to the National Finals, and they should be getting word on that any day now. There was only one very large obstacle to overcome.

Cole was at the arena, rebuilding one of the chute gates. He turned off the cutting torch and shoved the protective goggles up onto his forehead as she approached.

"What?" he asked.

"I have an idea. Just promise you'll listen all the way through and really think about it before you say no."

He squinted at her for several pained moments. Then he nodded.

That evening, she convened an emergency meeting of the Jacobs Livestock board of directors around her mother's kitchen table. Her mother and Lily were openly curious, her father wary, and Cole a complete blank.

Violet cleared her throat. She smoothed a hand over her notes, incredibly nervous considering this was just her family. "Cole and I have been talking…as you're all aware, we need a hundred thousand dollars cash money to buy out Buck McCloud without putting ourselves in a serious pinch. Dirt Eater is worth at least five times that much. If he's picked for the NFR this year, his value will go up considerably." She raised a hand to ward off their protests. "By my reckoning, we could sell shares up to forty-five percent, buy Buck's stock, and have enough liquidity to operate comfortably."

They stared at her for a moment. Then her father said, "But we keep the bull."

Violet looked at Cole, who was staring down at the table, before answering. "First—and most important—no matter who buys in or where he bucks, we would require that Jacobs Livestock always be listed as the main contractor."

The ramifications took a moment to sink in.

"We don't keep the bull," her father said slowly. "You're proposing that we sell shares to another contractor. Somebody who'll take him to the really big shows."

"Yes. But we'll still be the majority owner, so we'd be included in any and all decisions, and…" She glanced at Cole again, and now he was watching her. "We would be able to have someone there with him whenever we wanted."

"And every time he bucks, they'd announce our name," Iris said, a glimmer of excitement sparking in her eyes.

Lily reached over to squeeze Cole's arm. "Are you okay with this?"

He flattened his big hands on the table top, as if counting his fingers. "If it meant seein' my daddy's bull buck at Cheyenne or San Antonio under the Jacobs name… yeah, I'd like that. Especially if I could be there with him, now and again." Cole drew in a breath so deep it stretched the buttons on his shirt. "As long as you're all here, you should know I've been seein' Mrs. Davenport at the school."

"*Seeing?*" Iris echoed, shocked. "As in—"

"She's the special education teacher," Lily cut in, without peeling her eyes off Cole.

"Yeah. She did some tests, and it turns out I'm not just an asshole. I'm autistic."

Violet gaped at him. "But how—"

"Joe. He knows someone like me, and he gave me stuff—a video and some magazine articles. It fit."

Silence reigned as they all tried to grapple with this new bombshell. Then her father said, "So now what?"

Cole shrugged. "Mrs. Davenport says we can work on developing my social skills."

"She can teach you not to be an asshole?" Lily asked.

"Lily!" Iris smacked her arm.

"He said it first," Lily shot back.

Violet laughed. Once she started she couldn't stop because it was all too much and she'd been so twisted up with Joe and Delon and everything she just came unwound. Lily started laughing at Violet, and then Iris lost it, and the three of them practically rolled off onto the floor while her father and Cole stared at them like they'd lost their ever-lovin' minds.

Violet's phone buzzed and she had to wipe away the tears and try to sound halfway normal when she answered.

"This is Vince Grant," a gruff voice said. "I hope you haven't made any plans for the first week in December. We'd like to have that bull of yours at the Finals."

And with that, the Jacobs Livestock business meeting turned into a party.

Chapter 38

THE MOONLIT MEXICAN BEACH WAS DESERTED AT three a.m. No one to see or care how long Joe stared out at the waves. But rather than soothing him, the rhythmic roar of the surf only echoed the ceaseless pounding in his head. He'd tried to outrun it. First by taking his mother up on her offer to fly off to Mexico. Then mile after mile after mile on the hard-packed sand, in the sun, in the wind, at god-awful hours of the night.

No matter how far he ran, there was no escaping his thoughts. The memories. The dreams that stalked him on the rare occasions that he managed to sleep. Violet, warm and naked in his arms, then suddenly not, her answer a cold, cruel laugh when he begged to see her again. Dick, snarling and cursing about how he'd always known Joe wouldn't turn out to be worth a shit. In his dreams Joe hiked the hills of the High Lonesome. Then suddenly, it changed, and he was running through the Canadian river breaks, trying to catch up with Violet, but she kept disappearing, leaving him to stumble through the unfamiliar darkness alone. So he didn't sleep.

His mother was not helping. She hadn't batted an eye at the men who tried to flirt with her, and there were plenty. Roxy ignored them, content to read her book—a biography, for Christ's sake—sip a drink and bask in the sun. Roxy and Frank really were solid. And that was great. Frank was good for her, not to mention Joe's stock

portfolio, but her serenity only threw Joe's ragged edges
into sharper relief. A fine time for his mother to go and
grow up on him.

His fingers clenched tighter around the phone in
his hand. It had been almost two weeks since he'd left
Texas, and not a word from Violet. Not that he had a
right to expect any, the way he'd left, but every time
the phone chirped, his heart nearly exploded. Didn't she
worry if he'd made it home safe? Wonder how things
had turned out with Dick? Did she give the slightest
damn what he was doing at this very moment?

Nothing eased the ache. Not fatigue. Not distance.
Not time. If anything, the need to see her, to talk to her,
got stronger every day. He wanted to tell her he'd left
Dick. Hear her say he'd done the right thing. Maybe
she could tell him what came next, because he sure as
hell couldn't find a direction. He understood now how
an addict felt. *Just one call. One quick hello.* But it
wouldn't be enough. He'd want more. And it would be
that much harder to stop himself the next time.

His thumb caressed the Send button. Her number was
already there, on the screen. One touch and he could
hear her voice. He stared down at the phone for several
beats. Then he reared back and heaved it out over the
moonlit waves.

—⁓—

A week later, Joe parked his Jeep in front of Wyatt's
condo, went around the back and hauled out two black
trash bags full of clean laundry. That, plus a few boxes
of trophies and pictures, were all that was worth keeping.

Wyatt opened the door before he could ring the bell,

stood aside, then followed Joe into the living room. "What did you do, jog home from Mexico? You look like a starved greyhound."

Joe felt it, too. Hollowed out, whittled down, nothing but corners and angles that rubbed everything wrong. "I couldn't hold down solid food for three days after you showed up at the Mint."

The details were blurry, but around the time they'd drained the first bottle, Joe had started talking. Not about getting dumped—he wasn't that pathetic—but he'd spilled enough for anyone who was paying attention to figure it out. Wyatt was always paying attention, even when he was so hammered he couldn't sit up straight on Joe's sagging, secondhand couch.

Wyatt's couch was cowhide, with rolled leather trim and brass studs. The coffee table was a work of art, handmade by a local woodworker, the top an intricate pattern of inlaid swirls. The pictures on the walls were original watercolors. In the midst of all that class, Joe felt like a hobo.

"Why is your phone out of service?" Wyatt asked.

"I dropped it in the ocean. I have a new number. Which room?"

"The one with the attached bath."

Plus a whole set of dark wood furniture and a flat-screen TV. Throw in a minibar and he could be staying at the Holiday Inn. Joe dumped his bags on the bed and wandered over to look out the window. The condo was perched high on Pendleton's north hill, with a view of the Blue Mountains to the east, and a line of sight down the steep slope into the Roundup grounds ten blocks below. In Pendleton, the higher up the north hill you lived, the cooler you were. Wyatt liked cool. He also liked real estate with high appreciation potential.

Wyatt propped a shoulder against the door frame and hooked his thumbs in the front pockets of his jeans. "I'm ordering out for dinner. You want Chinese, ribs, or chicken?"

"Whatever."

Joe wandered over to the dresser to finger the buttons on the television remote. Satellite, with DVR. Good to know he'd have a couple hundred channels to choose from during those hours he used to waste on sleep. He pushed the remote aside and picked up the manila envelope underneath.

"Those are the contracts for the rodeos we agreed on," Wyatt said.

Joe considered dumping it in the trash, but what was the point? "I'll read and sign them later."

"Already done."

Joe shot him an irritated glare. "You forged my name?"

"How could anyone tell? You write like a chicken on meth."

Joe peeled back the flap and dumped the contents out on the dresser. His guts twisted as he saw the names. The dates. Wyatt had him working somewhere in Violet's vicinity every six weeks from January to October. An entire season of torture.

"I suppose it's too late to weasel out," he said.

"For the first two rodeos? Yeah." Wyatt cocked his head, studying Joe. "I can find a replacement for the rest, if you can give me a valid reason that you're not already in Texas."

"She doesn't want me there."

"What makes you so sure?"

"I said, 'I'd like to come back sometime' and she said, 'I don't think so.' I took that as a no."

Wyatt frowned. "That can't be right."

"It's never right." Joe mashed the balled-up envelope between his hands, the stiff paper digging into his palms. "For guys like us, this is as good as it gets."

"What do you mean, guys like us?"

"Some people aren't made for the marriage and family thing. It's better for everyone if you just accept it."

"And what? Live with you for the rest of my life?" Wyatt shook his head. "Not fucking likely. Decent human beings deserve better."

"Who are you calling decent?"

"You, dipshit." Wyatt paced over to the window and braced his hips on the sill. "Who else would crawl out of bed at two-thirty in the morning and drive to Butthole, Idaho, to pick me up when my sweet little wife dumped me at a rest area?"

"Athol," Joe muttered.

"What?"

"It was Athol, Idaho."

"That's what I said." Wyatt glared at him, impatient. "Give yourself a chance, Joe. So your dad bailed out on you. Your mother wasn't exactly the poster child for healthy relationships. My family traded basic compassion for social standing about five generations back. That doesn't mean you and I have to settle for half a life."

Joe snorted in derision. "What, one wreck of a marriage wasn't enough for you?"

"No." For once, Wyatt's expression was completely unguarded. "I want the whole goddamn works. In-laws.

Out-laws. Holidays from hell with a house full of screaming kids and five dogs."

Joe stared at him for a beat. Then he said, "They'd definitely be hell on that fancy leather sofa."

"Fuck the sofa. I'd rather have a family."

Since when? First his mother, now Wyatt—the two people he could count on to be as dysfunctional as he was. Joe tossed the crumpled envelope into a brass-and-leather wastebasket. "Bash your head on the wall again if you want, but people don't stick, Wyatt."

"How would you know?" Wyatt dragged frustrated hands through his hair and laced his fingers on top of his head like it might pop off. "You're gone before anyone gets close enough to try. We probably wouldn't even be friends if you could outrun me."

He should be running now. Fast and far before Wyatt talked him into some new form of self-mutilation, but he was just too damn tired.

He slumped onto the side of the bed. "Why me? Out of all the guys you could've picked to torture."

"You're the best. In the arena or out."

"I'm just a hick from the sticks. You went to *Yale*."

"That only means I'm more educated. It doesn't mean I'm smarter."

Joe snorted again. "You are so full of shit."

Wyatt jabbed a finger at him. "*That's* why I need you. Because I am full of shit and you're not afraid to tell me so, while everyone else smiles and nods and backs away slowly." The old gleam came into his eyes. "Violet isn't afraid of me, either. Something else you have in common."

"It's not enough," Joe said flatly.

"So she's mad at you. Apologize. Grovel, if necessary."

"She's not mad." That was the whole problem. He gripped the edge of the dresser so tight his knuckles cracked. "I acted like a lunatic and she should've been furious, but she *didn't care*. Just shrugged and dumped me off at the airport, good riddance."

"You've got to be reading her wrong." Wyatt shoved off the windowsill and started for the door. "I'll get the real story."

No damn way. Joe scrambled to block his exit. "You can't call her."

"I'm supposed to just let you sit here and rot?"

"Yes." At least this way, he had a shred of pride left. Joe held his ground, chest to chest, refusing to budge out of the doorway. "She already said no. Don't make her repeat herself."

Their eyes locked, Joe's desperate, Wyatt's measuring.

"I'm not kidding, Wyatt. Promise me you won't call her." Then Joe remembered who he was talking to, and added, "No letters. No texts. No emails. You do not contact Violet, even by fucking carrier pigeon."

"Fine. Christ. Make it difficult." Wyatt gave him a shove and side-stepped around him. "I'm going to order food. State your preference or eat what you get."

"Ribs," Joe said, because the sauce irritated Wyatt's ulcer but he'd slather it on anyway. They might as well both feel like they were bleeding internally.

Joe turned to unpack his bags. He made a couple of halfhearted attempts to loosen the first knot, then ripped a hole in the side, scattering socks and underwear across the bed, tempted to just kick them off onto the floor instead of putting them away. This wasn't his place. For all intents and purposes, he was homeless. His body was parked in Wyatt's guest room, but his chest was still hollowed out, as if his heart had been incinerated and the ashes scattered, half on the High Lonesome, half across the Texas Panhandle. He couldn't visualize a future where he would be whole again.

"Here." Wyatt strode through the door and shoved a blanket into Joe's hands. "Helen dropped that off. She decided to follow your example and told Dick to take a leap. She's moving up to Yakima to live with her sister, but she wanted you to have something to remind you to stop and visit once in a while."

Not just a blanket. A quilt, patchwork squares of soft flannel on one side and plush, velvety stuff on the other. He slid his hand between the folds and it wrapped around his arm, as soft and warm as a hug from the woman who'd made it. Joe clenched his hands in the fabric, run clear through by a pain so sweet and sharp he could taste the blood.

Wyatt folded his arms. "Tell me again how nobody cares fuck all about a worthless bastard like you? I'm having trouble seeing it."

Chapter 39

EVERYTHING VIOLET HAD EVER WANTED WAS SPELLED out in the paperwork scattered across her desk, but she couldn't concentrate. Possibly because she'd done nothing but paperwork for the past two weeks. As of yesterday, the McCloud deal was final, with twenty percent down and the remainder due after Dirt Eater sold. They already had commitments from half of Buck's rodeos for next year, and another quarter were strong possibilities.

Violet should be downright giddy. She was, most of the time. Underneath the smile, though, there was still a low throb of pain, like a bad tooth. She frowned, annoyed with herself. She'd decided against regrets. Waste of time and some damn good memories. Besides, moping was selfish considering everything Joe had done for them. Dirt Eater was going to the Finals and Cole... well, that remained to be seen. He was still Cole, anal and stiff-necked, but his relief at having a name to put to his struggles was obvious. So, no. She would not regret bringing Joe Cassidy into their lives, even if she had to suffer for it.

She propped her chin on her hand and stared at the copy of the *Pro Rodeo Sports News* on her desk, open to the current rodeo entry information. Upper right-hand corner, in bold black, the listing read *Redmond, Oregon*. The first performance was tonight. The last on Sunday.

And down at the bottom, under personnel, the bullfighters were listed. Wyatt Darrington and Joe Cassidy.

For the first time since his plane left Dallas, she knew exactly where Joe was. Fifteen hundred and thirty-four miles from where she sat, according to the internet map site. Might as well be the moon. The words began to dance before her eyes. She blinked, then reached underneath the paper for her vibrating phone.

"How's the wheeling and dealing going?" Melanie asked.

Violet tipped back in her chair. "I'm trying to estimate an advertising budget. What's up?"

"We-ell…I called because I learned something today."

Her tone made Violet sit up, as if she might need both feet solidly on the floor.

Melanie spit it out in a rush. "Joe and Wyatt are working the rodeo in Amarillo next fall."

The announcement was another jab to a heart that felt like a dartboard. The rodeo wasn't until next September, almost a year away, but still…

"Wyatt called me," Melanie added.

Violet almost dropped her phone. "Wyatt *Darrington*?"

"The one and only, and wow. You were right. The man is scary. How did he find out who I am and where I work? That's borderline creepy."

"What did he *say,* Mel?"

"He wanted to talk about their contracts. I tried to tell him I don't handle those things, I'm just the facility coordinator, but he said he wasn't allowed to get in touch directly and he knew he could count on me to pass along a message, which was when I finally got a clue that we weren't talking about contracts."

"What message?" Violet demanded, the pounding of her pulse shifting to a different gear. "From Joe?"

"Not exactly. Let me look at my notes."

"You wrote it down?"

"I wanted to be sure I got it right. Plus Wyatt said, 'You should write this down.'" There was a rustle of paper, then Melanie quoted, "'Joe wants to back out. He says someone told him they didn't want to see him around there again.'"

"I did not say—" Violet protested.

But she had. She cringed, remembering that evening over at the other place, when he'd asked to see her again and she'd been too scared to say yes.

"Okay, I did say that, but it was before I…I mean, we…" She trailed off.

"And yet you say nothing to your best friend." Melanie clucked her tongue in disapproval. "I'll be needing details, Miz Violet, but not right now. So, you blew him off. Twice. At any point did you actually look him in the eye and say, 'I take it back'?"

"Well, no, but I showed him…"

Melanie chuckled. "Honey, as soon as you showed him the girls, he went deaf and dumb. Didn't the two of you talk afterward?"

"I meant to, but he bolted."

"And you didn't try to stop him?"

Violet huffed out a breath. "Remember when we were in the fifth grade, and tried to corner that calico barn cat of yours because it was so pretty?"

"I still have a scar on my arm."

"Joe had that exact same look in his eyes."

"Oh." Melanie paused a beat. "Well now, that would make a girl take a step back."

"You see? I thought he just needed space. A little time to adjust." Violet tilted her chair back to glare at a cobweb in the corner of the ceiling. "I can't believe he's dumb enough to think I'd jump him if I wasn't serious."

Melanie snorted. "Did I mention he's a man—and a cowboy? That's clueless squared. Wyatt said, and I quote again, 'Joe is going through some major personal and professional changes that have affected him deeply. He won't go back to Texas unless he's convinced he's welcome.'"

"Idiot," Violet muttered. She'd practically thrown the man over her shoulder and hauled him into her motel room, and he wasn't sure she wanted to see him again? Then she blew out a guilty sigh. He *had* asked to see her again. Offered her exactly what she'd told her sister she wanted—an occasional no-strings fling—and she'd tossed it back in his face. Twice. So who exactly was the idiot?

But on the other hand, what had changed? She'd always known Joe wanted more than one night. And she knew more than ever that part of him wasn't enough. "What difference does this make, if he's still chained to Dick Browning?"

"This is why we take notes," Melanie said, with exaggerated patience. "You weren't paying attention, Violet. I repeat—*Joe is going through some major personal and professional changes.*"

Oh. God. Did that mean—hope flared, a small but stubborn flame that had never quite died. "If he left Dick, why hasn't he come back? At least called? He must realize it changes everything."

"As I believe I mentioned earlier—man, cowboy, clueless?"

Violet drew a deep, resolute breath. "Then I guess it's up to me to educate him."

"Atta girl," Melanie said. "And Violet? Good luck."

"Thanks." She might need every bit she could get.

As soon as she hung up, she pulled Joe's number out of her contact list and hit Send, before she lost her nerve. She tensed as the phone clicked, but instead of Joe's voice, a recording declared, *"The number you dialed has been changed, disconnected, or is no longer in service. If you feel you have reached this message in error..."*

Violet frowned, grabbed the *Sports News*, and fumbled through the pages to the classifieds at the back, where Joe was listed with the other contract personnel. The number was the same. She keyed it in from scratch, just to be sure, and hit Send again.

"The number you have dialed has been changed—"

She jabbed the Off button and flung the phone down on her desk.

"Is something wrong?"

Violet jumped, startled by the deep rumble of her father's voice. "Uh, no. Nothing important."

Just life or death for that little ray of hope. Then she took a good look at his face, flushed with something between anger and confusion.

"Is something wrong with you?" she asked.

He settled into the chair in front of Violet's desk, making the springs squeal in protest. "I just got a really strange phone call."

Join the club.

"It was Dick Browning. Called right outta the blue, goin' on about how I stole his bullfighter when Joe was only supposed to be taking a break." His face darkened as he spoke, a visible measure of his rising temper. "Made it sound like he gave Joe leave to come down here."

"As if! After what he said in Puyallup?"

"I know, but I couldn't get a word in edgewise. He kept rantin' and ravin', sayin' Wyatt told him Joe quit because he had a better offer in Texas." He squinted at her with a touch of impatience. "Did you hire him again without telling me?"

"No! I wouldn't…I haven't talked to Joe since he left."

"Why would Wyatt say so, then?"

Because Wyatt had some kind of nerve, and he was covering all of his bases. And then the full impact of what he'd said hit Violet square between the eyes. "Joe really quit?"

"Obviously, or Dick wouldn't be on such a tear."

And that meant there really was nothing holding Joe in Oregon any more. Not Dick Browning. Not the High Lonesome Ranch. Violet rested her elbows on the desk and pressed her throbbing forehead into her palms. "Why can't he just pick up the damn phone?"

"Maybe he doesn't know how."

"To dial a phone?"

Her father scowled, shifting in his chair. "To talk about feelings and such. It ain't that easy dealin' with women. Even you."

She rolled her eyes. "What's so hard? He dials the phone and says, 'Hey, Violet, sorry I jumped you and ran, can I make it up to you?"

"See?" Her dad stabbed a thick finger at her. "This is why fathers and daughters shouldn't discuss this crap. Now I feel like it's my God-given duty to kick his ass, even though your mother insists I'm supposed to respect your independence. Why can't y'all just leave me out of it?"

"I'm sorry. But honestly, I don't understand why he hasn't…" But she did. She'd rejected Joe not once, but twice, and despite all that had passed between them since, she hadn't verbally taken it back. Another man might have assumed, but vulnerable, skittish Joe—her Joe—needed the words even more than she did. She hissed out a curse and let her chin drop to her chest. "I never even tried to stop him."

"I don't think you could have. But you might've made it so he could see his way back." His voice gentled. "From what I hear and what I saw, he hasn't had much practice at belonging, and he sure as hell didn't learn anything good from that son of a bitch Browning."

Or the man who was supposed to be his father.

Her father gave his chin a thoughtful rub. "Might be he needs someone to put up a fight for him."

Violet flopped back in her chair with an irate huff. "I'd be happy to try, but his number is out of service. I suppose I could get it from Wyatt, though."

His brow furrowed, considering, then cleared. "No. This kind of thing is better done face-to-face."

"But he's in Oregon…"

"Yup." He tapped the rodeo listings with one finger. "And you know right where to find him. Better get crackin' if you intend to get to Redmond by Sunday."

She watched in stunned disbelief as he stood and ambled out of the office. As he opened the door, a thought struck her. "What did you say to Dick Browning?"

He planted one big hand on the knob and smiled at her. "I told him Wyatt was right. There ain't nothin' better in the whole wide world than what Joe found down here in Texas."

Chapter 40

JOE BOUNCED ON HIS TOES, IMPATIENT FOR THE NEXT BULL rider to nod his head. How long could Rowdy diddle around before the chute boss smacked him upside the head? The anticipation that had been building event by event, ride by ride, was going flat despite a packed house and Guns N' Roses blasting over the sound system. The crowd could only hang on the edge of their seats for so long before their butts went numb.

Beside him, Wyatt dropped a disgusted F-bomb. "If that dumb bastard plays dead again, I say we let Hotshot stomp his guts and drag the body back to the catch pen."

The bull would be happy to oblige. He was a snaky, man-hunting son of a bitch. Finally, Rowdy nodded. Hotshot whipped around right in front of the chute. Rowdy survived the first nasty duck, but his hips slid back off the rope, and on the next jump, Hotshot launched him into the rafters. Or would have, if Rowdy had opened his damn hand and let it come out of the rope. Instead, he whiplashed to the end of his arm, slammed against the bull's shoulder, then hung there, boneless as a sock monkey.

Joe jumped for the bull's head, giving Hotshot a target for his slinging horns while Wyatt threw himself onto the bull's shoulders, cursing Rowdy and all of his ancestors as he yanked at the tail of the rope. Hotshot stayed hard into his spin, each jump close to a one-eighty. Joe scrambled to keep up as Wyatt gave the rope one last yank and Rowdy dropped…and took Joe out. He tucked his head as he went down, hoping to somersault clear, but the bull stayed right on his ass.

All Joe could do was throw his arms over his face as a massive front hoof skimmed past the end of his nose. A rear foot skidded down the outside of his hip, taking a layer of skin along with it. He heard Wyatt yelling "Hey! Hotshot!" and pulling the bull off him. Saw more legs and hooves flashing past as the pickup men rode in to rope Hotshot and make sure he didn't come back for another round.

And then it was over. Joe stayed put, inventorying body parts as he sucked in a careful breath. Head? Check. Ribs? Check. Knees? Check. Ass stung like a bitch, but didn't feel like anything was broken.

"You okay?" Wyatt asked, leaning over him.

Joe opened his eyes. "If he's not dead already, I'm going to kill that fucking Rowdy."

He scrambled to his feet, the hot stab of pain fueling his fury. He shouldered past the athletic trainers coming to his aid and went straight for the cowboy.

The moron rolled to his knees, taking his own sweet time about getting up. "Thanks, Joe—"

"Run, you little bastard." Joe grabbed the back strap of Rowdy's chaps and the collar of his shirt and threw him toward the chutes. "You hit the ground, you get up and fucking *run!*"

"What the—"

Rowdy stumbled two steps before Joe cleated him square in the ass. The force of the blow bounced Rowdy off the front of the chutes, but a hand hauled Joe back before him could kick him again.

Rowdy spun around. "Who do you think you—"

"I'm the guy who just got his ass stomped on your behalf," Joe yelled, fighting the arm that locked around his chest. "And I'm fixin' to return the favor."

More hands grabbed Joe's shoulders, jerking him away as Wyatt shoved between them, chest to chest with Joe.

"Not in the arena. You want to kick the crap out of him, we can take turns outside the bar later."

Joe gave Rowdy one last hard look, then wheeled around and stalked off to the other end of the chutes. Wyatt followed, limping more than he had been.

"You get tagged, too?" Joe asked.

"Just landed on it a wrong," Wyatt said, flexing his bad ankle. "Where'd he get you?"

Joe grabbed the water bottle one of the chute crew handed him, took three big gulps, then dragged an arm across his face to wipe away dirt and sweat. "He stepped on my ass."

Wyatt laughed. "Figures. They always hit you in the sorest spot."

Back in the locker room, Joe threw his cleats in the corner and peeled off his jersey, Kevlar vest, and the sweat-dampened T-shirt underneath and heaved them all at the wall. He was so damn tired of being tired. Tired of being pissed off. Tired of hurting. He kept thinking he'd hit bottom. *Splat!* Then he could start gathering up the pieces and see what was left. But this was like falling off of one of the mesas in Palo Duro Canyon then rolling down the scree slope, getting beat to shit by the rocks and sagebrush with every bounce. Down, down, down, with no end in sight.

He shoved an ice pack into the back of his shorts, hissing when it slid across the fresh scrape, then flopped face down on the padded treatment table the committee had thoughtfully installed in the bullfighter's dressing room. *Bless their hearts*, as they'd say in Texas.

Wyatt sat on the bench against the wall, peeled off his sock, and gingerly rotated his foot. A puff of swelling surrounded the ankle bone. "That's gonna raise hell with my dancing."

"So we'll just drink. And pound on Rowdy."

Joe punched the plastic-covered pillow into a ball, barely noticing the frigid burn of the ice against his flesh. He'd slapped on so many cold packs over the years he'd learned to crave the burn, or at least the numbness that would follow. Too bad he couldn't ice his brain.

Wyatt hooked a toe in the strap of his duffel, dragged it close enough to root around inside, and pulled out a glossy piece of paper that he tossed on the table next to Joe's head. "I found a stack of these at the rodeo office earlier."

Joe turned the paper over and his breath seized up in his lungs when he read the words emblazoned across the top, recognized the picture. *Offered for sale by Jacobs Livestock. National Finals bucking bull.*

Joe felt like his guts had been sucked out through his navel with a drinking straw. "They're selling him," he said numbly.

"Not really. They're offering forty-five percent interest with a list of conditions so long they'll be lucky to get half of market value. Who does that?"

Violet. She would do exactly that, with her family

behind her one hundred percent. Just like his stupid *Kiss it better* joke, she'd taken his wrong-headed advice and turned it into something shiny and good. Staring at that flyer, hearing Violet's voice loud and clear in every word of the bold print, he missed her so bad he wasn't sure how he could continue to breathe.

Wyatt fished out his phone, punched a few buttons, then got up, hobbled over and dropped it on the table in front of Joe's face. Violet's number was on the screen. "Call the woman, for Christ's sake."

"We already talked about this."

"Joe. Come on. You just tried to knock some sense into a *bull rider*. I'd say that calls for an intervention." Wyatt shoved the phone with one fingertip, so close it touched Joe's nose, making his eyes cross. "*Call her.*"

Joe covered the phone with his hand but didn't pick it up. One touch. One little tap of his finger and he could hear her voice…

Wyatt snatched the phone, punched Send, and shoved it back into Joe's hand. "Geezus. Do I have to do everything for you?"

"Oh f—" Joe cut the curse short as the phone started to ring. His pulse screamed into overdrive. He couldn't hang up. She'd see it on her caller ID, figure out it was an Oregon number, and who else could it be? Maybe that's why she wasn't answering.

The voice mail clicked on. *"You wanna talk to my mommy, you gotta go through me,"* Beni declared, then added more politely. *"Please leave a message."*

When it beeped, Joe's mind went blank. He squeezed his eyes shut. "Uh, hi, Violet. It's Joe. I, um, just wanted to call and say hello—"

"Hi."

At the sound of her voice, his heart jumped straight up and smacked into his vocal cords, rendering him speechless. She sounded so close. Like she was standing in the room with him, instead of half a country away.

"It's about time," Wyatt said. "I was starting to think you weren't coming."

Joe's eyes popped open. The phone clattered onto the concrete floor as he stared at Violet. Blinked. Stared again.

"What are you doing here?"

She flinched, but her chin came up a notch. "You said if you failed to show up, I was supposed to come pounding on your door. Consider this your wake-up call."

"Atta girl." Wyatt heaved to his feet, slung his bag over his shoulder, and limped toward the door. "I'll just leave you two alone."

Violet narrowed her eyes at him. "You're the one with all the advice—got any now?"

Wyatt glanced over his shoulder at Joe, then back at Violet. "Stay between him and the door."

He toasted them with his water bottle and limped out, leaving them to it.

Joe shoved off the table and to his feet, the abrupt change in altitude making him dizzy. Or it might have been Violet, standing in front of him, wearing that red shirt under a denim jacket. The combination was so perfectly *her* it made him want to laugh. Or cry. Or just grab her.

The ice pack slid out of his shorts and plopped onto Wyatt's phone, water pooling around it. Good. Served him right. "I told him not to call you."

"I haven't talked to Wyatt since he left our ranch," she said, almost without blinking.

So Wyatt had weaseled through some loophole Joe had missed, and somehow convinced Violet to come all the way to Oregon. "Why *are* you here?"

"I told you. I came for you."

His heart did a big *ker-thump*. Violet watched him, her eyes steady, but her fingers fidgeted with the bottom brass button on her jacket. Three steps and he could have his hands on her. Bury his face in the soft curve of her neck, let her hair slide cool against his cheek. She'd smell like strawberries and feel like heaven. But how would he ever let her go again?

When he didn't move, didn't speak, she said, "That bull freight-trained you pretty good. Do you have a concussion?"

Because, yeah, he was acting like a man with a brain injury. "I'm fine."

"Well. That's a relief." Her smile was quick, a little wobbly. "I can sympathize with your mother. It looks a lot worse from the stands."

Her gaze slid down, over Joe's bare chest and stomach, shying away before it got any lower. "So much for that fantasy where all I had to do was show up and you'd throw yourself into my arms."

He wanted to. It was killing him, having her so close and not putting his hands on her, but…

"Violet, I—"

She gave a quick shake of her head. "No. This is better. There are things I should say, and I lose my ability to make whole sentences when you're touching me."

She reached over and swung the door shut. Then

she grabbed a chair, planted it front of the door, and sat down.

Panic trickled cold into Joe's blood. "What are you doing?"

"Takin' a load off. Plus I don't want you disappearin' again if I look away." Her drawl was more pronounced than he remembered, thick and sweet as molasses. She tipped her head back and closed her eyes. "Lord, I'm whupped. I've been travelin' since yesterday afternoon. Spent the night in the Atlanta airport."

"Atlanta? Why?"

"Last minute reservation usin' Daddy's credit card miles. I had four connections."

And she'd done all that for him? He intended to ask why Steve would want her anywhere near him, but she folded her arms and everything sort of lifted and he could see clear down to the red lace in her cleavage. He exhaled, long and shaky. "That shirt is not fair."

"Lily said it would bring back fond memories, but Mom made me promise to wear the jacket so people up here didn't think I was a hussy."

Joe stared at her in disbelief. "What did you do, call a meeting to discuss it?"

"Pretty much. Melanie said…" She paused, took a deep breath, and opened her eyes to meet his. "Melanie told me to just tell you straight-out how I feel."

Her gaze was anxious, but steady. "That night after we went dancing, I was all set to get naked and you walked away. I was hurt, and I was mad, and I realized I was hooked on you. I've never been really hooked on anyone in my whole life, Joe. It scared the hell out me, and there you were, dead set on high-tailing it off to the other side of the country. But you weren't the first one to run away. I bailed out on you." She snorted in disgust. "As if it wasn't already too late, and my heart wouldn't get broke quite so bad if I just stopped right there."

His head spun so hard he had to grab onto the edge of the treatment table to keep from falling flat on his aching butt. "When I asked if I could come back sometime and see you—that's why you said no?"

Violet ducked her head, doing some kind of complicated weaving thing with her fingers. "I imagined you popping in for a few days, then gallivanting off again. In between, I'd never hear from you or know where you were or who you were with, and it would've killed me—killed me *dead*—to picture you with someone like that girl in the Corvette."

Joe had to put a second hand on the table, because his skeleton seemed to be dissolving and he wasn't sure how long he could remain vertical. "And when I took off the morning after—"

"Possibly the worst dismount in the history of sex," she pointed out helpfully.

"Why didn't you say so? Chew my ass, call me names, whatever?"

"I didn't know you needed me to, or believe me, I would have been more than willing." The glint in her eyes suggested she might still consider obliging him. "I thought if I gave you time to calm down, you'd get used to the idea of…us."

Blood pounded at the base of his skull, obliterating his ability to think. Reason. Make her see. "Why me,

Violet? Of all the men you could have. What do I know about relationships?"

"About as much as me, seein's how I've never had one worth counting, but I figure we can't be any worse together than we are apart. I'm miserable and you look like you've been marched to Hell and back on short rations. I can count your ribs, for crying out loud. Doesn't anybody up here feed you?"

Joe looked down, remembering he'd stripped to the waist. He spun around, grabbed a reasonably clean shirt out of his bag and wrestled it over his head.

"It's backwards," Violet said.

He checked, cursed, and nearly strangled himself fumbling it around the right direction. "You shouldn't have come. I'm not...I can't...I'll screw up, Violet, make some stupid mistake."

"What kind?"

"Huh?"

"What kind of mistake?" she repeated. "Sleeping with my friends, beating my kid, what?"

"No! I would never—"

"Those are the only kind of mistakes I couldn't get over."

He clenched his fists, desperate to make her understand. "I don't want to hurt you. Or Beni."

"Then quit making this so damn hard." Her bravado melted and her eyes filled, the tears welling over. She swiped at them with the back of one hand. "I'm sorry. I'm so tired—"

Her sniffle hit Joe like a roundhouse punch square in the gut. He shoved off the table and staggered over to drop to his knees, hands cupping her face, the pain in his hip obliterated by the throbbing in his chest. "Don't do that. Geezus, don't, please? Whatever you want, it's yours, just stop doing that."

Which only prompted another spurt of tears. She planted her palms on his chest, hands fisting in his shirt, and gave him a shake, and even that felt good because finally, *finally,* Violet was touching him.

"Damn you, proving Cole right," she said, shaking him again. "He said forget all the yakking, just work up a few tears and you'd cave."

Geezus. Even Cole? Joe shook his head, amazement trickling through his panic. "They're all okay with this? You being here, me being with you?"

"Yes, dummy. They actually like you." She used a fist to catch a tear that had trickled down to her jaw. "Except maybe Hank. He's still sore about his phone."

"Served him right." Joe wiped her face with the pads of his thumbs. "I can't stand doing this to you."

"Then stop!" she said, and punched his shoulder.

Stop. The word exploded in his head. So simple. He had a choice. He didn't have to keep running, didn't have to hurt either of them anymore. He could just…stop.

She stroked away the hair that had grown long enough to fall over his forehead. "I know it must've torn you apart, leaving the High Lonesome."

"I just…I had to." The aching void opened inside him again, thinking about it. "I couldn't go back and find a way to make it seem right. But God, Violet, it's been so hard, not being there…"

Violet slid her arms around his shoulders, her hands strong and sure, and he realized he was shaking. She stroked his cheek, the touch smoothing the ragged ends of his nerves. "I can't give you the High Lonesome, Joe, but I can give you a home, and a place where a whole lot of people care about you." She drew back to give him another wobbly smile. "Including Beni, who keeps asking if you can come visit because his dad is no fun at *all* since he got hurt."

Joe smiled, hearing the words exactly as Beni would moan them, dramatic sigh and eye roll included. "What about Delon?"

Violet's gaze dropped, and her voice was tinged with regret. "He understands that we'll never be together, with or without you in the picture. Things aren't great between us right now, but we'll be fine once he gets back on his feet. Delon's a reasonable man and Beni is his number one concern."

Joe wasn't as sure. He couldn't imagine how bad it would be, having Violet even as a pretend wife and then losing her.

She reached up to cup his face, the emotions in her eyes so naked and honest he could barely stand to look. "I chickened out before, and let you go without giving you the words you needed. I swore I wouldn't do that again, so listen close. I love you, Joe Cassidy. And you're gonna have to deal with it, because there's nothing you can do or say to change my mind."

His heart just crumbled, along with the doors and walls and feeble excuses he'd tried throw up between them. He collapsed against her, wrapping his arms around her waist and pressing his face into the silky softness of her hair, drinking in the scent and the feel of her that had tortured his dreams for weeks.

Thank *God*.

The relief of finally having her in his arms again was so enormous, it shattered the last of his self-control. He kissed her neck, her temple, her cheek, every inch of her he could reach, then braced his forehead in the curve of her shoulder to steady himself when it was all too much—and still not enough. His throat was so tight he could barely force out a whisper. "I don't think I was gonna make it without you."

Her laugh vibrated against his skin, but her voice was choked with the tears that trickled down to drip onto his cheek. "Well, lucky for both of us you don't have to."

His mouth found hers and she took him in, absorbed all of his need and his desperate hunger, and returned it twofold. He kissed her until he felt sane for the first time since he'd started running.

Until his knees screamed in protest.

He paused long enough to catch his breath. "If we don't stop, I'm going to be lame for life."

"Good thing you kept your knee pads on," she said, nibbling her way along his jaw, hands pushing at the hem of his T-shirt, burrowing underneath.

He groaned as her fingers found bare skin, waking a different kind of need, and kissed her again. What the hell. Walking was overrated. Finally, though, he couldn't take it anymore. "I have to stand up. But I think I might need some help here."

She laughed and held out her hands, palms up, to support him. "You can lean on me."

He could. Now and always. He knew it as sure as he'd ever known anything in his life. Violet was a pickup man. She would save his sorry ass or go down trying.

The thought made him dizzy all over again, but in a

good way. He kissed her chin, her nose, her forehead, then pulled away far enough to see a smile that was like a magnet for all those tiny, lost pieces of his heart, drawing them together into a battered, but determined, whole. He would never be half the man she deserved, but if she had her heart set on him, he'd do his damnedest to be sure she never regretted it. The words he hadn't even let himself think just tumbled right out. "I love you, Violet."

"I know."

He laughed at her smug grin, got himself upright, then pulled her out of the chair and into another kiss. She broke it off to skim her fingers ever so lightly over his sore hip. "Is this where it hurts?"

"Mostly."

Reaching behind her, she turned the deadbolt on the door.

"What are you doing?"

She pressed her palm to his chest and her voice dropped to a husky, wicked drawl that matched the gleam in her eyes.

"I'm fixin' to kiss it *all* better."

Epilogue

VIOLET STOOD IN A CORNER OF A CONFERENCE ROOM in a Las Vegas hotel at the annual meeting of pro rodeo stock contractors and committees, soaking it all in. For the first time, she was one of the chosen few who would have stock bucking at the National Finals, and Jacobs Livestock was the biggest news in town until the rodeo kicked off tonight and the real stars took the stage. Every second person who passed stopped to shake her hand with congratulations on the success of the Dirt Eater sale, for an amount of money beyond her wildest dreams.

She was now business partners with someone she'd watched on dozens of movie screens. They had Wyatt to thank for the infusion of Hollywood money. Scary he might be, but extremely well-connected. And speak of the devil…

"You're looking very confrontational for a woman who's got everything she wanted."

She narrowed her eyes. "If Dick Browning doesn't stop glaring at me, I'm gonna have to throat punch him."

"I'll hold your purse," Wyatt said, and tossed a brilliant smile in Dick's direction. Dick snarled and turned away.

Violet grinned. Wyatt took some getting used to, but his fierce loyalty to Joe made him impossible to dislike. Besides, as Melanie had pointed out, "As long as he's on our side we should be safe."

Safe being a relative term.

"I'm glad you stayed for Thanksgiving dinner," she said. "You really didn't have to sit at the kids' table."

"I wanted to."

For reasons known only to the good Lord and Wyatt. "Sorry about the food fight. I suppose that jacket was Armani or something. My cousin swears her kids never act like that unless Beni's around, but I've heard rumors to the contrary."

"They're all awesome. I want ten."

"Now I know you truly are insane. And I will warn you once again." Violet leveled him her sternest Mama Bear glower. "No matter how many times he asks, or what line of BS he feeds you, Beni does not get a ride in your airplane."

"I'm an exceptionally good pilot."

"And still—no." She turned away before he could lure her into a debate she would surely lose and focused her attention on the world's most unlikely marketing team. Across the room, her father and Joe were chatting with the committee chairman from Tucson and a man who might be the greatest stock contractor of all time, Harry Vold. Violet was beginning to realize there was no one in upper echelon of pro rodeo that Joe didn't know.

"I may have created a monster," she said.

"You wanted to expand."

"Well, yeah, but who knew Daddy would take *that* bit in his teeth and run?"

Or, more accurately, saunter. In a room littered with distinguished men, Steve Jacobs stood—in most cases literally—a head above the rest, at least in Violet's admittedly prejudiced opinion. Dressed for business in a western-cut jacket, starched shirt, bolo tie and spotless white hat, he carried himself with a stately confidence that made the people around him stand straighter and pay attention.

Beside him, Joe looked lean and agile and slightly disreputable in spite of his dark jeans, polished boots and a black button-down shirt plastered with sponsor logos. It was the hair. Violet had made him promise not to cut it short again without her leave, and that would be a long time coming. She planned to spend many, many more hours running her fingers through that hair. And over that body…

Wyatt laughed. "Okay. *Now* you look like the girl who's got it all."

"Not yet." She lifted her eyebrows with vintage Joe Cassidy arrogance. "But give me a few years…"

With the unnerving way he had of feeling her eyes on him, Joe glanced over, caught her gaze, and smiled, and her heart tumbled all over again. Damn. Six weeks of spending nearly every day together and he could still knock the breath clean out of her from thirty feet away. With Cole's blessing, Joe had taken up residence at his family's place. Wyatt had made himself at home there, too, while they trained for the National Finals and helped rebuild the rundown corrals, the extra pens a necessity with the addition of the McCloud stock. As a nod to Cole's daddy, they'd decided to make that the bull facility.

And bless his heart, Wyatt was a genius at finding excuses to drag both Cole and Beni out from underfoot for at least a couple of blissful hours every day.

Her father turned, too, and waved Violet over. When

she joined the group, he rested a proud hand on her shoulder while he made introductions. "My daughter, Violet. She's the brains of the operation. These gentlemen would like to know if we're interested in sendin' some stock to the rodeo in Tucson next spring."

"I'm sure we can figure something out." Violet whipped out her ever-present tablet, punched up the calendar, and got down to business.

Twelve hours later, she watched the first of ten performances of the National Finals Rodeo wind down. She stood in the big center alley between the bucking chutes, holding the backup pickup horses, a job Joe had wrangled for her. There were no insignificant chores at the NFR. The man opening and closing the gate was a world champion all-around cowboy.

And in three days, Cole and her daddy would be on the back of the chutes when one of the top fifteen bull riders in the world climbed down on Dirt Eater's back and the chute gate flew open on Jacobs Livestock's virgin trip at the biggest show in rodeo.

But not their last. Her pulse did a happy jitter at the possibilities opening up where not so long ago she'd seen only walls. She propped her elbows on a metal rail, peeking through the foot-wide gap between the big yellow *Wrangler* sign and the top of the gate. Her eyes gravitated to Joe. She would to have to stop going soft in the head every time she looked at him once they were working in the same arenas again.

Joe had signed on for half a dozen of next season's rodeos—and yes, he was working cheap. He said the fringe benefits more than made up for lower wages. By which, he hurried to assure her parents, he meant cheap rent and Iris's home cooking. Her father pretended to believe him.

At the moment, Joe had one hand hooked on the front of a bucking chute and the other propped on his hip, talking with the chute boss as they all waited for the final cowboy to nod his head. The bull reared, slamming his bulk into the back of the chute as hands dragged the cowboy to safety. The bull sank onto his belly, and the chute boss pulled the sliding gate, allowing the bull to right himself and move forward a slot.

"How does this matchup look to you, Joe?" the rodeo announcer asked, to fill the gap while the cowboy reset his rope.

Joe flipped on his wireless headset. Honest to Pete, what were they thinking giving him a microphone in front of eighteen thousand fans? Violet held her breath every time he opened his mouth.

"This bull should go right into J.W.'s hand, and settle into a nice spin. I'm betting he'll spur the hair off him."

"Sounds like a winner." The announcer segued into a sponsor plug as the cowboy eased over the bull, tugging his rope into place.

Joe retreated a few steps so he was directly in front of Violet. And there it was—that look, that smile, the way his eyes lit up when they landed on her. He closed his hand over the microphone as he spoke. "Good night?"

"The only way it could be any better is if I was out there," she joked, nodding toward where the pickup men sat waiting for the chute gate to open.

"Well, hell, if that's all you want—"

Before she had time to draw a breath, Joe had

ducked out the gate, handed the horses off to a surprised bystander, and dragged Violet into the arena.

"Joe! What are you—"

"Hey, Boyd," he called out, holding tight to both of her wrists as he cut into the announcer's patter. "There's somebody special I'd like you all to meet. Ladies and gentlemen, Violet Jacobs is the only female pickup man currently working in professional rodeo."

Oh no. He did *not*…

She looked up and felt her knees turn to water. Yep. There she was, her face big as a billboard on the massive video screen. She gave a feeble smile. The audience responded with a ripple of applause.

"Pickup *man?*" the announcer asked.

She tugged at his grip, trying to hiss words through a smile and pitch her voice too low to be picked up by the microphone. "*Joe! Stop it.*"

Joe only cocked his head, as if giving Boyd's question serious consideration. "My mistake. Pickup *lady.* And a damn good one. But the rest of you are gonna have to stand back, because this lady is all mine."

And then he kissed her. A roaring sound filled Violet's ears, punctuated by whistles and the stomping of feet. She started to cringe, then tipped back her head and laughed instead. Joe Cassidy was just as bold and brash and shameless as the day they met—and she wouldn't have him any other way. She fisted her hands into his jersey, yanked him close, and kissed him back.

And the crowd went wild.

*Read on for a sneak peek at the next book
in Kari Lynn Dell's Texas Rodeo series*

TANGLED UP *in* TEXAS

Chapter 1

DELON SANCHEZ WOKE UP PISSED OFF AT THE WORLD.
Which was pretty much like every other morning in the
past four months. For the official Fan Favorite Cowboy
two years running and the unofficial nicest guy in pro
rodeo, it was like being trapped inside someone else's
skin. A person he wasn't particularly fond of.

He made a fist and beat on his pillow as if it had
caused his dream. That stupid, pointless dream where he
didn't get hurt at the very end of the best rodeo season of
his life. Didn't feel his shot at a world title disintegrate
along with the ligaments in his knee. The dream where
he went on to the National Finals Rodeo and walked
away with the gold buckle, heavy and warm and so
damn real he could still feel the shape of it when he
woke up.

Empty-handed.

He jammed his fist into the pillow again. His sub-conscious was a cruel bastard, and a whiner on top of it. Every year an injury yanked the trap door out from under some cowboy's gold buckle dream. That was rodeo. Hell, that was life. Delon was no special flower fate had singled out to trample.

He flopped onto his back. A spider sneered at him from the corner of the ceiling, lounging on a web Delon had just knocked down the day before. He was tempted to reach down, grab a boot and fling it, but the way his luck was running, he'd just miss and it'd bounce off and black his eye. He stuffed his hands behind his head with a gloomy sigh. They should have drawn a chalk outline in the arena where he'd fallen, because the man who'd climbed down into the bucking chute that night was nowhere to be found.

Gone, in the twenty-two seconds from the nod of his head to the moment of impact. He'd timed it on the video out of morbid curiosity. Less than a minute before the paramedics jammed a tube down his throat and re-inflated the lung that'd been punctured when the horse trampled him, wiping out his knee and busting two ribs. Three days before he'd checked out of the hospital. In that short time, his entire life had disintegrated.

Or had been an illusion all along. But that was his fault. He'd let himself want too much, dream too big. Other people could reach up, grab the world by the throat, and make demands. Every time Delon tried, he got kicked in the teeth.

Whiner.

He flipped the spider the bird, kicked off the blan-kets, and got up to dress for another therapy session that would accomplish nothing except forcing him to absorb one more unwelcome change. He doubted this new therapist could fix him either, but maybe she wouldn't be afraid to tell him the truth.

He slipped down the back stairs, escaping his apartment above the shop at Sanchez Trucking without seeing a soul, but was forced to stop at the Kwicky Mart for gas. With only two thousand people in Earnest, Texas, the face at the next pump was bound to be familiar.

And it would have to be Hank. The kid hopped out of his pickup, so nimble Delon wanted to kick him. "Hey, Delon. How's the knee feelin'?"

Like he'd torn it up so bad even Pepper Burke, surgeon to the stars of professional rodeo, couldn't make it good as new.

"Fine." Delon turned his back, hunching his shoulders against the bitter January breeze as he jammed the gas nozzle into the tank of what his brother jeeringly called his mom car. Well, screw Gil. If he'd paid more attention to safety ratings, he'd be flaunting a gold buckle by now.

Hank lounged against the side of his dad's one-ton dually while it guzzled four-dollar diesel like sweet tea. "Looks like it's getting' pretty serious between Violet and Joe. Think they'll get married?"

Delon made a noncommittal noise and mashed harder on the gas nozzle. Short answer? Nope. When the shine wore off, Joe Cassidy would be gone, back to Oregon. Bad enough he'd leave Violet in pieces, but there'd be one brokenhearted little boy, too. Delon's boy. Until now, Delon had just shrugged and laughed at Violet's dating disasters. She couldn't seem to help herself, so he might as well just let her get it out of her system—but she'd never brought her disasters home before.

Beni worshipped Joe, along with every bull rider in the pro ranks and most of the buckle bunnies. The bull riders had good reason. Joe's job was to save them from getting stomped, and he was damn good at it. And a whole lot of those women had admired him from real close up, too. So no. Delon didn't think Joe was the marrying kind.

A red Grand Am whipped around the corner and the little blonde Didsworth girl—Mary Beth?—distracted Hank with a smile and a finger wave. He returned it with a cocky grin. "I hear she's got a thing for bullfighters."

"Don't they all?" Delon muttered.

Even Violet, who should know better, being a stock contractor's daughter. What was it with women, lusting after men dumb enough to throw their bodies in front of large, pissed off farm animals? Sure, it was exciting, but the long term career prospects were not great. *Said the guy who got a knee reconstruction for his twenty-ninth birthday.*

Mary Beth parked down the block, climbed out of her car, and made sure Hank and Delon were watching as she sashayed into the drug store.

Hank gave a low whistle. "I gotta get me a piece of that."

"She's a human being, not an apple pie," Delon snapped. "And she's still in high school."

"Old enough to know what she wants." Hank turned his smirk on Delon. "Like you've got any room to talk. Everybody knows about your hot blonde."

Tori. The memory slammed into Delon. Another of

those times he'd made a grab for something *way* out of his reach. And fallen hard.

Hank shot him a sly grin. "You were seein' her for what—five, six months? And you never brought her around, not even to meet Miz Iris. Sounds like a booty call to me."

Delon had to choke down his fury for fear of sparking the gasoline fumes. Besides—damn it to hell—he couldn't argue.

"Can't blame you. I seen pictures." Hank made a show of wiping his brow with his sleeve. "She was *smokin'*. Melanie and Violet and Shawnee called her Cowgirl Barbie—said she had the perfect outfit for every occasion and roped like she was afraid she'd break a nail."

Tori was definitely not made of plastic. Delon would know. He'd examined every inch of her on multiple occasions. Had planned on doing it a whole lot more, until he'd called her one last time.

I'm sorry, the number you have reached is no longer in service...

"Too bad she wasn't the one you knocked up. Senator Patterson's daughter? That's some serious cash."

Delon slammed the nozzle back onto the pump and wheeled around, biting off a curse when pain stabbed through his knee. "Honest to shit, Hank, why someone hasn't strangled you yet is beyond me."

Hank gazed back in wide-eyed bafflement. "Why? What did I say?"

Only the gas pump between them stopped Delon from running the little bastard down as he drove away. He reached over to the passenger's seat, grabbed a Snickers bar and ripped it open with his teeth, but even the blast of sugar and chocolate couldn't ward off the memories. Tori, with her silky blonde hair, endless legs and eyes as blue as her blood. Who'd left without so much as a *Kiss my ass, cowboy, we're through*, never to be heard from again.

And he'd been stupid enough to be surprised, even after seeing how it'd ended for his brother. Except it never ended for Gil because he *had* knocked up the rich blonde, and he had to fight tooth and nail to be a part of his son's life. At least Delon didn't have to drive clear to Oklahoma to see Beni. He just had to share him with goddamn Joe Cassidy.

Delon crammed the rest of the Snickers into his mouth and punched up the playlist he'd labeled *The Hard Stuff*. The bass notes vibrated clear down into his gonads as he thumped his fist against the steering wheel in time to the beat. He might drive a mom car, but he'd match the custom stereo system against any gang banger in Amarillo.

He pulled into the parking lot at the clinic and sat for a moment, dreading the upcoming appointment. Victoria Hancock was probably better than average or Panhandle Sports Medicine wouldn't have hired her, but he was so damn tired of rolling with the punches. Taking the crumbs he was given and pretending he was satisfied.

Don't kick up a fuss now, Delon. Your mother can't come visit if you're gonna throw such a fit when she leaves.

He scowled, drop-kicking that memory into the distant past as he climbed out of the car. On the worst days along the rodeo trail—beat-up, exhausted and homesick—he'd always been able to paste on a happy face. He was the guy who could work the crowd, the sponsors, the rodeo committees, trading on the face God had given him to the tune of as much sponsorship money as some of the world champions. Now he could barely manage a smile for the receptionist.

Beth—a faded redhead with tired eyes who didn't have much luck hiding her prematurely gray roots or the hard miles that had put them there—smiled back. She clicked a few times with her computer mouse. "Got you checked in, Delon."

"Thanks. Can I go ahead and warm up?"

She shook her head. "Tori said she wanted to do a full evaluation first thing. She'll be right out."

His heart smacked into his ribs. Tori? Couldn't be. Lots of women named Victoria shortened it to Tori. He was just jumpy because Hank had mentioned her. She had been studying physical therapy, but what were the odds…

The waiting room door opened and a woman stood there—tallish, slender and almost plain, wearing khakis and a white Panhandle Sports Medicine polo shirt. The floor tilted under his feet.

"Hello, Delon." Tori didn't smile. Didn't…anything. Her face was as blank as if they'd never shared more than a cup of coffee. "Come on in."

She turned to lead the way without checking to see if he followed. Delon squeezed his eyes shut, taking a moment to steady himself. Here he'd been thinking his life couldn't get much more screwed up.

That'd teach him.

Chapter 2

DELON WAS STILL GORGEOUS. WHICH, OF COURSE, TORI had known. He'd been one of the top bareback riders in the country for years, and fans and sponsors alike swooned over that face, that body, and that way he had of making every person feel like he'd been waiting all day just to smile at them.

He wasn't smiling now. Tori pointed him down the hall toward one of the four private treatment rooms and followed behind. He walked with the distinctive, slightly duck-footed gait of a bareback rider who'd spent a lifetime turning his toes out to spur bucking horses. The view was spectacular, despite loose-fitting nylon warm up pants and a plain navy blue T-shirt. His body was denser, the way men got as they matured. The changes only made him more attractive. More…there.

She'd never seen him in workout clothes. Hell, she'd barely seen him in clothes at all, back in the day. Most of the time they'd spent together had involved the opposite of dressing for the occasion. She poked at the memory, the way her dentist poked her cheek to see if she was numb enough for him to start drilling. *Can you feel that? No? Great. We can go ahead then.*

Ah, the blessed numbness. It had settled around her like thick cotton batting, layer after layer, down the long highway between here and the Wyoming border. By the time she crossed into the Panhandle, she couldn't feel anything but the most basic biological urges. Eat. Drink. Pee. Sleep…well, she was working on that one.

Everything else was muted to near silence. Grief. Guilt. The gossamer thread of anger that wound through it all. She was vaguely aware of their presence, but from a safe distance. For now, survival was enough. An induced coma of the heart, so it could finally rest and heal.

If anyone could penetrate her cocoon, it should have been Delon, but she had looked him straight in the eye and there was…not exactly nothing. But what she felt now was an echo, the ping of a sonar scanner detecting the shape of something too far in the murky past to be more than a blur on her emotional screen. Which meant her concerns about whether she could effectively function as his therapist were ungrounded, at least from her perspective. From Delon's…hard to tell, since he had yet to say a word. He hesitated at the door to the treatment room, as if unsure about being trapped in the confined space with her.

"Climb up on the table," she said. "I want to take some measurements."

He didn't budge. "It's all in my chart."

"I reviewed Margo's notes, but I prefer to form my own opinions." When he still didn't move, she added, "You won't be charged for the evaluation, since it's solely for my benefit."

She held her breath as he stood for a few beats, possibly debating whether to turn around, stomp back to reception and demand to be assigned a different therapist. Being fired by a star patient wasn't quite the impression she wanted to make on her first day. Damn Pepper for insisting that she take over Delon's rehab when she transferred to Panhandle Sports Medicine, but she'd rather hang herself with a cheap rope than explain to her mentor why she shouldn't.

Delon finally moved over to the table, but rather than sitting on it he braced his butt against the edge and faced her, arms and ankles crossed, a posture that made all kinds of muscles jump up and beg for attention. A woman would have to be a whole lot more than numb not to notice.

"So, you're back from…"

"Cheyenne," she said, filling in the blank.

He blinked. "Wyoming?"

Was there any other? Probably, but only one that mattered. "Yes. I did my outpatient clinical rotation at Pepper's place and he hired me when I graduated."

"Pepper *Burke*?"

"Yes." The man who'd performed Delon's surgery, also in Cheyenne, where Tori had made damn sure their paths hadn't crossed. "I've worked for him since I graduated."

She watched the wheels turn behind Delon's dark eyes, connections snapping into place. Cowboys traveled from all over the United States and Canada to be treated by Pepper and his staff. "Tough place to get hired on."

"Yes." She gestured toward the table. "If you're satisfied with my credentials…"

He blinked again, then squinted as if he was seeing double, trying to line up his memory of college Tori with the woman who stood in front of him. She could have told him not to bother. She'd shed that girl, layer by superficial layer, until there was barely enough left to recognize in the mirror.

Whatever Delon saw, it convinced him to slide onto the treatment table. She started with girth measurements—calf, knee, thigh—to compare the muscle mass of his injured leg to the uninjured side. As she slid the tape around his thigh, she felt him tense. Glancing up, her gaze caught his and for an instant she saw it all in his eyes. The memories. The heat.

Her pulse skipped ever so slightly, echoing the hitch in his breath. Her emotions might be too anesthetized to react to his proximity, but her body remembered, and with great fondness. A trained response. No more significant than Pavlov's drooling dogs.

"Lay flat," she ordered, and picked up his leg.

Halfway through the series of tests she knew Pepper's concern was justified. If anything, Delon's injured leg was slightly stronger than the other, testament to how hard he'd worked at his rehab. Four months post-surgery, though, he should have had full range of motion, but when she bent the knee, she felt as if she hit a brick wall a few degrees past ninety. She increased the pressure to see how he'd react.

"That's it," he said, through gritted teeth.

Well, crap. "How does it feel when I push on it?"

"Like my kneecap is going to explode."

Double crap. She sucked in one corner of her bottom lip and chewed on it as she considered their options.

"Is there any chance it's going to get better?" His voice was quiet, but tension vibrated from every muscle in his body, for good reason. He was asking if his rodeo career might be over. It wasn't a question she could, or should, answer.

She stepped back and folded her arms. "I'll give

Pepper a call. He'll want new X-rays, possibly an MRI..."

"What will an MRI tell him?" His gaze came up to meet hers, flat, black, daring her to be anything less than honest.

"Whether you've developed an abnormal amount of scar tissue, either inside the joint or in the capsule."

"And if I have?"

"He can go in arthroscopically and clean up inside the joint." But from what she felt, she doubted that was the case.

"What about the joint capsule?"

She kept her eyes on him, steady, unflinching. "You had a contact injury with a lot of trauma. The capsule may have thickened and scarred in response, or adhesions may have formed between folds. There are ways to address the adhesions."

"But not the other kind."

She saw the answer in his eyes before she spoke. "No. And there are limits to how much we can improve it with therapy. You'll have to learn to live with a deficit."

A shorter spur stroke with his left compared to his right leg, in an event where symmetry was a huge part of the score. How many points would the lag cost him per ride? Five? Ten? Enough to end his career as he knew it.

"Worst case scenario, we can get you to at least eighty percent of normal. Then we can look at your biomechanics, make adjustments…"

He gave a sharp, impatient shake of his head. "The judges aren't stupid. They'll notice if I try to fake it."

She didn't argue. After the thousands of hours he'd spent training his body to work in a very precise groove, telling Delon he had to change his riding style was no different from informing a pitcher they couldn't stay in the major leagues unless they changed their arm angle, or a golfer that they had to retool their swing.

The tight, angry set to Delon's shoulders suggested it might be a while before he would consider trying. Well, he was in luck. He'd found a physical therapist who knew all about adapting to loss. One of these days she might even get around to finding her new style.

Delon sat up abruptly and swung his legs off the table, forcing her to step aside. She pulled out a business card and scribbled a number on the back.

"For today, stick with your regular exercise program. If you want to go ahead with the X-rays and MRI, let Beth know on your way out and she'll make the arrangements." She handed him the card. "That's my direct line if you have any other questions."

He turned the card over and studied the front for a long moment. Then he looked at her, his face a wooden mask. "What does your husband think of Texas?"

"I wouldn't know."

His fist curled around the card. "Sorry. Divorce?"

"Dead," she said, and walked out the door before he could join the legions who'd expressed their heartfelt sympathy when they didn't know fuck all about Willy except what they heard on the evening news.

Chapter 3

DEAD.

There were less brutal ways to say it. *Widowed. Passed away. I lost my husband last...*year, summer, whatever. But Tori had deliberately picked that flat, ugly word, and said it with her eyes empty. Abandoned. Set in a face Delon barely recognized. Leaner, harder, her cheeks hollowed out like a person who'd been ill. Or heartsick.

She was Tori, but not Tori. He realized now how much of her beauty had been manufactured. Platinum blonde hair, push-up bras, perfect makeup. Even the intense sky blue of her eyes must've been colored contact lens. Now she'd let her hair go a dark caramel color, and her eyes were more gray than blue. The color of mist. Or ghosts.

He slammed the heel of his hand on his car's center console. He wanted to rage. He deserved it, goddamnit. His fury had built, coal by glowing coal, the entire time she'd examined him like nothing more than a specimen under a microscope. No explanation for her disappearance. No apology. Then she'd looked at him with that cool, blank expression and said yeah, his knee was probably fucked. He wanted to curse her for confirming his worst fears. For waltzing off to Wyoming and getting married and never looking back. Cheyenne, for hell's sake. All the times he'd competed there in the past six years...

You might have to learn to live with a deficit.

Live? Sure. He could *live* just fine. But ride? When she'd said those words, the fresh wash of panic had spilled into a vat of old hurt and humiliation, and he'd been two seconds away from exploding. And then she'd stolen his thunder.

Dead. Dead, dead, dead. One grim syllable he couldn't spit out. It left a taste like ashes in his mouth that he couldn't smother with chocolate. His body felt as it was constructed of a thousand coiled springs. One wrong move and he would fly apart.

As he pulled through the gates of Sanchez Trucking, the wind kicked up dust from beneath his tires and sent it whirling across the gravel lot, spinning and skittering like his thoughts. He parked, turned off the car, and just sat there, trying to breathe. The yellow steel shop was two stories tall at the peak to accommodate semis, trailers and the chain hoists that dangled from steel beams above, and wide enough for three pull-through repair bays. The far right side housed office space at the front and a one bedroom apartment upstairs. Home sweet home.

People asked why he didn't get a house, more space, but they had an entire shop for Beni to run tame under the watchful eyes of the mechanics. Beni loved the trucks, and hanging around with the drivers. Besides, Delon was gone—used to be gone, he corrected himself bitterly—more often than he was home. Might as well save some cash and stay here…where he could still pretend to be a real part of Sanchez Trucking.

The front door banged open and one of the drivers stomped out, strode over to an idling pickup, slammed into the cab and roared away, spewing an angry rooster tail of gravel and dust. That couldn't be good. And if there was smoke at Sanchez Trucking, ten to one Delon knew who'd started the fire.

He slung his gym bag over his shoulder and walked through an open bay door, past an engine they'd pulled the day before for a total overhaul, and into a dusty, wood-paneled hallway, the concrete floor tracked with grime. At the far left end were a break room and bathroom for the mechanics. Next to that was the dispatcher's office. Directly in front of him was the beat up metal desk that served as their reception area.

Their secretary barely spared him a glance as she bustled around, collecting stacks of trip sheets, delivery receipts, bills of lading and invoices, most already scanned. Cloud backup be damned, Merle Sanchez insisted they keep paper copies of everything. The computer system did allow Miz Nordquist to run their office from home, though, rather than "That stinking shop." Given that she had the face and disposition of a thundercloud, no one objected.

"What's wrong with Jerry?" Delon asked.

She jerked her head toward his dad's office, at the front of the building. "Your brother."

Bingo. Delon found his dad slouched behind the desk, elbow on the armrest of the big leather chair, and chin in hand, expression grim. Gil stood at the window, a narrow slice of darkness through the square of sunlight.

"What's up?" Delon asked.

His dad blew out a weary sigh. "Jerry got an offer from an oil company up in the Bakken."

"North Dakota?" Delon shivered. Closest he'd ever come to freezing his ass off was in Valley City in March. "Must've been one hell of an offer. When's he done?"

"Now," Gil snapped.

Delon jerked around in surprise. "He's due to load out for Duluth tomorrow night."

Silence. Delon looked from his dad to Gil, and cursed. "You cut him loose and left us hanging?"

Gil slapped his hand against the window hard enough to make the pane vibrate. "I've been bustin' my ass, working the loads so he could get home more since that new kid was born, and this is how he repays us."

"So you booted him out the door?" Delon let out a growl of impatience. "For Christ's sake, Gil. He's a good operator and he's HAZMAT certified."

Gil wheeled around to glare at Delon. "He quit. I just accelerated the process."

"He won't stick in the oil patch," Delon argued. "Just long enough to get a jump on paying for that new truck, then he'll be out of that frozen hellhole, headed south."

"And I'm supposed to welcome him with open arms?"

"Guys like him are hard to find—"

"The kind who takes advantage of you then spit in your face?"

Their dad straightened, cutting his hand through the air to signal *Enough!* Lord knew, he'd had plenty of opportunities to use it over the years. What did Merle think when he looked at the sons who wore the Sanchez name so much more easily than he did, with his ginger hair and freckled skin? Did he search for some piece of himself in them, or curse the dark skin and hair of the woman who'd deserted him?

Merle sighed. "We need to figure out who's gonna take his load. What do we have for a truck?"

Delon stared at his dad in disbelief. He wasn't even going to try to salvage the situation? "The white Peterbilt is ready to go."

"Then we just need a driver. I'm hauling hay to Quanah till the end of the week."

"I can get Miz Nordquist to cover dispatch and take it myself." Gil scowled. "It'll cost me."

Mostly in beer for all the drivers and mechanics who had to deal with the woman in person. Delon let it hang for a minute, debating whether to let Gil off the hook he'd buried in his own ass, but it came down to doing what was best for the business. And a chance to get out of town, even if it was to Duluth. After ten years of criss-crossing the country on the rodeo trail, he was going stir crazy in Earnest.

"I'll take it."

"What about Beni?" his dad asked.

"Violet asked to keep him a couple of extra days. Joe's gonna be here."

Another silence. Someone else's family might ask how he felt about that, but the Sanchez men didn't discuss feelings unless they involved the latest idiotic mandate from the Department of Transportation. Building up this business from a single worn out cattle hauler hadn't left Merle Sanchez much time for the touchy-feely crap. He'd kept his boys fed, clothed, and mostly out of trouble. The rest they'd had to figure out on their own.

"You sure your knee is up to it?" his dad asked.

"I'll stop and walk out the kinks when I need to."

"Works for me." But Merle looked to Gil for confirmation, as if he had the final say.

"The paperwork's at the front desk," Gil said, starting for the door. "I've gotta go make some calls, find someone to take Jerry's HAZMAT loads until I can get a permanent replacement."

The hitch in his gait was more pronounced than usual as he walked out, pausing at the front desk to grab a folder before he disappeared into his lair. On the door that slapped shut behind him an engraved plate said *The Dispatcher*. Below it, one of the drivers had taped up a handwritten paper sign that declared *Enter at your own risk*.

"You're welcome," Delon muttered.

His dad gave him a wry smile. "We do appreciate the help."

We. As if there was a them, separate from him. And he'd let it happen. As he'd built a name among rodeo fans, the demands for autograph sessions and sponsor appearances had increased, eating into the time between rodeos. At home, he'd spent every available moment with Beni, as often as not at the Jacobs ranch with Violet and her family. Meanwhile, his brother had slithered into the position at Sanchez Trucking that Delon had always assumed would be waiting for him. Gil, who'd once said he'd rather have his balls cut off than be chained to a desk. Which left Delon…what?

"I can talk to Jerry," he offered. "Smooth things over before he leaves."

Merle shook his head. "Your brother is right. We did everything we could to keep him. When—or if—he comes back, we can't make it easy for him. Otherwise, he'll just use us again and take off soon as he gets a better offer."

Hell. Delon couldn't argue with that logic.

Merle shifted in his chair, visibly switching gears. "What did you think of the new therapist?"

"She's…different." Which wasn't a lie. Tori was nowhere near the same girl he used to know.

"Is that good or bad?"

Odds were, it didn't matter. Delon fought to keep the cold punch of misery from showing on his face. If the joint capsule was scarred beyond repair, the best therapist in the universe wouldn't be able to fix what ailed his knee. Whether he could stand to see Tori twice a week until they admitted defeat…

"I haven't decided yet," he said. And that was the honest truth, too.

Please enjoy this sneak peek at Nicole Helm's

TRUE-BLUE COWBOY Christmas

available October 2016

BIG SKY CHRISTMAS

Thack Lane has his hands full. For the past seven years, he's been struggling to move on from his wife's tragic death and raise a daughter all by his lonesome. He doesn't have time for himself, much less a cheerful new neighbor with a smile that can light up the ranch.

Christmas spirit? Bah, humbug.

With Christmas right around the corner, Summer Shaw is searching for somewhere to belong. When her neighbor's young daughter takes a shine to her, she is thrilled. But Thack is something else altogether. He's got walls around his heart that no amount of holiday wishes can scale…and yet as joy comes creeping back to the lonely homestead, Summer and Thack may just find their happily ever after before the last of Christmas miracles are through…

Chapter 1

FOR SUMMER SHAW, HAPPINESS WAS MADE OF SIMPLE pleasures—a place to call your own, a little patch of land, the big open sky and food in your stomach. All that was why the Shaw Ranch wasn't just happy, it was heaven. Here, she also had family—as evidenced by the tiny week-old niece she held in her arms.

"She's just the most beautiful thing I've ever seen."

"So you've said, approximately three hundred times." Mel sighed, closing her eyes and sinking into the living room couch. "Today alone."

"Why don't you go take a nap? I can handle Lissa for an hour or so."

"No, I'm fine." Mel yawned, curling her legs onto the couch. "I'll just close my eyes for a few seconds."

"Of course you will," Summer placated, cradling the baby in one arm while she draped an afghan across Mel with the other. "Your mama needs to learn that she can't do everything," Summer whispered to the bundle in her arms.

"I heard that," Mel mumbled without any heat.

Summer tiptoed out of the room. With any luck, Mel really would relax and sleep—at least until Lissa needed to eat again. Mel and Summer's tentative relationship still had its moments of awkwardness, and had since Summer had showed up on the doorstep of Shaw over a year ago. But the changes that came with Mel's pregnancy and Lissa's birth had smoothed over those last pockets of distance.

They finally had something to bond them together, that could get them past being so wary of each other.

Summer hummed to the beautiful baby girl, walking her to the den at the end of the house. It was a cluttered, messy room that smelled of old magazines and dirt. Summer liked how it held the distinctive signs of the most recently married Shaw couple: her brother Caleb's ranch magazines and her new sister-in-law Delia's gardening tools stored for the winter.

This space had everything she wanted—the comfort, the evidence of family and the big window that looked out over mountains, barns and so much of Shaw.

Winter held Montana in its grip, the mountains heavily snow-peaked, the world around her white and glittering. She missed the warmth of summer, but she couldn't bring herself to miss California, even as she entered her second Montana winter.

It was harsh and long, but the upcoming holidays would warm up this interminable season. Her family would gather, and they would celebrate.

A family who treated her as though she were a person. Maybe a person they didn't know what to do with, but it was hard to push. It was mainly just her father treating her with distance, at this point.

He'd apologized, after all, for treating her with silence when she first showed up. For knowing that Summer's mother had been pregnant with her when Mom had left him and Montana, and doing nothing to stop it.

Even so, Summer wasn't one hundred percent sure what to do with that apology, or with the dread that lived in her heart. Because who knew which of her mother's stories were true? She might *not* belong here. Summer winced at the little prick of conscience. She had been at Shaw for almost a year and a half—she couldn't let that possibility ever take this away.

The Shaws were her family now. They never needed to know that there was doubt.

Summer took a deep breath. She'd spent a lifetime—short though twenty-three years might be—learning to soak up life's good moments. She'd learned every deep-breathing, positive-thinking, centered-life meditation, practiced them with every fiber of her being. She breathed, day and night, through thick and thin, happy and sad.

That had kept her going, all through the unpredictable prison that had been her life with Mom, and the new freedom she'd found in Montana and Shaw.

Still. Nothing was perfect. Even in moments like this one, holding this newborn—her *niece*—in front of the most beautiful landscape she'd ever seen, the joy could be jarred. A knot formed in the pit of her stomach. Tiny at first. A little pebble. But eventually it would grow until she had a boulder sitting on her chest.

Because a life spent collecting these few-and-far-between perfect moments had taught her one thing. Just when she thought she was on the right track, happy, peaceful, *home*…

Life would have other plans.

She closed her eyes against the certainty. *Please don't take Shaw away from me. I can handle anything but that.*

Anything but that.

A beat. A breath.

Summer opened her eyes, and her gaze drifted toward the tree line around her caravan. Well, that was something no one could take away. Her little home. Her ability to survive. Those were all hers.

Lissa fussed and Summer began to sing, one of the slow country love songs the regulars at Pioneer Spirit tended to drift off to.

At second glimpse of the caravan, way off in the trees, she didn't pay much attention to the little dot of red. The vehicle was a colorful thing as it was. She'd repainted the outside this summer, a vibrant purple and blue to mimic the sky at dusk.

But red was off. She squinted, noticing the dot of color was moving. It was too big to be a bird, too red to be…well, anything else, but so far away it was impossible to make out clearly.

Her stomach dropped with the sour fear she thought she'd gotten over, except for in her dreams. Surely it wasn't big enough to be her mother. Surely, *surely* Mom wouldn't have followed her here. But that bright vibrant red had always been one of Mom's favorites.

Run.

Panic bubbled up in Summer's chest, and she backed away from the window. She couldn't let Linda get up here, especially couldn't let her talk to any Shaws. Linda would turn them against Summer, and ruin everything Summer's life had become. Who knew what damage she could inflict on the Shaws, on this place Summer was finally beginning to think of as home.

Summer turned on a heel. She wasn't going to run. She'd promised herself she would never run away again. So, she'd fight.

It was not her mother.

After settling Lissa back with Mel, failing to stay calm or nonchalant, Summer dashed across the snow-packed land that separated the Shaw house and her caravan. She arrived breathless and near tears, only to find a little girl. A little girl dressed in red. Red coat, red boots, even her pants were red. She had a shock of unruly curly blonde hair, and she stared at Summer with big blue eyes.

Summer wasn't great at guessing ages, but the girl had to be old enough for elementary school, though probably not much older than that.

"Hello," Summer offered once she could breathe almost normally. "Are you lost?"

The girl continued her wide-eyed staring.

"Are you okay?" Summer pressed, taking a few uncertain steps toward her. She didn't know of any neighbor children; a few families around the ranch made sure not to associate with any of the Shaws. There was a lot of not-so-pleasant history there, mainly involving Caleb being a bit of a ne'er-do-well as an adolescent.

"Are you a fairy?" the little girl whispered.

Summer's eyebrows shot up. Maybe the girl was really lost—days lost and delirious. "No, sweetheart. Are you cold? Hungry?"

"Are you an angel?"

"No, just a human."

Summer carefully knelt in front of the girl. She knew what it was like for strangers to approach you, touch you, speak to you and leave you uncomfortable.

Summer swallowed a lump in her throat, swallowed away old, bad memories, and resisted the urge to touch the girl to see if she was shivering. It was far too cold for a little girl to be left wandering around.

"Is that yours?" the little girl nodded toward the caravan.

"Yes."

"It looks like a fairy palace."

Summer smiled. "Fairy palace" might not have been the aesthetic she was going for, but *colorful* and *free* meant different things to different people. Maybe that description was about right.

"It's a little cold to be walking around alone. Can I help you get back to your house?"

"I got a little lost." She bit her bottom lip, the downy pale slashes of her eyebrows drawing together. "Daddy will be mad." The little girl's big blue eyes filled with tears.

The chill in the air was no match for the chill in Summer's heart. Angry fathers weren't something she had any experience with, but angry parents or adults who scared children—she knew them, and the memory was disturbing.

She felt immediately protective of this lost and scared little girl. Poor thing. She needed a friend.

"I'm Summer. What's your name?" She held out her hand. An offer, if the girl felt so inclined to take it.

The girl opened her mouth, but before any sound came out, a man's voice bellowed through the trees. *"Kate!"*

Instinctively, Summer stepped between the trees and the girl. The little thing didn't need an angry man yelling at her when she was lost, teary and scared, no

matter if he was her father or not. Parentage wasn't a
get-out-of-being-a-monster-free card, for anyone. "If
you want to hide—"

But the dot of red darted around her.

"Daddy! I'm here!" Kate waved her red mittens and
jumped up and down, then got distracted by the snow
puffing up in drifts as she jumped. She giggled, kicking
the snow in powdery arcs, any threat of tears gone.

"Katherine." The man burst through the tree line. He
was obviously furious and frustrated, but the predomi-
nant emotion on his face was neither of those things.

He was *terrified*.

Summer knew she should soften. A man who felt
terror as he searched for his missing daughter was
more than likely not the kind of man who would hurt
her as well.

Or so one would hope.

But Mom had been loving and thoughtful one minute,
quick to raise her hand the next. Everything inside
Summer coiled in a tight, tense ball. It took a great feat
of strength not to reach out and grab the bundle of red
away from the man. A lot of people were very, *very*
good actors, after all. She had found people who were
honest, and good as well. She just had no idea which
one he was.

The father sank to his knees in front of the girl, grabbing her shoulders. "What are you doing? You can't
keep doing this to me." He ran his gloved hands down
her arms, over her face, as though he were checking for
an injury. Once he was satisfied, he pulled the bundle of
red against his chest. For a few quiet minutes, he simply
held her there, his eyes closed, some of the tension in

his shoulders draining away, clearly moved and relieved that she was unharmed.

"I'm sorry, Daddy. But look!" She pointed at Summer, a bright smile showing off two missing front teeth. "I found a fairy palace!"

For the first time, he looked at Summer. He got to his feet, his mouth tightening into a frown. He was a tall man, a broad man, and neither the puffy work jacket nor the cowboy hat that now shadowed his face could do anything to hide the obvious—that he would be far stronger and more powerful than her.

"Who are you?" he said. No, that was too kind—his tone was all demand as he stepped in front of Kate as if he could shield her from Summer.

Summer wanted to shrink away, or hide, but she'd learned something about standing up even when it was the scariest thing you could imagine. "Maybe I should be asking *you* that?"

"Why are you talking to my dau—" Kate grabbed the hem of his coat and he stopped.

"Daddy," she whispered, tugging on his coat. She grinned up at Summer. "She's a fairy *queen*. Just like in the bedtime book."

"We're going home." He moved her by the shoulder, steering his daughter toward the trees. They separated Summer's clearing from a fence that she'd never crossed. She'd never even given a thought to what lay beyond it. Because Shaw had been enough. Shaw felt safe.

For some reason, nothing beyond that fence ever had.

Acknowledgments

This is where you normally thank your family, your writer friends, your agent and editors, and I do owe a huge debt to all of the usual suspects—you know who you are. However, there is another group of people who, in my case, deserve priority.

On May 8, 2014, I was diagnosed with Stage IIIC ovarian cancer. This book and I are literally in existence due to the efforts of an amazing group of medical professionals—Dr. Melanie Bergman and the staff of Cancer Care Northwest; the surgical and nursing staff at Sacred Heart Medical Center in Spokane, WA; Dr. Grant Harrer, David Brost, P.A., Tosha, Nanette, Sharnai, and the rest of the exceptional staff of Sletten Cancer Institute. I wish I had time and space to list you all by name because you have earned my everlasting gratitude. With luck, we will to continue to see as little of each other as possible.

To my stylist, LeeAnn Burke, who smoothed an emotionally rocky road by keeping me looking as close to normal as I ever get. I may be the only person in history who had better hair when I was bald.

To June Yearwood and Janet Yearwood (I had to flip a coin for who got to be listed first), my eagle-eyed beta readers, whose unflinching critiques finally brought this story into focus, along with everything I've written since. Plus Megan Coakley, who hooked us up, and is my hero just for surviving every day with humor and class.

And finally, to Janet Reid, who back in 2012 dragged me and this book-that-was-not-working into her conference room and spent two days of her precious time helping me deconstruct it, chapter by chapter, to root out the flaws. We may not have fixed it, but knowing someone of her caliber would devote that much time and effort to us kept me from giving up on this baby.

And to Ryan the Intern, who was trapped in that room with us, I'm sorry if you were scarred for life. Consider it a favor. You're probably making more money and drinking a lot less in whatever profession you chose that was not publishing.

About the Author

Kari Lynn Dell is a ranch-raised Montana cowgirl who attended her first rodeo at two weeks old and has existed in a state of horse-induced poverty ever since. She lives on the Blackfeet Reservation in her parents' bunkhouse along with her husband, her son, and Max the Cowdog. There's a tepee on her lawn, Glacier National Park on her doorstep, and Canada within spitting distance. Visit her at karilynndell.com.